The Angel Blade Series
by Carrie Merrill

A fast-paced, paranormal adventure, the *Angel Blade* series follows Nikka, a young woman who was dying of cancer until a stranger provided a cure in exchange for becoming a demon hunter. As the seraph, Nikka now wields the power to exorcise and destroy demons, but she must face the most powerful forces of Hell that will try to bring about the End of Days.

Angel Blade
Book I in the Angel Blade Series

What readers have said about *Angel Blade*:

"Fast paced with rich imagery."

"Keeps you engaged and wanting to read "just one more chapter."

Daemon
Book II in the Angel Blade Series

"She's done it again with the page turning suspense and the nail-biting cliffhangers. One more page turned into several hours and chapters later."

Archangel
Book III in the Angel Blade Series

Archangel

Carrie Merrill

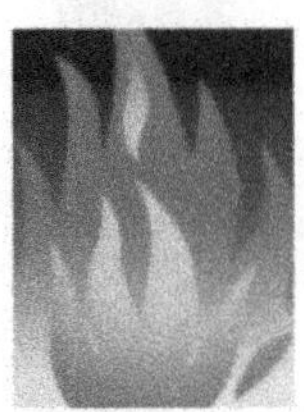

SOUL FIRE
PRESS

an imprint of
Christopher Matthews Publishing

Boston, Massachusetts

Archangel

Editors: Jeremy Soldevilla
Cover design: Neil Noah

ISBN 978-1-945146-28-2
ebook ISBN 978-1-945146-29-9

Published by
Soul Fire Press

an imprint of
CHRISTOPHER MATTHEWS PUBLISHING
http://christophermatthewspub.com

Boston

Printed in the United States of America

This book is dedicated to my parents, who always said when times get tough, that "angels could do no better."

Acknowledgments

This book is yet another collection of love and hard work, made possible by so many people. First, I need to thank my family again because they have gotten me to this point and made me who I am. They provided the support and guidance I needed to get this far in life.

Without the great crew at Soul Fire Press, you wouldn't be holding this in your hand. So, thanks to Jeremy Soldevilla for being willing to give me a chance to bring the world of angels and demons to life. Thanks to Neil Noah for such a great cover.

Beta readers make this world go round, so thanks to my betas: Honey, Natalie, Shanien and Sunny.

And a special thanks to a wonderful fan: Shelby, my favorite Comic Con fan. Your story of beating childhood cancer is so inspiring. You're the real hero.

In the Beginning

Archangel is the third installment of the Angel Blade series, the dark story of Nikka Connors, who was dying of cancer until she became a seraph, a powerful being able to exorcise and destroy demons. After she saved Jason from possession by the demon Abaddon, he fought at her side against the demon horde that had infiltrated the government and planned a massive EMP explosion to disrupt life throughout the world. Nikka thought she had lost Gideon, her mentor and her first love, but instead learned that he now had the power of his alter-demon, Pazuzu and led the forces of Hell toward an apocalyptic future.

With only Jason and two FBI agents as her allies, Nikka fought through the army of demons that orchestrated the launch of a missile carrying the EMP device. But they were too late, and the rocket launched, detonating the device in the atmosphere, plunging the world into darkness.

Gideon decimated their small group and tortured Nikka until he had removed her marks and left her powerless. In one small moment of defiance, she fought back with the last of her strength and forced a soul back into Gideon's body, driving the demon away from him. This act of her last vestiges of power opened a rift into Heaven, and the cherubim took her from the earth, leaving Jason as the next seraph and Gideon to be his mentor.

Part Six

"It is easy to go down to hell; night and day the gates of Dark Death stand wide; but to climb back up again, to retrace one's steps to the open air, there lies the problem, the difficult task."

—Virgil, The Aeneid

Chapter 1
Jason

Jason pressed back against the wall, cold in the heat of the night. Blood still trickled from the laceration across his ribs, flowing into his shirt and looking like black oil in the midnight darkness. The navy blue T-shirt that had become a part of him over the last several days was now just another casualty of war, torn from the claws that had inflicted the wound to his ribs. He placed a hand against the cut and pulled it away. Okay, not totally soaked with blood. It'll heal. It was the last of his worries right now.

Not even close.

The demon stalking him down the hall was probably more of a concern.

Jason held his breath—not an easy task since he had just run up three flights of stairs with a pack of drones close behind. The first two he took out with the sword, but the third one doubled back, and he lost it in the shadows of the building. The place echoed of emptiness, like so many buildings since the power had died, and there was nobody else around to hear the growl of the creature that skulked in the shadows. He halted in his position, crouched against the wall and held his breath to listen for any footsteps. That thing was out there somewhere; no way it would just let him go once it saw the tattoos along his arms and up his neck, trailing toward his skull until they got lost in the locks of blonde hair that fell close to his shoulders—the same tattoos that had appeared in the place of the art that used to adorn his skin.

Silence.

Only the occasional rattle of the windows in the nighttime breeze carried any sound through the halls.

The drone was out there somewhere. It had smelled his blood, and it wouldn't give up until he was dead. After all, every demon out there dreamed of killing a seraph. If demons dreamed at all.

Jason stood and listened into the corridor, the pounding of his heart as loud as a freight train. His fingers ached to reach for the sword. But if he unsheathed it now, the blue light would give away his position. Not yet. He just needed to listen.

Then he heard the creak of a floor board just beyond the space where he crouched. He braced back against the wall and held his breath again.

Another creak.

It neared the doorway.

Just two feet to his left, the wall exploded in a shower of drywall and wood splinters. Jason ducked and rolled away from the falling debris as a shadow moved through the breach in the wall. The creature had tricked him. Somehow it had moved down to the end of the hall without him knowing and ambushed him. Jason stopped in a crouch and turned to face the beast that shook its head free of the falling debris. Its dark eyes, hidden in a human skull, turned toward him and the demon smiled, black oil dripping from its lips. The person it possessed hung over the bones of the demon like a horrible Halloween costume, its wrinkled, gray skin tearing at the edges. Then it charged at him.

His fingers twitched for a moment, and Jason reached to his back and found the hilt of the sword. As it unsheathed, the room lit up into a halo of blue light, and shadows danced in the corners. Jason stood to face the creature that now came at him.

The beast charged, its claws still dripping with Jason's blood from their last encounter only minutes ago. Jason swung the sword through the air just as the demon came at him, but the beast dodged back, its neck arching just enough to miss the tip of the sword. Its claws swiped back as the blade whistled past its ear. Its claw caught Jason's wrist, and he almost dropped his weapon.

The drones were getting smarter, and this one was being particularly difficult.

It skittered across the floor on all four limbs, stopping just inches from Jason's side. He lunged back as the creature tried to kick his legs out from under him. This gave Jason the ideal moment to catch it.

Jason's boot swiped under the demon, clearing its supporting arm from holding its weight. The creature stumbled for a moment, giving Jason the millisecond opportunity he needed. He shoved his boot against its torso, twisted into a crouch and landed on top of the demon, his knees pinning the arms of the demon to the ground.

The beast shrieked and wailed, a sound so awful and high-pitched it shattered the window next to them and showered the room in fragments of glass. Jason clenched his teeth against the cry and placed his open palm against the demon's chest, his fingers pressing against the creature's ribs.

"In the name of the seraph, I demand your name," he said.

It opened its mouth wide and screamed in agony at the words. The black oil sputtered and splashed from its throat, gushing in gray bubbles against Jason's arm. He held his hand in place, waiting for the moment that the demon could no longer hold its tongue. It continued to thrash under his weight, but he knew he had it now.

"Your name!"

Legs kicked and bucked against him. The demon choked on the black fluid and opened its dark eyes. The ebony orbs searched for his face, the blue light of the sword reflecting in the oily depths. It took in a wet breath and lifted its head from the ground.

He saw its black stained teeth below serpentine lips. It almost smiled as it cocked its head to the side. "Namtar."

Jason felt his fingers sink into the demon's flesh as soon as the words escaped the creature's throat. The ethereal body felt empty, like reaching into a barren closet. But then he found the leathery, firm thing that had brought him to this place. He wrapped his fingers around the creature, and it fought back. They always do. He pulled, feeling its insectoid arms reaching for anything to hold on to, anything to keep it from being torn free. The creature ripped out of the man's body with a sound like splintering wood.

Once he had it free, he struggled to hold it until he had his sword ready. The thing whipped its black body and thin tail around like a scorpion, with claws and teeth snapping toward him.

This was the best part. This is what he had learned from watching the seraph before him.

He threw the creature down to the ground and pinned it against the cement with his boot as he swung the sword through the air. The blue light shined against its black carapace just before he decapitated the beast. The blade almost moved itself as though it knew its own purpose. It finished the deed and settled cleanly in the palm of his hand.

The demon's body shuddered for a moment and then went still as the head rolled twice toward the corner of the room. Then both pieces quivered into ashes that drifted in the breeze blowing through the shattered window.

Jason stood still for a moment and caught his breath. The last of the ashes settled on his boot, and he shook them free before he stepped back and pressed against the wall. He slid to the ground, his hand reaching up to the laceration across his ribs.

Three down.

How many was that now? Fifty? A hundred?

The pain of the battle settled into his bones now that his faded from his muscles. He was definitely going to hurt tomorrow.

The moonlight poured steady silver light into the dark room, falling on the face of the man who lay motionless on the floor. Moments ago, Jason had pulled the demon from his body. Now, his still eyes looked to the right, directly at him.

Removing the demon didn't help this man. All it did was kill him in the process. The man had been ridden too hard by the beast before Jason could save him.

Jason closed his eyes and leaned his head back against the wall as he felt blood ooze from his wound. The sight of the man's dead face had burned into his retinas, though. Just like every one of the people he couldn't save.

Unlike his kill tally, that was a count he didn't want to remember.

CHAPTER TWO
JASON

Jason stepped through the darkened corridors of the abandoned building, the wound at his side now clotted but still uncomfortable. Each step brought him closer to the outside world blanketed in night, but the heat of the desert still radiated from the ground. His truck waited out here, equipped with his first aid kit and a light to see the damage the drone had inflicted on him before he evaded it.

And his teacher waited out here, too.

Jason exited the building, hoping that he would feel cooler air hit his face, but that wasn't the case. The summer heat in the desert never let up, not even at night. His pace quickened, and at first, it was involuntary, but he realized that he hurried toward the back of the truck because he saw the passenger door open. *Dammit. Not now.* He really didn't need a lecture, especially from *him.*

It took everything in his power to not pull the sword and point it directly at him as the other man rounded the back of the truck.

"That was a foolish thing to do," Gideon said as Jason opened the tailgate and reached for the large duffel bag.

Jason clenched his teeth and his fingers absently smoothed across the goatee that framed his mouth. *Don't say a word.*

He unzipped the bag and fished around until he found the first aid kit. The box had enough rolls of gauze since he had taken a bunch from the abandoned urgent care clinic they had found last week.

Gideon still faced him. "Following those two without knowing where the third was located . . . you could have gotten yourself killed."

Jason pulled his shirt over his head and leaned toward the moonlight to get a better look at the damage and to face away from Gideon. The blood caked around the huge gash in his ribs looked black in the dark, staining the curved sigil tattoos that coursed down his torso. Gideon took in a breath as he produced a flashlight from his pocket and shined it at Jason's cut.

"You are wounded," Gideon said and reached a hand to inspect it.

Jason slapped his hand away. "Get off me." He meant it to sound as harsh as it did. Gideon's help was the last thing he wanted right now.

"Very well."

Jason grabbed the flashlight from his hand and placed it on the truck's back gate while he cleaned the laceration with a bottle of alcohol. The cold fluid burned and stung in all the wrong places. Another splash of the stringent sent the blood in red trickles down his side. He bit his lip against the pain until he had cleaned the last of the dried blood from the wound.

He could still feel Gideon's eyes on him, though. Well, Gideon could look at him all he wanted. It wasn't going to change anything. With a heavy pad pressed against the wound, he wrapped a round of gauze about his chest.

Then he looked up at Gideon. "I got them, didn't I? So what's the big deal?"

Gideon hesitated for a moment. "I am charged to protect you. To guide you. I cannot do that if you do not heed my warnings."

Jason tied the end of the gauze wrap and felt the dressing fit securely around his chest. He dug around the bag until he found another T-shirt and slipped it over his head. Gideon watched him as if he waited for him to respond, but he wasn't about to. They had had this argument so many times in the past that it had become just motions in a play. He wasn't even sure why Gideon still insisted upon trying to control anything. He lifted the gate of the truck and locked it into place.

"Or do you not wish to listen to me because you seek death?"

There it was. This made Jason stop in his haste to the driver's side door. His hand clutched to the edge of the truck bed, fingers tight against the metal.

There were so many reasons he didn't want to listen to Gideon. Now or ever again. Even with his eyes on him now, he felt his skin ripple, and the muscles in his shoulders tighten. So many times he had wanted to hit him, to pound his face into something unrecognizable, just to shut him up so he would never have to hear his voice again. Every day was a struggle to keep going, to learn as much as he could from him. And every morning he awoke, wondering if this was to be the last day.

Jason flashed a glance up at him. Gideon's face remained shadowed with the moonlight at his back. Flakes of old paint crumbled under Jason's grasp against the truck. With his seraph strength, he knew he could probably even crush the metal in his fingers. As soon as he felt the metal begin to warp in his grasp, he let up and turned his gaze away from Gideon.

"Get in," he said and jerked open the driver's side door. He climbed into the truck and started the engine. The old diesel rumbled to life.

He didn't wait for Gideon to shut his door before he pressed the gas pedal, the tires spinning against the gravel and taking them off down the dark road.

They rode together in silence back to the small, empty ghost of a town they had left in their chase of the demon pack.

Just need to get back and get some sleep. Maybe that would help to ease the ache in his side. But it wouldn't get the image of the man's dead eyes out of his head. He remembered each and every one just like that body, cold and lifeless because he was too late to save them. The truck lights spanned across the road ahead of him, but beyond that, he saw only darkness. Darkness, and the eyes of that dead man.

The truck maneuvered into the streets of the town. It was like any small town that they had passed. A single main street. A variety of streets flanking both sides of the town. A scattering of homes surrounding the area. And like so many they had found in the last several months, there wasn't a soul to be found. Abandoned and dark.

Cars and trucks lined the roads, still in the same places they had been on the night it happened. When everything went to hell.

No street lights shone on the road as the truck moved down the street. Jason drove off the main street and parked in the shadows behind a two-story house, dark and abandoned like everything else. He climbed out and stepped around to the back of the truck, where he grabbed the duffel bag. He slung it over his shoulder but listened at the same time. The area around the town remained quiet. Dead and silent.

Gideon slipped from the truck and moved behind him as he stepped to the front door of the house. Jason didn't have time to worry about him right now as he peered through the windows that looked out toward the town. The curtains had been drawn but still left a gap between them. Only darkness within the house. Nothing moved.

He tried the doorknob, and it turned without hesitation. The door opened with a creaking of its hinges, but Jason stood at the threshold, feeling the warm and closed air that breathed out from inside the house. He held his breath, listening for any sound coming from within the space.

Nothing.

But he had been fooled before. A demon knew how to hide from detection, even from him. He reached behind his back and withdrew the sword. The tattoos along his arms tingled and sparkled with light as he held the weapon out in front of him, lighting the room with the blue fire along the blade. The room remained still and quiet, though.

He stepped past the threshold and let the bag slip from his shoulder. It landed on the hard wood floor with a heavy thud. The sound didn't stir anything from the shadows behind the couch or the dining room chairs that still stood around a table in the next room.

"Looks clear," he called out to Gideon and stepped fully into the room.

This would be their shelter for tonight. Maybe a few nights. Jason never knew these days.

Gideon crossed over into the room and turned on his flashlight while he inspected the kitchen and down the hallway to other rooms. Jason rested back against the couch and pulled his bag closer to him. When he found everything he needed, he fired up the lantern he kept, lighting the room well enough to chase the shadows away.

The living room looked like it hadn't been touched in months. A layer of dust had settled over the coffee table and lamps. The stale air around him smelled heavy and thick, like a stagnant swamp cooler. At the opposite end of the room stood a bookshelf decorated with books and photos in little handmade frames. As he looked at them, he saw the faces of a family with two children—two little girls. A family that had just up and left, like everyone else. The entire town had vanished.

Most towns now looked like this, too. Except for the cities, and those were places that you didn't want to enter because that's where most of the demon hives clustered. It was far better to stay off the main roads and freeways, but that's how he found so many of these kinds of places.

Gideon stepped back into the room. "Two rooms upstairs, one down. It does not appear to have been looted. There is food in the cupboards."

His voice stirred Jason back to the emptiness of the house. "Fine. Take what you want. I'll eat something later."

Gideon nodded. "Very well. I will sleep upstairs if you wish."

Jason waved him off. *Whatever.*

He stood and peered through the curtains and out the window. The street was dark enough that he couldn't see everything on the other side. Just more empty houses. Nothing in the streets but dead cars. Those could wait until morning for him to drain the gas tanks. Sometimes, when there was enough light, they would find a body or two in the street in various stages of decay. Hopefully, this wasn't one of those towns.

As he backed away from the window, his arm caught the edge of the lamp. It nearly toppled to the ground, but he caught it just in time and placed it back on the table. As his hand steadied it, though, he looked at the lamp and just stepped away. Such a useless thing. It hadn't worked in months and would probably never work again. The power had disappeared the night that the EMP had detonated. The EMP that he had tried to stop. That he and Nikka had tried to stop.

Don't do this.

His vision grew cloudy.

Just stop it. Right now. There was no use in thinking about that anymore.

He clenched his fists and pressed them against his temples until his head hurt. Anything to fight away the memory of that night. He blinked his eyes clear and shook his head. *Stop thinking about that. It only creates pain and nightmares and insomnia.*

The ache in his head throbbed enough that he couldn't organize his thoughts. He glanced up to the kitchen and paced to the cupboards. There had to be something in here. Usually, they were lucky when they found a place like this, untouched from the looters that had affected most towns. He pulled open the doors in a frantic look for the thing that would help him ward off the memories that plagued him.

Cans of soup. A box of crackers. Spices.

Not what he needed.

His fingers searched in the dark through each cupboard as the cans and other items toppled from the shelves and onto the kitchen counter. It didn't matter if things clattered to the ground with such a noise. Not until he found it. He crouched to the lower cabinets and pulled them open.

Jackpot.

His fingers wrapped around the neck of the bottle that he had spotted behind several canisters of sugar and flour. The glass felt cool, even in the heat that had spilled into the house. He withdrew the bottle and leaned back against the refrigerator. In the lantern light, he read the black label across the face of the large, full and unopened bottle: Jack Daniels. Not his favorite, but it would do if this was the only thing here.

His memories played back to him as he sat there, the bottle in his hand. The flash of light that filled the sky that night seven months ago. The feel of her hand in his. The last kiss, frantic and desperate, before the demon horde overtook them.

Tears filled his eyes, and he found the cap of the bottle. His fingers curled around the bottle as he unscrewed it and placed it to his lips. The bottle tipped, and the liquid slipped into his throat.

He saw her eyes, her face twisted in pain as her flesh was flayed from her body. Each tattoo cut out in painful strips.

A drink of the cold liquor.

The gun shot ran shrill in his ears just as he saw the bullet enter into Agent Wolfe's head first and then Agent Cavanaugh. A pink spray of blood and brain matter speckled the side of his face.

Another drink from the bottle.

Nikka's face streaked in tears as she collapsed in a pool of her own blood.

Another drink.

Gideon's hands on her, pulling her toward him as she fought him. He almost raped her until she stopped him with light and power and such a pained screaming.

Another drink.

The images began to blur just enough that he could close his eyes and not see her bloodied body lying in a mess of rubble and concrete. The memory faded, and then he could see her face now, her bare head adorned in beautiful black tattoos. The copper scent of blood had vanished, and it was only the two of them standing in the dark, only the moonlight existed between them. Her hands touched his face as she smiled and kissed him and finally said that she would marry him. It was one of the last things she ever said to him.

The liquor took over now and allowed him to slip into a quiet lull, away from the sounds of screaming and the smell of blood.

CHAPTER THREE
GIDEON

Gideon heard the thump from downstairs, loud enough to wake him up. The sound only came once, but something about it unnerved him. In a ghost town, nothing should be making sounds any more.

The moonlight poured through the windows of the bedroom, a room that looked like it had once belonged to a ten-year-old girl. Despite the princess-themed décor, the bed was so much more comfortable than the cab of the truck. Gideon pulled himself to his feet and stepped into the hallway. The carpet muffled the sound of his footfalls as he moved to the stairs and listened down to the first floor. Everything remained silent now. The light of Jason's lantern still illuminated the area from the living room, steady and bright.

Things were so quiet down there that the silence crawled against his skin, making the hair stand up on his arms. Something was not right.

He moved down the stairs and stepped out onto the main floor. The lantern light cast his shadow against the far wall as he entered the living room, but there was no sign of Jason there.

Perhaps he had decided to leave. Just like he did last month, and Gideon could not find him for almost four days. Not that he would blame him. In fact, he was surprised that Jason had come back to the little hotel where he had left him alone and without any transportation. But he showed up and never said a word about where he had been. And Gideon never asked.

And then there was the time that Jason had ditched him again, but something nagged at Gideon's brain until he gave in and searched for him. Luckily, he had heeded his feelings. He had found Jason in the lobby of an abandoned urgent care clinic, raiding the medicine cabinet. He had just swallowed about thirty Xanax that he had found in the back cabinet. With enough struggle and force, Gideon fought with him until he had vomited the pills back up and then collapsed in a heap of silent tears.

But Jason had eventually pushed him away and sulked in the back room that night until dawn came. Gideon had saved his life. There would have been no coming back from that if he had not shown up when he did. But Jason never thanked him.

And Gideon never expected it, not after what he had done.

He only did what was planned for him. This was his penance for a goal that he knew he would never attain—redemption.

Now, the prickles of concern tingled down his spine, just like they had the night the Jason overdosed on the pills.

He moved to the window and peered out into the dark, but the pick-up was still parked in the driveway. If Jason was going to leave him again, he would have probably taken the truck. He looked back into the living room, to the duffel bag that sat still unzipped on the floor. He would have taken the bag too. There were too many personal treasures for him in that bag for him to leave it just lying there.

Gideon's gaze moved to the back room, beyond the dark dining room and to the edge of the kitchen visible around the corner. That was when he saw it.

The tip of a boot lying on the ground.

Jason's boot.

He hurried into the dining room and rounded the corner. More of Jason's leg became evident as he entered the dark room. There he was, slouched against the refrigerator with a bottle of liquor in his hand. He must have finished the entire bottle because it had tipped against his leg and there was no liquid spilled over the floor.

Gideon crouched down and placed his hand against Jason's cheek. Still warm. And he was breathing.

He shook his head as he looked at him. He should have known better and checked the cabinets before Jason walked into the kitchen. Of course, he would have drunk anything he found there, just like he took the pills that night. Whatever he could find to silence the memories.

With a steady hand, he pulled the bottle from his hand and placed it on the kitchen counter. Then he drew Jason's arm around his neck and lifted him to his feet. Jason groaned and barely opened his eyes, but he tried to balance him on his legs. Not that it helped much, though. His gait was like jelly at best as Gideon walked him to the master bedroom on the main floor and dumped him onto the bed. Jason moaned again, unaware that Gideon helped his feet onto the bed and then stepped away.

But he watched him sleep, still smelling the scent of the liquor hanging over him like a raincloud.

Gideon was no fool. He knew why Jason abused himself like this. He knew that Jason wanted to kill him by the end of each night. What was he waiting for?

Every day that passed, Gideon wished that he would just do it, even though he was not sure that it would work. He had already lived for over two thousand years at this point, but things had changed seven months ago.

Oh, how they had changed.

Something had happened to him that night. That horrific and unspeakable night, filled with things that he would never forget, no matter how hard he tried. He remembered everything that he did during the months before that night as well. Something had manipulated him into doing them, but that made no difference. He still hurt so many people in that time.

But he hurt Nikka the most.

The things he did to her . . .

Somehow, in her last effort of strength, she did something to him. The one sigil that he had not flayed from her body channeled a power he had never seen before. It struck him and sent him to a place, ever so briefly, that altered him forever.

And, if he did not know better, he could swear that he awoke with a soul.

Maybe that meant he could die now. Maybe that meant that Jason could kill him. So, why did he not do it already?

He could see that Jason struggled every day with the things that had happened that night. Of course, he did. Gideon had forced himself on Nikka when he first came back and then tried to rape her again in front of Jason. He had murdered two of Jason's companions and then destroyed Nikka. And she was taken away from them. Heaven had sent a cherub and taken her back.

What Jason did not know was that Gideon was well aware of Nikka's secret. The very thing that Jason had discovered after that horrible night: Nikka had been pregnant. Jason had tried to hide the pregnancy test from him, but Gideon found it the next night among Nikka's things in the duffel bag. To this day, Jason kept it hidden in there. And he was sure that it was the result of that test that drove Jason to take those pills and drink anything that he found in these dead little towns. That small life, just weeks old, was also taken from both of them that night. The life that could have belonged to either of them. Now, they would never know.

Gideon never expected forgiveness. He did not deserve it. Not from Jason. Not from anybody.

So he would do his job and keep Jason alive, for as long as possible. He would save him from anything, even from himself if needed. He would do it for Heaven. He would do it for Nikka and her baby.

Chapter Four
Jason

His head felt like it had been struck by a sledge hammer. And that was before he had even opened his eyes.

Jason turned to his side, and one eye cracked open just enough to make him nauseated. The dizziness still swirled around his brain, but he knew he had to open his eyes again, even if it hurt. The sounds of birds chirping just outside the window encouraged him to face the light that poured into the room.

At first, he wasn't sure where he had slept. There was a roof over his head and a soft, comfortable bed under his body. None of this looked familiar, though. He lifted his head from the pillow and felt a sharp ache against his ribs. The events of the previous evening finally began to collect in his memory. The three drones. One of them had snagged him. He came back to town with Gideon, and they took shelter in a house that didn't seem too looted.

And he had found a bottle of Jack.

That's why he was nauseated, and his head pounded.

But how did he get to the bed? The last thing he remembered was lying on the kitchen floor. Maybe he crawled into the bedroom somehow.

He forced himself upright and sat at the edge of the bed, his elbows on his knees and his head resting in his hands. *Need to take things slowly. Just try not throwing up this morning.*

At least his head had cleared. No more memories right now.

Despite the spinning room, he stood and stumbled to the door. The morning light came through every window in the house like a blazing white lantern filament, so bright that he found it hard to keep his eyes open. He stepped toward the kitchen and saw Gideon standing at the counter, removing the contents of the upper cabinets.

"Feeling better?" Gideon said, but he didn't look away from his work.

That guy was the last person he wanted to talk to right now. He moved to the kitchen table and sat at one of the chairs, resting his head in his hands again.

The sound of ceramic against the table made him look up to see a porcelain cup just under his nose. Gideon stepped away from the table, a small smile on his face. The warm steam hit him first: coffee. Hot coffee.

"A good remedy for a hangover," Gideon said and turned away from him, going back to the kitchen. "It is only instant coffee, but it was what they had in the cabinet. It will have to do for now."

So Gideon must have found the bottle in the kitchen—the Jack Daniels he had finished off in one sitting. Jason sipped at the coffee. Not bad, especially since they hadn't found any coffee in months, instant or otherwise. As it hit his stomach, the queasiness eased a little.

"We did not have a chance to review the events of last night," Gideon said. "Did you get a name from any of the drones?"

Jason cleared the thickness of bile from his throat. "Namtar."

He nodded, his forehead creased as he looked back at him. "You are sure?"

"Of course I'm sure. Namtar."

"A name of Sumerian origin. Interesting." He turned back to analyzing the things he had removed from the cupboard. "It has been some time since we found one from that era. I will note it."

Whatever. Jason didn't care what he did with the names he collected. Like it mattered, anyway. Most of the drones ended up dead at the end of his sword long before he could get their names. It was probably better that way. Most of the possessed didn't fare well after exorcism these days.

"What's the plan? We staying here or what?" Jason asked after he took a deep drink of the coffee, feeling the pounding easing in his brain.

Gideon turned back and shook his head. "There is nothing here. It has been too long since we found a significant human population. We are no good to anybody out here."

Jason wanted to laugh. *We're no good, period.* There was no helping anybody, no matter where they went. Since the night the lights went out, the demon army had vastly increased in numbers. Portals had opened throughout the world, large gates that released thousands, if not hundreds of thousands of demons, onto the Earth. Without any electricity, apocalypse came and it came quickly. The cities were hit first, where looting and violence took over long before the demons needed to do anything. Chaos reigned. There was no law anymore. No national military. And then ten days later—only ten days—the first nuclear reactor blew. Without power to cool the reactors, the cores just exploded. Large numbers of the population got hit within hours.

And that was just the first two weeks.

Seven months later, he and Gideon still roamed the western half of the country just looking for anybody. Every so often, they found a few people here or there, hiding and just trying to survive. Nobody trusted anyone.

That's because the demons had taken over. The earth was now their playground. The horde had so many fingers in the government, orchestrating this apocalypse, that they now had control. There were a few vehicles still on the roads, and most of them belonged to the demons. Entire hunting parties, usually drones and headed by a few lieutenants, searched the towns as well, looking for any fresh bodies. They wanted anyone worth possessing. Humans had become livestock to them.

And that was why Gideon insisted they keep going, like lone warriors trying to save humanity. If they could save as many people as possible, if they could fight off the hunting parties, maybe they alone could save the world.

Jason didn't buy it, but he went along with it for now. At first, they had found small communities huddled together, trying to keep the monsters from their doors. And Jason was able to keep them safe. But it was only for a short time. They were eventually lost, and he had failed.

So now he stayed on the road, finding these smaller abandoned towns. He knew Gideon thought that they would find a few people in places like this. Jason only wanted to find the next bottle hiding on the bottom shelf, just until he was ready to rid himself of Gideon for good. He just hadn't found the right opportunity yet.

Jason sighed and finished off the cup of coffee. "Whatever you want to do."

Gideon spent the morning going over the canned goods and other minimal food items left behind in the cabinets. Just enough food to keep them stocked in the truck for the next few days, or at least until they found another town. While Gideon searched the rest of the house, Jason took the truck out to the middle of town. Sure, the thought of driving away again was tempting, but today was just not one of those days. His head pounded, and he wasn't in the mood for feeling even slightly guilty for stranding him like this. Not today. He just needed to find some diesel fuel to siphon into the truck and fill the gas tanks in the back.

When he had filled everything, Gideon loaded the back of the truck with the fresh blankets he had taken from the beds and the boxes of food he had collected from the kitchen. They left the abandoned town behind them and headed north on the empty highway.

Gideon had navigated most of their way already, using his collection of maps that he had taken from one of the many gas stations they had found in their journey. He poured over a single map, his finger trailing along a line through the patches of green on the paper.

"From what I can determine, we can stay on this highway for about eighty miles. It will take us into Utah. We have not been there yet."

"You think there will be more people up there?"

"It is worth a try."

Sure. Anything might be worth a try. But they still won't find anybody, at least anybody that will survive. The demons would have taken all of them by now. "Fine. Utah it is."

He pushed the truck further, weaving occasionally around an abandoned vehicle that had just stopped in the middle of the road, an end to a destination that it would never reach. The road had been dusted over with layers of sand and red dirt, swept through during times of storms but never able to clear now that nothing drove the highway anymore. The distant hills turned from bland shades of yellow and brown to rich red and chocolate the further north they drove. Joshua trees dotted the landscape, having escaped from the realm of cacti and rocks.

The signs along the highway told Jason that they were nearing something he had never seen before: Zion National Park. He didn't remember ever seeing a national park as a kid. *Well, better late than never.* After stopping at another lot of abandoned cars, they filled up the gas tank again before he drove into the winding road that entered the park. The auburn rocks that surrounded them and covered the roadside edge shone brilliantly in the evening sun. He found himself driving slower through the winding road, watching the beauty of the rock formations around them.

"There is a campground ahead," Gideon spoke, stirring Jason from admiring the area around them. "A possible place to stop for the night if you wish."

The truck curved around another bend and the scenery looked like it had dropped away into a huge canyon along the side of the road. It was everything that he imagined such a place could be. But, as the truck moved on and the sun set, he knew it would be dangerous to keep driving with such a narrow road in the dark. And nobody was out here. Not a single human or demon.

"Okay," he said. "We can stop for the night."

He followed the signs to the upcoming campground and pulled into a collection of trees. A few other vehicles had been left there, but no other souls populated the place. The best thing, though, was the rows of small cabins and the few water pumps scattered around the campground. They could pump fresh water and fill their bottles. And he could have his own bed in his own cabin, away from Gideon.

He shut down the truck and unloaded his duffel bag from the back. The first cabin to his left looked just fine, and before Gideon could say anything, he took off and walked to the front door. The lock still held, but it was flimsy and didn't take much to pick it until the door opened to him. The dank, musty air hit him first, but this had become so commonplace lately that he barely noticed anymore. The cabin was small, but it had a mattress that still looked like it hadn't been eaten by mice. That was good enough.

"You will need these for the evening," Gideon's voice said behind him.

Jason almost jumped when he spoke. He turned to see a collection of blankets and a box of food in his hands. As Jason looked at him, the furrows began in his brow. The guy didn't need to wait on him; he could get it himself.

"I got it," he said and accepted the items. Gideon hesitated for only a second and then turned away just before Jason shut the door on him.

He settled down on the mattress and turned on his flashlight as he looked in the box of items that Gideon had taken from the house. A few cans of soup. Box of crackers. An unopened box of Cherry Pop Tarts. A few cans of generic soda pop. *Awesome.* He tore into the box of Pop Tarts and rested his head back against the cabin wall as his stomach grumbled. He hadn't eaten much all day, not after the night of heavy Jack Daniels use.

Too bad that he couldn't have found another bottle to take with them, just for tonight. Just in case he started to have the memories again.

At least he was alone in the cabin and Gideon was out there somewhere, fending for himself.

Chapter Five

Jason

The touch against Jason's face first stirred him from the fitful dreams that haunted his thoughts. It might have been a cool breeze, but then he realized that it wasn't cold as much as it was almost liquid, like a breath of frost. Then he smelled the faintest hint of lavender float into the air. Perhaps it was the edges of the dream that still caressed his face.

Then he tasted a hint of peppermint and strawberry. Just like the lip balm that Nikka used to wear.

But it wasn't just a brush or a breeze.

No. It was a kiss. A kiss that grew deeper as he took in a breath. The lavender scent surrounded him as the touch on his cheek grew more tangible.

If this was another dream, he didn't want to wake up. He kept his eyes closed and felt the lips move over his, pressing more firmly and taking his breath away, just like she used to.

Then it stopped, and the hand moved from his face. She was gone, but the lavender fragrance still hung in the air like a spirit.

He had to do it.

Jason opened his eyes to face the darkness of his cabin. There was nobody there. No female hand. Not Nikka's face or her touch.

But he could still smell the floral scent.

Jason bolted upright to see the cabin door was wide open, silver moonlight pouring into the small room. It hadn't been that way when he went to bed. He had made sure he locked it because he didn't want Gideon bothering him about anything. Now it stood open.

There was something else there, though. Beyond the door, down the steps and toward the grassy center of the campground, shadowed in trees. Something stood in those shadows, looking at him.

His ribs ached with the rapid breaths that moved in and out of his lungs. The beat of his heart almost deafened him as he gazed out into the center of the grassy lawn. As the trees swayed in the breeze, strips of moonlight moved over the figure, covered in a billowing white fabric that seemed to envelop it, the edges drifting in the breeze and dancing over the dark grass. Jason moved to his feet and stood at the doorway, ready to unsheathe the sword.

The figure began to move, almost glide, over the grass and away from him. But he could sense its eyes locked onto him. The lavender fragrance drifted over the breeze and lingered at the doorway. The figure moved into a patch of moonlight, and the glow settled on its features like sparkles of silver on a pond at night.

He felt his knees weaken. It had to be a dream.

The light danced over her bare head, now empty of any tattoos. Her slender neck curved down to her pale shoulders where the white robe started and hugged her torso, covering her swollen and pregnant belly. The form—maybe the spirit—looked at him with the same eyes he had gazed into for so many moments before she was taken. Then she raised her hand and reached her fingers out to him, curling them around to beckon him toward her.

It wasn't possible. She was gone, yet there she stood like some ethereal being in the moonlight of the campground, urging him toward her. Everything in his soul wanted to be there with her, but how could she be standing there right now?

Her fingers curled around again, and a gentle smile appeared on her lips that appeared blue in the faint light.

He had to know if it was really her, consequences be damned. Maybe she was here to finally take him away, to take him to the place where she had gone these many months. He bolted from the door with his bare feet and glanced down at the steps as he stepped onto each one. But as he looked back up, she no longer stood in the patch of grass.

No. She can't be gone. Not like that.

His hands trembled as he searched around the space where she had been standing. Nothing, not even evidence of footsteps in the grass.

But the woody, floral scent drifted toward him again.

His eyes darted around the campground, into the shadows between each of the cabins and around his quiet truck.

Then he saw her, the spirit dressed in white, at the far end of the campground near the edge of the trees. She looked at him and turned away, walking into the thick of the trees. The figure began to fade under the shadows cast by the overhanging boughs. Jason felt his heart jump into his throat as he pushed forward, sprinting toward the woods where the spirit had just entered.

He nearly stumbled as he crossed the edge of the woods and jumped over a fallen tree. The little slivers of moonlight barely illuminated this place, and he couldn't see each step he took. It would only be a matter of time before he stumbled and rolled down a hill. The place was so dark, and he lost her again.

A flutter of white flickered at the edge of his vision. He turned toward the movement and saw her again, further down a small slope and standing beside a large tree. The moonlight fell on her form just enough that he could see her face again, her beautiful face. But her abdomen was no longer swollen. Something about her had changed.

Then he saw that she held something to her chest, something wrapped in the same gossamer white fabric that surrounded her.

In the moonlight, he could see the form of a baby held to her chest.

The spirit turned away from him again and plunged into the dark of the forest. He had to find her. To stop her. There was no way he could let her go now. He darted into the trees, calling out her name. The pine needles, rocks and twigs tore at his feet as he ran over the forest floor toward the figure that moved in and out of the slivers of moonlight. It slid behind a tree, and then he could no longer find her in the woods. Darkness surrounded him, his path back to the campground lost.

He called her name again and again until his throat was raw and he could taste blood. The breath caught painfully in his lungs as he gasped for air. His knees trembled, and he crouched down, ready to collapse to the ground.

The lavender fragrance played around his head. He looked up to see a shimmer of white along a knoll in the distance. She stood there, looking at him with the same smile of contentment on her face. The white cloth drifted in the breeze about her ankles. She no longer held a baby in her arms, though. The spirit just looked at him as though she waited for him to come to her again.

Another figure moved beside her, and she looked down to her right. This being, also dressed in white, stepped next to her and clung to her side. It was small, less than waist-high, but Jason could see it's pale skin and big blue eyes. This was a young child, and the spirit touched the child's head with a loving hand.

She looked up at him, reaching her hand out once again, curling her fingers to beckon him to her.

Jason awoke with a start, bolting upright in bed, his breathing fast and painful in his wounded ribs. Sweat had beaded against his temples and soaked through his shirt. His eyes darted to the cabin door, but it was closed and locked, just like he had left it. The air smelled musty, not the comforting scent of lavender.

The dream still hovered behind his eyes, enough that it made his hands shake and his abdomen quiver. He could still taste the peppermint on his lips and feel the ache in his feet from running over the forest floor.

Even as the peppermint faded from his memory, though, the pain in his feet did not. His fingers fumbled around the bed until he found the flashlight he had left there. He flicked it on until he had a faint light filling the cabin space. He pulled back the blankets from his body and felt his breath choke in his throat.

Dirt, dead leaves and twigs covered his feet. As though he had been running through the forest in the middle of the night.

In the dark of the cabin, the edge of the flashlight beam caught something along the door. He pulled himself out of the bed and held the light in his shaking hand as he approached the thing he hadn't noticed when he first closed up the cabin for the night. Pinned to the door was a yellowed and frayed piece of paper, like a page torn from an old book. His fingers tore it free of the silver pin that held it in place.

He looked down at it and shined the light over the words, a song that had been removed from a book and stuck on the back of that door. As he read it, he nearly dropped the paper:

Last night she came to me, my dead love came in.
So softly she came that her feet made no din
As she laid her hand on me and this she did say:
It will not be long, love, 'til our wedding day.

He held the paper in his hand as he opened the cabin door. Someone must have slipped in while he slept and pinned this to the door. A waft of fresh air laced with the scent of pine drifted across the threshold as he looked out into the empty campground. Only night and darkness. Just enough moonlight to see the truck. Nobody else out there.

But he knew that she had been there, if only in a vision. She had left this for him, and the things he saw told him so much more.

Nikka was out there somewhere, with her child, waiting for him to find her.

Chapter Six

Gideon

"Our Father, who art in Heaven, hallowed be thy name," Gideon muttered the words, his eyes closed and his hands clasped before him. The words felt empty tonight. The road had been long and barren, but without this moment, he knew he would never manage to find sleep.

"Thy kingdom come, thy will be done, on earth as it is in Heaven."

If only they still heard him.

In two thousand years, he had hoped for redemption, every day knowing that he did what was asked of him in order to find his way back to his home. But now, he was no longer sure that anyone even cared. Whatever Nikka had done to him on her last night ensured that he now had a soul.

A soul is bright thing, wonderful and awful at the same time.

That is what they told him when they brought him back from the brink of Hell. He had been swallowed up in evil, surrounded by so many fallen angels, with the Devil whispering the most terrible things in his ear. Then Nikka did something, and he found himself surrounded by a host of seraphs long since dead as they guided him back from the darkness.

And when he awoke, he felt the pain of a soul for the first time in his long existence.

"Lead us not into temptation, but deliver us from evil," he whispered and clutched his hands tighter.

There was so much more to the prayer, but this was the only part that mattered to him, especially if nobody else heard him. Now that he had a soul, he needed to care for it and never let it fall. It was a heavy task, and he now understood the burden of Man like never before. The angels no longer spoke to him. He had crossed to the existence of mankind, and he knew he must live as they did. They needed faith because they could no longer hear the voices of Heaven. He never understood how faith worked until now.

Nikka's face still haunted his thoughts every time he closed his eyes, and far too often her eyes were filled with tears that he had caused. He tried to shake those memories free and return to a time before any of that, to the place where they lived together. The place where she taught him to watch movies on his computer and when she touched his face like she never wanted him to leave. In a thousand lifetimes, he had never imagined that he would love a human, but she proved him wrong on so many occasions. He knew every pain that Jason suffered because he understood it too well, only he had no right to relieve it in himself. Jason had earned it; he had caused it.

The sound of the truck gate opening outside of his cabin made his eyes flash open. It may be the middle of the night, but somebody moved about around the truck. If it was Jason trying to leave him again, he needed to be swift in order to stop him.

Gideon moved quickly to his bare feet and rushed to the cabin door. The warm desert air of the park drifted over his closely-trimmed scalp as he gazed through the dark to see a flashlight moving around the vehicle. Jason stepped around the side of the truck and opened the passenger side door.

"Is everything all right?" he asked as he stepped over the rough stones of the driveway.

Jason's eyes were wide and wild as he searched through the glove compartment of the truck. His breathing had quickened like he had been running a marathon.

"I need the map," he said.

"I have it with me in my cabin," Gideon said, motioning back to his quarters.

Jason looked up before he pushed past him and rushed toward the cabin. Gideon followed as Jason moved into his lodging and shuffled through the papers on the table.

"What can I do? I do not know how to help you," Gideon said.

Jason continued pushing around papers until he found the folded map, the edges worn from use. The map unfurled across the table, and he gazed over it with his flashlight in hand. "If we keep on this highway, what other towns will we drive through?" he asked.

Gideon stood beside him. He had studied these state maps so many times that he almost had the routes memorized.

"Not much on this route." Gideon placed a finger along the thin line of the highway they had travelled all day. "That is why it was the best route for us to take at this time. But it will meet with I-70 here."

Jason looked over the lines, and his finger began to trace along the roads, away from the interstates, to smaller routes and highways back into Nevada. His hand trembled so slightly that Gideon almost missed it.

"Something troubles you." Gideon did not want to pressure him. That usually only resulted in Jason shutting down or abandoning him for a few days. He had learned not to trigger any further misguided feelings in him.

Jason shook his head and reached into his pocket, producing a yellowed page that had been torn from a book, and handed it to him. Gideon held it to the light and read the words of an old song.

"I am familiar with this piece," he said. It was something he recalled hearing about 200 years ago, or thereabouts, while he lived in Ireland. These were the lyrics to a sad ballad that was often sung around a fire or during a funeral. And this particular stanza appeared to be especially poignant, given the trials they had both endured.

"This is from a song called "She Moved Through the Fair." I do not understand. Why do you have this?"

Jason seemed to hesitate, halting his breathing before he spoke. "Something just happened."

As he related the vision, Gideon felt the unsettled jittering in his gut. He did not usually experience that unless he was hiding from a hunting party while Jason had gone to fight. This was what anxiety felt like, and he had still not gotten used to it. The things Jason told him, about the figure in his vision with the child, were so much more than just the images in a dream. That, coupled with the verses on the page, indicated that this was a prophecy. A seraph vision.

"We must go," Gideon finally said after Jason had finished. Jason looked at him as though he held more answers, but Gideon had nothing more. None of these images pointed them in any particular direction, nor did it prove that they would find anything when they got there.

Jason stammered, looking like a lost child now, helpless and alone. "Does this mean she's alive?"

In the millennia that he had existed, Gideon had only seen Heaven return one soul back to this world once it had crossed the eternal plain, and it was in Jerusalem over two thousand years ago. The hosts of Hell always had ways of escaping, and the seraph was created to prevent that from happening. But nobody ever wanted to leave Heaven. Nikka was on the brink of death for the second time in her short life the night she was taken. The cherub would have ensured that her spirit had moved through the rend in between the realms, never to return.

But he had no way of explaining the symbols in his vision. A pregnant Nikka that then held a child who eventually stood at her side? This definitely seemed to indicate that there was a chance she may have survived.

Jason must have seen the look of uncertainty pass across his face because now he smiled. That was something Gideon had not seen him do in months. For just that moment, he looked at him with hope instead of hate and anger.

"If she is alive, then you must trust your instinct that you will find her," Gideon said.

"How do I do that?"

Gideon looked down again at the map, to the intersecting lines of highways and freeways that stretched across the western states. Thousands of miles to search. "Go to the first place that feels right. Let your power tell you."

Jason nodded and let his eyes slip closed. His hand spread out on the map, and Gideon could see the muscles in his face relax. He said nothing, the flashlight glow casting shadows through his blonde goatee and over his nose and eyes. The room seemed heavy with the silence as Gideon watched him.

The black markings that snaked up and down his arms began to shimmer and sparkled with faint points of light that undulated just under his skin. Gideon took a single step back and watched Jason's face turn upward, as though he listened to something in the dark. His hand lifted from the page and hovered over the mapped landscape across the table. Fingers twitched. The glow of the tattoos intensified. His index finger curled downward and then planted firmly to the map.

Then the lights disappeared as Jason opened his eyes. Gideon moved closer to him again and heard Jason suck in a little breath.

"Carson City," Jason said. "That's where we need to go."

CHAPTER SEVEN
GIDEON

Gideon helped Jason load the truck with the last of the supplies just as the morning sun began to peek at the edge of the horizon. With the jagged mountains and vast canyons surrounding them, the sky grew light long before they could see the first glimmers of the sunrise. The campground had provided very little to take except the fresh water from the pumps. Once they had packed everything, Jason was more than eager to get on the road.

The look in Jason's eyes was something Gideon had never seen before, and he welcomed it. They finally had a goal that both of them could agree on, even if Gideon secretly felt that it would be only another empty place. The dream—or vision—lit him with a fire that pushed him further toward their purpose. If this is what it took to get them to a place to help people, then Gideon gladly accepted it.

He navigated with the map as usual while Jason drove, his eyes focused and squinting in the summer sun. The road curled through the mountains and beyond more abandoned towns until it opened up at Interstate 70. They had yet to travel this road, but with such a busy freeway in the time before the power died, it proved to have many more vehicles permanently stalled along the path. There was nothing they could not maneuver through as they continued west until Gideon found the exit to the highway that would take them into Nevada once again.

They had just left Nevada a few days before, hoping to never return. That was where everything had gone to Hell, almost literally. As long as they stayed clear of the large cities, and never go back to Las Vegas, they should be okay. This far out into the middle of the desert, they saw nobody else on the roads as the day moved on toward evening. And the time spent checking out vehicles that had fuel they could siphon took more time away from getting to their destination.

"Getting dark," Jason finally said after hours of driving.

Gideon trained his eyes on the map, needing his flashlight now in the coming twilight hour. "It looks like there is a town just up ahead. Austin."

"We'll have to stop there," Jason said as he glanced down to the gas gauge. "Hope it's big enough to find gas."

And shelter, Gideon thought. Even if they were in the deserts of Nevada, hiding under the safety of a roof was far superior to sleeping in the truck, exposed and vulnerable.

The road curled up a small foothill, exposing the empty village of Austin with a smattering of homes nested along the hillside. Jason drove the truck slowly along the abandoned streets as they both inspected the dark windows and doors of every building along the road. The street opened onto the main thoroughfare, just like every small town that they had passed through.

Even in the fading light, Gideon could see the buildings along the street and that a part of this place had been an actual ghost town before everyone had abandoned it.

"Jeez," Jason said, peering at the buildings. "This place is like right out of the old West."

The churches, windows dark and some of them broken, looked to be over 150 years old. At one time, he could tell that the ghost town had been restored, but it now was as empty as the modern buildings surrounding them.

Jason stopped the truck in the center of town, along the side of a hotel. As Gideon stepped from the vehicle, his legs stiff from the long ride, he glanced around and counted at least four churches in the small town. The spires rose high along the hillside and appeared as dark silhouettes against the setting sun. Maybe in one of these buildings, he might find a small measure of peace, a place where he could find a moment to kneel.

He glanced back at Jason, who now worked on picking the lock of the hotel. The door opened to him with little resistance. His gaze fell on Gideon just before he walked inside, and then he too looked toward the nearest church.

"Go ahead," Jason said with a sigh. "I won't stop you."

Gideon nodded and watched him disappear into the dark of the hotel. He turned toward the nearest church and stepped up to the front door that rested open. Beyond that, he only saw darkness inside the building. In these times, though, he knew that even a church could hold certain dangers, and wild animals in these desert hills could be just as precarious as any of the demons that hunted them. He placed his hand on the door and pushed it open. The hinges squealed as the heavy wood tilted to the side. The smell of dry wood and old books drifted past him from the shadows that had settled over the building. For a moment, he stood at the threshold and gazed into the chapel that stretched far away from him.

Rows of tall, narrow windows allowed some light of dusk to illuminate the pews still set along the chapel floor. At the far end, a dais stepped up to a single altar. All of these things appeared untouched, with a layer of dust that coated everything.

Gideon stepped inside, the sound of his boots echoing in the large space. As his eyes adjusted, he saw a single cross standing upright atop the altar. The cross was made of simple wood, no intricate designs or paint. Just a polished, dark wood crucifix held upright in a stand.

He moved to the foremost bench and settled his eyes upon the cross. Even though it had been abandoned, this place still held a power that he could feel, even within that small icon on the altar. This was a place of protection.

The chapel grew darker as the orange hues of the sunset drifted away. He closed his eyes, just listening to the silence. The rumble of the truck still buzzed in his legs, but he tried to focus on only the quiet of the chapel.

Until the harsh click of a shotgun chamber echoed in the room.

"Don't move," a voice called out from behind him.

Chapter Eight
Gideon

Gideon froze, every muscle in his body now tight. The sound of careful footsteps from the door of the church rebounded against the walls of the chapel. Gideon opened his eyes and looked to his side, his head turning slightly.

"I said don't move," the woman's voice came again.

"Okay," he said. "But I am unarmed. You have me at a disadvantage."

The steps shuffled closer to him, and a figure moved around the pew. The fading light fell on her just enough for him to see her shoulder-length auburn hair. The barrel of the shotgun glinted in the light as she trained it toward him. She raised her other arm, and the harsh beam of a flashlight suddenly shone in his eyes. He squinted and held his hands up against the light.

"Are you one of them?" she said, a slight tremble in her voice.

The flash of the light still hovered behind his closed eyes, but he tried to force them open. She needed to see that his eyes were normal, not the oily black or pale white of the demons. When he opened them, he tried to gaze away from the light just enough for her to see.

The flashlight faltered for a moment, and she drew it away from him, but he could still see the shotgun pointed toward him. Lucky for her, he was not a demon anymore. She must not have realized that the eyes do not always give away the monster, that sometimes they can appear as normal as he did now.

"We are just passing through," Gideon said, his hands still up. "But I wished to pray before we went any further."

He heard her breath stop for a moment. "How do I know I can believe you?"

"You cannot," he said. "That is what faith is for."

"What are you, some kind of priest?" The barrel of the gun drifted downward.

"Not exactly."

She pulled the gun away and stood in the faint light of the window. Her face was pale, with bottle-green eyes that he could barely see. She had to be about twenty-five, but he was never a good judge of someone's age. Anybody could look at him and think the same thing, but he was far older than that. The woman bit her lip like she wanted to say something more, but she hesitated. She placed the gun in the crook of her elbow and held out her hand to him.

"I'm Amy," she said.

He shook her hand. "Gideon."

"Wow, that's an old-school kind of name." She smiled and looked away for a second. "I just haven't seen anybody around here in a long time, nobody except those awful things. They're the only ones with cars that I've seen. I just thought you guys were more of them."

Gideon stood carefully, his hands still up in case she still remained skittish with her gun. But she only stepped aside.

"You say you're just traveling through?" she asked, and cocked her head to the side, her green eyes looking hopefully at him.

"Yes, indeed."

She glanced at the ground as her toe tapped at the edge of the pew. "Any chance I could hitch a ride?"

Gideon let his hands fall. "Excuse my saying so, but you do not even know us. How can you just assume that we will be safe companionship?"

"You just told me to have a little faith, so here it is." She looked up at him. "I don't know about your friend hiding out in the hotel, but you don't seem half bad. If a guy would rather go into a church to pray than to smash out the windows, I'm kinda thinking I can put some faith in that guy."

"I suppose that would be true."

"And you sorta talk funny, like you're an English teacher or something."

It was difficult not to smile a little at her innocence, but he forced himself to maintain his composure. "Very well. I can introduce you to Jason, but this will really need to be decided by him."

She smiled, showing her perfectly straight and white teeth. "Awesome."

They had never come across another person in the last month no matter how long and far they searched. But for one to come to him as he prayed was nothing short of a miracle. Perhaps they would not find the thing that Jason sought, but at least they found someone. Someone that needed their help. After all, that was why they were still walking this earth. That was why Jason had not been able to kill himself just yet, no matter how hard he tried. Their task had not been completed.

"Gideon," she called to him as she stopped at the church steps. He turned to face her through the dark. "There's just one more thing. I have a son, and we both need to get out of here."

Chapter Nine
Jason

The sound of the main doors opening reverberated down the hall, but Jason paid little attention to it. He had broken open the door to one of the lower rooms near the front desk. Unfortunately, these doors had magnetic locks, and since there was no electricity, brute force would have to do. A broken door didn't matter, though. The king size bed was made with comfortable sheets and blankets despite the dust that had settled on everything. The lantern light illuminated the room well enough that he could see into the duffel bag as he searched for the bottle of water he had placed there earlier.

His head throbbed from the full day of driving with the sun beating down on the hood of the truck, but just a little sleep might help drive it away. And then tomorrow they would begin the search for more diesel fuel and other essentials. He opened the bottle and put it to his lips when the knock sounded on the broken door behind him.

Jason turned back to shoot Gideon a glare, but he saw the woman first. She stood next to Gideon, entering the room behind him. She chewed on her lip like she was anxious to talk to him. The woman, with a flash of brown-red hair falling to her shoulders, looked at him from around Gideon's back. And then he saw the boy at her side, a kid that stood no taller than her hip, with the same red hair and a pattern of freckles across his nose and cheeks.

"Hey," Jason said, the bottle still hovering around his lip. That felt stupid, but what else do you say when you haven't seen another human in weeks?

"Everybody," Gideon started, "this is Jason. Jason, this is Amy and her son, Dylan."

The woman gave him a nervous half-smile, and her hand clutched at her boy's shoulder. The kid twirled the string that dangled down the edge of his hoodie in his fingers as he just watched him.

"Hi," Amy said and gave him a quick little wave of her hand.

"They need our help," Gideon said.

ஜ♂☯ℰ♂

"We just stayed in my apartment at first," Amy said, sitting on the couch while her son wandered through the room. Her hands fidgeted around her knees, but at least she had taken off her thin jacket. Her tank top looked more comfortable anyway, especially in the warm evening. "Right after the power went out, there was so much looting that we couldn't leave. It just wasn't safe. But we knew we couldn't stay in Vegas, it was too dangerous. It was only a matter of time before somebody broke in. After a few days, we just started walking because none of the cars would start. But with Dylan," she said as she glanced at the boy, "it was difficult. I mean, he's only six. And we were out there on our own. We had no food or water unless we stole it."

Jason rested his elbows on his knees as he sat at the edge of the bed and listened to her.

"We finally found a group of people that took us in. They were travelling north too, planning on going to Salt Lake City. We were out there with them for so long, I lost track of how long. But we were halfway there when we got ambushed by those . . . those things—"

Her voice cracked when she recalled the attack. She glanced down at the floor.

"It was dark, and they came with three big trucks, like military trucks. Lights and guns and everything. When they started shooting, I grabbed Dylan and ran. We hid in a culvert out in the desert until the sun came up. The trucks had long gone by then. I told Dylan to stay there, and I went back." Her eyes rose to look at Jason. "They had killed all of the older people. But they took everyone else. The kids. Men. Women. Everyone was gone."

Gideon flashed a knowing look at Jason. They had seen something like that as well. The demons had started to collect people, but for what purpose, he didn't know.

Tears glistened around her eyelids. "I took Dylan, and we just kept going until we found a town. And then we hid there for a while until it was quiet enough to find the next town. We've been doing that for weeks. We've only seen a few people since then, heading the same way. Until tonight."

Jason waited for her to wipe the tears from her eyes before he spoke. "You realize that you're headed the wrong way if you're going to Salt Lake City."

She looked at him and then to Gideon. "We're not going there anymore. We're going to Oregon."

Jason's brow furrowed. "What's in Oregon?"

"I guess you wouldn't know if you haven't seen anybody," she said and looked back at him. "I heard there's a community up there, walled away and protected from all this. And there's some kind of preacher and his wife living there who's organized a militia and everything. I've heard that it's been preserved from all this . . .." she said as she held out her hands to the dark room.

"So you want a ride to Oregon," Jason said.

"We won't be any trouble, and we can fend for ourselves," she said quickly. "I can pay you."

"Money is no good in this world anymore," he said.

She shot a glance to her son and lowered her voice. The trembling returned in her lip as her head hung, the words caught in her throat and then came out in a whisper. "I can pay you . . . in other ways."

Jason's spine straightened, and he felt like he almost choked. Money didn't have value, and Amy was smart enough to know the value of companionship in this dead world. "What? No, that's not what I meant."

Her glassy green eyes looked up at him. They had grown wide and worried. "Please, I need to get my son to safety. We're barely making it out here on our own."

"Looks like you're actually doing pretty well," he said as he ticked his head toward the shotgun resting by the door.

"Oh, that?" She smiled a little. "I don't even know how to load the damn thing. It's just for show."

Jason stood and paced toward the door while he ran his finger over his goatee. Two more bodies, and a little kid at that. He really didn't need anything slowing them down on their way to Carson City, but they were so close already. Maybe it wouldn't hurt, and Gideon had been on his back for weeks about needing to help people. It was their mission or some shit like that. He glanced over at the boy, with his red hair and bright blue tennis shoes.

Without him and Gideon, these two would never make it in this world. That kid was as good as gone. They were exactly what the demons were hunting.

And he was a seraph. They would probably die without him.

"We're going as far as Carson City," he said.

Amy smiled and stood, her hands clutched together. "Every mile helps. Thank you."

He turned to face her. "You might as well stay here with us. Just pick any room you want."

The tears flowed freely down her cheeks now. She signaled for Dylan, and the two left the room hand in hand, but Gideon lingered at the doorway. He continued to watch them until they had gone far enough away from earshot before he turned back to Jason.

"What?" Jason said and shot him a quick glance.

"We cannot just leave them at Carson City."

"I'm not going to Oregon."

"Why not?"

Jason let out a fast breath. "Because there's nothing there. This oasis she describes doesn't exist. And I'm not a chauffeur."

Gideon hesitated for a moment, half in and half out the door.

Jason turned away, keeping his hands busy with the bag at the end of the bed. He wasn't looking for anything in particular; he just didn't want to talk to Gideon. He moved a few of his T-shirts around and saw the flat, white, plastic stick at the bottom of the bag. The little test with the tiny "+" sign still imprinted in the window. He tossed the shirts back over it. That wouldn't help him at all, and it would have been better if he hadn't seen it just now.

"I'm no savior," he said, his voice dropping. "That was Nikka. Not me."

He wondered if there was anywhere around here that he might find another bottle of Jack Daniels.

Chapter Ten
Jason

To his surprise, Jason slept last night without the aid of the alcohol, but it wasn't without trying. As soon as Gideon had left his room, he slipped away and wandered around the dark town, looking for anything in a cabinet, however, anything with even a hint of proof had been taken long ago. So he had collapsed onto his bed and waited for the anger to subside and then he had fallen asleep.

He must have been fatigued because the sun shone hot and bright by the time he had opened his eyes. Maybe it was the bed, but his muscles ached far less than they had when he went to sleep. As soon as he had pulled his shirt over his torso, he stepped out of the hotel and squinted into the bright light. Amy stepped around the back of the truck and spotted him as he emerged from the shade of the hotel awning.

"Good morning," she said with a wide smile.

It was too early in his day for being so cheery. He only gave her a brief wave of two fingers.

Then Gideon appeared around the corner, carrying a laundry basket filled with supplies. He placed them in the back of the truck and eyed Jason.

"Ah, you have finally awakened," he said.

Jason wandered stiffly to the edge of the truck bed and gazed inside. Amy stepped up beside him and leaned in with a whisper. "He wanted to wake you hours ago, but I distracted him." Then she backed away with a wink of her eye.

"What's all this?" Jason said, glancing over boxes of what appeared to be canned and boxed food, bags of cereals and grains, gallons of water and a basket full of fresh clothes.

"My contribution," Amy said. "We've been here a while and I just sort of collected these things, thought we could use it. Didn't want any of it to go to waste."

He rested his arms against the side of the truck while he fought to fully wake up. There was a lot of stuff here, including two more five-gallon red gas cans.

"Oh," she said as she watched him scan the bed of the truck. "Found some more tanks. I filled those and the others you had back here. Diesel, right?"

Damn, she was already earning her way.

"Yeah," he said, but he felt like there should have been more he could say to her.

"I told you, we won't be a burden."

"I believe you," he said, feeling Gideon's eyes on him. He wasn't ready to hear an *I told you so* speech from him.

"Okay," he said. He rubbed his eyes and took in a deep breath. "On to Carson City."

The sun pounded down as hot today as yesterday, maybe hotter. Jason drove the truck down the highway with Amy and Dylan in the cab. Gideon had offered to ride in the back, to avoid the uncomfortable closeness of having four people in the front. Good enough. It was sort of refreshing not having to sense him right next to him for hours on end. Only thirty minutes into the drive, the kid started talking.

"What's your name?" "Why are you out here?" "What's your favorite color?"

After so many questions, Amy tapped him on the shoulder. "He doesn't need to have the twenty questions, okay?"

"Sorry," Dylan said.

Jason glanced at him and then back to the road. The boy had found an action figure somewhere back in Austin and played with it on his knees. "What'd you find back there?"

He held up the figurine. "It's Spiderman."

"Oh, yeah," Jason said. He wasn't sure why, but the name made his stomach fall a little.

"Yeah, I like the comics. I have the last five issues ever made," Dylan said with a smile.

The comics. Nikka loved Spiderman too.

Jason just nodded for a moment, trying to avoid the constriction that started in his throat. "I—I had a friend that liked Spiderman."

"He's my favorite."

From the corner of his eye, Jason saw Amy tug on the kid's shirt as if to say that he needed to be quiet. She wasn't stupid; she was well aware of what happened in the driver's seat as she saw his eye twitch and the single swipe of his hand across his damp eyes.

"I'm sorry," she said.

He glanced at her for a moment, and her eyes had creased around the edges. It was the same look you give someone when you don't know what else to say.

"Your friend; you mean the woman Gideon told me about."

Jason's eyes flashed to the rear view mirror, to Gideon sitting in the bed of the truck. He had no right to talk about Nikka, especially to a stranger. His fingers clutched around the steering wheel until his knuckles turned white.

"What did he tell you?" he said through clenched teeth.

"You know," she stammered, seeing the color drain from his hands, "we don't have to talk about this."

"What did he tell you?" he said more forcefully.

She swallowed first. "That you lost someone, your fiancé. I'm really sorry I brought it up. He only told me to warn me that you might be a little . . . sensitive about it."

The muscles in his jaw had tightened until they hurt. He forced open his fingers on the wheel and let them relax. "It's all right." Then he shot a glance toward her and felt his jaw loosen. "It's true. Her name was Nikka. It happened the night of the power loss."

"I'm really sorry," she said.

"It's okay. It's just . . . we haven't talked about it since that night." He realized he hadn't even said her name aloud since then either.

"Well, I'm all ears if you need to," she said as she looked away from him and to the road while Dylan played at her side. She didn't say anything else about it.

The road continued on in silence between them, with only the occasional random question from Dylan. For a while, Amy rested her head back and slept while he drove the road to Carson City.

Jason slowed the vehicle as he started to see the first evidence of Carson City. When the truck decelerated, Amy awoke and gazed out the window.

The town was larger than most that they had passed through lately, and with the larger towns came more evidence of looting. The place looked abandoned, just like the others, but the windows in most of the buildings were shattered, cars along the streets looked like most had been gutted for stereos or speakers. As if any of that would work now. Some of the buildings had been completely burned out. This place was definitely no utopia.

Jason drove the truck slowly down the main street, curving through the town and past casinos whose lights would never illuminate again. The greatest degree of destruction rested at the doors of the casinos where the windows were shattered and slot machines had been thrown out onto the streets. Looters had obviously raided these places first to get to the money, but cash was useless in this world. They still saw no sign of any people, though. Just evidence of chaos that had long since passed.

"This is nothing like I thought it would be," Amy said as her arm held tighter to her boy.

Jason had thought the same thing, but the apprehension kept his lips closed. He turned the truck around a burned out mini-van in the middle of the road, and the capitol building came into view. From this distance down the street, it looked like it hadn't suffered as much damage as the rest of the town. He continued to drive until they neared the outskirts of what appeared to be a mall.

"You can probably stop here," Amy said.

He looked at the building, the front entrance open to shattered glass and with evidence of scorch marks around the pillars.

"I'm not so sure about that," he said.

"The parking lot's full of cars," she said. "There's a better chance of me finding a working car here than anywhere else."

The gnawing pull of guilt began to build in his gut as he turned the truck into the lot. He drove down many of the rows of parked vehicles, but none looked old enough to have survived the power outage. The car had to be at least pre-1994, and those were really difficult to find nowadays.

He stopped the truck, and before he could say anything, Amy stepped from the vehicle and shaded her eyes with her hand. Dylan jumped out after her and began to run around the lot, playing with his action figure. Gideon climbed out of the back as he gazed around the side of the mall.

"We cannot leave her here," he whispered to Jason.

As he watched her walk among the cars, gazing into windows for any keys, he began to nod his head. "I know."

He felt a weight building on his shoulders. They had made it to Carson City—the long anticipated destination that had promised to be something amazing. They were supposed to find their hope here. At least, that's what he felt after he had his dream. Or vision. Or whatever it was. Why would he have the urging to come here, to this burned-out, desolate hell-hole if there wasn't something to find?

"There's nothing here," he said, glancing at the vast expanse of town around them. He didn't expect Gideon to say anything, nor did he want him to. "I was wrong."

Jason wanted to sit, maybe just climb into the back of the truck and stay there forever. All of this was for nothing after all. Maybe it had only been a dream. It wasn't ever a vision. Nikka wasn't here.

Then he heard a sound, a whistling that rang out into the air. The moment he realized what it meant, it was too late. A fireball exploded just three cars away from them, sending the vehicle careening into the air. The impact wave from the rocket hit him and Gideon like a storm, throwing them back against the pavement.

Chapter Eleven

Jason

Jason hit the pavement hard, his spine crunching back toward the hard cement along the back row of cars where his truck had been parked. The sound of the blast still rang in his ears and reverberated in his skull. For a moment, he didn't know what had brought him to his back, but then he saw the plume of fire and smoke arise accompanied by a shower of debris. He rolled to his side and saw the parking lot, bumper after bumper of abandoned cars.

Then he saw the olive green Humvee driving down the next row, a half dozen men standing along the running boards and one standing with the rocket launcher in the back. Even from where he was he could see their faces, black oily eyes and rotting teeth. Demons.

The vibration of the blast still skittered through his bones, but he pulled himself to his feet and saw Gideon by his side. He had fallen next to him and struggled to get up.

The ringing in his ears faded as soon as he heard Amy's scream.

He looked around the other side of the truck and saw her, but her face creased with fear as she shouted toward Dylan. Jason followed her gaze and saw that the boy had wandered to the far end of the parking lot long before the blast had hit. He must have started running when he heard the explosion, but the Humvee closed in behind him. Amy scrambled to her feet and rushed around the side of the truck, but Jason stopped her before she could get too far from him.

"Let me go," she cried as she watched the vehicle bear down on her son.

"If you go out there, you'll die," he said, struggling to hold onto her.

"I don't care. That's my son out there."

She pulled and clawed at him as she watched her child run, and Jason looked down the row of cars. The Humvee drew closer, but they were all out in the open now. The hunting party wouldn't just stop at the child. As soon as they grabbed him, they would be next.

Gideon got to his feet and stumbled toward the front of the truck. Jason released Amy's arms, but grabbed her wrist and shoved her toward Gideon.

"Both of you need to hide, now," he said and looked back at Dylan. *Damn it.* If he did this, there might be no coming back from it.

"What are you going to do?" Gideon said as a trickle of blood slipped down his temple from a fresh laceration along his scalp.

"I have no idea," he said as the trucks moved faster. "Go, now."

Before he even knew where they would go, Jason bolted down the row, toward Dylan as he cried to escape the oncoming hunters. The boy looked back and saw the vehicle coming closer. Jason pushed harder, hearing the roar of the Humvee straight ahead. Each step against the pavement pounded in his head.

Dylan looked up at him, his eyes wide with fear and his face streaked in fresh tears. The boy cried out again just as Jason neared him, but the truck accelerated. The demons inside laughed and screeched as they saw him. There was no mistaking who he was in the bright mid-day sun, with the black tattoos apparent against his arms and up his neck. He grabbed the boy into his arms and spun on his heels just as the Humvee barreled just feet from him. It drove so close behind him now that he could feel the heat blowing through the front grill of the truck.

He dodged right and ran between two parked cars as the Humvee rushed past him. The child clung to his neck, his weight heavy in Jason's arms. He pushed harder as he heard the squealing tires of the Humvee spin against the pavement and turn back around to come at them from the other side. The hot Nevada air burned in his lungs with each step.

From the other side of the lot aisle, between two abandoned trucks, something came out toward him, an engine blaring loudly. He hadn't noticed at first, but when he did, it was too late. A drone on a motorcycle raced out in front of him, the creature grabbing Dylan and tearing the child from his arms. The momentum of it pulled Jason off his feet and threw him to the ground. He hit the pavement hard for the second time. Then, another motorcycle circled around, two engines screaming like harpies that waited for more vultures to arrive. The roar of the Humvee came close, and he heard the screech of the tires as it came to a halt.

He hurried to his feet again just as the drones from the Humvee jumped to the pavement and rushed at him. They had every weapon imaginable: guns, staffs, axes, cross-bows. And the business-end of everything pointed at him.

"A seraph," one shouted as he swung his staff around in front of him. His lips had almost gone blue with the dark ooze that trickled at the corners of his mouth. "Oh, Lila's gonna love this."

The rest of them circled as the one who had grabbed Dylan pulled the child back toward the Humvee. Jason could hear the boy's screams for help, but with the crowd of drones that surrounded him now, the kid would have to wait.

He planted his feet and eyed the circle, each drone pulling in closer. The smell of sulfur and rot hovered like a cloud around them. As they drew near, his tattoos itched and quivered. He reached behind his back, felt the hilt of the sword, and withdrew it. The flames came to life with his grip as did the sparkling lights that inched through every tattoo on his body.

"Let's play," he said.

With that, the drones came at him from all directions. The sword moved smoothly, striking the first demon. Another came, a volley of movement and foul odor. Something struck at him, and the sword blocked at his side. Hands grabbed him around the neck from behind and pulled him back. He almost lost his footing but twisted just in time to free himself. He stabbed toward the demon that had him, but it dodged to the left and swung his axe. This knocked him off balance, and he felt another land on his back. With the sword tight in his grip, he lunged and sliced through the torso of the first demon. It crumbled to ashes as he turned and threw the next one off his back. Just as it fell to the ground, he brought the sword down through its chest. The beast screeched before it collapsed into embers and char.

Another shift of movement came from his right as the demon with the staff rushed at him. He blocked, and then felt a blow to the back of his head. For just a second, the world had gone black, and his entire body felt numb. No stars. No pain. When he opened his eyes, he lay on the ground, his face pressed to the pavement, and the sword had fallen out of reach. He reached his hand out to grasp it, but his fingers couldn't touch the hilt.

A military-style boot stepped right in front of his face as he heard grinding laughter come from all around him. Then, another blow struck him in the head as the world went completely dark.

Chapter Twelve
Jason

When Jason opened his eyes, in the few moments he was lucid, he saw the back of the Humvee and the remaining drones that had ambushed him. Dylan was there, held in the front of the Humvee by two demons that had bound his hands. The glint of his sword in the hands of a drone next to Dylan caught his eye. The next thing he saw was the dark space the Humvee had driven into before they pulled him out of the back of the truck.

The hands that grabbed him forced him to his feet, but his eyes could barely focus through the swirling image that danced in his vision. The last blow to his head must have been a good one. They shoved him forward into the darker space where the sounds of other things echoed down long passages. They forced him up a series of steps, and his head begin to clear. There were more voices now, more than could be accounted for by the small band of hunters that had taken him and Dylan. When he felt that his legs were no longer so unsteady, he pushed forward until he felt the muzzle of a gun at his back. The gun nudged him onward, flanked by a squad of drones on all sides. He glanced back just once and saw Dylan in the grasp of another demon at the rear of the group.

A pair of double doors opened, and he almost stumbled through the vast entryway of what used to be a large casino and hotel. A grand atrium with white pillars now looked like the gates of Hell, with a large bonfire in the center of the room and torches on the walls. The atrium opened through the center of the hotel in a column that rose up several floors, and the once-glass ceiling had been shattered to release the smoke of the fire. Hundreds. No, probably thousands of pairs of eyes now watched him from each level of the hotel. Black eyes, seething with hatred at the seraph that had been captured by the hunting party.

His escorts moved him through the atrium as demons walked around, their necks craning to see him. At first, he wasn't sure what he saw at the far end of the room that had probably once been the casino floor, but he slowed as he watched. They were people, regular and unpossessed, crowded together and inspected by a group of demons as if they were cattle. They must have been humans collected from outside and brought there, but for what purpose?

The gun prodded him on further. "No stopping," the drone behind him said.

Three men moved into their path, and Jason could see the demons slithering behind their faces. The entourage stopped and faced these men, who looked like they were not much older than him, but their dark eyes and cracked lips told him they had been possessed for a long time. They were dressed in black, as seemed to be the wardrobe for this den of devils. The man in the center smiled with a twitching lip, his black hair rising in a low Mohawk of long locks tinged in strands of bright red.

"What have we got here?" he said and grabbed Jason's chin, who tried to jerk away from the demon, but the gun at his back pressed painfully into his spine. The two drones at his sides grabbed his arms and held him fast. "No way you found a seraph."

"We did—Belphagor, and he's our trophy," the drone to his left said, the guy's shaved head filthy with dirt and axle grease. He shoved Belphagor away. "We're taking him to Lila."

"Fine," Belphagor said, "but I want his sword."

Shaved Head stiffened at his side, and Jason could see the glint of the blade in the man's hand as he tugged it against his leg. "I caught him, so it's mine."

Belphagor's lip twitched again, his eyes even blacker. Jason could feel the air temperature plummet, cold enough to make his breath escape in puffs. The argument drew more demons, all drones, around them. They gathered like wolves surrounding a dying animal, eyes never wavering from him and inspecting the tattoos along his arms.

So many demons in one place. He had never seen a hive like this before, and he would probably never see another one again. Trying to save the kid got him into this mess, and it was bound to be the last good thing he ever did.

Carson City wasn't meant to be a haven for him like he had thought. It had turned out to be his final mistake.

He had gotten distracted enough by the circling demons that he hadn't noticed the argument had escalated too far. Belphagor jumped at Shaved Head, claws tearing at each other. The other drones surrounding them cackled in delight. The scuffled crashed against him, and he fell back against the white granite floor. The fight had turned into absolute chaos in a room full of demons. Jason turned to his side and worked at the duct tape on his wrists. He bit at the bonds, trying to pull them free. The tape frayed at the edge as he pulled harder and faster.

Screeching and howling filled the atrium, carrying up to a dozen balconies that overlooked from the hotel tower.

Then hands grabbed at him and dragged him across the floor. He glanced up to see several demons surrounding him, clawing at his flesh as if they were ready to tear him to pieces. These were not the same entourage that had brought him here, either. These were more drones that just wanted to end the seraph. Cold hands wrapped around his throat. He saw rotting teeth flashing in the firelight. Black claws. Dead eyes.

The sound of a gun blast exploded into the room, and everything fell still and quiet. Even the hands around his neck and the claws that tore at his T-shirt now froze. All faces turned to the source of the sound, at the distant end of the room.

"What is this noise?" a woman's voice, angry and sharp, shouted out into the atrium.

The claws around him receded as bodies scrambled away, leaving him in the center of the atrium with his hands still bound in front of him. The crowd of a hundred demons parted along the main walk from him to the woman who stood at the base of a collapsed pillar, a shotgun in her hand, and the muzzle still smoking.

In the firelight, he saw the gun in her slender hand. Her ebony skin looked unblemished, adorned in a black leather halter top. Her black hair had been cut short, but a long swath of hair swept over her right eye, barely concealing the glowing red behind her pupils. The cold that came off of her body chilled him more than it did around the drones. Two creatures settled at her side, beasts with hulking bodies and standing on all four legs, twisted horns spiraling from their skulls. Hell hounds. He had seen another one like these in his apartment right after the Hell portal opened back home.

This must be Lila, and she wasn't just another mindless drone. She was a general.

"Master," Shaved Head said and cowered before her as she looked at the mass of demons. He scrambled toward Jason and pulled him to his feet. "I have brought you a gift."

The demon yanked Jason forward by the tape at his wrists. In all his time since he had been the seraph, he had never fought a general. Plenty of drones and an occasional lieutenant. He hadn't sensed this degree of evil since he felt Abaddon take over his body and hold him hostage for six months. It was a feeling that he hoped to never know again.

She drew the shotgun to her side and took a step forward, the hounds moving with her. Her dark lips split into a grin. No black ooze or foul odor dripped from her like with the drones. She was pure evil power.

"You found a seraph," she said, her ember eyes moving over every inch of his skin. "How wonderful. Excellent."

Then her eyes drifted to his left, to Dylan in the clutches of the drone across the room. "And this one was with him?"

"Yes, Majesty," Shaved Head said.

Those embers moved back to him, and the chill moved down his spine. "I know who you are. You were once Abaddon's vessel. I would recognize you anywhere. This will be interesting." She stood straighter and glanced to the entourage of drones that had brought him into this nest. "Take him to be prepared. The little one, too. Destroy the sword and remove the tattoos. If Pazuzu taught us anything before he was lost to us, it is that the seraph's power lies in the marks. I will notify the Master."

She nodded her head, and the entourage rushed toward him, grasping his arms and dragging him back through the atrium. The woman watched him for only a moment before she turned away with her Hell hounds. The drone holding Dylan raised him over his shoulder and carried him along to wherever the general had demanded. The room of demons howled with delight as they watched the group move toward the staircase that led down to the deeper levels of the hotel.

The light of the bonfire faded with each step down to the lower floors. Demons surrounded him now, each clambering to grasp his arms or shove him forward, ecstatic that they were going to "prepare" him, whatever that meant. Torchlight illuminated the dark corridors where the entourage moved him. They entered another pair of double doors that opened into a large dark space.

The smell of the torches changed to the tart odor of motor oil. No torches down here. This had probably been the parking garage to the casino at one point. But it had been transformed into a factory or a staging area for something greater. White lanterns hanging from the surrounding cement pillars illuminated the space in harsh white light. They moved beyond a scattering of Humvees and motorcycles, just like the ones that he had seen with the hunting party. Beyond the parked vehicles, the garage opened into a wide space arranged with a few tables and racks adorned with a variety of tools, weapons and guns. At first, he thought these were instruments for the vehicles, but as he neared, he saw that they looked more like surgical tools. Blades, saws, retractors. Surgical-grade steel. The tables in the center of the room weren't just tables, either. They were metal slabs, and they were streaked in blood.

When he saw this, Jason instinctively pulled his arm free. His heart pounded in his chest as he heard Lila's words to them: 'remove the tattoos.' She knew to do that because that's exactly what they did to Nikka, and she had lost her power when they had flayed every mark from her body. They knew what to do because Pazuzu—Gideon—had shown them. His legs wouldn't move forward anymore. The air in his lungs seized as he looked upon that table.

Cold hands dug into his arms. A dirty rag wrapped around his mouth from behind his head, gagging him. The drones lifted him from his feet and threw him against the slab. Claws tore his shirt and the bandage around his ribs from his torso and held him supine against the cold metal slab. He shouted against the gag in his mouth, the vision of pools of blood at Nikka's feet from every cut made on her body now roaring in his head.

He heard Dylan scream, and as the demons pulled Jason's bound hands forward, he glanced to his left and saw the drone carry Dylan to another slab. A demon stepped up to the table with a blow torch and an iron brand in his hand, clicking the blue flame of the torch to life.

Cold hands against his bare skin brought his attention back to his own slab. Shaved Head leaned in closer to his ear as the other held him down. He heard the slink sound of a steel knife being pulled from the far wall. Shaved Head breathed against his ear, the stink of it almost making him gag.

"Oh, this is gonna be good," he said. "You'll be one of them, once a seraph and now a breeder. I knew she would have a plan in mind."

The demon holding his hands pulled harder, stretching his arms in front of him. That meant the first cut was coming soon, and as soon as they started, he didn't know if he would still be awake to feel the last one. He heard Dylan cry out, but he could no longer see him through the throng of demons that had gathered around his slab.

He remembered hearing Nikka's cries that night, and there was nothing he could do. Bound and helpless then, just like now.

Don't give up. It was almost like he could hear her voice in his head.

They had his sword, and he had no way of fighting off this many demons. *Get up.*

The smell of rotting flesh surrounded him. Claws dug into his flesh where they held him tight against the metal slab.

Get up now.

He could hear her voice, urging him. Like she stood right there, and he could feel her hand on his face.

Through the smell of oil and smoke and rot, he noticed something else, the faintest thing. The feel of an icy blade touched the first mark on his back. He closed his eyes, and then he smelled the lavender.

I love you.

His eyes flew open at the moment he thought he heard her voice. The tattoos rippled with light as he felt the surge of power rise from his gut, the strongest current of it he had ever felt. He didn't know where it came from, but it energized every muscle in his body. He jerked his arms toward his body, and the demon holding him lost his grip. With bound wrists, he wrapped his arms around Shaved Head and smashed his face down against the metal slab. This was enough to distract the others, and the hands holding him down loosened. He yanked the gag from his mouth and tore the tape free from his wrists with a quick swipe against the edge of the table.

Jason leaped to his feet and hurdled over the demon that held the knife. The power fueled his limbs, guiding him with each movement as he turned. He wrapped his arm around the demon's neck and grabbed the knife, plunging it into the demon's chest. The rest of the drones fought their way around the slab, but he stepped on the body of the demon he had just stabbed and flipped over the other edge of the table.

The two drones that held Dylan had stopped and now glanced over at him. As though fate intervened on his behalf, he saw the sword in the hand of the demon that held down the boy. The blow torch drone turned toward him and swung the iron brand at him. Jason kept his forward momentum but ducked back as the brand whistled through the air. The power surged into his core where he felt it explode through his arms. He landed a strike into the demon's throat as he stood and kicked him back against the wall of tools. The drone crashed into the racks, sending a thousand pieces of steel, knives and guns tumbling to the floor in a cacophony of sound. That would surely be enough to alert the rest of the hotel that something had gone wrong down here.

That meant he had to move faster. He slid across the slab and kicked the other drone away from Dylan. As the demon fell, he grasped the hilt of the sword. The blade came to life, illuminating the small space around them in blue light. And lighting the faces of the rest of the drones that rushed at him.

The tattoos lit up in a firework of shimmers as soon as his hand felt the cold metal of the hilt. He looked toward the onslaught of demons with eyes glowing an electric blue as well. Dylan lay frozen on the slab, gazing at him with his mouth agape. Jason pulled him off the table and shoved him down under the slab as he faced the demons that rushed them.

The power coursed down his muscles, sizzling under every tattoo. He lunged toward the attack, the sword slicing through the air. The demons screeched with each surge. Claws rushed at him, and he saw blackened teeth snapping. The blue light cut through the onslaught, bursts of ashes fell around him as he beheaded one after another. A demon shoved the slab toward him, trying to send him off balance. A drone jumped at him from behind, but he turned and cut through him before he could strike with the knife in its hand. The slab crashed at him, and Jason leaped over the edge to see the last demon rush at him with its outstretched claws. He spun and led with the sword in his left hand, cutting through the demon's neck as he lunged toward the drone.

The last thing he heard was the sound of the ashes falling on the overturned slab. Everything in the garage had fallen silent, but it only took seconds for him to hear the sound of more demons coming down the corridor. Something had alerted them that things were not going well in the garage.

Jason rushed around to crouch in front of Dylan. He saw the frightened boy huddled below the table. "We've gotta get out of here," he said, trying to catch his breath.

The blue glow of the flames cast light over the boy's face, and he looked at Jason's blue sparkling tattoos. His eyes had grown wide, and tears soaked his cheeks. Without a word, he just nodded his head and took Jason's outstretched hand.

Before he stood, Jason rifled through the mess of tools that had crashed to the ground until he found a lever-action shotgun. He opened the barrel: loaded. He tucked the gun under his arm, put the sword behind his shoulder and ran with the boy's hand in his, away from the staging area and back to the vehicles he had seen in the dark section of the garage. The sounds from the corridor grew louder and closer. He ran to the first thing he recognized, something he knew he could use quickly.

The motorcycle was just like the Harley he had long before all this happened. He straddled the bike and pulled Dylan behind him, storing the shotgun between their bodies. Shouts echoed down the hallway, just feet from the doors that would open into the garage.

He put Dylan's hands around his bare torso. "You've gotta hold tight, okay? And close your eyes. Don't open them for anything. Got it?"

Dylan nodded. "Got it," his little voice said as he pinched his eyes closed.

Jason glanced back at the doors. He stood on one leg, his other foot on the kickstarter. One thrust down, but the bike didn't start. Another. Another.

The doors crashed open to the throng of crazed Drones that poured into the garage.

He thrust the starter down again, and the engine finally roared to life.

Demons rushed toward them as he gunned the throttle. The back tire spun out when he turned the wheel, and the bike surged forward into the dark of the garage. The feel of the motorcycle moving them into the dark coursed through his veins like the power in his tattoos. He maneuvered the motorcycle onto a ramp that spiraled up to another parking level that he hoped wasn't blocked in some way. The lot opened up, and painted arrows along the ground illuminated by the headlight of the bike pointed his way to an exit that he prayed was still open.

Just under the roar of the engine, he heard another set of motors come to life from the lower level of the parking garage. He throttled hard, feeling Dylan press tighter to his back. The motorcycle rushed through the main level until he could see the open access into the garage. He drove faster, plunging into the oncoming twilight that had descended over the desert. The surrounding city had left behind a maze of abandoned cars that he maneuvered around but still tried to maintain his speed.

Then he saw the headlights of a Humvee appear behind them, rushing from the garage and plowing down the street, crashing into the obstacles of abandoned cars.

He hit the throttle harder and turned down another street that opened up toward the highway. The bike moved faster down the road and beyond the edges of the city. The engine screamed as he pushed it down the highway. In the rearview mirrors, he saw the Humvee turn onto the highway and barrel toward them. There could have been more, it was too hard to tell and keep his attention on the dark road before him. But the truck moved faster than his motorcycle, and it was only a matter of seconds before it caught them.

Dylan clutched his little fingers around his waist, and he felt the boy's head pressed against his back. Jason released one hand from the throttle and grabbed the sawed-off end of the shotgun. He pulled it free and levered it until he felt a shell lock into the barrel. The Humvee grew closer in the mirror.

He took one look at the road ahead, long enough to know what the next quarter mile looked like in the light. Then he hit the brake, swinging the back tire around, and planted his boot against the pavement. Dylan's hands grasped around him even tighter with the sudden stop of the bike, The Humvee roared toward them as he aimed the gun and fired it toward the right front tire. The rubber exploded, and at that speed, the vehicle swerved against the blown tire, sending the truck into a deadly roll across the road. Jason didn't wait to see it land in the ditch. He throttled the motorcycle and spun the back tire. With the sound of shearing and metal scraping along the road, he rode further down from the crash and the hive of demons that would continue to search for him and the kid in the dark.

He tucked the gun back between their bodies again and kept the engine fast down the highway. Dylan had finally loosened his grip when he realized that there was no more noise behind them and no more gunshots. Night had descended upon the desert, but Jason could see the highway signs that would lead him back to Carson City. He had no idea, though, if Gideon would still be there with Amy. It was the last place they had been, and he hoped that they would be able to find them there. And he hoped that another hunting party hadn't already found them.

The empty road continued into the dark, and he checked his mirrors for any sign of lights behind him, but the road remained quiet at least for now. By the looks of the road and the signs, the demons had taken them to Reno, but he didn't remember it being this far. They must have hit him in the head harder than he thought.

The night grew darker until he finally began to see the outskirts of Carson City. All he could do was retrace his steps, to go back to where they had last seen each other. He drove the motorcycle deeper into town and toward the mall parking lot.

The bike's headlight cast out before them as he slowed in the lot. He saw his grandpa's truck, the doors gaping open just as they had when the rocket explosion had distracted everybody. He pulled the bike to a stop and dropped the kickstand. Dylan slid off the back first. Jason finally stood, his muscles stiffening from the exertion of the fight. Without a shirt, his skin felt cool from the ride, and he felt a small shiver start up his spine. Was that the cold, or was it the worry that he might not find Amy and Gideon?

Dylan walked to the truck, his eyes looking into the dark beyond the light of the motorcycle. Jason gazed into the cab to see that everything was still there and all of the supplies were still in the back.

He had told them to run, to hide. Hopefully, that's what they did because they definitely didn't come back for the truck. They could have taken it and continued on, but knowing Gideon, he wouldn't want to leave him.

"Where are they?" Dylan called from the front of the truck.

Jason sighed as he gazed over the untouched supplies. "I don't know."

"Where did my mom go?"

Dammit. He didn't want to tell the kid his mom was just gone.

Then a sound came from the far end of the lot. It intensified, and he realized he heard shouting. A woman's voice.

The kid turned toward the sound when he heard her shout his name.

"Mom!" he called and ran into the dark parking lot toward her.

At first, Jason felt his spine stiffen, but then he saw two figures emerge from the abandoned mall. The muscles in his shoulders and neck loosened as they walked closer. Dylan rushed into Amy's arms as she ran to him and crouched down among the rows of cars. He heard her crying and saw how puffy her eyes had become since he last saw her. With a sore knee and back, he limped toward them and saw Gideon step beside her in the beam of the motorcycle headlight. His hazel eyes looked at him with relief.

Amy cried and wouldn't let her son go as she buried her head in his hair. "I didn't think I was gonna see you again." Then she pulled away just a little and placed her hands on his cheeks. "I love you so much."

Jason watched her hold and kiss him over and over until Dylan finally started to laugh. Then, he turned away from them and limped back toward the truck. He just needed to lie down somewhere, but they also had to get away from Carson City and soon. The demons would surely come back to comb the streets looking for them.

He leaned against the side of the truck, feeling the cold metal against his skin. Maybe it was the night or the feel of the wind against his bare chest during the ride back to Carson City, but he felt chilled to his deepest sinews and joints. It wasn't just the adrenaline, either. Something trembled and quaked inside him, aftershocks that still rumbled in his memories. The worst thing that he had tried to forget was seeing Nikka tortured and flayed, watching her power be stripped from her until she had nothing left. Not only did he have to relive that, but he experienced her helplessness, if even for a moment when the demons had him in their grasp.

Need to drown those memories. Can't think of them ever again.

His fingers began to shake, so he clutched them into fists and pressed them against the side of the truck.

Gideon's voice interrupted his concentration. "Are you okay? What can I do?" He approached the truck.

He glanced at him but kept his fists against the metal. The shaking ebbed a little, just enough for him to feel more steady on his knees. "Let's just get on the road."

When Gideon didn't move or say anything for a moment, Jason turned to him to see the satisfied smile on his face. Jason cocked his eyebrow. "What?"

"You saved that child's life," he said.

"Don't." Jason turned away from him. He didn't need Gideon doing that. Nothing special had happened. He just saved his own ass and brought the kid along with him. A second or two later, this would have ended very differently.

"I do not understand."

"Don't look at me like I'm some kind of hero."

"Thank you," Amy said and stood with Dylan's hand in hers. She stepped toward the truck with him. "I would have lost him if it weren't for you."

Jason nodded, the ache in the back of his head starting to climb toward his eyes. "You're welcome."

"He's a hero, Mom," Dylan said as he tugged on her arm.

"He was very brave." She looked down at him with a smile.

"No, like Spiderman," he said and let go of her hand. He moved in front of her, his eyes wide and his hands making shapes in front of his chest. "With all this blue fire, and he glows, and he has a really cool sword."

Amy's brows knit together. "Honey, I don't understand."

"He's a superhero, mom."

Gideon glanced at Jason again, and Jason could tell what thoughts ambled through his head. He had that "I'm so proud of you" look that he never asked for.

Amy looked up to both of them. "What is he talking about?"

Jason held his breath because he knew it was coming. Gideon crossed his arms over his chest. "I think it is time you show her."

"Show me what?"

Nobody else knew about him beside Gideon and whatever demons were now in that hive. And now Dylan. This power wasn't something to just display, but the kid just kept going, and then he looked at Jason like he really was the superhero that he believed Jason to be.

Fine. With the dried sweat chilling against his bare torso, he bit his lip and reached behind his shoulder. His fingers found the invisible hilt of the sword and withdrew it. Their small space in the dark parking lot now glowed with a ghostly blue that came from the sword in his hand. His tattoos began to shimmer in ethereal dots of light.

The blue light shone on Amy's pale skin, making her lips look purple and cold. Her eyes opened wide, unblinking as she gazed on him. He heard her take in a halting gasp.

"See, Mom," Dylan said, his face spread in a wide smile as he jumped with his fists in a fighting stance, ready to fight an army. "I told you. He's a real superhero."

Chapter Fourteen
Gideon

The truck moved smoothly and languidly down the highway, despite the rumbling of the diesel engine. It had been so long since Gideon had driven that he was more than happy to oblige when Jason offered him the opportunity.

Jason, instead, wanted to keep the motorcycle, which he now drove in the lead. It was likely that he wanted to be alone and that was his way of doing so. And he was correct, of course. They needed to leave Carson City as soon as possible, and when all other options fell to the side, it began to look like the trek north to Oregon for Amy's utopia was the best course of action. Jason no longer acted as though he needed to part ways with the woman and her son, especially not now that the boy looked at him like he was the most amazing person he had ever met.

Gideon watched the motorcycle down the road ahead of them in the headlights as Amy rested her head back, stroking Dylan's hair from where he lay asleep on the seat next to her. She remained quiet, contemplative since she had seen Jason reveal the sword. The promise of a ride out of Carson City was enough for her, but she would need an explanation before too long. For now, she seemed content to just stay with them even if she had no idea what to expect. After all, Jason had just saved her son's life.

He glanced at her for a moment, seeing the reflection of the headlights in her eyes. Her face looked so pale and rigid.

"Are you doing all right?" he said.

She didn't look at him, almost like she tried not to. "I'm not sure."

"You are safe with us. I want to reassure you of that."

Her eyes closed. "I don't know what to think anymore, but," she said and finally looked at him. "I have seen a lot of things since the world changed. I've never seen anything like him before." She nodded her head toward Jason in the distance. "You talked about faith, so that's what I'm going with right now. I know you two are nothing like those other things out there."

"No, we are not. But we have killed our fair share of them," he said and smiled as he followed her eyes toward the motorcycle. "Well, mostly him."

"Are you like him, too?"

"No. I am just his teacher. A mentor."

"Well, if you taught him all that stuff, then you're pretty badass too." He could hear the smile in her voice. She cleared her throat and sighed like she hesitated to speak. "If you're his mentor, then why does he hate you so much?"

Gideon's smile faded, and he did not want to meet her eyes. He just watched the road and the rear reflectors of the motorcycle. "That is a long story."

"I'm sorry, I didn't mean to pry."

"It is all right. I just did not think you would notice."

"I might not be very book smart, Gideon. But I know people. I was a bartender, and it was my job to read faces. The moment I met you, I knew you were an okay guy. I saw it in your eyes. Okay, but really sad, and not just because of the world we live in. There's something else going on in that head of yours."

He felt the center of his stomach fall. The woman was intuitive; no doubt about that. The air in the truck grew heavy, like trying to breathe water.

"See," she said, and he could feel her eyes on him. "There it is again. Sadness."

Gideon felt his hands tighten around the steering wheel. He did not want to talk about these things with her. He had no right to speak about his past. Those things could never change; he was only able to try to atone for the things that had happened.

"And what about him?" he said as he nodded toward the motorcycle, trying to change the subject. "What do you read about him?"

She looked through the windshield. "Oh, he has sadness too, the kind that just tears you up inside. I imagine that's why he's so angry. Maybe it was the woman he lost. What I don't get, though, is why he hates you so much. Unless . . ." She grew quiet for a moment, and he could hear her hold her breath as she turned her gaze to him. Her eyes bore into him like probes that searched his thoughts.

A sigh fell from her lips. "Oh my gosh. I totally get it now."

He had to lift up from the accelerator just a little because the speedometer began to increase while she talked. The truck slowed back down as he glanced at her.

"I didn't see it before, but it makes so much sense now."

"What?"

Her voice dropped. "You were both in love with the same woman, and he blames you for her death."

Gideon set his jaw and watched the road again. Amy discerned far too much about their situation, but he was almost relieved that somebody could finally vocalize what he could not.

She cleared her throat. "I'm sorry," she said. "I won't bring it up again."

"No, it is all right." He could not believe that he said it. "He will not talk about it, nor will he allow me to speak on the subject."

"That's gotta be hard."

"But he is right. I should not dwell on it. He gets very . . . difficult . . . when he thinks about it."

"I'm sure. He's got a lot of things to work out."

"But I fear that if he does not settle with the things that happened, it will end him."

Amy said nothing to that. She only clutched the back of her son's shirt like she never wanted to let him go.

The motorcycle slowed a bit, and Jason pulled off the main highway to a dirt road that veered off toward the hills. The lights began to show on a collection of trees that surrounded a darkened farm house surrounded by barns and corrals. The hour had grown late, and it was never a good idea to travel in the dark. If this place was abandoned, it would make a good location for them to stay the night.

Gideon stopped the truck beside the motorcycle and opened the door. Jason had approached the house, its windows dark, and the front door ajar as though the inhabitants had left in a hurry. He disappeared into the building and emerged a few minutes later to declare that it looked empty. They unloaded their essentials from the truck and took shelter in the house among the few beds and couches that still remained untouched.

They gathered everything in the living room to make beds and settle down, but Jason left them and sat on the porch while he watched the road. Gideon watched him leave, saying nothing as he did so. He noticed that Amy observed him too, but Dylan ran outside to talk to him again while they put out the blankets they had and found a little something to eat.

"He worships him now," she said with a faint smile. "Dylan will be okay out there with him, right?"

"Of course," Gideon said. "I am sure that he is planning to keep watch tonight."

The child would be safe with Jason. He had no concerns about that, but he did worry about Jason disappearing again. It was certainly possible that he could be gone when they all awoke in the morning, especially that he now had a motorcycle of his own. But he knew that if he walked out there to talk to him, it would just end in an argument that Amy and Dylan could hear.

The boy returned with a smile on his face, saying 'goodnight' to Jason before he shut the door. He nestled in beside his mother on the make-shift bed. Amy rested her head against the pillow and looked at Gideon.

"Goodnight," he said to her as he moved to extinguish the lantern.

"Goodnight," she said with a smile, "and thank you for everything."

Chapter Fifteen
Jason

Jason felt a tapping on his shoulder first. When it became stronger, he let his eyes open enough to let the morning sunlight in and to see Dylan's face. The stiffness in his neck bit back at him from where he rested against the side of the house. At some point overnight, he must have fallen asleep, which was a surprise given the memories that raced through his brain. But they had quieted enough to give him rest, at least for a few hours.

The kid looked at him and smiled as soon as he opened his eyes. With the action figure clutched in his hand, he crouched down as though he needed to get more one-on-one with Jason. "Mommy says to come inside and get some food."

That didn't sound like a bad idea since his stomach began rumbled at the sound of it. He couldn't remember the last time he had eaten, except for maybe the Pop Tarts he had back at the campground. So much had happened since then that eating became less of a priority.

He nodded to Dylan and spoke, the gravel in his voice more pronounced this morning. "Okay. I'll be right in."

The boy jumped to his feet and ran into the house as Jason tried to stand up and felt every muscle and joint argue with him. He gazed out over the barren landscape around the farmhouse. The truck sat in the middle of a gravel driveway surrounded by fences and trees. Beyond that lay rolling hills of rock, sand and Joshua trees.

Another day of this. They would drive for hours, away from the Hell-scape that was the casino hive and toward an uncertain destination that held no promise of salvation. Just another empty town with broken windows and shattered lives.

Little knuckles rapped on the window behind him. He turned to see Dylan's face brighten when he saw him, signaling Jason to hurry into the house.

If that kid only knew who he was and what he and Gideon had done, then he wouldn't be so optimistic about everything.

He took in a deep breath and turned toward the door, then he entered into a place where Dylan wanted to be at his side every minute, even if he said nothing to him. Amy's watchful eyes followed him everywhere when her son was nearby, afraid that he might just snap one minute. He settled back against the couch and ate the peanut butter and jelly sandwich that Dylan had insisted upon bringing to him.

Amy sat across from him, a paper plate in her lap and her eyes turned to him. He could feel it coming. It was bound to happen.

"So, what the hell are you?" she said to him, her green eyes boring into him.

"Mommy said the H-word," Dylan whispered to him from his place next to Jason on the couch.

The comment almost made him laugh, but he still felt her gaze pinned to him and he held it back. He felt his tongue go dry. The word just wouldn't come out.

"You must first understand something," Gideon said, throwing him a glance. At least he was better at explaining things than Jason. "Those creatures out there that took your son, the ones that killed your friends. They are demons."

"Demons?" she said and laughed a little, but her eyes didn't look amused. Worry had settled into the lines around her face. "Like the devil. You mean literal demons."

"Yes," he continued. "They caused the events that turned the world into this." He opened his hands out to the abandoned house around them. "They want people. To possess them. To use them. And they have been successful enough to now rule the world."

Her face had gone pale.

"Jason is one of the few who can destroy them. He is a seraph."

Her green eyes turned back to Jason, and he could barely look at her.

"I am his guide and his guardian. He is protected by angels, and with their power, he is able to remove the demons from existence completely."

She swallowed against a dry throat. "So are there others out there like you?"

"I'm the only one," Jason said. "And when I die, another will take my place."

"That sounds like a lonely road," she said and looked down at her hands. "How can you ever possibly hope to win?"

That was the same thing that he had pondered for months now. "I don't."

Gideon looked down as well. He must have thought it as well.

"Then, what?" she said, her voice cracking. "We just go on like this until we eventually die? Until the world burns? What's the purpose of all this? Of you, if there is nothing that can be done?"

He had no answer to that, and he never hoped to find it. Those were the kind of thoughts that drove him into an empty clinic in the middle of the night. The thoughts that made him down a bunch of pills, hoping that he would never wake up again. But Gideon had to ruin that too.

Amy sniffed once and stood. She wiped the back of her hand against her cheek and rushed from the room, probably to a bathroom where she could cry in solitude without anyone seeing her. Dylan stood up and hurried after her. Jason only let his head hang. He had eaten half the sandwich but it no longer satisfied him.

"That could have gone better," Gideon said.

"What do you think I should've done? Lie?"

Gideon shook his head slowly. "No. The truth is painful, but it is only now that I realize that you believe it too."

"I always believed it, even when—" He stopped before he said her name.

But Gideon wouldn't let it go. "Even when Nikka believed she could save everything."

Jason stood and placed the paper plate on the couch, no longer hungry. He stepped back out the front door, feeling the air getting slowly sucked from the room. The fresher air outdoors didn't get caught in his throat. He hurried to the truck and found his duffel bag in the back. *Just keep the thoughts on something else*, like putting on a shirt since the last one lay in shreds back in the casino.

But Gideon followed after him. The guy always seemed to be there, making him think things he didn't want to remember.

"I am sorry," he said. "But you are clearly troubled after yesterday. I must know what you saw out there."

Jason rummaged through the bag until he found a gray T-shirt. He pulled it over his head, feeling less exposed than he had been all night. Gideon was trying to make him talk about painful things again, things that reminded him of her. And especially in that hive, he thought he had heard her voice. It was the only reason he got out of there alive.

He clenched his fist until his nails dug into the palm of his hand. "There was a nest, thousands of demons. And I met a general."

Gideon halted, his brow furrowed. "Who?"

The memory of her ember eyes made his skin grow cold. He remembered the movement of the Hell hounds at her side. "Lila."

"I know of her," Gideon said. "She served at Abaddon's side during the Fall from Heaven."

"There were so many drones. And I saw hundreds of people, gathered like cattle. They're collecting them, keeping them alive down there."

Gideon rubbed the back of his neck. "Keeping them for possession, I imagine."

"Or worse," Jason said and let his voice drop. "They said something about breeders."

The color drained from Gideon's face. "Of course. Most of the human population is gone now. That makes for fewer bodies for possession. They plan to create more."

"I don't like the sound of that."

"All the more reason to keep Amy and her child out of their hands," Gideon whispered as the front door of the house opened.

Jason stood straighter and watched her approach, her eyes red but tear-free now. Dylan held her hand as they neared the truck.

"Okay," she said and tossed her pack into the cab of the truck. "Ready to go."

She looked more defiant than she did when she ran from the living room during their conversation. Her demeanor had changed enough that she might be ready to start a fight if anybody disagreed with her.

"Well," Jason said and leaned back against the truck. "Do you know the way to this new world utopia that you want to find?"

"I think so," she said. "Just show me the map, and I can get us there."

"All right, then. Let's go."

CHAPTER SIXTEEN
JASON

The dust that occasionally drifted off the back of the truck made Jason keep the motorcycle back just far enough to see them in the distance. The hum of the engine lulled him, and the solitude it brought helped him to clear his thoughts. Wind blowing through his hair. And no sound from Gideon. This might have been the best of the last few days, even though he hadn't gotten much sleep the night before.

Maybe finding this paradise that Amy described might be the best thing, at least for his conscience right now. He couldn't leave her and the kid back there, but if they find something in Oregon, any semblance of a group of decent people, then he wouldn't feel so bad leaving them there. Maybe Gideon would want to stay there, too. He and Amy seemed to be getting along fine. That way, he could be free of all of them. Nobody to tell him what to do. Nobody to bring up the past.

The air grew a little cooler the further north they went, but it was still summer, and the heat off the black pavement curled up in ribbons along the horizon. This particular road had fewer little towns along the way, which brought less of a chance of being hunted, but it also meant fewer opportunities to find any usable fuel. They made one stop, but if Amy was wrong about her utopia, they might be stretched a little thin for their gasoline.

Sunlight moved across the sky until the heat peaked and the light grew orange-red on the horizon. The highway wound through a mountainous terrain, surrounded by thick green trees. They had been driving through hours of national forest at this point, and it reminded him of hunting with his grandfather when he was just a kid, climbing among dozens of tree-covered hills. The road curled through the trees that overhung and shadowed the way around each curve.

He watched the truck in the distance and slowed the bike when he saw the truck's brake lights illuminate. The vehicle moved over a hill and disappeared from his view. In the early evening light, the trees opened up at the top of the hill, and as he came to the top, he saw the truck stopped in the center of the road. He pulled the bike to the side of the truck and gazed out over the small valley at the base of the hill.

Amy's utopia did exist after all—the town that had resided in this small valley surrounded by forest on one side and a lake on the other. The place was well-hidden on this distant road, far from any large cities that attracted scores of demons. In the seven months since the power outage, somebody had erected a vast structure of iron walls around the town, equipped with watch towers and all. From this distance, he could see people standing along the walls, patrolling each corner of the town, guns in hand.

"Looks like it's real," he said.

The others gazed out through the truck's dirty windshield, eyes bright despite the long drive. *Good.* He needed them to want to stay here forever. It would be better that way when he leaves them here tomorrow.

"I guess we just go up and knock on the front door," Amy said with a smile.

Jason nodded and took the lead. As expected, the moment any of the people along the walls and towers spotted motorized vehicles moving toward their encampment, a volley of bells and shouts start from somewhere behind the walls. The town had gathered enough assault rifles and handguns that now aimed down at them from along the outer edge of the south wall. Jason pulled his bike to the front gate, killed the engine and held his hands up as he gazed toward the faces that looked down on him. At least twenty people up there. That was a good sign this place was well-protected, just like Amy had said.

"We're looking for sanctuary," Jason called up to the wall, to anyone who would listen.

Gideon stopped the truck across the road and kept Amy and Dylan far enough back in case these people didn't want visitors.

"How many in your party?" a man's voice shouted down to him.

"Four. Three adults and a child," he said. Maybe the presence of a kid would soften them up.

A gate opened before him, two great steel doors with metal sheeting locked from the inside. It parted just enough to allow three men through, two men with guns and another with a gallon jug in his hand.

The assault rifles aimed at his chest made him keep his hands in the air and his position next to his motorcycle. Each of them wore Kevlar vests and other tactical wear like they had once been with a S.W.A.T. team. The man with the jug eyed him as though he memorized every tattoo he saw on his arms and neck.

They stopped just a few feet from him as the man looked at him.

"Open your mouth," he said with little emotion.

Jason's brow furrowed. "What?"

"I said open your mouth."

"Why?"

The men with the guns stepped forward just a little bit, and the fingers on the triggers twitched.

"Hey," Jason said. "Okay. No problem." He opened his mouth as the man stepped closer and gazed at his teeth. Satisfied, he glanced back to the gunmen and nodded. They seemed to relax enough to pull back but not to lower their guns.

The man opened the lid to the jug. From what Jason could see, it was probably water, but he wasn't sure.

"Hold out your hands."

Jason was ready to protest again, but he saw the men behind him growing impatient. He brought his hands down before him and opened his palms. The man lifted the jug and splashed the liquid over his skin. But there was nothing, not that he had expected anything. Maybe it was just water.

Then, he realized what was happening.

Holy water.

These guys know what's out there. Somehow, they understand the threat outside their walls, and holy water is the best way to tell if someone is possessed unless they have his power. Holy water would burn when it touched the skin. It wouldn't do much as a weapon, but it would stun a demon for a second, which might be just enough to get free from it. And they recognized that the demons would rot the host from the inside out, teeth and all.

The man glanced back to the people at the top of the gates and gave a large hand gesture. Then he turned back to Jason.

"You're clean," he said with a smile and patted him on the shoulder. "The name's Dave, and welcome to Garnet Falls."

Jason felt his shoulders drop a little, and then realized how tight he had become with all those guns aimed at him. He signaled the others to come as well, and Gideon drove the truck toward the gates. Dave gave each of them the test as well before he let them all drive into the village gates.

The community was clean and looked so white. White fences. White walled homes and businesses. Even a white church with a single spire in the center of town. No burned out cars or broken windows. People came out of their homes to see who had just arrived. Children. Mothers. Fathers. Whole families stood along the sidewalks. Jason just found some place to stop his motorcycle and gaze around the area. Amy and Dylan climbed out of the truck, and she had the widest smile he had seen on her yet.

Dave met them with his two men at his side. He greeted everyone as they gathered around the back of the truck.

"I take it you've come a long way," he said.

Jason only nodded as he watched the people milling around the town square in the center of Main Street, necks craning to see them. They all looked so healthy and content here in this space.

"My people can get you settled," he continued. "Dinner is starting in about an hour, and we'll have someone show you where it is."

"There's dinner for everyone?" Amy said and peered around the corner to Main Street.

Dave nodded. "We work together here. Everybody pitches in, and nobody goes in need. We all eat together."

Some men approached the truck, eager to meet the new arrivals. Dave immediately put them to work to help unload their supplies and take them to a place to stay for the night.

"You can stay as long as you want, we just ask that you help us keep the peace." His eyes drifted to Jason as he eyed his long hair, tattoos and the Harley he rode in on. "No fighting."

He didn't need the guy's judgement. Jason watched him as the man glanced back at the others and encouraged them to follow him to their lodging. He grabbed up his duffel bag before one of the other men could take it. Nobody was touching his stuff but him. He kept his distance but examined the street as they moved toward an inn at the end of the main road. Dave and his guys left them alone once they found a few rooms they could sleep in for the night.

He entered the first room at the end of the hall with a window that opened out onto the main street. It wasn't anything special—the usual kind of hotel room that he had been sleeping in for the last several months. A single bed. A bathroom. But it was his, and Gideon wasn't here to ruin it. He could find his own room down the hall. He closed the door to the room and dropped the duffle bag on the floor as he sat down on the edge of the bed. The hum of the motorcycle still buzzed in his hands and legs as he ran his fingers through his hair—his dirty blonde hair that smelled like diesel fuel and road dust.

And then he wondered if they had running water. *Damn, it would be nice to have just one shower.*

He stood and paced toward the bathroom door and reached around the threshold for the light switch. As soon as his fingers found it, he turned it upward. He almost jumped back when the dome light in the ceiling flashed on. *They have electricity!*

An involuntary smile formed on his lips as he squinted into the light. Then he stepped up to the sink and reached for the faucet. If they had power, there must be some kind of generator. And with power, there could be running water. He turned the dial of the faucet, and the water poured into the sink, just as he had hoped.

And it grew warmer with each second.

Running water. Hot running water.

His fingers danced below the faucet as the water cascaded into his hands, washing away the grime that had built up over his nails, when a knock sounded at the door. He turned the faucet off and shook the water from his hands before he opened the door to see a woman standing in the hallway. He had seen her when Dave and his men brought them into the hotel. She must be the caretaker of the place, and she looked like she had probably been so for many years. Her long hair was pulled back into a severe bun of mixed gray and drab brown hair. The skin around her eyes puckered into furrows that were familiar with her smiles.

She pulled the glasses from her nose and let them dangle on the chain around her neck. "Hi there," she said with a nervous laugh. "I see you got some water working. The generator is on here at the hotel for only an hour at night. I know you all are just getting settled in, but it's dinner time, and you folks don't want to miss it."

Jason forced a tired smile back at her. "Okay."

"It's just across the street at the park," she said, pointing down the hall to the front entrance of the hotel. "There'll be plenty of people who are just dying to meet you."

"All right," he said and stood at the door as the woman lingered in the corridor with the broad smile on her face. She reminded him of someone, maybe his grandma. She had always smiled like that when she met new people.

"Okay," she said and started to turn away, her wrinkled hands clasped together with nervous excitement. "You know," she started again. "There are some nice young ladies here who would just love to meet you as well."

Ah. The sweet old lady was already trying to fix him up with somebody.

He nodded with a forced smile. "Well, I will let everyone know that dinner is ready."

She finally turned away and hurried to the front door and out to the gathering throngs of people that he saw walking past the hotel.

All he wanted to do was lie down and get some sleep, but his stomach rumbled at the mention of dinner. Well, he could show up with his group and make an appearance at the town meal, even if it was to just grab a few bites and then come back to his room and crash for the night.

He stepped out into the hallway, knocked on the doors to Gideon's and Amy's rooms, alerting them of their need to join the rest of the town for dinner.

As a group, they left the hotel together, Gideon taking the lead as they walked out of the hotel. Once they stepped out onto the street, throngs of people moved in the same direction toward the park at the end of the block. Eyes drifted toward him, curious glances and whispers danced around the crowd. People smiled and nodded, occasionally holding out a friendly hand and dropping their names.

Evening had turned into twilight since they had arrived in Garnet Falls, leaving the street a little shadowed as they walked toward the park. A central bonfire burned in a fire pit, lighting an area of tables and chairs. A single long row of tables set with the food in a buffet-style line bordered the east end of the park. Voices chattered happily among the townspeople, as though they had become accustomed to such communal living. They felt safe here.

Gideon even appeared distracted enough by this that he left him alone for a while. No concerned glances. No talk of plans for the next few days. Amy blended in well, and Dylan had already found a group of boys his own age that ran and played along the monkey bars under the trees. This was perfect. These people might be a little too cheery for him, but it was just right for the others. He could leave them in the morning and never have to look back.

Chapter Seventeen
Jason

Jason gathered enough food on his plate to feed an army as he followed Amy back to a bench where they sat with Gideon. Dylan insisted upon sitting next to him, as usual. To his surprise, so many people came by, and others sat down with them. Men and women, children, all wanted to know about them, where they had come from, how bad things had gotten out there. Amy did most of the talking while Jason just ate.

As overbearingly positive as these people were, their food was amazing. He must have downed a gallon of mashed potatoes like he had never eaten them before. The bread was that crusty homemade stuff that was still warm and soft in the middle. Even the water tasted like it was fresh from a mountain spring. He needed to take it all in now because he wasn't planning on any of it again after tonight.

"So are you two a thing," the woman next to Amy said, her dark brown hair pulled back into a ponytail. She wagged her finger between Amy and him.

Amy almost choked for a second and Jason just looked up at her, his mouth too full to answer. "Oh no," Amy said like it was so unreasonable. "No, no. Um, they just found me and Dylan in the middle of Nevada. They were kind enough to give me a ride."

The woman flashed a smile at Jason. It was more than just a smile, though. He could see it in the gaze that lingered just a little heavy on him. "Oh. So you guys are a couple of saints then."

"We were more than happy to help them," Gideon said, formally nodding and everything.

Jason said nothing and kept chewing. As long as his mouth was full, he didn't have to talk to these people. That's why he was beginning to appreciate sitting next to Amy; everybody wanted to talk to her, and she was more than content to talk right back. Kept him from having to say anything.

"Well, I'm Ellie," the woman said. "And I live just down the street. If you guys need anything, please don't hesitate to let me know. Are you gonna stick around after dinner for the message?"

Jason looked up at her and saw the confusion across Amy's face as well.

"Message?" Amy asked.

"Well, it's Friday, and Brother Max always gives us a message after dinner on Fridays."

"Who is Brother Max?" Gideon said.

"He's the guy that pretty much built this whole place," she said as if they didn't know. "Without him, we would probably be dead or taken. Well, him and his wife. She's really the one that helped protect us. She figured out what those things were. The holy water and all the crosses around the gates, that was her. She knew that those things were demons and prepared us all much earlier than the rest of the world."

Jason glanced at Gideon and gave him a look to ask, *do you know about Max?* But Gideon just shrugged.

"It's like God speaks through them," Ellie continued.

"Well," Amy said, "I think we would love to hear what he has to say, wouldn't we?" She glanced at Jason, giving him a nudge with her elbow and a piercing glare.

"Sure," he said before she could stab him with her eyes. She wanted this to work out, and of course, he would make sure that it would for her. As much as he didn't really want to hear some preacher expound on the meaning of life and the grand purpose of nearly being killed by demons, he would go if only for them. Just this once.

He could have continued eating, but most of the people had finished, and he heard the murmurings of all the people as the crowd began to rise and head as a group toward the church. With Gideon, Amy and Dylan at his side, he stuffed his hands into his pockets and kept his head down as he walked down the street. The sky had grown dark, but as they neared the outskirts of the church, he looked up and saw strings of white twinkle lights glowing steadily in sweeping arcs across the darkened street lamps. The crowd chatter now dulled to a low whisper. He looked up at the lights, which must have been illuminated by the same electrical power that seemed to keep this place alive.

The people moved in reverent silence now, and looking up at the small wonder of something electric gave him goosebumps. He wasn't sure if the others sensed it, but the air felt charged like it had been given a boost of electricity as well. The hairs on his neck rose, and he had to look down at his marks. The sensations prickled over his skin almost like the moments when his tattoos began to glow. The last time he felt like this was when he was a little kid, sitting in front of the Christmas tree in December and hearing his grandfather read the story of the Polar Express. There was something almost magical about that moment, just as there was now as he moved toward the church.

He glanced to his left, where Gideon walked beside him. His hazel eyes sparkled with the lights above him as he gazed up in wonder, and he could have sworn that Gideon sensed it too.

Maybe this guy Max had something after all.

The hushed crowd settled into the chapel, filling each pew to standing room only in the far back of the room. Ellie had stayed with them and made sure they had the best seats, in the center pews, about five rows back. No standing for the new people. No way.

Jason had never really attended church. Sure, he might have stood at the door during a Christmas mass or maybe sometimes at Easter. Before the world died, he wasn't even sure he believed in God. He thought that would have changed when he became a seraph. After all, angels had kidnapped him and placed their sigils all over his body. But he never saw God. He never heard his voice or even had evidence of him. And with the way the world looked now, it only reaffirmed his stance.

But he had never felt anything like the buzz in this room as he sat looking up toward the dais. There was nothing special about this chapel. The usual stained glass windows. Crosses on an altar. He had no idea why he sensed the profound feeling of some great power here, but it surely wasn't because of the architecture or the décor. Something else dwelled in this space, unseen and charging the ions in the air that he breathed.

The room fell into absolute quiet just moments before a man rose from the center front pew and stepped up to the altar on the dais. As he gazed out over the people, Jason didn't think that he was remarkable in any way.

Probably in his mid-40's, light brown hair with just a hint of gray in his temples, clean-shaven, lean with kind brown eyes.

"Thank you for joining us this evening," he said.

This must be Brother Max.

"The message I have prepared for you tonight is on Hope," he began.

As he continued to ramble on about his religious nonsense, Jason knew that the sensation dancing over his skin wasn't coming from this preacher. He was just like any other dude giving a sermon. Lights didn't shine from his ass or explode from the altar around him, although that would have been pretty awesome. He still had no idea why the air seemed to sizzle against his skin. Jason shifted in his seat, wanting to move, to absorb the energy around him. If this guy would just get to the point already so he could stand and just feel what bathed him in its invisible light.

"Faith is the confidence of things that we hope will happen, and gives us assurance about things that cannot be seen," Max continued. "This faith and hope brought us here, together as we are now. It keeps the enemy from our door. And by God's hand, we will be saved from that enemy so long as we have hope."

A murmur of amens moved through the crowd, and this drew Jason's attention back to the speaker.

"I would like to conclude this message with a prayer for you all," Max said, his hands clasped before him.

Oh great. A prayer.

"And my wife wishes to join me up here for our prayer tonight." He smiled to a woman sitting in the front row, her head covered in a thin, white, gossamer shawl. "We're getting awfully close, and we need all the prayers we can get." A small murmur, with the occasional giggle, flowed from the front to the back of the chapel in response to the preacher's last comment. He stepped to the side of the dais and reached his hand out to her. The woman accepted it. Her back stayed toward the congregation as she stood from the pew, the thin white shawl falling over her shoulders and down her narrow waist like angel hair. She rose as she took his hand and stepped up the few short stairs to stand at his side.

The energy in the room grew so intense that Jason itched at his skin like a thousand ants were crawling over his flesh, fierce and almost painful.

The woman turned, and her slender hands pulled the shawl back from her head.

Electrical jabs coursed into Jason's tattoos like static. And when he looked at the woman, he could no longer breathe.

Her blue eyes looked out at the crowd, and everyone grew silent and still. It was like looking at the face of an angel. Smooth skin and pale porcelain lips. Far younger than the man at her side. The shawl fell away to her shoulders, revealing very short and light blonde hair like it had only just begun to grow a few months ago. Like she had recently been bald.

The thin shawl dangled from her long fingers that moved down like the hands of a ballet dancer to her abdomen. Her pregnant abdomen.

Though her skin was smooth and unblemished from the blade of a knife that had once cut away her marks, he knew beyond any doubt that this was Nikka, alive and breathing and very pregnant.

Chapter Eighteen
Jason

He looked at Gideon, whose eyes had now fixed on the woman upon the dais, her head bowed and her mouth moving, but neither of them heard the prayer. Jason needed to know if he truly saw what he thought was up there, and with Gideon's transfixed gaze, he was sure that Gideon saw it too. He shifted enough in his seat that Gideon grabbed his arm and tried to hold him still.

The prayer ended, and the people that filled the chapel began to rise from their seats. The silence that had previously dominated them now turned into a loud chatter. Jason stood quickly, peering between shoulders to the woman, who now shifted with the preacher as he held her hand. They moved across the dais, and the security force that had such a presence at the gate earlier tonight now escorted the woman and the preacher to the rear door of the chapel. Jason couldn't see her anymore, although he saw the preacher's face as he shook the hands of the people that clambered to see him before he left as though he were some celebrity.

He felt his heart hammering against his ribs and glanced to either side of the pew where he sat. People were too slow at exiting from the place and more interested in chatting with each other. Smiling faces. Laughter. Hand shaking. They didn't move fast enough, and he couldn't get out unless he shoved his way free. And Gideon wasn't helping, either. He just stood, staring forward between the people to the preacher and the woman as they made their way to the exit.

No more waiting. He had waited for seven long months to see her and he couldn't let her go this easily.

Jason shoved past Gideon and anybody else who stood along the pew. He ignored the many comments about how rude he was and emerged out into the aisle still teeming with parishioners. Something brushed his hand, and he realized that Gideon was close on his heels. The guy had shoved his way through right behind him. Jason kept going, pushing through the crowd until he reached the entry doors that they had gone through to get into the chapel in the first place.

That electric buzz still remained fresh on his skin, and now he knew why. His power was telling him something, that she was Nikka and that he needed to find her. Everything that had happened in the last few days led him to this place because he was supposed to see her here like this.

He pushed out into the night air, under the boughs of sparkling twinkle lights that curved overhead. The crowd thinned enough that he could run, and his feet sprinted against the grass around the side of the church, to the rear exit that opened into a darker part of the town. She was back there; he could feel it in his bones.

The security entourage moved along the outskirts of the sidewalk, away from the fading artificial light. But deeper into that group, Jason saw the preacher and the woman who walked beside him. He pushed harder, hearing Gideon's footsteps right behind him.

The head security officer turned as soon as he heard the steps and Jason saw Dave's face. He stepped out into the street and intercepted him, but Jason shoved him aside and kept going.

"Whoa," Dave said as he spun about, catching him in the ribs with a nightstick.

Jason felt the blow first and then saw more of the black-clad officers approach him. The group stopped as Jason felt Dave grab his arm and try to maneuver him to the ground. The preacher turned around and looked at him just before he went down into the shadows of the men that began to surround him.

It couldn't end here. Not like this.

He closed his eyes as Dave twisted his arm at the wrist. Deep inside his gut, he felt the well of his energy just waiting for him to use it. These weren't demons, but he could manipulate his power now, just like Nikka used to. He willed it into his limbs and felt the first tingle of energy begin to undulate along his tattoos. It filled every vessel, feeding his muscles and giving the power he needed to fight back.

The first spark of it started in his legs, and he knew it was time. He pushed back and turned, catching Dave off guard. Jason forced his head back quickly, catching Dave in the face with a strong head-butt. The grip on his wrist loosened and Jason broke free. More hands fell on him, but he lunged through the group, sweeping the legs out from one man and catching another's ribs with his fist. Gideon was still back there, but he couldn't worry about him now.

Jason almost fell as he pushed through and caught his balance with his hands against the pavement before he sprang toward the preacher. But somebody else caught his foot and twisted. He hit the ground and tried to pull free. Another body leaped on top of him, then another. They had both his hands now forced behind his back. Somebody else pressed his face against the pavement.

They were going to stop him, and there was nothing he could do. He was going to lose her again.

"Nikka," he called out with his last breath before he felt a knee in his back.

Cold metal clamped against his wrist. Handcuffs. He had felt them before, the first time as a 15-year-old kid.

"Wait," the woman spoke out. "Stop this."

It was her voice. He would know it anywhere.

The men halted their aggression on him. He felt the knee move from his back, and he could finally breathe again. The space around him grew silent. Jason lifted his head, and he heard footsteps come toward him. In the dark, he couldn't tell who it was, but he saw a man's shoe step before him. The man crouched, and he finally saw the preacher's face.

Concern filled every line of the preacher's face as he whispered, "Do you know her?"

Jason breathed hard with his chest pressed against the ground, his wrists bound behind him. "Yes."

The preacher said nothing more and stood. "Bring them inside." Then he moved away from him.

Hands lifted Jason from the ground but kept the cuffs in place. At first, the world swirled with vertigo, all black and light and no color until he reoriented his balance. By the time he was on his feet, the preacher and the woman that accompanied him were far down the sidewalk with the rest of the security officers and then turned to enter the front gates of a house down the block. Dave stepped in front of him, his nose bloodied and bruised from the head-butt Jason had given him. He held a white handkerchief under his nose and looked at him, his eyes narrowed, and his jaw clenched.

"You heard Max," Dave said and nodded to the men that held him. "Let's go."

As the men pushed him forward, Jason glanced back and saw Gideon walking with the group, his hands also bound behind him. They walked with the entourage down the darkened street and toward the two-story, Victorian-style home with an open porch. In the dark, he nearly stumbled up the stairs into the front door.

Lanterns had already been lit in the foyer, spreading bright white light over the furniture that looked like it had been here for over a hundred years. The smell of freshly baked bread filled the place. The men shoved him through the living room area and through a set of double doors that opened into a formal dining room. A dark wood table surrounded by intricately carved chairs sat in the center of the room. They moved him and Gideon to one end of the room and forced them into the chairs. They stepped back, keeping their eyes on them and their hands close to the guns at their belts.

The room glowed with candles set in the center of the table and along the shelves that lined the walls, turning the harsh white lantern glow into something softer and more subtle. The other end of the room remained empty, waiting in silence for the next thing that was about to happen. Jason shifted his gaze to the men that stood behind him as he sat at the edge of his chair, ready to move at any time. But Gideon only sat there, his eyes fixed forward with that knit of worry between his eyebrows. It was that same look he got whenever Jason came back with a fresh wound. He had also seen it the time when he found him after he had taken the pills and tried to end everything.

Dave moved around the far end of the table with the handkerchief at his nose. He said nothing but only stared at him.

The door opened, and this made Jason sit straighter, but it was only the preacher. Compared to his security team, the man was slight with smaller shoulders and hands. No wonder he needed a pack of bodyguards. He was definitely not a fighter. Rolling up the sleeves of his button down shirt to his elbows, he stood at the end of the table and looked at both of them.

"Who are you?" he said, his voice even but soft.

Jason's eyes shifted to the door, waiting for her to come through. He felt his mouth go dry as the door never moved, but he knew she was out there, somewhere inside this house. He could feel her gliding behind the walls like a ghost, listening into the dining room at their conversation.

He felt a sharp nudge in his back from one of the guards that stood behind him.

"Jason," he finally said and ticked his head to his right. "This is Gideon."

"I understand that you just arrived here today," Max said. "Where did you come from?"

When he didn't answer right away, he felt the nudge again.

"Nevada."

"Why did you come here?"

"We brought—"

"Not you," Max said, and his eyes shifted to Gideon. "You. Do you speak?"

Gideon's hazel eyes flickered in the candlelight. "I do. We found a woman and her child who said she needed to come here. She wished to find sanctuary."

"And what about you? Do you desire sanctuary?"

Gideon only stared forward for a moment, and Jason held his breath. Why wasn't he saying anything? The light continued to dance in his eyes, and that wrinkle between his brows only deepened.

"I do not deserve it," he said and looked at Jason. "But he needs it more than anyone."

Jason turned his gaze away from him. He didn't want to see the sorrow that had spilled from him; that only made him angrier, and that wouldn't help them out of this predicament now.

Max stood, his expression blank, and stepped quietly out the door, leaving them with the security officers that glared down at them. Several minutes ticked by before he heard shuffling just outside the room and then a woman's voice. His heart raced as the doors opened and Max stepped into the room. He saw a woman's form fill the threshold, but as she stepped inside with him, Jason felt as though the ground had fallen away from his feet.

He didn't come back with Nikka, but he had brought someone else.

Max entered the room with Amy, whose glance shifted all around the room, to each of the security officers with hands on their guns. With her fidgeting hands clasped before her, she took small steps into the room and sat in a chair at the table with them. Her eyes widened as she saw them sitting there, handcuffed.

"You came with these men?" Max said.

Her glance moved back to him. "Yes, sir." Her voice trembled.

"Tell me about them."

"Well," she said and glanced back at them once more. "They found my son and me in Austin. We had been there for weeks, just hiding and barely surviving. I needed a ride, and they helped me. He," she said, pointing to Jason, "saved my son from hunters. He risked his life to save him. Without him, I don't know what we would have done."

She turned her gaze back to Jason, her eyes wet and shimmering in the candlelight. "He's not a bad person, even though he thinks he is. Please, whatever they did, I'm sure they won't do it again."

"Thank you. I think you've helped me greatly," Max said and waved his hand to one of the officers, who moved to her side and urged her out of the room. Before the officer showed her out the door, she glanced back and met Jason's quick gaze. The worry had also settled in her eyes as she held her stare on him for only a second. Max stood, and this drew her attention away. The preacher accompanied them from the room and closed the door behind them.

What was this, a character investigation? Jason looked at Gideon once more and saw that same forward stare. Every minute they had to sit here, the further away Nikka felt.

The door opened again, and Max stood there, the light at his back, as he stared at them. He seemed to study them, considering his options and his next move, like a man playing chess. He glanced back into the room beyond the dining area, whispering into the room. Then he moved into the dining room again, but this time he held a hand. The woman entered with him.

The energy in the room came to life, tickling across his tattoos and zinging up his spine. She held onto Max as though she was afraid to let him go. He helped her into a chair, settling into it as though it might be a little difficult with her pregnant abdomen. She didn't look at either of them, but only down at her abdomen covered with her dark gray T-shirt. Max touched her shoulders gently and sat in the chair beside her.

It was her. Jason could feel it from across the room. She didn't have her tattoos anymore, and she had hair growing on her head, but it was definitely her.

Chapter Nineteen
Jason

The cold metal of the handcuffs dug into Jason's wrists. Fighting with them would only get him into more trouble, but he wanted to rise, to go to her. The others must have sensed it too because he felt a hand on his shoulder that pressed him into his seat.

The woman didn't look directly at them, but leaned in toward Max and whispered in his ear. He nodded and then looked at Dave.

"Take off the cuffs," he said.

"But, sir—"

"Please," Max said and glanced between Jason and Gideon. "We are ready to have a civil discussion here. Take them off and leave us alone for a while."

The officers behind them grabbed the cuffs a little more forcibly than necessary, unlocked them, and then the group exited the room. Jason rubbed the soreness from his wrists and settled his eyes on her again.

Max watched them, but Jason could tell that he waited until the last of his security detail had exited the room. "How do you know this woman?" he started, his hand holding hers as she looked down at her abdomen, as though she was afraid to look at them.

Jason turned his gaze to Gideon. As with the last time he opened his mouth, he seemed to settle the room down better than he could. Gideon met his glance and understood what he needed.

"I was her mentor," Gideon started. "Her teacher. I have known her the longest. She was very sick at the time we met." He touched his own closely-trimmed hair. "She has more hair now than when we last saw her."

Her eyes darted up to them and then back to Max, a knowing but silent exchange between them. She leaned toward him and whispered at him again. He nodded, and his eyes moved to Jason. He could tell the man looked over the tattoos across his arms.

"Your marks," he said, "where did you get them?"

Jason looked down at his arms. "I'm not exactly sure," he said and looked directly at her. This time, she met his gaze and didn't turn away. "But you had them once too. You lost them just before you disappeared."

"Are they all over your body?" Max asked. "Do you have one here?" He placed his index finger in the center of his chest.

Jason shook his head. "I have them everywhere, except there. But you did." He pointed at her.

Her lip quivered just a little, and a shimmer of wetness appeared in her eyes.

Max turned his gaze toward her and gave her a little nod. For a moment she hesitated against whatever he had indicated that he wished her to do. She bit her lower lip, and her hands moved to the neckline of her shirt. He could see that her fingers trembled. She pulled down the neckline, exposing the skin of her chest.

The black round curving tattoo with the tribal edges was there, just like it had been since the moment she exorcised Abaddon from his body. It was the only mark that Gideon/Pazuzu had not cut from her flesh.

She covered herself again and leaned forward, her elbows on the table.

"Who am I to you?" she said, desperation edging her voice.

This was definitely Nikka, but he could see the confusion in her eyes. These questions, from both her and Max, began to make sense. She had no idea who she was.

"You don't remember," Jason muttered.

"Who am I?" she demanded again.

"Nikka," he said. "Your name is Nikka Connors. You were born July 26th. You would be about 19 years old now. You saved my life, so many times that I can't count." The words flowed out of him like he couldn't stop. "We lived together, hiding from all of this. You and I were there when this all happened. We tried to stop it, but it happened anyway."

His voice faltered for a moment. "I asked you once to marry me, but you disappeared before you gave me your answer."

If he said anymore, he would probably have to rush to her. To hold her and prove to her that she knew him. He would make her remember.

Her lips hung open, and her eyes swam in tears as she sat back against the chair. She looked at him as her trembling hands moved to her abdomen.

She wanted to speak, but her voice trembled. "Are you the father of my baby?"

The question hung in the air, heavy and dangerous. The darkness outside of the candlelight felt blacker than usual as Jason looked away from her. From the corner of his eye, he saw Gideon. Now Gideon no longer stared forward, but hung his head and pressed his face into his hands.

"I'm not sure," Jason said, still seeing Gideon out of the corner of his eye.

She sucked in a little breath and looked at both of them, and he knew that she had come to understand the thickness that had settled in the air between the three of them. It was the burdened mystery that had risen to the surface, something that none of them could answer.

Jason turned his gaze back to her, not wanting to see Gideon anymore. Maybe it was a good thing she couldn't remember any of this, especially what Gideon had done to her. With him sitting there, wallowing in his shame, Jason wanted him to feel every bit of it.

"I hope I am," he finally said to her.

She turned to Max, her voice shaking. "I have to go," she said and struggled to rise to her feet. The chair tipped a little, threatening to fall, as she shoved away from the table and moved out of the room as tears streamed down her face.

As she left, he felt his heart tear from his chest to follow her. Max stood, his eyes watching her leave. Then he looked back at them, his face drawn and tired.

He held his hands out before him. "I am sorry about all the security. I've had to do it since we started this place." He moved around the table to sit closer to Jason. "I tell people she's my wife to keep her safe. Until now, nobody knew differently. You see, about a month after the lights went out, I found her. She was naked and bald and wandered to my doorstep. She had no recollection of who she was. My real wife had died a couple of years before that. I had no children. I was alone in that house, afraid to go outside. Things were terrible. Looting had torn up the entire city. And then there were the hunters."

Max looked back to the door where she had just exited. "She knew things, though. She could tell when the hunters were coming. She knew how to fight back, but she didn't remember why she knew it. So, we packed what we could, and we traveled together until we came here. These people had no idea what to do with themselves. With her help, we fortified this place, and so far, it's worked. It wasn't long after we got here that it became obvious that she was pregnant. So, we thought she would be safest if people believed she was my wife."

Max ran a finger absently along the edge of the table. "It's obvious that you know her, but she has been safe here so far. For now, I will allow you to stay in Garnet Falls, but she will stay here in the house, and you two will remain in the inn."

Jason felt the hair on his neck try to stand. "No."

"Please," Max said, his voice calm and even. "She's not going anywhere. Just, please understand it from my standpoint. I have fought to protect her and this baby for months now. Then you two just wander in. She doesn't remember you, she doesn't trust you."

Jason tried to stand and speak, but Max held out his hand. "Give this time. If we force her back with you, she'll resist. Please, I beg you to take this slowly. For her sake."

Gideon lifted his head. "She is happy here?"

"Yes. I have made sure of that. And don't worry," Max said. "We are purely platonic. I've never laid a hand on her. I keep the security team around her to make sure she is always safe. For now, leave her where she is familiar. Come back here tomorrow, and if she wishes, you can spend more time around her. Let her get to know you again."

Jason bristled, his hands clenched and his jaw tight. How could he just walk away now, knowing that Nikka was just outside this room? He had come too far to just give up now.

"We will do that," Gideon said.

Jason shot a glance to him, but Gideon's expression remained soft. "We will come back tomorrow," he said as he looked at Jason.

The two of them stood, but Jason rose on stiff knees. It took everything in his will power to not run out of that room and find her again. But seeing Max's gaze, as he extended his hand to shake, made his resolve tremble. He took the man's hand and shook it. Then Gideon led him from the room and out of the house.

The security detail stood around the porch and watched them leave like guard dogs ready to attack. Jason eyed Dave, who looked out from his swollen nose. Gideon urged him forward, to not make eye contact and just keep going. They stepped out into the dark street, getting further and further away from the house.

Jason looked back, to the upper floors of the house. He wasn't sure why he did it. Perhaps it was the tingle on his neck or along the tattoos, but something made him search the windows. And then he saw her, gazing down at him from between two white curtains. She watched them walk away, leaving her alone with those strangers.

Chapter Twenty

Nikka

Her name was Nikka. That didn't feel right, but at the same time, it felt like that had been it the whole time. They had called her Jane for so long that she had just started to get used to it. Jane Doe. So generic. Nikka felt like it was the name for someone who mattered.

She shut the door of her room at the top of the stairs and locked it. Living with Max, she never felt like it needed to be locked, but it did now. Whatever it took to be as far away from those strange men as possible.

Things hadn't been this difficult since the day she awoke.

She sat on the edge of the bed and held her hands up to her face. Tears flowed down her cheeks, soaking her fingers. This was not how she imagined it would be: the day she found out who she was. There was supposed to be a big reveal, and her mind would suddenly open up, and she would remember everything that she had forgotten.

And her baby would finally have a father, and there would be an answer to that great mystery. The moment she saw him, she would just know, and they would be together forever.

There was nothing. No spark of a memory. No big fireworks.

Just those two men, who looked raw and worn and fierce, claiming that they knew her name and where she came from.

And her baby still had no father.

Just another lingering question.

But what bothered her most were those marks on the man's arms. Jason was his name. They were just like hers, and that frightened her. With her head in her hands, she cried harder. That could only mean that they were telling the truth: they knew where she came from, and this mark came from the same place as his. And she wasn't sure she wanted to know any more.

She could still see Jason's eyes from across the table, the way he looked at her so desperately. Like he would just steal her away from Max's house at any moment if he had the chance. Everything about him screamed intensity. How could someone like that really love her like he claimed? Maybe she had run away from him, and that was why she had disappeared and forgot everything.

And then there was Gideon, quiet and withdrawn. He was hiding something, and she wasn't sure if Max knew it or not.

Something awful must have happened. She knew deep in her gut that she never willingly left these men. Whatever it was, it had torn her away from them and taken away her memory. Maybe it was better left unremembered.

The flutters began in her abdomen again, and she glanced down, her hand over her navel as she felt the kicks. The movements had grown more frequent, more intense since the moment those people walked through the gates. As the baby jostled around inside of her, she stood and padded toward the window. She had no idea how, but she knew they had left the house. She could feel them on the street.

Nikka opened the curtain and gazed down to the road just outside the house and saw the men walk away. The baby continued to kick, each jab into her ribs growing more uncomfortable.

Then, the blonde man stopped and turned, his eyes gazing up at the window as if he knew she stood there. Their eyes locked for a moment. The baby kicked harder, and she let the curtain fall back again as she stepped into the shadows of the room, her heart pounding against her ribs. But through the thin white fabric of the curtain, she could still see them walking further down the street.

CHAPTER TWENTY-ONE
JASON

Jason turned away from the window when she closed the curtain and backed away into the darkness of the room. Every step from the house took more effort, and he felt it in the muscles along his arms. They grew tighter the further he got.

Gideon walked beside him, but he never looked back. "The clergyman is correct about everything."

Jason stopped in the middle of the street, his eyes burning into the pavement at his feet. "You don't even know him. We have no idea what's happened to her in there. She could be a prisoner for all we know."

Gideon turned to face him. "She looked well. If she has no memory, then it would be best to leave her as is."

"How can you say that?" he said, clenching his fist and looking up at him. "How can you just walk away, knowing that she's there?"

"She will not be going anywhere tonight."

Jason seethed, walking up to him, his spine straight and adrenaline pumping in his veins. "She's right there, waiting for us. With my baby."

"You do not know that for sure," Gideon said.

That was the wrong thing to say. Jason felt the surge in his gut first, and then it sprang forward through his arm. He struck Gideon swift and hard across the face. He stumbled backward and reached out an arm to break his fall against the pavement. Jason lingered over him, his shadow cast over Gideon's body. Watching him fall like that made the pain in his fist just a little better, justified.

"Get up," Jason demanded.

Gideon spit blood onto the pavement and shook his head. "I will not do this with you."

"Get up."

He looked up at Jason. "Strike me if you must."

There was no pity for him. Not ever. Jason swung his boot and kicked him in the ribs. Gideon fell to his side and coughed as soon as his ribs expanded again.

"You did this," Jason said, kicking him again. "All of this is because of you."

He was ready to do it again when a voice called out to him. The flash of Amy's red hair caught the light of the twinkle lights around the church. She shoved herself in front of him, planted her hands against his chest and shoved him away.

"Stop this," she shouted at him, her green eyes raging and her mouth in a tight grimace.

Jason towered over her, gazing down at Gideon. She never moved her hands, though, keeping him from stepping forward again. He didn't want to hurt her, so he pulled in his anger and backed away. He watched Gideon move to his hands and knees and spit more blood from the laceration near his mouth.

"I should have killed you a long time ago," Jason muttered and stepped back again.

The shouting drew the attention of the security team, who now came running down the street. Jason wasn't going to fight them this time. They had every right to detain him, and they probably should before he did something even worse to Gideon. Dave rushed to his side, shoving him down to his knees and twisting his wrist behind his body. He never let his gaze drift from Gideon, watching as he looked back at him. Dave clamped handcuffs on him again and then forced him back up to his feet.

"All right," Dave said as more officers surrounded him. "Let's go, asshole."

They pulled him away from Gideon and Amy, taking him deeper into the town. He didn't pay much attention to the route. The thought of Gideon on the ground replayed over and over again. There had been so many chances for him to do that before, he had just let it build until it finally exploded. He always knew it would happen that way, and if it hadn't been for Amy, it probably would have ended very differently.

The officers forced him into the darkened corridors of the City Hall, where they flicked on their flashlights to take him to a solitary room at the south end of the building. Dave opened a door and shoved him inside.

"This isn't county jail," he said as he worked at the cuffs, his voice sounding pinched through his swollen nose. "I assume you've had some experience with jail before."

He placed a hand on Jason's shoulder and shoved him into the single chair in the room. With all the officers surrounding him, this felt familiar, and he didn't need to look at them to see the hatred in their eyes.

"But this will have to do," Dave continued. "Gonna keep you here tonight. I'll have one of my boys bring you a bedroll. It's time to cool off."

Jason turned his eyes up to him. "Aren't you going to read me my rights?" It probably wasn't wise to antagonize him, but he didn't have anything else to lose.

Dave leaned down, his hands on his knees. "I'm not the damn police."

He looked away from the officer and stared toward the blank wall on the other side of the room. Police or not, they were all the same. Judged and sentenced him before they even knew the facts.

Dave nodded to his men, who left the room. Then he stepped toward the door. "You already broke the only rule I gave you. I wouldn't plan on staying in town much longer if I were you." He moved out of the threshold and Jason heard the door lock behind him, leaving him in a dark and silent room.

Alone in that space, he now felt his knuckles throbbing. The shaking in his hands worsened the longer he sat there. He let his head fall, his face buried in his hands. Behind his eyelids, surrounded by the dark, he saw her face again. Not like he saw her tonight, but before, when he touched her cheek, and she would smile at him. Back when she wasn't frightened and lost in her amnesia.

Chapter Twenty-Two
Gideon

The pain in his jaw throbbed anytime he moved it, but at least the cut inside his cheek stopped bleeding into his mouth. Amy wrung out another cloth in the basin of cold water and brought it to him. She placed it against his face, and he winced.

"Sorry," she said with a cringe.

"It will be okay," he said and rested his head back against the wall. He stretched his legs out over the bed and closed his eyes. Amy continued to work with more cold rags to place on the growing bruises over his ribs.

"None of this is okay," she said, shaking her head. "He had no right."

Gideon opened his eyes again. The woman would never understand Jason, not like he did. "Yes, he did. He needed to do this."

She turned back to him and placed a hand on her hip. "Why do you keep defending him? He has treated you like crap the whole time I've known you guys."

"He is in pain."

"I know that," she said and brought him another cold rag. She sat at the edge of the bed, and the motion of the mattress made the muscles in his ribs spasm. She lifted his shirt just a little and placed the rag against his skin. The cool water made him gasp.

Amy hesitated to speak for a moment, but he could see it lingering just at her tongue. "That was her, wasn't it? You thought she was dead, but she's here. Right?"

Gideon nodded and drew the rag away from his face. "Yes."

"I guess seeing her just made him flip out."

"It is more than that."

"And," she said. "I had no idea she was pregnant. I assume that he had something to do with that . . ."

Gideon looked away from her and let his head hang. Amy was so kind to him, much more than he deserved. He grasped her hand and pulled her away from him. She had seen enough at this point in their journey, especially Jason being a seraph and she understood what he was. Maybe he should tell her everything.

"Jason is troubled, and it is because of me, because of things that I did," he said as she sat straight on the bed. "I will tell you things that will be difficult to hear, and I will understand if you wish to leave and never see either of us again."

Her head tilted a little to the side as she studied his face. "You saved my life and my son. I would never abandon you."

"You have a good heart," he said. "But it is not the same with everyone. You see Jason as he is now, but you would look at me far worse if you knew more. He deserves to have your sympathy. I do not." Gideon pulled his legs around to sit at the edge of the bed, facing away from her. "You see, Jason has suffered since Nikka died—because I killed her."

"I know he blames you—"

"No," he said and looked at her, his eyes glistening in the candlelight. "He blames me because I did it."

She remained silent for a moment, and she pulled back from him. "I don't understand."

"You have seen that he is a seraph. You know about him now. What you don't know is that I am a demon, like the hunters."

Amy quickly stood and backed away from him. "That can't be true."

He shook his head. "At least, I was a demon. For two thousand years, I walked this earth, working for my salvation back into Heaven. I had made a grave mistake by following Satan, and I fought so hard to earn my way back. I did so by working with archangels to create the seraphim. It has been my duty to teach them, to mentor them. And then, I was pulled back into Hell."

His gaze had drifted toward the candles, and he heard Amy's breathing quicken. "But I came back. I came back with a terrible secret that I could not share. I heard the Devil's voice in my ear every second of every day."

He grimaced as he remembered the day he had returned. He had been so frightened until he saw Nikka and she had calmed the voice in his head for a short time.

"I loved her before I fell and I love her still, but when I came back, the Devil's voice was stronger than my own will. I separated her from Jason." He looked up at Amy, who pressed back against the wall. "It was not difficult, but as soon as I had her alone, I did it."

"Did what?" she said, her voice shaking.

"I raped her," he said. "I hated every second of it, but I had no choice. It was what I was supposed to do. To this day I do not know why my Master wanted that to happen. And then he snapped his fingers, and I was his again. I was Pazuzu, in all my former glory. I knew exactly what I was doing when I went to Nevada. Of course, Jason and Nikka tried to stop me, but they were no match for me. I did terrible things to her; I had no idea she was pregnant at the time." He grimaced as he remembered the strips of her skin that he cut from her body. He pressed his hands to his temples and squeezed, trying to get the memories from his head. "But she stopped me. Somehow, she stopped me, and she changed me. Before she vanished, she gave me a soul."

He stood and faced her, the pain pulsating in his jaw. "I did all of this. I am the cause of the world's death. Jason should have killed me a long time ago."

Amy's hands clenched into trembling fists. "Why do you stay with him?"

Gideon shook his head. "It is my duty. He has become the seraph, and I must teach him until the day he decides to end me. I have no idea if I will ever earn my way back into Heaven, but it is the only thing I have left."

Her hand reached for the door knob. "I have to get some air." She pulled the door open and nearly stumbled out of the room.

He watched her leave, and he fell back onto the bed. That was the first time he had vocalized what had happened to anyone but God. No matter how many times he prayed for forgiveness, the guilt had never purged from him. It still remained, but saying it to someone had relieved some of the pressure that had built for over seven months, pressure that had increased the moment he saw Nikka's face in that chapel.

CHAPTER TWENTY-THREE
JASON

The door opened, casting light into Jason's small cell that had once been somebody's tiny office space. If he had been sleeping, the bright yellow sunlight would have awakened him, but he had slept restlessly on the thin bedroll for hours now, and it left him with only a sore shoulder and hip. A figure filled the space at the door, blocking out a person-shaped silhouette in the morning light. Jason squinted toward the sunshine as Dave leaned against the door frame.

"Rise and shine, buttercup," the security officer said.

Jason pulled himself to his feet and ran his fingers through his hair. Dave's swollen nose looked like a purple and blue sausage in the middle of his face this morning, but at least it wasn't bleeding anymore, not like the gusher from last night.

"Cutting you loose today, as long as you can contain yourself," he said, his nightstick pointed at him. "But stay away from the preacher's house. You make any moves that way, I'm booting you out of town myself. Got it?"

"I have to talk to her—" Jason said.

"She doesn't want to talk to you," Dave said, keeping his nightstick up. "She was very clear about that."

The sudden drop of his heart into his feet made his knees weak, and he steadied himself with his hand against the wall. The thought of going one more day without seeing her made his ears ring as he felt his blood pressure rise, each pulse pounding in his temples.

"When she says so, then I escort you there myself. No sooner. She wanted to talk to the other guy first, so you'll just have to see if she changes her mind. In the meantime, you are to stay confined to the hotel."

Of course. Gideon was going to ruin this. He should have expected that. His hands clenched into tight fists as his nails dug into the palms of his hand, the simple action of it sending ripples of pain from the bruises on his knuckles into his forearm. His hands had taken as much of the punishment as Gideon had last night.

"Now," Dave holstered the stick into the slot on his belt. "We have a deal?"

Staying in this tiny room was no way to spend to rest of the day, and he would never be able to see her like this. *Get it together man, take it easy.* The tendons in his fingers eased as he let his fists open, but he had to look away from the security guard just in case he saw the smirk on the guy's face.

A single deep breath later, he said, "Sure."

Dave stepped aside and, with a nod of his head, indicated that he was free to step from his cell, just like the warden of a prison. Total control and one swipe of the nightstick to the back of the knees would be enough for you to know that he was in charge. Jason wasn't ready to test that theory yet. He stood on his stiff knees and squinted back out to the sunlight streaming through the door. Dave remained at the edge of the door as Jason walked out, his step careful and even should the guard decide to try the nightstick on him. But the man just eyed him as he stepped into the corridor and continued behind him as they moved out of the building, no further words were exchanged for the duration of his exit from the prison he had just left.

The walk across Main Street with Dave at his back made him nervous, especially knowing that the preacher's house was just a block away. One look, though, would probably earn him more detention, or worse, a one-way ticket out of town. So he kept his eyes forward, always pushing away that urge to just give one glance back there in case Nikka watched from the window again. They neared the inn, and he stepped into the lobby, where Dave turned away from him without a word but gave him a single glare that made the tendons in his fists go tight again. Then the security guard left him in peace, but he was sure Dave or his men were out there keeping an eye on that hotel door.

Jason wandered into his room where he had left everything that he owned. At least his duffel bag was still here and untouched. He sat down on the edge of the bed and rested his elbows on his knees, his fingers stretched into his dirty hair. The knuckles on his hand still throbbed, but the pain had improved a lot since last night. He hoped that Gideon's face still hurt worse, though. Thankfully, Gideon was gone right now. Looking at that guy might just send him into another rage and get him kicked out for good.

A knock sounded at his door, and it opened just a little by the time he had looked up to see Amy peering into the room.

"Knock, knock," she said. Usually, the little lines around her eyes hardened when she looked at him, but now they were smooth and almost absent as the corner of her mouth curved into a faint smile. "Okay if I come in?"

"Sure," he said and looked down at the floor again, his body aching for rest on a softer bed.

"I brought you something," she said and stepped fully into the room. She held a plastic plate in her hand covered with tin foil. "You missed breakfast this morning, so I got you some." She uncovered the plate, revealing scrambled eggs, sausage, biscuits and pancakes. She had heaped so much onto the plate that he would be eating all morning. His stomach grumbled as soon as he saw it.

"Wow," he said and accepted the plate. "Thanks. You really didn't need to do that."

"It's okay. You've done a lot more for me."

He rested the plate on his knees and started in on the eggs with the plastic utensils she handed him.

"You do okay last night?" she said, lingering by the door, her fingers fidgeting around the door knob.

"I guess so," he said with a full mouth. "Had a roof over my head, even if the door was locked."

"So," she said, her lip curling just under her teeth. "I'm sorry about everything that happened."

"Don't worry about it."

"I didn't mean to get you arrested."

"Well, they're not really cops, so—"

She sighed and smiled. "You know what I mean. And . . . Gideon told me everything last night." The pause in her voice remained heavy and lingered between them. "Everything."

Jason stopped chewing and looked up at her. The smile had faded from her face, and he knew what she meant by that. For some reason, Gideon couldn't keep quiet and spilled his guts to her, and now she looked at him with pity.

"Everything, huh?"

She moved into the room a little more. "Yes, and I apologize. I misjudged you."

"Well, I didn't even know you judged me at all. So no harm, no foul."

"It means something to me. He told me everything about her, about Nikka. I didn't know she was pregnant."

"Yeah," he said and felt like he was ready to choke on the food. This was definitely something he didn't want to rehash. "Well, she is. And now she doesn't want to talk to me. Only wants to talk to him, and she can't even remember what he did to her."

"I know you can't go out there right now," she said. "Let me help you. Maybe I can talk to her—"

"Don't worry about it." His appetite had vanished in the last few seconds. He placed the half-full plate on the bed and stood, stuffing his hands in his pockets. Hopefully, that was enough to signal that he needed to be alone for now.

She nodded and looked away as she stepped toward the door. "Okay. If you need anything, just let me know."

"Fine," he said and watched her walk out the door, closing it behind her.

He didn't need anybody else's help. He just needed to figure out how to get Nikka to talk to him without going outside the hotel, or at least without Dave seeing him go out. There had to be something he could do to get her to remember him without pissing off the local law enforcement.

Chapter Twenty-Four
Gideon

When the security team came to Gideon's hotel room, he was not sure what they wanted. They only said to follow them, and he never questioned this, lest he get escorted to the same prison where they kept Jason overnight. He slipped into his shoes, and they led him down the street. As soon as he saw the preacher's house come into view, he knew where they were going.

They showed him around the side of the house and to the back gardens, where he saw a bench among the ivy trellises. He sat on the bench, and the security team stepped away, not saying a word about why he was there. Perhaps this was something about the fight that he and Jason had had the night before. By now, the entire town seemed to be buzzing about it. Even at breakfast out in the park with everyone, he could feel their eyes on him, wondering what had happened to the other man in his group.

The officers exited through the gate into the back yard, leaving him alone with his thoughts. With the security team just down the street, this was probably going to be the conversation about leaving town, why he and Jason cannot stay and can never come back.

A squeak of a rusty hinge caught his attention, and he glanced up at the door on the back porch. He had expected to see the preacher's face, but when he saw Nikka, he quickly stood, his hands wringing, and his feet unable to stay still. She stepped out onto the porch, and when the sunlight settled on her face, the flutterings began in his gut.

The light shone in her pale blonde hair and sparkled in her blue eyes as she stepped down from the porch and onto the grass. Her white tank top curved around her abdomen. When she touched down to the lawn, she stopped and clasped her hands in front of her, like she did not know what to do with them.

She looked right at him as though she wanted to remember him like there was nothing to fear from him. It was the same look she once gave him when he saw her in the hospital for the first time, and she had nothing else to lose. Oh, how things had changed since then. That look only brought him pain, and he turned his eyes down to his feet.

"Hi," she said, a quiver in her voice. "I hope this is okay. I didn't really want Dave's guys to go get you, but they insisted."

He nodded. "It is fine."

"It's just . . ." she said and took a step closer to her, but he turned away and placed his hands in his pocket. She has no idea what she is doing; she does not know what he was capable of because her memories had abandoned her.

She stopped and bit her lip. "It's just that I wanted to talk to you, alone."

"Very well. I am here."

"It's Gideon, right?"

He gave a little nod, but never glanced up at her.

"Can we just sit for a minute?" she said and hastened over to the bench beside him. She had moved quickly enough that it caught him off guard. "Please. I won't bite."

He smelled a fragrance on her skin as she brushed past him, something woody and floral. Something entirely wonderful. If he sat there, he would be close enough to touch her. And if he touched her, he may not ever be able to get her out of his head again. But there she was, beckoning him to take the space next to her on the bench.

"Please," she said again.

He felt every muscle in his back go rigid. "All right." The back of the bench touched his legs, and he settled into the seat, keeping his gaze on the door of the house. "What is it that you want of me?"

"I asked both of you last night, and only he answered. But I need to know, who am I to you?"

A lump formed in his throat making it hard to breathe. "I told you, I was your mentor—"

"I know what you said, but that doesn't tell me who I was . . . to you."

"Nothing more." That was the hardest lie he had ever uttered.

"I don't believe you. Not for a second."

"Why must there be more?" he said, feeling his shoulders grow tight. He took in a careful and deliberate breath, pushing his emotion deep into the furthest recesses of his mind. "I was your teacher. I taught you to fight. I taught you about this world before it died. I taught you how to survive."

"Then why are you so afraid of me?" she said, the tremble in her voice stronger now.

"Because—" he started but then held his tongue. He needed to control himself, but that was much harder than he had expected. "Because I am not the one to whom you should be speaking right now."

"You mean the other guy, Jason?" She let out a sigh. "I don't think I'm ready for that. I saw what he did to you last night."

Her fingers drifted toward the bruise on his lip, but he pulled away before she could touch him. That was too close. He stood and took a step away from the bench.

"He is the one who deserves this conversation," he said. "I would suggest that you focus your attentions on him and stay far away from me."

She stood, which took some effort with her pregnant belly. "Why? I can see it in you, Gideon. You're afraid of me because you feel something for me. I saw it when you first walked into this house. I don't remember who I am." Her voice rose and grew forceful. "Believe me, I've tried for months. Don't you think that I would want to know where I came from, how I got this way?" She opened her hands around her abdomen. "I have wanted to know for so long what happened to me, and now that I find someone, he won't tell me."

She had no idea what she asked of him. He pulled further away and could not look at her. "I . . . cannot. Please do not ask this of me."

The ache in his chest released pressure into his head. Everything that he wanted to say resided there, trying to push its way out. But he had to keep it there, safe from her. She didn't remember the horrible things he had done to her, and if he could contain it, she never would find out. Not from him, anyway.

"I—I'm sorry," she said and took in a breath.

Then he heard her gasp, a pained sound that had come from nowhere. It took him only a second to lose his focus and glance at her. She had curled over her abdomen, a hand along her side and her face twisted in a grimace. A few quick breaths escaped her lips as she moved her hand to the front of her stomach.

Something was wrong. She did not move. She did not make another sound, but only hunched over in pain.

Gideon stepped toward her, feeling as though the ground had fallen out from under him like he had plummeted into a dark hole. She was in pain, in a way that he knew nothing about, and he did not have the power to help her. His hand reached to her arm and touched her fingers.

She suddenly grasped his hand, standing straighter and her blue eyes flashed up at him. The grimace was gone now, and a small grin of victory had settled across her lips.

"I knew it," she said. "You still care about me."

It took only a second for him to realize what she had just done, and in that moment, she held his hand, and he caught her gaze. She still carried those deep blue eyes that he had gotten lost in once before. He tried to pull away, but she held him there. Of course, he could have tried harder, but he did not want to. She had just tricked him, and he was okay with that.

Then she took in another quick and surprised breath and turned her eyes to her abdomen. Was she trying to trick him again?

"Oh my gosh," she said and moved his hand to her belly. Before he could stop her, she had grasped his hand palm-down over her belly and placed her warm hand over his. "You've got to feel this. It's going crazy in there."

He held his breath, just feeling the warmth of her hand over his and her blue eyes drifting toward him. The scent coming off her neck filled his senses again, and with her being so close, he stepped a little closer.

And then he felt it. Like a little rumble under his hand, he felt the rhythmic movements vibrate through her body from inside her womb. Even if he tried, he knew he would not be able to move his hand away from her now. That little life moved inside her and almost touched his skin. He had never felt anything like it.

"It likes you," she said. "It's never moved like this before." She smiled, that same delight that once lit up the room around him.

He could not help but smile with her as he felt that tiny movement in her body. As he touched her, he wanted to stay like this forever and revel in every experience that this life brought to her. There was no town around them. There was no dry and dead world outside this space in the back yard of the Victorian house. Right now, there was only the three of them—Nikka, him and the baby inside of her.

The baby that might be half demon.

The baby that might be Jason's.

He pulled away from her, freeing his hand from under hers, and turned his eyes from her again. The smile faded from her lips as she watched him slip away.

"I am sorry," he said, trying to keep his voice even. "I cannot do this."

Gideon turned and hurried to the back gate, but he heard her voice as he touched the latch.

"Don't go," she pleaded.

Losing her was the hardest thing that had ever happened to him, and he knew it was about to happen again. But it would be best for her and him. He had fallen before, more than once, and he had tried so hard to redeem his soul. He could not risk it by putting her in danger again. "You must stay far away from me."

He opened the latch and rushed out of the gate, trying not to look back. The subtle flutters still vibrated in his hand, and he curled his fingers around his palm, hoping that he would never forget that feeling for the rest of his days.

Chapter Twenty-Five
Jason

The morning had wandered into afternoon as Jason sat back on the bed of his house-arrest prison. The door cracked just a little, and he lifted his head enough to see Amy peering into the room.

"It's dinner time," she said. "Everybody's gathering. Want me to get you a little something?"

He gave her a half smile. "You know, you don't have to do that."

"Just try and stop me."

Jason propped himself up on his elbow. "All right. Do what you have to do."

"Okay. But if it's any consolation, we'll probably get rained out. Looks like a storm's coming."

"Actually, yeah. It is a consolation," he said. "I hope it pours on all of them out there, soaking all their pansy asses."

"There you go," she said with a laugh. "Way to stay positive." She moved to leave the room, but then she hesitated and glanced back at him. "Oh, and Gideon's hanging out in his room too. He didn't want to go either. Maybe you two should talk."

Jason turned away from her. "I don't want to hear anything he has to say."

"All right, I get that," she said. "But you know I've gotta keep trying."

He reached his hands behind his head and looked up at the ceiling. "I know."

She slipped out of the door and shut it behind her. What she didn't see was the little smile that had formed on his lips after she left, even though he tried to suppress it. He had to give her props; at least she acted like she cared.

Like everyone else in town, she went with the throngs of people for their big community dinner. They were probably all crowding toward the park now while he stayed here, just feet away from Gideon in the next room.

The sound of thunder rumbled across the valley and rattled at his window. The oncoming evening cast a green-blue glow into his room from the window facing the street, and a flash of lightning illuminated across his bed for only a fraction of a second. But it was enough for him to sit up and pad toward the window to gaze out at the horizon. Just as he had suspected; he watched the crowds gathering at the edge of the park across the street, chatting and happy as they conversed with each other about nothing important, he was sure. None of them had been touched much by the outside world, and their clean clothes and bright eyes showed it. Amy slipped into the crowd easily, with Dylan's hand in hers. She had started to look just like them, even after only being here for a couple of days. With the oncoming evening, somebody had already starting lighting the lanterns around the park and the street to illuminate it for everyone coming toward dinner. Everyone except him, and apparently, Gideon.

As he watched them, his eyes drifting to every face that walked along the street and feeling the desire to stay away from them, he saw Nikka. She walked beside Max with the security detail around her. Jason leaned his head against the window sill as he watched her, her arms covered in a thin, long-sleeved white T-shirt that hugged her abdomen. The camo green cargo capris hung loosely about her hips, and the hems danced over the sandals that decorated her feet. She looked happy and healthy just like the rest of them, the short hair on her head so light it almost appeared white. He had never thought of her as a blonde. Funny. He had actually never thought about the color of her hair and it felt strange seeing anything on her head at all. She held Max's hand, and that simple gesture sent pains into his chest.

The small entourage walked under a lantern just before turning into the park, when she slowed and then came to a stop. Her eyes lifted and turned toward him as though she knew he watched her. He never turned away, though. He had to let her see him. The smile faded from her lips, her small hand still in Max's. The preacher stopped as well and glanced back at her, following her eyes to the window of the inn. He said something to her, but she didn't move. She only looked at Jason now, studying him through the glass like she wanted something but was too afraid to ask.

For a moment, he thought she would pull her hand free and run across the street to him. But maybe that was only what he wanted. She stood there, watching him until Max tugged on her arm one more time, and she turned away. The security team surrounded her again as they disappeared into the crowd of the park, far beyond his reach.

Sure, he could go out there and try to find her again. But he was smart enough to know that it would just land him either back in his cell or outside the walls altogether. Being patient was not his strongest trait, but he would just have to suck it up.

He stepped away from the window and fell back against the bed again but felt the tug of his heart back across the street. This is how he would have to live for now, trying to bide his time and distract himself. And he would do it for her. Whatever it took.

The list of books available in the lobby of the inn sucked, but it was enough to keep him occupied over the next few hours, even after Amy came back from dinner with plates of food for both him and Gideon. Having her and Dylan around helped distract him as well, especially when the kid wanted so much attention from him. Even spending a night in that makeshift jail wasn't enough to make Dylan like him any less.

The lanterns outside in the park and on the street finally grew dark as the park became quiet again. He promised himself he wouldn't linger at the window, waiting for her to pass by. He wasn't a stalker.

The lines of the book he read jumbled into just collections of letters and words, too boring to continue and reading by the light of a flashlight gave him a headache. He finally closed up the book and rested back against the bed. With his eyes closed, he let his memories wander over the vision of her face. For the first time in months, he welcomed those thoughts and didn't try to push them away. He would remember her as she was then and see her as she was now. Even if she didn't want to see him, he would give her a reason to want to. He would let her remember him, even if it took him years to do it.

Those thoughts drifted away into dreams, overtaking him as the rumble of thunder grew closer, and the lightning flashed into his room.

Chapter Twenty-Six

Jason

The vibration first began like an undulation just under his skin, writhing to the surface just below the tattoos. The sensation blended into his dreams until it grew, the intensity building until the discomfort was too much to take. The pain stirred him from his sleep and coursed through his limbs, moving up and down like a tidal wave of warning alarms. As soon as he recognized it, he bolted upright in bed and stared into the dark room.

Even through the closed curtains, he saw another flash of lightning. It illuminated the corners of his room, casting long, black shadows over his bed. A rumble of thunder trembled along the floor, and then everything grew silent again. There was nothing in the room, not even a sound that suggested anything was wrong. But the vibrations in the tattoos intensified until they itched.

He rose from his bed and pulled on his boots while the marks on his body seemed to come alive with movement. The T-shirt that he had draped over the single chair in the room felt cold against his skin as he drew it over his head and walked to the window. He pulled back the curtains and stared out into the darkened street. All the lanterns had been extinguished hours ago. Nobody walked the streets, and very little moonlight lit anything against the thunderstorm that had descended over the valley. Rain spattered on the glass, cascading down in streams as another flash of lightning pulsated over the small town.

Quiet had descended upon everything except the beginning of the storm. But the vibrations in his marks told him otherwise. At this late hour, he could risk going out into the street to investigate, but it could land him back in the cell, or worse, outside the walls. Something was wrong, though. He had to take that chance.

Jason stepped outside his room, down the corridor of the inn and through the front lobby. He could barely see into the center of the room, and without any power to the lights, it looked abandoned. When he opened the front door in the lobby, the scent of fresh rain hit him first, tickling across his skin and drifting into the hotel. Other than the next wave of thunder and the slight breeze against the trees, the town remained peaceful and still.

As still as the bottom of a grave.

He took a single step out the door and peered down the darkened streets. At the far end of Main, a few men stood at the watch towers along the inner side of the city walls. Fortunately, they were too far away to notice him. But those men wouldn't have caused him to awaken with such a start. And the tattoos continued to vibrate and burn under his skin, alerting him to some other yet unseen threat.

The breeze moved over his skin, and he closed his eyes, sniffing into the dark. No brimstone. No decay in the air.

The sensation under his skin caused an unsettling in his gut, like swarms of bees that grew angry with each passing second.

A flash of lightning. He opened his eyes, and as the last milliseconds of the lightning flash ebbed away, an explosion sounded from the outside of the wall, right at the gates. The plume of red and orange rose into the night, and the sound of the bomb rattled the windows of the inn.

Jason froze for a moment, not sure that he actually saw the fire that grew above the edge of the gate. The bells in the watchtowers rang out. His legs wouldn't move at first, but his fingers clutched at the doorframe. He knew what was just outside those gates now, beyond the plume of smoke and fire that grew along the wall. The power in his sigils had warned him. And if the hunters got through the gate, this city would be like a buffet table for them.

He had to move.

The shouts of men at the wall diminished as he rushed back into the hotel with the one thing he had to do. He ran down the hall and shoved his shoulder into the door until it gave way. He crashed into Gideon's room and hurried to the side of his bed. Gideon still lay fast asleep, the bruise on his lip fresh in the fading light coming through the window. Jason grabbed his shoulders and shook until his eyes flashed open.

"We've got a big problem," Jason said.

Jason could tell the moment he understood what was happening as he saw Gideon's eyes open wide at the sound of the bells ringing from down the hall. There wasn't enough time to explain things. Gideon jumped out of bed and followed Jason from the room. As they emerged into the corridor, Amy's door opened, and she stepped out.

"What's going on?" she said as Jason ran past her door. More shouts rose from the street.

Jason dashed back down the hallway with Gideon and Amy at his heels. By now, the security team had collected at the end of the street. People stood at their doorsteps, gazing with wide eyes toward the sound of the bells and the smell of smoke.

Another explosion, and the impact was much larger than the first one.

The city must have had a plan in place should something like this happen, and every man in town ran down the street toward the wall. They each had some kind of weapon in hand—guns, knives, axes. Anything that they could use to defend their city.

A larger plume of fire and smoke arose from a third explosion, and now he could see a breach in the wall.

Jason's nails dug into the door frame from where he stood. The gate started to collapse, and these people wouldn't be able to hold out much longer.

He turned back to Gideon and Amy, who watched out the window with wide eyes. "Get everybody into the church."

Gideon glanced at him and nodded, the unspoken understanding flashing between the two of them. Jason ran out into the street and the pouring rain that descended onto Garnet Falls. The church sat a half block away, and the men ran toward the chaos, leaving everybody else in their homes. He signaled Amy down one end of the street and Gideon down the other. Hopefully, they could alert enough of the people to get to the safety of the chapel. At least in there, the demons couldn't get to them as long as the threshold stayed protected.

Another throng of men rushed past him as he heard the sound of metal-on-metal scraping from the gate. The flames bloomed above the top of the wall and engulfed the east watchtower. The gate bowed inward until the hinges finally shattered. As soon as the gate fell, he saw the flames just outside the walls and the silhouettes of two big trucks roar into the perimeter of the city, accompanied by a swarm of motorcycles. Shots rang out in a clatter, and the gunfire he heard came from either the people or the hunters. He wasn't about to stop and find out.

In the rush of men that ran toward the falling gates, he saw Max, his face drenched in rainwater and a rifle in his hand. Jason rushed to him and grabbed his arm.

"Where is she?" he shouted over the sound of thunder and gunfire.

"In the cellar," he said, pulling free. "She'll be safer there than out here."

Max ran toward the wall, blending into the crowd of dark figures that ran to face the fight. But Jason stepped back, against the wave that rushed down the street. He turned on his heels and darted through the crowd, his heart pounding against his ribs. Nikka was alone in that house, and the hunters were coming.

The roar of engines moved into the city, blending with the sounds of fierce howling like wolves storming a hen house. The rumble of motorcycle engines echoed against the walls all around him as he sprinted down the street. Screams and gunfire came again. It all sounded like chaos behind him, but he couldn't look back, not until he found her and made sure she was safe.

By the time he had reached the preacher's house, the group of men running toward the gates had left this area unprotected and desolate. There wasn't another soul here that could see him force a kick into the locked front door until it broke free at the deadbolt. Splinters of wood showered around the floor of the quiet atrium as he stepped into the dark room. The house seemed empty and quiet; no sign of Nikka. Max had extinguished the lights, probably as soon as the explosion happened. From his last visit here, he knew where the living room and dining area was, but he had no idea how to find the cellar.

"Nikka," he called for her, running into the dining room and through the back entrance to the kitchen as he listened for any indication that she was still here.

He turned another corner, but it led out onto the back porch. The old house proved to be a maze of doors and hallways that curved around and continued to dump him back into the same place he started. He turned and felt his hands along the dark walls back into the kitchen. His fingers found a seam in the textured paint of the wall that made him stop. The house was old enough that it probably had one of those hidden spaces in the wall. His great-grandmother's house had something like that, and his parents had kept him away from it when he was a little kid.

He worked at the seam until he could fit his fingertips in enough to pry it open. The wall opened, just as he had hoped. The space beyond it, though dark, felt deep and cold like a cavern as the air of it breathed out against his rain-soaked skin. It had to be the cellar.

Jason called her name again, his voice reverberating back to him from the space below the grand house. He held his breath and listened into the darkness. It only took a second for him to hear a shuffle and then a click as the beam of a flashlight erupted into the dark. The white light fell upon her small face, casting sharp shadows over her nose and eyes. Her pupils were huge and black as pits as the light shook in her hands.

"I've got to get you out of here," he said and walked down the first few steps into the cellar, reaching his hand out to her.

The light shone against her wide eyes, the beam of the light shaking in her hands. A spattering of gunfire clattered outside, and she jumped with a gasp. That was enough to get her legs to move. Her hand caught the railing of the stairway, and she dashed up each step, her sandaled feet clacking against the wood. She caught his outstretched hand without hesitation. As soon as he felt her in his hand, he turned and rushed with her into the kitchen.

When they moved into the light from the kitchen window, a crash sounded from the back porch. A figure leaped into the house, eyes black and mouth wide with rotted teeth. The drone under his skin slithered as soon as the demon saw him. Its claws reached for Nikka just as Jason pulled her close to him, feeling the curve of her pregnant belly against his arm, and braced against the kitchen counter. He kicked the demon back through the door and turned with her still in his hand. They dashed together from the house and into the pouring rain. With each step, her hand in his, he could only think of protecting her child and getting her away from all of this.

They rushed down the steps to the front sidewalk. The feel of her fingers tight around his hand had distracted him enough that he didn't see it coming. Something moved in the dark to his right and struck him from the side. He fell hard as the figure slammed into him, losing the grip he had on Nikka's hand. Wet, muddy grass hit his head and coated his back as the creature on top of him lifted off, another drone wrapped its cold fingers around his throat. He tried to pull and fight at it, but its claws had him pinned tightly enough that he couldn't even reach back to grasp his sword.

Nikka screamed, and he glanced away from the demon that had him pinned to see that another drone had his hand on her ankle, crawling toward her in the mud as she tried to get away from him. The demon at his neck squeezed harder, and the ringing began in his ears, the sound that came before a person blacked out altogether.

Chapter Twenty-Seven

Nikka

The sound of his voice sent shivers rattling down Nikka's spine. He was the last person she expected to see here right now, staring down at her from the top of the cellar stairs. The moment Max had left her here with the flashlight, something had told her to run. That this wasn't the right thing to do. The mark on her chest burned and itched, and this didn't happen very often. But when it did, she never ignored it.

With the flashlight clutched in her hands like it was a weapon, he reached his hand out to her, the one they called Jason. He knew, just as she did that she had to leave this place, even if it was with him. She rushed up the stairs and took his hand before she could think of the consequences. For a moment, it felt like the mark in her chest had calmed down when she first took his hand, but it was hard to tell when everything outside sounded like World War Three.

Then the burning of her mark came again as soon as something crashed through the back door. Jason acted fast, pulling her away and kicking the thing right back out of the house. She couldn't think, but he did and pulled her away and back out into the night.

She screamed when the thing collided with him as soon as he stepped out onto the street. Whatever it was, it looked big and dark and smelled like rotting meat even through the torrential rain. Then the second creature came out of the shadows from behind her, grabbing her around the chest and pinning her arms. It pulled her into the dark of the trees, its cold breath on her neck. The tattoo on her chest almost burned right into her ribs, through her heart.

The creature dragged her further away from where Jason fought with the first demon. It had him down, choking the life from him, and there was nothing she could do about it. The arms that held her moved around her torso and threw her to the ground. She fell against her hip, trying to catch herself on her hand. The demon seemed to slither over her like a cold, wet serpent, and in the flash of lightning, she saw the face of a young man no older than herself. His black hair wet with rainwater, but bright red locks of hair fell around his eyes and danced around his shaved temples. Dark eyes looked at her with fierce hunger. He climbed over her, pulling her toward him through the mud with such strength that she knew he couldn't be human.

The moment she saw his face and felt his tug, she lifted her leg and planted it in his chest. With a surge of adrenaline, she kicked him away and turned to pull herself onto her feet. He grabbed her ankle firmly, though, and drew her back toward him. Her fingers grasped at anything to stop her descent, but they only raked through mud and wet grass.

Not like this. She couldn't let her or her baby die like this.

She lifted back on her hip and swung her fist at his face, but he caught her wrist with the speed of a ninja, anticipating the move. The rain and mud had left a slick of moisture over her skin, and she wriggled free. When she tried to crawl away, he reached around for her arm but caught the neckline of her T-shirt. The force of him pulling her back tore the fabric free, exposing her chest down to the edge of her bra, revealing the mark tattooed there.

The demon stopped his advance on her with a sudden jolt, his eyes wide as he looked at the mark. His mouth dropped open, and his dark eyes turned up toward her face, a fierce look of awe in his black demon eyes

"It's you," he said with a grin. "You're the one Lila's been looking for."

His hand moved to her leg, and she took this one moment of distraction to turn around and kick him in the face, sending him back into the mud. She scrambled to her knees and crawled away as she turned back to see Jason twist and dislodge the demon on top of him. He shoved it far enough that he could turn and rise into a crouch. From the shadows all around him, things moved into their circle, surrounding them from all sides. She watched as Jason turned and laid eyes on the demon that had just spoken to her, and a phantom of recognition passed across his face.

The demon with shocks of red hair atop a wet mohawk stood, his form rising tall in the rain. He looked back and forth between her and Jason, a wicked grin twisting on his lips. "I should have figured you would be here with her."

Demons materialized out of the shadows now, a dozen closing in around them, faces pale and eyes dark. The mark scorched against her skin as more of them appeared from the darkness.

The demon walked backwards, beyond the surrounding creatures and smiled at both of them as he swaggered into the dark.

"Lila will be pleased," he said.

Just as he slipped back into the shadows, he gave a flick of his wrist, and the surrounding army fell in. Nikka knelt down into the mud and clutched her cold arms around her torso, trying to hide the mark on her chest. There were too many of them, and nobody else was coming to help them. She pressed herself back against the tree and Jason stood just feet from her, his back to her as he watched the army encroach. He might have had good intentions in finding her tonight, but they were both going to die at the hands of the dozen demons that now surrounded them.

He turned his head back to her just enough that she saw the edge of his angled cheek and the shadow of his eye, rain dripping from his hair and off his goatee. His blue eyes lit up in the flash of lightning, as though he wanted to tell her it would be okay. She looked at him, shivering in the rain and curling around her belly to protect it before the creatures came at her.

Then he turned back to the demons. His hand reached behind his shoulder, and she couldn't believe what she saw. Like something from her dreams, a sword materialized from behind him and the space around them lit up in an electric blue fire that emitted from the weapon. The power behind that fire moved into his arms, lighting every tattoo on his body into sparkling blue lights as well. The weapon moved with him, like they were one, as every demon descended on him at once. She watched him move in a dance of fire and shadow, the sword cutting through the air. Demons howled and screeched, some disappearing in a burst of ashes and embers.

Nikka shielded her head with her hands as ash scattered over her from the swipe of the sword. Another demon destroyed. Jason moved, his body lunging and dodging each demon that came at him. He moved across the yard in a leap over their heads like he had wings and landed as the sword came down, decapitating two at once. Four more rushed at him, and he arced backwards as one came at his throat.

Fire swirled around the tip of the blade as it dispatched the last of them. Then, with a downward swish of the sword, Jason stopped, his chest moving with his rapid breathing. Everything grew still in that moment. The rain still fell hard, but she moved her hands from her face and looked at him, the shaking in her shoulders now painful. The lights still undulated under his tattoos like a thousand blue fireflies that danced in his skin. He glanced back at her, the lights shifting across his face.

Still breathing hard, he moved the sword to his back, and it disappeared, as though it never existed. The lights under his skin extinguished with the replacement of his weapon. He stepped toward her and fell to his knees, his chest rising and falling with each exhausted breath. The light that had shone from his eyes no longer lingered there, but now his blue eyes turned up toward her in the dim light as if he begged her to remember him.

The mark on her chest no longer burned, but her skin now felt like ice in the pouring rain. As she looked at him, the slump of his shoulders and the way he eyed her with such desperation, she felt something stir in her memory. She knew what déjà vu was, but she had never felt it like this before. She could have sworn she once saw him like this, just him in the dark. Maybe she saved him, or he saved her. It felt familiar.

His hand moved toward her, and for a moment she thought he reached for her hand that clutched tightly to her chest. But his fingers touched the torn edge of her shirt and moved it back across her chest, covering the mark that lingered there.

He didn't touch her, and for the first time since she saw him within the city walls, she wanted him to.

Her teeth chattered now against her will, and she was sure her lips were blue, but she looked up at him from the tear in her shirt. At that instant, the recognition that swam in her thoughts was undeniable. His hand finally slipped to the back of her neck, and he pulled her gently toward him. As cold as she was, she forced her arms to unlock from around her torso. She slid them around him, and he pulled her close, her face pressed into the warmth of his neck. Despite the shivers, she felt his heat through her wet shirt as his arm moved around her back.

Everything that she had just seen, the blue sword and his marks, would have to wait for an explanation until later. For now, she just needed this moment without words and without the sounds of war around them. Her fingers clutched onto the wet T-shirt at his back.

Then she felt him whisper in her ear. "Are you okay?"

Nodding would have to do because she wasn't sure that the words would come out.

Sounds of shouting came from down the street, and she realized that the roar of engines had disappeared. People began moving from their positions and into town. Nikka peered over his shoulder in time to see Max running back toward the house, the rifle still in his hand. He had a streak of blood running down his face from a cut along his hairline. Her usual security team ran with him as well.

She pulled away from Jason, and as she tried to meet his eyes, he turned away and stood up. Max rushed onto the lawn, his arms reaching out for her. She felt arms all around her, lifting her from the mud. At some point, a blanket fell over her shoulders, all while she tried to see Jason from around them, but he had backed away and into the shadows. The arms drew her toward the house, voices chattering away that she needed to get inside and dried off and the baby will be okay and that everything was safe now.

But she still looked for him, until she saw the back of his form walking away down the street, away from Dave's team and probably back to the inn where he had been ordered to stay as far away from her as possible.

And now she could only think about his hands around her, holding her and never wanting to let him go.

Chapter Twenty-Eight

Nikka

The shivers rippled over Nikka's skin despite the blanket and the cup of hot tea Max had prepared for her. It was probably that her hair was still wet and she could hear the rain spattering against the window of her bedroom. And her blue lips probably didn't help convince Max that she was okay.

He knelt in front of her and held her hand that peeked out from the edge of the blanket around her shoulders. "I'll get Justine to come check on you."

"I'm fine," she said. She didn't feel like getting the only nurse in town involved with her chills tonight. The woman had already taken such good care of her throughout this whole pregnancy, and a little thing like shivers seemed ridiculous. "I'm not injured, just cold."

"Are you sure?" he said and placed a hand on her forehead. "The baby's moving?"

"Yes," she said and pulled her head back from his touch. "I just need a little time. And space." Her eyebrows rose as though telling him that he needed to go.

He smiled and nodded. "I get it. I'm smothering you again." That same look of paternalistic care appeared on his face as he stood and stared down at her. "Just get some rest."

"I'll be fine. I'm sure Dave and his hit squad are waiting for your orders downstairs."

After all the chaos of tonight, she didn't have to see the security team to know they gathered somewhere in the house. The people of this town would need to know that their leaders had a plan to stop this from happening again, and she didn't want that affected by her ridiculous problems.

Max turned away and stepped out the door, but not before turning back one more time. "Get me if you need anything."

"Bye," she said, with her head wagging and her eyebrows raised again.

As soon as the door closed, she sipped at the tea and felt the hot, sweet liquid slip down her throat. She pulled the cup away from her lips and examined the mark on her skin just under the hemline of her clean tank top. The shirt she had worn now lay in the trash, torn and muddy and wet. But the edge had been ripped away to reveal the mark, and that demon had reacted oddly when he saw it. The tattoo had been there since the day she woke up and wandered to Max's front door, and she never had a clue what it meant.

And it was similar to the markings Jason had all over his body like it had been made by the same hand. The same markings that lit up tonight when he fought against the demons that had attacked them. The same tattoos that matched the intensity of the sword he had produced out of nowhere. Everything was connected to her own baffling tattoo.

Even though she never understood what the mark meant, she had known it was not just some artist's makings across her skin. This had always been something special. The mark had been the first thing that had alerted her about the presence of the demons on the first night that Max had taken her in. They had followed her to his house, and she knew they were there. The tingling burn she felt in the ink always told her when something was near.

Now, there was somebody just down the street that could hold the answers to the mark on her chest. Maybe it was time to actually talk to him, even if he made her a little nervous. Even if she felt familiar in his embrace.

Nikka pulled the blanket from her shoulders and placed the tea on the nightstand as she stood and peered through the curtains of her window. The end of the inn was visible from her bedroom, and she could see a faint light shine through the window of the room he occupied—the same room she saw him gaze out of earlier tonight. Max would hate it, but she knew she had to see Jason again. Now.

She shuffled through the items in her closet until she found a thin jacket that fit over her shoulders. It was enough to keep the rain away from her skin when she went outside, even though it was a little big for her. At least someone had donated it, along with the few other clothes that she had since coming to this place. The goosebumps raised the hair on her arms under the sleeves of the jacket.

When she opened the door, she heard the men speaking in hushed tones, and the noise sounded like it came from the dining room. Max must have closed the doors in order to keep the voices from carrying upstairs and concerning her. He always treated her like she was so fragile, but he had no idea how much she actually heard when he talked with Dave and his men. She always knew what was happening at the front gate and how much she would have to worry. That's how she had heard about the new people who had arrived just a few days ago.

She stepped from the door and crept down the stairs, avoiding the one step that squeaked when someone walked over it. The voices still came uninterrupted from behind the doors, and she eyed them as she stepped through the kitchen and out the back door. The rain pattered against the slick material of the jacket hood over her head, but the downpour had softened to just a thin drizzle. She moved around the side of the house and into the street, keeping the faint light coming through the window of the inn in her sight.

The lobby of the hotel was dark, as always. The woman who owned it didn't really run it as a hotel anymore, but rather as a boarding house for any new people until Max could establish better housing for them in town. And since nobody new had shown up in over a month, they hadn't really prepared for more housing yet. She walked to the room at the end of the inn and stepped up to the door.

But then she stopped. She had been so ready to just go in and ask him what in the hell was going on, but something made her hesitate now. The faint tingle began along the mark on her chest, just like it had that night in the church when he and Gideon first arrived. It was enough to make her take notice, and not painful like when the demons are nearby. She placed a hand on the door and closed her eyes. Through the wood of the door, she could sense him in there, moving around at the far end of the room. Maybe he could sense her too, but how was that possible?

In all the days she could remember, she had never come across somebody that she could feel without actually touching them. But even now, through this door, she knew where he was like she could see his shape. Those broad muscled shoulders that tapered down his torso to his hips.

Stop it. What the hell? How did he get into her head so easily, with just one touch?

She bit her lip and shook the thoughts from her head. He had to have more answers, and she needed them, even if he was beginning to drive her crazy.

Her fingers slipped to the doorknob, and she turned. Unlocked. Nerves beat like moth wings in her stomach now. She pushed the door open, and the white light of a lantern poured into the darkened hallway where she stood. The room opened up to her, and she could see the bed next to the window, the linens strewn about like the bed hadn't been made up in. But it was empty.

She pushed the door further and edged herself into the room. A chair stood barren next to a desk, covered with an open duffel bag. All these things, and he was not there.

Then she heard a sound from behind the closed door of the bathroom. *Oh gosh.* He was in there, and she had just let herself into his room. If he opened that door and found her in his room, he would think she was the worst, snooping around his belongings. She had no business just barging in like this.

She turned on her heel and stepped toward the door when it happened. The bathroom door opened and a golden light poured from that room, shining over her like a spotlight. She froze and cringed as she saw his shadow fall over her from where he stood.

"Hey," he said, his voice expressing a little surprise but not with the horror that she had expected.

Nikka turned back and faced him, but felt her cheeks flush. He stood there at the threshold of the bathroom door, a large white towel wrapped around his hips. And nothing else. The moment she saw him, she tried to look somewhere else. The corner of the room. The nightstand. Anywhere.

"Uh, sorry," she said. And turned halfway to face the wall so he couldn't see the warmth that had developed across her cheeks. "I shouldn't have just let myself in."

"It's okay," he said and moved further into the room. She could smell fresh soap on his skin, and his hair was still wet, dripping on his muscled shoulders and over the tattoos that curved down his torso. "I'm glad you came."

He moved toward the bed and smoothed out the surface for her. "Please, have a seat."

"I'm not staying."

"Oh." The word fell hard between them.

"I just . . ." she started, but the words felt so hard to say when she tried to look at him, "just need to ask you something."

"Okay."

She looked at him from the corner of her eye. "Could you put on some clothes or something?"

"That's what you came to ask me?"

"No," she said and sighed with a smile.

"Hey, this is my place. You came to me, remember?" He took a step closer, and she felt the tingle intensify against her mark.

"Fine." She rolled her eyes and looked at him. The smirk still remained on his face, his eyebrow a little cocked. This was a lot harder than she thought it would be. The words stuck in her throat for a moment, but as they simmered there, she saw the faintest bruises and scrapes along his neck and shoulders. Those must have been from his scuffle with the demons that attacked them outside the house. He hadn't come out of that fight unscathed. Now she wondered what else he had suffered in that fight when he saved her from them.

"I'm ready to know," she finally said, her mouth feeling like cotton.

He lost the smirk, his blue eyes sapphire in the lantern light. "And what, exactly, do you want to know?"

"All of this," she said, her hands rising up and down at his side. "These marks. My mark. What is all of this? Why am I here? And why don't I remember you?"

He turned away from her and stepped to the desk, rummaging through the duffel bag until he produced a worn and weathered scrap of paper. The edges had been yellowed, like the rim of a book page. He held it out to her, and she accepted it, unfolding it with caution not to tear the brittle paper.

The words typed on the page were eerily familiar. Lyrics of a song that had inexplicably played through her head a hundred times.

Last night she came to me, my dead love came in.

"Where did you get this?" she said, reading through the lines and hearing the song in her head.

It will not be long, love, til our wedding day.

"You gave it to me, just about a week ago."

"That's not possible," she said, shaking her head.

"I saw you in a vision." He stepped closer again. "You were there, with your baby in your arms. And when I woke up, I found that."

"It can't be." She looked at the words, over and over, hearing the song in her head. The song first came to her in a dream. A dream that she had only a week ago. "This song won't leave my head. I was hearing it every day until you guys showed up."

"When I found that, I knew you were alive."

She couldn't look away from the page. "How? How can this be?"

"Because you, me . . . all of this—we are being guided by something else. There's some other force at work here."

Her fingers brushed along the worn paper, across the aged typeset. "What happened to me?"

She saw the shadow pass across his face, and he stepped back a little. "I don't think you really want to know."

"Yes, I do."

He bit his lip, which made the dimples at the edges of his goatee deeper. "I can tell you this: the powers of Heaven and Hell are fighting to claim this world, and we're caught in the middle of it. When I lost you, when I thought you were dead," he said, and his voice cracked, "something took you away, and you vanished."

"Something?"

"Gideon said it was a cherub."

"But I thought cherubs were those cute little baby angel things."

"Oh, no. There was nothing cute about it. It was a huge beast that tore its way into this world and took you. We had no idea what had happened to you, and we just had to assume you were dead."

"And what about this?" She pulled down the neckline of her shirt, exposing her tingling mark.

"It was a mark you had before you were gone. The only one left."

"What do you mean, *the only one left*?"

"You were like me," he said, his voice dropping. "No. Better. You were so much better at this than I could ever be."

"Like you? You mean—" Her eyes moved to the tattoos, and she remembered the sword at his back.

"Yeah," he said, taking a step back from her. He reached behind his back and his fingers curled around the hilt of the invisible weapon. As soon as he touched it, the blade materialized, and he pulled it out before him. The blue flames erupted along the length of the weapon, illuminating the room in neon light. He looked up again, the light sparkling in his eyes. "You were a seraph."

That word felt like something she remembered like she had always known what it meant.

"You had this power once. You saved me with it." He leaned down and placed the weapon on top of the duffel bag. As soon as his fingers left the hilt, the blue flames disappeared, leaving only the simple metal of an old sword, like the relic from an ancient time.

"Seraph," she whispered, turning away from the blade and facing him again. "And I fought demons, didn't I? I thought it was just a dream. I've seen myself doing that so many times. In my dream, I can always defeat them. All except one, and I don't know who he is. But he doesn't feel like the others. And he looks different, too."

"Who are you talking about?"

"I don't know," she said and scrunched her eyes closed. Maybe that would help her to remember the face that kept eluding her. "He's beautiful, but he scares me. I don't know what he is."

She felt his hand touch her face and she opened her eyes.

"I won't let anything happen to you."

"You said I was a seraph, just like you. I had the marks, just like you. But you don't have this one," she said, pointing to the sigil on her chest.

"I don't know how you got it. It was the mark you used to save my life once."

His thumb brushed against her cheek, making the tattoo tingle even more. She slipped her hand onto his wrist, feeling the heat of the warm water still on his skin. Those blue eyes looked deep into her soul.

"It's like, the mark brought you here," she said, feeling him draw closer to her.

"Back together." He leaned in, and she closed her eyes, tilting her head back as his lips touched hers.

This was exactly like her dream, the way he moved closer to her, his hips against hers and pulling her closer to him. Except her pregnant belly wasn't always in the way. Her hand slid down his arm and felt the muscles along his ribs and down his back move under her fingers.

Then, the tingling in her chest pulsated into her heart, a throb that coursed into her head and made stars sparkle under her closed eyelids. The sensation made her gasp, and she pulled back for a moment, but so did Jason.

They both opened their eyes, and she looked at him, his tattoos lit up in undulating blue light just like they did when he held the sword. A violet light shone from somewhere below her chin, and she looked down to her own mark. The sigil on her chest glowed with a neon purple halo that sent rivulets of light rippling into her veins.

She stumbled back and felt the baby jump in her abdomen. The light remained steady, and she felt the threads of it into her fingertips.

"What's happening?" she said, her hands trembling.

The violet light glowed against his skin and mixed with the blue light from his tattoos. "I have no idea."

The nervous moths rumbled in her gut, but she steadied her breathing. The light didn't hurt, but it actually felt good, like she had been running on clouds or flying with eagles. She saw his wide eyes and watched as the glow in his marks intensified when she stepped closer to him. With a steady hand, she reached out her fingers to his forearm. He remained still as she made contact with the tattoo on his arm.

A lick of blue fire, just like from the sword, leapt from his mark and connected with a similar violet ribbon that reached out from her fingers. The lights mingled and twisted, sending ripples of energy into her arms. The baby jumped again like it was dancing in her womb now. Jason moved his arm steadily toward her and touched his fingers to the mark on her chest, and the same thing happened. He looked up at her with a wondrous smile over his lips.

Her eyes had grown wide as she took in the swirling of ethereal light around them. "So, if you're a seraph," she said, "then what am I?"

"I don't know. I've never seen this happen before."

Chapter Twenty-Nine
Jason

The last aftershocks of sharing Nikka's light still ebbed in Jason's fingertips. The way she looked at him now was the same as before, like the night he took her out on their "official" date and danced in that little bar and grill. Even though she still didn't remember her past, he could see the hope in her eyes.

And now he lay beside her on his messy bed, but he was able to move the duffel bag and all the other stuff that came with it to make room enough for her to sit comfortably. She sat up with her back against the wall, and he stretched out beside her, his head propped up on his elbow and his other hand on her abdomen. Nikka had the sense to finally convince him to get out of the towel and into some real clothes. He hurried to slip on his jeans just in time to see her waving him over as her other hand rested on the center of her abdomen.

"Hurry," she said. "You've got to feel this."

He almost tripped on his way back to the bed but finally settled in next to where she sat. She guided his hand to her abdomen and placed her hand over his. Subtle vibrations and shudders bloomed from deep inside of her, radiating through his fingertips through the thin T-shirt that covered her torso. And it was like nothing he had ever felt before, that little thing moving inside of her.

"You feel that?" she whispered as she held his hand in place.

The smile across his lips would probably stay there for years. The brisk thump shook against his fingers. "Yeah."

"It's moving a lot more these last couple of days," she said.

"Why do you call it 'it'?" he said.

She looked down at him and shrugged. "I don't know. I guess I don't want to give it identity issues yet."

Jason laughed. "Can I call it a 'he'?"

"Sure. I guess I've wanted to call it 'he' also, but I also don't want to be surprised."

"All right . . . *he*."

"Maybe he knows," she said, the smile slipping from her face. Her eyes lost their spark if even just a little.

Jason pulled himself up and sat next to her, his legs crossed. "What do you mean?"

"I know you don't want to talk about it," she said. "But you said it when you first came here. This baby may not be yours, and neither of you will tell me why."

His hand moved to her chin, and he turned her face to look at him. "It doesn't matter. I'll be there for you, no matter what. I won't leave your side."

"And what about him?" Her head ticked to the side as she flashed a glance across the room, to the wall that adjoined Gideon's room. "He's tormented by something."

Jason saw the worry behind her eyes. He hadn't concerned himself with Gideon's thoughts since the day she had disappeared, and he still didn't care. She probably wouldn't either, if she knew the truth.

"He says he was my mentor, but I know he was more than that. I can feel it, the same way that I can remember the way I feel when I'm around you. If he was my mentor, that means he was with me when I was the seraph."

She was too smart for her own good. This would only take her down a path that could be dark and tumultuous.

"Maybe he knows what this is," she said as she pointed to her mark.

"He might know something." He had to admit it; Gideon's knowledge from centuries of experience could be valuable at times. But he hated to think that she would have to talk to him about these things.

She glanced out the window and groaned. "I've got to get back. Max will be worried to death if he sees I left."

"You snuck out of the house to come here? Does that make me the bad boy that Daddy won't approve of?"

Nikka laughed and shoved him back against the bed. "Don't flatter yourself." She planted a quick kiss on his lips and then stood from the bed, but it was a little difficult for her to lift up with her abdomen in the way. He stood with her and took her hand as he helped her up.

He stood in front of the door before she could open it. "What happened tonight, the thing with the light and stuff, that needs to stay between us for now."

"Okay," she said and nodded.

"And after those things breached the wall, this place isn't safe anymore," he said.

"Max's guys already have it fixed. They're pretty good at keeping it up."

"Not this time." Jason leaned in toward her. "I've seen that group of hunters before. They followed us here, and there are a lot more where they came from."

Her face had gone pale, and she averted her gaze like she wanted to say something.

His hand moved to her forearm. "I can keep you and the baby safe."

"It's not that," she said and looked up at him. "The demon that grabbed me, the one with the red hair—"

Jason remembered that drone, the same guy that antagonized him at the hive. It was the same demon that slipped away into the rain: Belphagor. There was something off about that whole thing. The demon just smiled and walked away, and then the remaining hunters just disappeared as though they had been defeated. But he knew something else was up. They had given up too easily.

"He saw my mark. He recognized it and said they had been looking for me."

This wasn't good. That hive in Nevada was huge, with the entire block of human slaves they kept in the lower levels, and the set up they had created. The group was controlled by a single general and her Hell hounds.

In the grand picture, he began to see the pieces fit together. They knew what Nikka was, even if he and Gideon had no clue that she held some as-yet-unknown power. Whatever it was, they were eager to harness it, which meant they would definitely come back, and if they did with the full force of the hive, Garnet Falls would be in ruins by the time they were done.

"We can't stay here. I have to get you out of this place," he said.

She shook her head. "I can't just leave. What about Max and the others? We have been safe from many attacks on those walls before."

"Not this time," he said. "Please, trust me."

"Just, wait," she said and backed away from him. "I have to think about this, okay? I can't just make a decision like that right now."

"Okay. I don't think they'll be back tonight. It'll take time for them to make it back to the nest and to get reinforcements. But they will be back, I promise you that. Tomorrow night, we need to be gone."

He could see that she wanted to just huddle in the corner and wait out this storm, but he had to make her understand how serious this was. She hadn't seen the inside of that hive and fought her way out like he had.

"Okay," she said and nodded. "But I need to talk to Gideon first."

"Fine. I think he's in his room. I'll go with you—"

"No." She interrupted him as she put her hand up. "I need to talk to him about this alone."

The flash of doubt settled over her face, and he hoped that he hadn't just lost her. If he tried to keep her from Gideon, she might just slip from his fingers again. He had to trust that she would be okay to deal with him on her own, but the thought of her and her baby alone with him left a bitter taste in his mouth.

The words were difficult to speak. "Fine. I won't follow you."

"Thank you," she said as he stepped away from the door and opened it for her.

Watching her walk out that door without him pained him like she took away a piece of himself as she turned back and smiled at him.

"Goodnight," she said and bit her lip like she wanted to say something else, but she held back.

"Goodnight."

He closed the door and leaned back against it, feeling the tingling of his tattoos ebb as she moved further away from him.

Chapter Thirty

Nikka

Nikka heard the door click shut behind her and the pull to go back in was overwhelming, like a tether that bound her to him. But the mystery of her mark and what it meant needed answers, and Gideon knew more than he was letting on. She didn't care how late it was.

His door remained closed, and she wasn't about to just walk in there like she did in Jason's room. She definitely didn't want to catch him in his bath towel, either. Just one of those tonight would have to do. She knocked on the door and then waited, listening through the wood for any movement inside. Nothing. She knocked again.

By the third knock, the door next to his opened, and the red-haired woman that had traveled with them peered into the corridor.

"Are you looking for Gideon?" she said with a yawn.

Nikka stepped toward her, her fingers fidgeting. She really didn't want anybody else to see her here tonight.

"Uh, yeah," she said.

"I think he's in the church," she said and extended her hand. "I'm Amy, by the way."

"Nikka," she said and shook her hand.

"Yeah, I know." Amy smiled, the faint freckles across her nose and cheeks making her look younger than she was. "I saw you at the house the other night when . . . well, when Jason made a scene and got himself handcuffed in the middle of the street."

A nervous laugh escaped Nikka's throat. "I'm sorry you got dragged into all that."

"No, it's okay. Those guys are all about you," she said.

Nikka didn't know much about Amy, other than she had arrived with them and she had a child with her. Max had told her that Jason had saved the boy's life, and she wanted to smile when she thought of that.

"Well, it was good to meet you," Nikka said and started to turn away.

"They both are still in love with you," Amy said. Nikka stopped and glanced back at her. "You know that, right?"

"What have they told you?" Maybe this woman had more information that would help her approach Gideon.

"Not a lot," Amy said and glanced back into her room as she checked on her son. She then stepped out into the hall. "But I know some things, things that are not my place to tell. That guy," she said, pointing across the hall to Jason's room, "has crossed time and space to find you. But Gideon—he would give anything to change the past. What happened between you and him, he feels guilty as hell."

She watched Amy wrap her arms around her torso as she shivered a little bit. The lines around her eyes had softened when she talked about them like she would if they were family.

Nikka smiled. "You kinda like them, don't you?"

A faint flush showed on Amy's cheeks. She glanced away. "I guess they sort of grow on you."

"You're probably right," Nikka said and started to turn away, but then she glanced back to her. "Thanks for watching out for them."

"No problem. I'm not sure that I helped much, though. And let him down easy."

Nikka's brow furrowed. "Who?"

"The one you decide to let go."

Then, Amy smiled and turned away, slipping back into the privacy of her own room. The first twinge of guilt sparkled in Nikka's gut when Amy disappeared. Of course, she was right. There was a lot of history with these two men, even if she didn't remember any of it. Even now, she wasn't sure what she was going to do or say when she walked into the church. Nikka stepped down the corridor and toward the darkened lobby with Amy's final words still lingering in her thoughts. But she was right. She couldn't keep holding onto the thought of both of them. And as soon as the baby was born, which could be any day, everything could change.

She tucked her jacket around her midsection and walked out into the night. The street was dark, except for the occasional light behind the windows of the houses. She glanced back up toward Max's house, when the porch door opened and the security team began to exit from the house. Their meeting had ended, which meant she didn't have much time before Max found out that she had gone. But she had to talk to Gideon, and this might be her only chance. Max would just have to understand why she needed to go out. He wasn't her father, just a good man with a good heart who had clothed and sheltered her.

And she might have to tell him that she was leaving. The thought of that almost made her sick.

She hurried across the street toward the front steps of the church. Candlelight from inside the building danced through the stained glass windows. Max never cared if someone wanted to use the chapel at any hour. That's why he always left the doors unlocked, and Gideon was using it now.

The chapel doors opened with a loud echo that reverberated deep into the church. She stepped inside, smelling the candlewax hanging in the air. Firelight flickered with the small breeze that drifted through the doors. Through the dark of the long chapel, see saw Gideon's form at the front pew, facing toward the bank of tea lights on the altar, and his closely trimmed hair making his head almost look bald. He didn't turn around when she walked in, although he must have heard her.

He must have expected her to come for him.

Chapter Thirty-One

Gideon

The moment he heard the door open and saw the candles flicker, Gideon knew it was her. The hesitant steps echoing into the chapel only solidified his suspicion. The air around him changed whenever she walked into a room, breathing in her vitality, and this was no different. He wanted to look back at her, but he tried to focus on the tea light candles instead, feeling her approach the front pews.

The lavender scent that she carried in her wake brushed past him when she sat on the bench across the aisle from him, facing toward the candles but glancing once at him. He was not sure how she found him, but it must have something to do with Amy or Jason. They knew he had taken people to shelter in the church during the attack. Amy had been with him, bringing in as many as she could. As soon as the dust had settled, the scared members of the town finally dispersed from the church, leaving him behind with Amy. She had tried to encourage him to return to the inn with her, but he needed to stay, if only for a little longer.

This place was peace and stillness, despite the chaos of the night that had descended on them. They had survived, though, and he was not exactly sure how. Of course, the hallowed ground of the church provided shelter from the demons that had attacked, but that was only a temporary reprieve. Instead, the remaining hunters just left the city, as though they had removed themselves to await further orders.

Gideon needed instruction now more than ever, and the angels had stopped talking to him since he had obtained the soul, the formless thing that Nikka had given to him.

"Are you okay?" she said, her voice small in this deep room.

His gaze never wavered from the candles. "I am well. A little battered, but everything will heal."

"Good."

"Why are you here?" That came out more irritable than he had intended, but he was not going to retract it.

She turned toward him. "I spoke to Jason, just as you had suggested."

So, she had found him, probably during the middle of the attack. Jason had gone to locate her, and he clearly had protected her. That was how it should be. At least, that was what he told himself, but a little stone of doubt settled in his heart. These souls made him feel things that he never wanted. Perhaps, this is what envy felt like.

"You did not follow my other suggestion," he said.

"And what was that?"

"I told you to stay away from me."

A small sigh came from her throat. "I know you don't really mean that."

"Yes, I do."

"Then why do you hold your breath when you see me? Why are you always afraid to look at me?"

Because it is just too difficult after everything that I have done.

She rose from the bench and stepped across the aisle. His fingers clenched into fists at his sides, and his spine went rigid as she settled into the space next to him.

"I'm not stupid, Gideon. I know you say these things because you think it's for my own good or something like that. But all that is in the past now. So much has changed. I'm not the same person I was, and I'm pretty sure neither are you."

"You could not possibly know that."

"I can get a pretty good idea."

Gideon stood, his joints stiff from sitting in one place for so long, he turned on his heel ready to walk away from her. She rushed around the pew and moved in front of him, blocking his way.

"I need to know," she said, placing her hands on his chest to stop him.

The warmth of her skin against his shirt melted into his chest, but he still tried not to look at her.

"I will not speak of our past," he said.

"You have to," she pleaded as he pushed against her and shifted to the side, but she stepped in his way again. "Jason says we're not safe here anymore. He wants us to leave first thing tomorrow."

"Good," he stopped his advance and finally met her gaze. "You must go with him. He is the only one who can protect you."

"I don't believe that, and I won't go unless you come with us too."

The candlelight danced in her eyes that now bore into him, her hands still pressed against his chest. He would give anything to hold those hands, to wrap his arms around her like he used to but that was a dangerous thought.

"I cannot help you anymore."

"Yes, you can," she said, her lips twisting in anger. She shoved him back hard enough that he lost his balance and stumbled backwards. Tears now glistened in her eyes as she marched toward him. "This baby might be yours, and I'm not leaving you behind."

Then, the one thing that would hurt her the most sprang into his thoughts like a poisoned apple. "If that child is mine, you would be wise to destroy it."

A gasp fell from her lips, and just as she did that, her hand came from the dark and slapped him hard across the face.

"How can you say that?" she said.

The sting of her strike still lingered on his cheek. Even when he had said it, he knew it would be painful, and that was how he had intended it. She needed to forget about him, and this was the only way he could get her to hate him.

He touched the sore place on his jaw and looked at her again. "I can say that because I know."

A tear fell from her eye and streaked down her cheek. It looked like glitter in the light of the candles. Her hand moved in the dark, and she tried to slap him again, but he caught her wrist and pulled her around to press her against the wall. She was so close to him now, his hand around her arm and holding her there, the woody scent against her skin filling his senses. He had not been close to her like this in months. For only a second his eyes locked with hers.

She wriggled her hand free and placed her fingers around the back of his neck, holding him fast. The feel of her skin against his made him freeze. He could have moved away from her, let her hand slip away from him, but he could not force his feet to move. Then she came at him before he knew what to do, pressing her lips against his and holding him against her with the hand at his neck. She kissed him hard like she just needed to know what it felt like.

The taste of her was familiar and sweet and pushed open that door inside of him that he had tried to keep closed for so long. He kissed her in return, and the moment he did it, he cringed at the guilt that surged into his memories. His hand reached to the hand at his neck and peeled her grip from his skin. He pulled away from her and met her desperate eyes again.

"You do not know what you are doing," he whispered.

"I don't care."

She reached for him again, and this time he did not stop her. Before she could grab him, he wrapped his arm around her and pulled her in. That door swung wide open, letting out all the emotion out that he had locked in there. Her lips moved against his as he felt the palms of her hands at his chest.

The first prickles like sparks moved from deep inside his gut. At first, he paid no attention to it, distracted by her touch. Then, he felt it grow like molten lead that pumped through his veins, escaping from that door within his psyche. It pulsed with each beat of his heart, like a familiar fire that rose from the dark, reaching its red tentacles into his fingers.

That sensation told him that he no longer needed to feel guilty, that she was his from the beginning. He found her. He created her. She and the baby belonged to him. To Pazuzu.

He found her hand against his chest and grabbed her wrist. The pulsing throbbed in his hands as he forced her arm back and pressed her against the wall. He tasted her, wanting to swallow so much more of her. He deserved everything he could take from her.

She gasped for only a second, but that was enough for him to open his eyes when he realized what he was doing. In that moment, he saw the violet glow from the tattoo in her chest as he looked at her through eyes that did not feel like his own. Like a nightmare, he saw her through the demon eyes that he had lost seven months ago. The soul had flickered out like a faulty bulb, and now he felt the fire of a demon residing in his heart, all fueled by the light of her tattoo.

Gideon jumped back from her and closed his eyes, forcing the pulsating fire in his veins to crawl back into the dark hole from where it had arisen. Nikka opened her eyes and saw the light of the tattoo in her chest. He collapsed to his knees with the effort it took to hold back the monster that raged just under his skin.

"What have you done to me?" he said and crouched at the base of the altar, afraid to look at her anymore, should that demon lust re-enter his thoughts and take over.

"Gideon—" she said, her voice breaking.

He opened his eyes and looked down at his shaking hands. They were still his own, and not the claws of Pazuzu. The fire coursing through his veins ebbed into small rivulets until he felt that it had dissipated. Then he turned to look at her, the tattoo on her chest still alight with only a few glimmers of violet now.

"What am I?" she said, tears now falling down her cheeks.

That mark had come to life, whatever it was. With what he had just seen, his initial suspicions about it now seemed more plausible. An archangel had given her that sigil, and Gideon began to realize what it may mean. It had the ability to call out a power he thought was far removed in him, but it had the potential to do so much more.

He tried to control the trembling in his voice and clenched his fingers, hoping to drive away the shaking.

"You were marked by an archangel," he said. "It is a sigil in the Enochian language. It means Master over Devils."

"What does that mean?"

"It means that Jason is right. You are not safe here. You need to leave with him as soon as you can."

CHAPTER THIRTY-TWO

NIKKA

The mark on Nikka's skin lost its light, leaving only the last vestiges of a tingling sensation just under the flesh. Then, there was the thing she saw in Gideon's eyes just before he pushed away from her like she was a bomb ready to go off. Maybe it was the reflection from her own violet light, but she could have sworn she saw an orange glow begin deep inside his pupils. It had already disappeared now that he looked at her, but she thought that something had ignited there. Just like it happened with Jason when the light first started, only Jason's light was blue and not the angry fire she saw in Gideon's gaze.

The way Gideon looked at her now made the guilt rise to the surface. She knew she shouldn't have done it, but she had to see what he was made of, especially after he just said such horrible things to her. If kissing Jason brought out that light, then she figured it might work on Gideon as well. She was right, and now she knew without doubt that Gideon kept a secret from her, something dark and sinister and she might have just had a taste of it.

But it still left the question about what it meant.

Gideon stepped toward her but remained at a comfortable distance in case she touched him again. "We have to get you out of here."

Nikka continued to look down at her shaking hands, wondering what she did that could trigger all of this to happen. "Where would we go?"

"I am not sure. But you need to go with Jason tonight." His hand reached toward her and grasped her hand with hesitation, as though she might burn him if he touched her. "Until we know more, we need to keep you hidden. Nobody else can know about this."

As he nudged her toward the door, she pulled her hand free. "I can't just leave like this. I need to tell Max. He needs to know what's happening. It's not fair to just go without telling him."

"Fine," he said with a sigh. "I will walk you there."

"I need to do it alone." Max was like a father, and she couldn't just drop this on him while Gideon waited in the other room like an impatient boyfriend.

"Then you must hurry," he said. "I will go to the hotel and begin preparations."

"All right." She hung her head, dreading the conversation she was about to have with the man who had kept her safe for so many months. And what was she going to say? She didn't even understand what was happening, so how could she explain it to someone else?

"This will be the best for everyone. As long as you stay here, you will put him in danger. Those hunters will be back for you."

"I know, all right." But that didn't make it any easier.

She walked with Gideon from the church, and he insisted that he walk with her down the dark street back to the house. The city had grown quiet in the last few hours since the attack, the kind of stillness that made the hair rise on the back of her neck. The only noise came from the occasional footsteps of the guards in the towers. As soon as she had approached the front steps, she looked back at him in the dark, still feeling the last remnants of guilt for kissing him.

Gideon didn't touch her again or say anything, but even in the shadows, she could see the lines of worry gathered around his eyes and settle between his eyebrows. He now looked at her like she was some kind of freak, something to keep at arm's length. Like an ugly secret. He disappeared in the dark on his way back to the hotel to let Jason know about the final decision to leave. And now that he had left her alone on that porch, she felt the shadows begin to crawl toward her in the late hour.

She walked up each creaking step leading up to the wrap-around porch as the cool of the night began to chill against her skin. Maybe it was the fact that she had to break this news to Max, but the butterflies began to flit around her stomach as she neared the door. The front windows were dark, but that wasn't much of a surprise since Max rarely lit the candles in the main room after dark. The rain had finally stopped, but it left a heavy, humid feel to the air which made it harder to breathe. The moisture-slicked doorknob felt cold to the touch when she turned it.

That was when she felt the sigil burn under her skin.

As the door opened, the air inside the house smelled odd—cold and coppery. The temperature inside the main room had dropped dramatically in comparison to the air just beyond the threshold. The little hairs on her forearms stood on end. All of the security guards had left several minutes ago, so the house remained quiet, as expected. But this was so much more than quiet. It was as still as a cemetery.

In the light cast through the kitchen windows and into the main foyer, she saw something on the hardwood floor. At first, she wasn't sure what she saw, but then it barely twitched in that shaft of moonlight.

She saw Max's face where he lay on his back, his lips quivering like he wanted to speak.

Nikka rushed to his side, almost tripping on his legs in the dark. The ground seemed to fall out from under her, making those bugs flitter about in her stomach like a swarm. Her hands reached for him as she knelt at his side, but a warm wetness touched her fingertips. She brought her hand to the light and saw the deep crimson blood coating her fingers.

"Max," she said as she looked down at him. "What happened?"

His lips moved like he wanted to speak, and his eyes had gone wide, searching for her through the blackness that had surrounded him. She felt his breathing under her hand, rapid and shallow, and each beat of his heart pumped more blood from the wound in his chest. His shaking hand rose and pointed into the dark behind her.

"He won't be saying any more tonight," a voice came from the main room, still shrouded in darkness.

Nikka's heart pounded against her ribs as the man moved behind her and came into the light. A man with familiar black hair with points of bright red. The demon smiled, his eyes turning black as he looked down to where she crouched. Then another movement at the far end of the room caught her attention. Shadows shifted all around her now. There were at least four of them in the house. They had come back much sooner than even Gideon or Jason could have anticipated.

She saw her breath come out in wisps of white like she had walked into deep winter. Four men moved toward her, passing through the light of the windows. They stood between her and the front door, and Max now lay bleeding at her feet.

Max shuddered once under her hand, and she glanced down at him. His wide eyes had tears at the corners that trickled down into his hair. He whispered one last thing to her. "Run."

His lips no longer moved and the pupils in his eyes dilated. But it was enough to make her breath stop short in her throat. Now she was alone in the dark with five demons surrounding her.

The drone with red in his hair was at least five feet from her now, and the kitchen was right behind her. She thought it through quickly enough that at first, they didn't see it coming. Nikka bolted into the kitchen, but she heard their footsteps hasten after her. She rushed around the center counter, grabbed a butcher knife from the block and swung it back at the demon that now ran around her left. The knife caught his hand, and he howled. The others stumbled around him as she darted back through the kitchen and up the stairs to her room. Footfalls pounded up the steps behind her, and she heard the first squeak of the weird step. She knew exactly how far behind her they were.

She hurried onto the landing, grabbed a chair that stood just outside Max's room and tossed it down the stairwell. In the dark, she heard the first demon trip over the wood and then smash it to broken wooden shards as he bounded up the stairs after her. She didn't stop to look back, but darted into her room and locked the door behind her. The butcher knife shook in her trembling hand as she felt them crash against the door. The puffs of white came from her lips faster now. They pounded on the door again and again.

It was only a matter of time before they broke through into the bedroom.

Nikka glanced to the bathroom and then rushed inside, locking that door behind her as well. Pale moonlight shone through the single window above the claw-footed bathtub. She glanced back through the glass and felt the last bit of hope simmer into her memory. The window was too small to fit both her and her pregnant belly through it, but there was something she could do. With a careful step into the tub, she reached toward the window and unlocked the latch at the sill. The wood argued back with her at first but gave way in a scrape of old paint against metal as she forced the window open.

The window looked out over the front porch, and beyond that, she could see the light from the inn through the windows of Jason's room. And she saw Gideon's form as he walked through the dark and into the front door of the hotel.

"Help me!" she screamed through the window. It was all she could do. She screamed again, crying into the night for anyone out there who could hear her.

The door crashed in behind her as she shouted again, the chill leaving her breath in a constant cloud at her lips. Then she felt the demon's hands around her, cold claws that pulled her away from the last hope she had left.

Chapter Thirty-Three
Gideon

The silence of the town mingled in the background as Gideon walked away from Max's home. The memory of what Nikka had just done to him, though, still lingered in his thoughts. It was only temporary. There were no permanent effects from what she did, but what exactly did she do? For a moment, he had felt the demon emerge from within him, from those mysterious places where so many people speculate that a soul resides. She had let it loose or commanded it to rise, but he had never heard of anyone who held that kind of power over a hidden demon. Nobody, except an archangel.

All of these thoughts presided over his senses, beyond the sound of the crickets in the background or the rustling of the leaves in the trees that lined the street. He watched the ground as she neared the hotel, seeing every small puddle along the sidewalk reflect the moonlight that now broke through the storm clouds overhead.

As he opened the front door of the hotel, one last thought percolated into existence. *Why would an archangel give her such power?* The mark on her chest was undoubtedly placed there by a Watcher, but it was unlike any he had ever seen. And it would certainly explain why she always smelled of lavender and trees, something that had never happened around her until now.

Then he heard another sound that stirred him from his thoughts. At first, it was faint, maybe the call of an owl beyond the city walls. But it came again, much more human this time. Howling and desperate.

It was a scream.

When he heard it the third time, he was sure. He turned back into the street and looked toward Max's house, where he had just left Nikka only a minute or two before. There was movement in the upper window above the porch. Something was not right.

As he quickened his pace toward the house, he felt the chill rush over the skin of his arms, leaving goosebumps across his limbs. The closer he got to the house, the colder it became. The kind of freeze that only a demon could create. He broke into a sprint until he neared the porch, and then bounded up the stairs to the front door that gaped open to the main room. Lying in the shaft of moonlight from the kitchen was Max, his face pale and lifeless.

An engine roared from behind the house, and then he heard the slap of the screen door from the back porch. He ran around the body in the foyer, through the kitchen, and pushed through the porch just in time to see the small Humvee in the back yard peel away into the darkness, toward a breach in the wall among the maple trees on the other side of the park.

They had come back for her. They found a way inside, a break in the wall that they had probably designed during the attack earlier in the night, and took her right from under them.

Chapter Thirty-Four

Jason

Gideon crashed through the door of Jason's room, breathing hard and fast.

"They have her," he said.

Jason jumped from the bed. "What?"

"I left her at the house for only a minute," Gideon said, his voice pressured and quick. "And I heard her scream. I went back and saw them take her through a breach in the east wall."

The ringing in his ears made it hard to hear anything more that Gideon had to say. He pushed past him through the door, every second wasted was more distance that the hunters had on him. Amy opened her door to the sounds and followed them both down the hall.

"What's happening?" she said, trying to keep her voice low enough not to wake Dylan.

"They came back," Gideon said as they ran from the hotel and into the dark street. He called out to Jason, who now moved farther from them into the dark. "You can't face them alone."

"I won't let her get any further away," he shouted back, running toward the motorcycle. He didn't care if Gideon followed him or if he had to go it alone.

The motorcycle was still parked along the curb, just where he had left it when they first arrived in Garnet Falls. He straddled the bike and kicked the starter to life. The tire spun out as soon as he pushed the throttle. With the sound of the engine, the men in the watchtower peered down at the parking lot, the security team alerted to a problem. He turned the bike toward the east wall and rode fast into the dark, plunging beyond the rows of maple trees that had obscured the break in the wall. He followed the two lines of fresh tire marks in the wet ground, leading out into the night.

Chapter Thirty-Five
Nikka

The demons that surrounded her had blindfolded Nikka as soon as they had her inside the Humvee. The vehicle moved fast, the engine roaring at top speed. None of them spoke, and they probably didn't have to with their coordinated plan in place. They bound her hands behind her and placed her in the center bench seat. With the cold coming off their skin, she sensed one on each side of her, two in the front, and maybe more behind her.

From the moment he had grabbed her and thrown her into the vehicle, she could feel the demon with the black and red hair next to her. The smell of rotting meat came off him, just like it did the others, but the scent around him was unique. Laced with the odor of char and blood. He kept her close to him, like his own personal prize. She felt his arm draped across the seat-back behind her, his fingers occasionally stroking the back of her neck, sending icy chills across her skin.

Maybe it was the feel of his hand on her, but the drive felt like it took far too long through winding hills and rough terrain. The Humvee began to slow, and she smelled something different in the air. The scent of water and wood. The vehicle stopped with a jerk, and as the doors around her opened, she heard the distant sound of lapping water against rock. A large body of water, probably a lake.

Then she felt his hand on her upper arm, cold and damp like a corpse. "Come on," he said.

She slid from the seat and nearly stumbled as she stepped out onto a gravel surface. The demon caught her and pulled her close to him again, his arm curling behind her back as he pressed her against his tall, lean form. The way he walked with her reminded her of the swagger of a rock star heading toward a throng of photographers, gloating in his popularity.

"You seem nervous," he said, leaning down to speak into her ear. She felt his rancid breath on her neck. "There is so much for you to see. They will be very happy that you're finally here."

Nikka tried to lean away from him, but he held her tighter, his fingers digging into her side. His other hand rested over her abdomen, and the baby's movements stilled for a moment. "They have been waiting for both of you."

He walked her forward through the entrance of a structure that sounded large and hollow, where he finally removed the blindfold. Doors closed behind them, and she glanced back to see the group of hunters that followed them, eyes black and staring forward as they obeyed orders to bring her in. The demon at her side slithered around until he faced her, his eyes as black as the others. He stood easily a foot taller than her and looked down at her as he stepped in close. Nikka held her breath and wanted to shut her eyes as he moved so near that she could feel the chill from his skin through her clothes.

His arm rose, and she heard a click. The glint of a switchblade in his hand caught her attention. The glint from the knife shone in the light of torches that glowed in the space where they stood.

This was it. This was how it would end.

She didn't turn away from him, even though she felt her knees grow weak and her mouth dry. The demon brought the blade close to her and touched the tip of it to her collarbone, the cold of the steel penetrating through her skin. She held as still as she could, ready for the tip to plunge into her flesh. But then he slid it across the skin of her chest. The blade caught the edge of her shirt, and he forced it down, cutting the cloth downward. Nikka almost cried out as she felt the tug on her clothes. His cold hand brushed against her skin again as he tore open her shirt enough to expose the mark on her chest.

"There we go. That's better," he said and slipped behind her. She felt the knife slide between her wrists as he cut her binds free. "You're our guest, not a prisoner." He stepped to her side again with a wicked grin on his lips.

His fingers wrapped around her arm and he pulled her forward into the dim tunnel ahead of them. Every ten feet, a torch had been placed in the thick cement walls. Bundles of cable ran along the upper corners of the tunnel, interrupted occasionally by large breaker boxes. With the moisture collecting on the walls and the smell of a lake nearby, they must have taken her to a hydroelectric dam, long abandoned these many months since the lights went dark.

The demon kept his arm around her as he turned a corner and pushed through a steel door that clanged open. The group that had followed them to this point now stayed outside the room as he forced her into the dark space, just her and the rock star alone.

A single dim flashlight on an old metal desk lit the lone chair that sat against the wall. The room was vast and hollow, but she couldn't see much further than the ring of light created by the flashlight. The air felt heavy, moist with a hint of mildew like a cavern. The demon pulled her to the chair and forced her into it just as she felt her legs ready to give out. Her hands found the edges of the seat, and she glanced into the vast darkness beyond the light.

The demon stood in front of her and crouched. His eyes lost their black oily film, becoming a deep brown of the man it possessed. A swath of black and red hair fell over his right eye as he looked at her. His hand rose to her face, fingers running along her jaw line. She wanted to pull away but knew it would do her no good. She could only sit there, shivering in that dark room and waiting for what fresh horror this demon was ready to let loose upon her.

His eyes moved over her face, examining every curve and color, like an artist studying his subject.

"Belphagor," a woman's voice echoed into the room as the door opened. "She's not yours to keep."

The demon stood and faced the woman, his hand falling away from her face. "I know that."

"Then stop scaring the poor girl." The woman stepped into the circle of light, and Nikka saw her ebony skin peeking from behind the tight black halter top and leather pants. She looked down at Nikka and smiled, a red glow starting behind her pupils like two coals in a furnace.

"So, you're the one," she said and placed a hand on her hip. "I would never have guessed."

Nikka couldn't stop the shaking that had taken over her limbs, but she faced them both as they hovered over her. "What do you want from me?"

"It's not our place to ask," she said, the red glow intensifying.

"I found her," the other demon asked. "I brought her back, just like you requested. Lila, you promised."

The woman turned to him. "Yes, I suppose I did." As her eyes sharpened toward him, Belphagor nodded, as if he understood the look on her face. He watched her with a steady gaze and moved to his knees as her hand rose and her palm settled on his forehead. His neck arched back, accepting the power that now glowed at her fingertips in ribbons of deep red fire.

"I, Lila, bestow this power on Belphagor," she said, her voice echoing deep into the room. "I raise you to the ranking of Lieutenant, here and now, by the power of Hell."

The fire reached from her fingertips, slithering down his skull and penetrating into his eyes and mouth. He screamed, and his body shuddered, in pain or delight, Nikka wasn't sure. Lila's eyes burned brighter as the fire extended along his spine.

Then, the light vanished, and she stepped back from him as he rose to his feet. He stretched his neck from side to side once and opened his shoulders wide. When his eyes turned toward her, they now had the same fiery glow that Lila had, and the temperature in the room dropped even further. She could see each breath and shivered as Belphagor looked at her with the renewed interest of a great white shark in a pool of blood.

"I said she's not yours," Lila said and placed a hand on his arm.

The demon turned to face her and growled, a deep guttural noise that came from his chest. Lila's eyes burned red again and shoved him back, her nails growing into black claws. But he caught his heel and faced her, his chest broad and his button-down shirt opened as he came at her again.

The darkness behind them shifted, just enough that Nikka held her breath. The two demons felt it too, and they stopped their bickering the moment it happened. They both gazed into the black abyss of the room, silent and still as they watched it form.

"He has arrived," Lila muttered and released her grip on her lieutenant.

Belphagor turned his gaze toward Nikka, his eyes wide and now tainted with a look of fear. He backed away from Lila, and both of them moved to the door, their eyes darting toward the darkness.

They slithered back through the door and closed it without a word, leaving her alone in the vast, darkened room with only the small flashlight shining into her eyes from the single desk. She shivered again, but this time she knew it wasn't just the temperature in the room. Goosebumps had formed all along her arms and prickled at the back of her neck. From the corner of her eye, she saw the shadows undulate again, and that was the moment she realized that something watched her from the abyss.

The flashlight flickered and dimmed as something drew the power from the light. Shadows drifted in and out of black. The prickles on her neck crept across her skin, and the tattoo on her chest burned like never before. The air around her collapsed in heaviness over her shoulders as the light dimmed. The black abyss expanded and surrounded her as the air weighed heavily on her chest.

The shadows coalesced, taking shape as the light faded. Like black smoke, they swirled into a form that towered toward her with hulking shoulders and great tendrils that reached out from the shadows.

This was the purest evil she had ever felt.

Nikka closed her eyes just as the flashlight blinked out, plunging her into absolute darkness. She turned her face away, feeling the shadow envelop her, its chill seeping into her bones. The thing in the black hovered around her; she could feel its breath on her neck. Every muscle in her body went rigid, but as still as she remained, it knew that she was there, its shadows all over her trying to burrow into her soul.

Its frozen fingers touched the mark on her neck, and she wanted to scream, to push herself off the chair and run to the door. The tendrils wrapped around her arms, curling up around her limbs until it held her fully in its grasp.

"I know you," it said, the voice deep and beastly. "Mother of light."

The tendrils slithered over her chest and settled around her belly. "Bringer of destruction. The Deceiver. Child of Pazuzu, my son. I will have my progeny."

The dark arms pierced into her soul, tugging at the fibers that kept her alive and sane. The cold raced into her chest, freezing the breath in her lungs. She screamed as the shadows choked her, reaching into her flesh and toward her baby.

Chapter Thirty-Six

Nikka

The smell of rancid meat first filled her nose, and her eyes flew open. The last thing Nikka had felt was the cold arms of the shadows crushing her and then she awoke to this. The darkness had dissipated into bright lights running along the ceiling, electrical bulbs burning just as they had before the power went out. The lights moved by in a stream of regular intervals. She felt a bump jar her entire body, and she gazed at her feet to see that she was lying on a gurney, her ankles and wrists strapped down. A demon at the head of the table pushed her down a long hallway, the walls a drab gray cement with cables running along the ceiling. Two other demons walked alongside the gurney, and the one on her right looked like Belphagor with his black and red hair.

Nikka tried to move her arms, but the bands at her wrists held her fast to the table. The clothes that she had worn were gone, replaced with a thin white hospital gown. The last vestiges of the cold tentacle that had surrounded her still burned against her mark, and she felt the pit deep inside her body where it had tasted her soul. She had no doubt what that darkness was and that it wanted her baby.

As the gurney moved down the corridor, they passed a series of rooms that had been modified with barred doors. Women stared through the bars at her. Human women. Scared and imprisoned. And each of them appeared to be pregnant as well.

"All part of our little project," Belphagor said as he gazed down at her.

She turned to look at him. He nodded his head to the cells of pregnant women that watched her go by.

"Breeders." The word fell like acid from his tongue. "If you haven't noticed, the human population is a little sparse lately. That makes for some difficulty when we have so many of our brethren stuck in the dark of Hell. These ladies, and so many like them in our camps around the world, will create the bodies we need."

Nikka felt the swell of nausea rise in her throat as she turned back to the women. But they all looked at her now with pity and remorse as they watched her traveling down the corridor to some terrible end.

"But not you, my dear," he said. "Don't worry. You will not share their fate. Tonight, you will bring us something new. It will change everything."

A drunken smile appeared on his face. The gurney moved through a set of opened doors, leaving behind the corridor of pregnant prisoners. The lights here burned brighter. The smell of alcohol and antiseptic drove away the dampness of the previous hallway. She lifted her head to see that the room had been converted into a surgical suite, equipped with silver trays and instruments. A man in a blue gown and mask stood beside the trays as the gurney moved into the room.

Nikka felt the first surge of adrenaline pump into her veins. She fought against the straps at her arms and feet as she neared the man behind the mask, his eyes black as he looked at her.

They meant to take her baby right now.

"No," she cried and tried to lift her body up from the gurney. Hands forced her down, but she pulled and tugged wildly at the straps.

"Fighting this will do you no good," Belphagor said as he leaned down to her ear. "Lucifer will take this child, no matter what it is—demon or seraph."

She screamed, knowing it would do no good, but she felt the tears stream from the corners of her eyes, and she couldn't help it. The sound ripped from her throat, desperate and angry that there was nothing she could do to stop them.

Hands pressed her shoulders to the table, and the surgeon moved in, his hands lifting the gown, exposing her abdomen. The cold steel of a blade touched her skin. She clenched her teeth through her cries, ready for the cut.

The doors of the operating suite flew open with a gust of warm wind, something that she had never felt around this nest of demons. Each of the men around her paused and turned their eyes to the entryway, but it was behind her and out of her line of sight. She could only see their faces, eyes widening. Belphagor growled, his eyes glowing red again, and he shouted to the others. The gust of wind turned into a hurricane force gale. The bulbs in the lights above her burned brighter as the breeze swirled into the room, blowing out the bulbs one by one.

The hands that held her down each lighted off of her as the bulbs ruptured into showers of sparks. As each of the lights blew out, the room should have plunged into darkness, but something else caused the room to illuminate in a blinding glow of white and violet. She closed her eyes against the light.

And then she heard the sound, a ringing that was subtle at first but rapidly grew in intensity, shattering glass beakers and jars around the room. The sound and the light pounded into her brain, and she screamed against it, but she couldn't hear her own voice.

A burst of wind sheared over her, and the straps on her arms and legs suddenly loosen. Despite the light and sound, she opened her eyes and held her hands up to her eyes to prove that she had indeed been freed. The cacophony intensified as she put her hands to her ears and closed her eyes. She turned on her side, felt the edge of the gurney and slipped from the metal surface, landing low to the ground. The wind that swirled around her collected the gurney and hurled it against the wall, clattering loudly even above the sound.

So much chaos and violence crashed around her, and she was too afraid to move. This was something even the demons fought against, and surely they couldn't even survive such a hurricane of wind and sound that had attacked the room. She huddled close to the ground, curled up around her abdomen and holding her hands against her ears. The screams still came from her throat, even though she could no longer hear them.

Something grabbed her up in warm arms, and the sound muffled, like hearing it through ear plugs. She felt arms around her, holding her against a strong and bare chest. The violence of the wind ceased, and she held her breath, waiting for it to start again. The thing that held her now shifted, and she felt it moving her as though it carried her through water.

She allowed her eyes to open and she saw his face, a man she didn't recognize, but deep in her soul, she knew him. Pale blonde hair cut short against his scalp, the same color as hers. His piercing blue eyes looked at her from under blonde eyebrows. Swirls of white and violet light surrounded him as though everything in the room had been put into slow motion.

Then she saw the tattoo on his chest. Curved marks intersected in a circle. It was the same mark she bore. His tattoo glowed a brilliant shade of purple, like neon, the same way hers had. She felt him moving her through the space of the room, even though everything had slowed. Outside of his sphere of protection, she knew the chaos still reigned inside that surgical room. He glided to the doors and placed her on her feet, his piercing steel-blue eyes never wavering from hers. Just as her feet touched the ground, he vanished into the whirlwind of light and sound that took over the room again. She stumbled backwards, her unsteady feet not ready to carry her weight after everything that had just happened. The sound and light took over the room as the doors swung shut.

The terrible hurricane that tore apart that room was bound to unleash itself into the rest of the compound, and she now watched from the front gate. She felt the surge of adrenaline that forced her arms to move. Crawling backward at first, she caught her footing on the cold cement floor and turned to face the long corridor. Bodies of demons littered the ground in bloodied messes, scattered down the length of the hall by the man in violet light that now tore apart the operating room. The sound behind her urged her forward, despite the bodies that lay before her. She picked up her pace, her bare feet turning into a staggered run as she held her hand around the base of her abdomen.

She rounded the corner and saw the cell doors and the scores of women that clung to the bars, their eyes wide as they looked at her. From down the hall, she heard the double doors crash open and the roaring wind and ringing rise from the room. She stumbled across another body, and a hand reached out to her through the bars.

"The key," the woman who had grabbed her said, her voice shaking and barely audible.

Nikka looked down, the woman's fingers clutching to the edge of her thin hospital gown. She pointed to the body that lay across the hall from the cells.

Whatever tore down that hallway now was coming straight for them. It would be upon these women at any second, and the kind of violence she heard would tear them apart. She hurried to the body, her fingers reaching into every pocket she found. The sound rose, piercing into her ears again. Her hands shook so badly that she couldn't feel anything.

The jingle in the last pocket made her fingers tighten, and she felt a ring of keys. She pulled them free and glanced up to see the light growing brighter just before it would turn the corner. Her bare feet slipped on the blood that coated the floor, but she managed to hurry to the doors, fumbling through the keys until she found the one that looked like it would fit the lock. The lock gave way, and she pulled the door open. A dozen women poured out of the cells, each of them at various stages of their pregnancy, but none as far along as she was.

Nikka glanced back at the growing light as she moved with the last of the women that ran from the cells. She turned away, the ringing sound louder, piercing into her head again. Some of the women looked back as they ran, their eyes wide in fear at what they saw in the distance. The light behind them filled the tunnel. It came too fast for her to outrun it.

She felt arms around her again. The light grew so bright that she had to close her eyes. The adrenaline pounded in her veins, and she covered her ears against the roaring wind and noise. She tried to pull back, but it held her close, plunging her into a whirlwind of violet light. She screamed again but made no sound above the roaring howl of the light.

CHAPTER THIRTY-SEVEN
JASON

The morning light first started with blankets of pink and orange on the horizon by the time Jason drove the motorcycle through the clearing. The road toward the dam and reservoir was the only route for miles that the Humvee could have disappeared into, and when he saw the vehicle parked at the edge of the side entrance, he stopped the bike and scanned the trees for any movement. The sound of water lapping at the edge of the cement dam echoed up to the walkway that led toward two steel doors. No birds or insects chirped in the coming morning light. Even though it was the middle of summer, the clearing around the dam was as cold as deep fall.

Within minutes of his arrival, the rumble of his grandpa's diesel pick-up moved down the road. Just as he turned, Jason saw the headlights darken and Gideon's face behind the wheel. Dave and five other men in their full Kevlar armor jumped from the back of the truck and jogged toward him. Gideon had actually come through and gathered reinforcements. Not that they could do much against a hive of demons, but it was something.

"You know they're in there?" Dave spoke low as he approached Jason.

He nodded. "I followed them this far, but I'm not sure how many. I've seen these guys before when we passed through Reno, and there were hundreds in a nest."

"And there are many within these walls," Gideon said as he stepped up to the group. "I can feel it."

Dave held up his assault rifle and clicked off the safety. "Well then, let's show them back to Hell."

The guns were a nice touch, but Jason knew that would only be a temporary measure. The demons could always return unless he had finished them off with his sword. At least, the security team would be a decent diversion until he could find Nikka.

The officers headed toward the door, eyes watching the tree line and guns at the ready, just like they would have a year ago if they had to storm a hostage negotiation. Things were different now, of course, but at least they could break down the door and begin the attack. The first two men pounded down the entryway, and the team went through, flashlights, shining into the dark.

The smell of decay filled the darkened corridors, edged with the heavy odor of extinguished fires. Jason stepped behind the men until they came to a fork in the tunnels. One curved down into the dark like a ramp descending to a stairwell. The other continued to the left, probably to the upper floors of the electric plant. Neither tunnel made a sound.

Dave signaled half his men to the descending tunnel, but Jason turned toward the dark corridor on the left. He listened, waiting for anything to encourage him either way. Gideon waited by his side and watched.

"We'll head this way," Jason whispered to Dave, who nodded and followed the rest of his team as they split down to the lower tunnel.

As their flashlights disappeared, Jason reached to his back and pulled the sword into the darkness, lighting everything in shades of electric blue. Each footstep echoed hollow along the long walls that extended the length of the building. Gideon breathed beside him, the sound carrying into the dark. They passed rows of closed doors with little square windows that looked into nothing. The further they walked, the more litter and debris was scattered over the floor.

Something had happened already, and Jason began to feel that they had missed it.

A click echoed down the hallway. He stopped and held his breath, listening into the dark, waiting for the sound to come again. Another shuffle and Jason stepped back against the wall, gazing down the hall the extent of the light until he saw something move behind the window of one of the doors.

He turned back to Gideon with a finger to his lips. Gideon nodded and followed with him as they stepped toward the door. Jason held the sword before him, ready to strike, but using the light to illuminate the plain door as they approached. The sound didn't come again, though, even as he touched the door handle. The metal was as cold as everything else in this place, but not frosted like he had seen so many when a higher level demon infested a building. He turned the knob and shoved the door open, his sword up and his foot planted, ready to kill whatever came out of that room.

The blue light flooded into the small area, cast into every corner. But he didn't see a demon. The glow fell upon a dozen women, huddled in the darkness of that room, squinting into the light of his sword. Their eyes turned toward him, one by one, and the way they looked at him said that they had each expected to see a demon. With dirty faces and trembling hands, they cowered in the corner, every one of them beaten down just like the people he had seen in the hive back in Reno.

He didn't know what to say, but he held out his hand to the nearest woman, her long brown hair falling over her face. For a moment she just watched him, her eyes flashing to the sword at his side.

A shaking hand reached for his, and the moment he felt her cold skin he pulled her to her feet. That was when he noticed her pregnant abdomen. As she stepped out of the room, he glanced at each of the women that now rose to get out of that place. Pregnant. Every one of them. They moved past him, and he searched beyond each face and into the shadows, waiting to see Nikka's eyes and her short hair.

As the last woman stepped from the room, he lifted his sword to light into the dark, but there was nobody left behind.

"There was another woman here," he said as he turned to face them. "Short blonde hair."

The last of the women looked back at him, her arms dirty and thin. She nodded. "She freed us." Her voice was shaking as she pointed further down the shadowy corridor. "We came from there; she was right behind us. And then there was a light and a terrible sound and then she was gone."

"Gone?" he said and lifted the sword toward the dark of the hallway.

"Disappeared," she said.

As Jason turned toward the darkened corridor, Gideon spoke to the women in tones that Jason could barely hear as he pointed them down the route back to the exit. Their bare feet ran along the floor in hushed tones until they had fled back to the truck, leaving them in the corridor alone.

"Light and sound," Gideon whispered. "That does not sound like demons."

"No, it doesn't."

Jason stepped down the hall, further away from the exit, listening for any other sounds in the dark. Shadows crawled along the walls as the light moved with them. They turned a corner and faced a bank of open, barred doors that had once been locked cells along the north end of the building. Lumps of dark, bunched clothing dotted the floor from Jason's light and into the dark. Bodies. Bloodied and broken.

Once he moved toward the first cell door, the tattoos along his arms began to sparkle and burn with the intensity of a magnesium flare. The pain burned into his muscles and made him stop as he looked down at his arms. The intensity of it grew enough that he gasped and bit his lip to distract himself.

Gideon grasped his arm, and his fingers squeezed around his wrist as he examined the marks. His eyes widened, and he glanced beyond him and into the tunnel. Despite the burn in his skin, Jason followed his gaze to the shadows beyond the rim of blue light.

The corridor remained dark, just as it had been since they arrived, but the shadows at the furthest end of the tunnel began to writhe and twist, growing blacker than they had been before. It pulsed and throbbed as the shadow folded in on itself and then expanded further, drawing all light away from it and stretching toward them. Even the edge of the blue light began to recede, driven back by the coming shadow. The air around him turned frosty, as cold as a deep freezer, and the hairs on the back of his neck prickled. A heavy weight settled over his chest and shoulders, making it hard for him to draw a breath.

Gideon's hand pulled him back. "Jason, we need to go."

Jason jerked his arm free and held the sword out toward the coming shadow, even though he felt his hand begin to shake. "Whatever it is, I will stop it. Nikka could be down there. We need to keep going."

"Not this time. We need to flee."

The shadows rippled just beyond the distant edge of his blue light. Like a low, deep bass, a growl rumbled against the walls.

Gideon shifted in the dark and grabbed Jason, shoving him back against the wall. The impact knocked the air from his lungs, and it didn't help that Gideon pressed his forearm to his throat. The blue light flickered in his wide, terrified eyes.

"I said we need to get out of here. Right now," he said, his jaw clenched.

Jason glanced back to the twisting shadow that grew closer. The growl rose and echoed down the corridor. The chill danced over his flesh, like the thing in the dark breathed ice and despair mingled with hate. The light of his sword faltered for a moment as the darkness pulsed out like ink in water. It tugged at his resolve, and the shivers rattled into his bones.

Gideon was right. Whatever this was, the two of them were no match for it.

The shadows moved closer, eating away at the dimming blue light of his sword. Jason turned to Gideon and nodded. The man didn't waste a second. He grabbed Jason's wrist, and pulled him away from the wall and they sprinted back down the hall.

The shadows shifted again, expanding down the hallway toward them, moving fast now. It seemed to sense their fear as though it fed from it. The chill sucked deep into Jason's lungs with every desperate breath he took as he ran close behind Gideon. The thing behind him growled again, now trembling along the walls enough to send a crack into the ceiling. They rounded the corner and nearly ran into Dave's team that had begun their trek down the left tunnel.

The sound grew into a howl. Jason's feet pounded against the cement with each step, feeling the shadow right on his heels. The security team turned when they saw the coming shadow, and they ran until the group burst through the exit door. Jason stumbled out with them, closing the doors behind him with a loud crash. He nearly fell into Gideon as he turned back and watched the exit, but nothing came through it. Only the cold that lingered in those corridors trickled out around the edges of the door, leaving a sheen of frost.

Whatever lived in that space now receded back into the darkness. He could feel it take the chill with it, leaving them, the security team, and the group of women that had gathered around the truck alone in the coming dawn.

"What was that?" he said and placed the sword on his back.

Gideon panted for air. "The First Evil."

Jason gave him a confused look. "What do you mean?"

"I mean that was Lucifer," he said, his eyes never wavering from the door.

"Like the Devil," Jason said, and his spine straightened. "And Nikka's in there with him?"

"No," Gideon said and took in a steady breath. "Those women said there was light and sound before she disappeared. She is not in there."

"How do you know that?"

"Because light and sound is an angel. An archangel. And I think it plucked her out of that place because Lucifer is in there."

Part Seven

"There is love in me the likes of which you've never seen. There is rage in me the likes of which should never escape. If I am not satisfied in the one, I will indulge in the other."

—Mary Shelley, *Frankenstein*

CHAPTER THIRTY-EIGHT

NIKKA

The light entered Nikka's eyes in a hazy glow at first as she blinked. The fog in her brain lingered, though, like she had taken a sleeping pill. She forced her eyes open and squinted against the bright sunlight that shone through the window. No curtains blocked the light from the four square panes of glass set in a pine wood sill. This wasn't her bedroom in Max's house. The smell of fir trees and firewood lingered around this place, unlike the old Victorian home.

She pushed herself up onto her elbows, and a blanket slipped from her body. A black tank top covered her torso. That was new. She swung her legs over the edge of the bed and saw that she had been clothed in long black pants. Someone had dressed her while she slept. Her bare feet touched the wood floor, and she stood to face the open windows.

The building, a custom cabin with a second floor, looked out into a bank of trees that opened toward a broad lake. Bright daylight shimmered over the water, and a breeze that smelled of pine drifted through the open window. A single door stood closed at the far end of the room, decorated in oil paintings of wooded landscapes and waterfronts. She stepped to the door and pressed her ear against the panel, listening for any movement on the outside of the room, but she only heard the rustling of the trees outside the lodge.

Her hand moved to her abdomen with a quiver of movement under her skin. That sensation brought the memory of a bright light into her vision. Sudden and harsh. There had been a sound so loud that she thought it pierced her eardrums and deafened her. That was the last thing she remembered. And now she was here, in this quiet place where her hearing worked well enough and she was away from all that chaos. Away from the demons that almost cut the baby from her body.

How had she ended up here, though? She couldn't remember anything after the light and the terrible noise.

Well, she remembered that someone else had been there and grabbed her just as everything went still. More demons. More monsters. Whatever it was, she didn't want any more of it. She was alive, that was the most important thing. Now to get back to Garnet Falls.

She turned the knob and let the door open just enough to see beyond the bedroom. The room was on an upper floor, opening to a landing that looked down onto a main level. Large, broad windows allowed the daylight into the lodge across rustic-looking pine furniture with thick dark green cushions decorated with the silhouettes of bears and pine trees. And just like everything else, it was covered in a layer of dust collected over months of emptiness.

She crept out onto the landing and down a curving staircase that opened into the large main room. Just as she stepped onto the hardwood floor of the room, she froze, feeling her heart jump into her throat. Her gaze fell on the face of a man, sprawled out on his back and unconscious on the floor next to the sofa. His long, lean and muscled torso was bare, revealing a tattoo on his chest.

The familiar black markings of two arcing lines intersecting in a circle. A tattoo just like hers.

Although he appeared to be either asleep or unconscious, the up and down movement of his ribs reassured her that he was still alive. Blue and purple bruises had begun to form along his arms and hands, probably from the fight to get her out of that place. Her gaze moved up to his face, and she felt her eyes linger there for far too long. Short, white-blonde hair cropped close to his scalp, the strong angle of his jaw. Why did he look so familiar? She remembered seeing him in the light when he freed her from the operating table, but she could swear she had seen him even before that. Like she had known him all her life; someone who was always there just out of sight.

When she realized how long she had stopped to stare at him, she shook her head clear of the thought. Whoever he was, he must have also taken her from that place and away from the dark thing that lived there. She wasn't sure how he could have done that, but he must have had something to do with all the light and noise that she saw before she woke up in the lodge. If he rescued her, maybe he was someone she could trust, especially since he bore the same mark that she did. What if he had answers to explain all of this? The mark. The strange power she had recently discovered. What if he knew why she had lost her memories?

But why not just take her back to Garnet Falls?

The last thought made her stomach flip uneasily, and she stepped around him as she watched his breathing. It didn't matter what he was. She knew that well enough now. Gideon was right: she needed to get away from all of these people. She just needed to find Jason and go somewhere that nobody could find them. And if she could get back to him, maybe Gideon would know what this man was.

She moved high on the balls of her feet around the man, her bare feet stepping over the floor boards. Her foot touched the throw rug stretched over the floor, and the board underneath it creaked with a loud snap. She stopped, her eyes moving to the man.

His breathing stopped, and his head rose, his icy blue eyes flashing around the room in confusion until he turned his head and looked at her. The muscles along his shoulders bulged as he twisted and pushed off the floor toward her.

Her heart raced, and she shoved herself forward, running through the room and back toward the kitchen. There had to be an exit back there somewhere if there was any logic to the construction of this place. Her feet landed on stone tiles in the kitchen, and she saw the door that led out to the back driveway, but she also heard his footsteps behind her. Whoever he was, he moved quickly for someone that was unconscious just a second ago. She turned the corner and reached for the door.

Arms wrapped around her from behind as his strong frame pressed against her and pulled her back through the kitchen. She could scream and cry out, but she had seen the wooded surroundings of the lodge. Nobody would hear her. But it didn't mean she wouldn't fight back. She threw her elbow back at him, catching his ribs, but that made no difference. Like hitting a statue, it only seemed to bruise her elbow with little damage to his ribs. He held her fast, pinning her arms to her side and lifting her off her feet.

He carried her back into the main room and dumped her onto the couch as he stood before her, the sunlight pouring down through the cathedral windows and onto his hair from behind him. It almost looked like a halo of fire, surrounding him as he stood there, catching his breath.

"I will not hurt you," he said; his voice had an odd and formal accent about it.

Nikka wanted to turn and run back around the couch, but it would be of no use. She didn't have the stamina to move that fast anymore, not with the baby having grown so much in the last month. Even the act of running to the door had winded her.

"What do you want from me?" she said, looking up to where he towered over her.

He crouched down, lowering enough that she could see him clearly without the glare of the sun behind him. When he moved, he carried the scent of lavender and fresh trees with him, something that made her thoughts float as if she had just taken a Valium. The blue of his eyes was like something she had never seen before, except perhaps at the edge of a glacier in those pictures from the arctic. This man was beautiful and mysterious, even though she couldn't determine his age. His features were so timeless that he could have been anywhere from his late twenties to his forties.

"I only want to protect you and the baby," he finally said after several seconds of looking at her.

His penetrating stare made her press back against the couch and pull her arms up around her chest. "Who are you?"

"I am called Samael." His eyes drifted to the mark on her chest, and his steady hand reached for her. She tried to back further away from him, but his finger extended toward her skin and touched the mark. Violet light began to flicker at the edges of her tattoo, and his began to sparkle as well. The light intensified, sending warmth into her chest and down her arms. "I am your creator."

He pulled his hand away and met her eyes again. She saw the faintest glimmer of violet light pulse within the depths of his black irises.

"What do you mean by that?" she said, sitting upright from the back of the couch. He didn't flinch but allowed her to move closer to him. She was sure that the flicker in his eyes was not an illusion when she saw it again. "What are you?"

Samael stood and towered over her again, taking a single step back, but his gaze never wavered from her. "I am an archangel, and I created everything that you are."

Chapter Thirty-Nine
Nikka

"When I found you," Samael said and turned away from Nikka toward the sunlight that flowed into the room, "I knew you were perfect." Nikka felt her mouth go dry. She couldn't move for fear she might startle him, and he would stop speaking.

"I knew you would be the one that could end the war," he said.

She finally shook her head. All of this gave her such a headache like she had been pounding it on a wall that just wouldn't give in. "What war? I don't even know who I am. Only who people tell me I am. How can I end some war if I can't even remember who I am?"

He turned toward her, a trace of sadness in his eyes. "Forgive me."

"For what? Why won't anybody tell me what's going on?"

Samael stepped toward her again and crouched down. His hands reached to touch her face, but she pulled back from him. He said and acted like he knew her so well like she was his lost love, but she remembered nothing about him and certainly didn't want him touching her like that.

His hands hesitated, balling into fists as they hung in the air. "Forgive me, for I am the one who stole your memories."

This man—an archangel, as he says—took everything from her, and he expected forgiveness. She swiped her hand across his wrists, pushing him away and she slid from the couch, turning from him. Maybe he wouldn't let her run from him before, but she wanted to get away from him even more now. She paced around the couch and back toward the kitchen, but he had moved much faster than he should have. He now stood right in her path toward the door.

"I want to go," she said, but she couldn't look at his face, at those icy eyes that seemed to know everything about her.

"I cannot protect you out there."

"Well, I don't trust you in here. I don't even know you."

"And where will you go?"

"Away," she said and tried to move around him, but he stepped in her path again. "Am I your prisoner?" She finally looked up at him, her eyes narrowed as she glared at him.

"Will you go back to Jason? To Gideon?" The last name almost fell from his lips like acid.

"That's none of your business." She tried not to wince when he spoke their names. Somehow, he knew who they were as well.

"They are the cause of all your pain." He spoke and stood there, the words not hateful or angry. Only honest.

"You know nothing about them," she said, trying not to let the tears well in her eyes. The tickle of them began first in her nose and throat, but she forced them away.

"And neither do you."

His words stung, raw and sharp. This was not a discussion she wanted to have with a stranger. Max was the only person she had trusted in this world, and now he was dead. It left her with only the choice of Jason and Gideon, who had come to Garnet Falls with promises that they could help her, and one of them was the father of her child. Somehow, Samael knew all of this.

"They can do nothing to protect you from what is coming," he said, his voice dropping. The air in the room began to thin, and the light from the windows dimmed, as though a storm had settled around the lake. "All the forces of darkness know about you and that child. Nothing can stop them. Nothing, except me."

Nikka saw the glimmer of violet in his eyes again. She remembered the thing in the dark that threatened to consume her, the purest evil she had ever felt, and it filled every corner of that dark room where she had been kept. She had been all alone to face that thing without anyone else to help her. Neither Jason nor Gideon had been able to come to her aid.

Only Samael. He took her out of that place just before they had tried to take her baby.

"What do they want from me?" The tears finally came flooding and running down her cheeks.

"That child is very special."

Her brow furrowed and her hands touched her abdomen. "It's just a baby."

Samael took a step toward her, the violet in his eyes a definite glow now. "It is so much more than that, and you know it."

"I don't understand."

He moved closer, and she could smell the fragrance coming from his bare shoulders again. "I will show you." His hands reached up toward her face, and this time she didn't pull away. "I will give every memory back to you now, and you will come to understand why this has happened."

Every memory. Everything that Jason and Gideon had tried to keep from her since she met them. Something terrible lived in there. She grabbed Samael's wrist and stopped him for a moment.

"Do you wish me to stop?" he said and tilted his head to the side as he looked at her.

That was such a hard question to answer. Whatever he was about to do would reveal her entire past. Up until now, she had loved this baby no matter what. She was just some unfortunate pregnant woman that Max had taken in, and she had learned to accept her lost past. She had even thrived, until Jason and Gideon showed up, throwing everything into chaos.

"Will it hurt?" she said, a tremble starting in her voice.

"The past will always hurt."

That wasn't very reassuring. She felt the baby kick and flutter just under her ribs. For the sake of that baby, she needed to know what was coming and why. She released the grip around his wrist, and he moved his warm hands to her face. The light in his pupils grew, and he stared at her. The entire world around her turned dark, like the storm clouds moving in across the mountains. Dark, except for the violet light ahead of her.

Air rushed through her body. Not around, but directly through her torso as she felt herself being lifted into a shaft of light as though someone carried her from the darkening room. She couldn't breathe as the air moved faster through her body. Lights flickered so brightly around her that she pinched her eyes closed. But she could still see, despite how tightly she held her eyes.

Images rushed past her. At first, they were like still photos and then morphed into reality all around her. At some points, she felt as though she were standing in the middle of the scene, where others she only watched as an invisible observer as her life unfolded before her.

A man and woman stood there. Her parents. She remembered her parents.

They laughed with her as she blew out the candles of a birthday cake. She was ten years old.

Then they cried, taking her hand, as a doctor said something, his voice muffled but clear at the same time. "Cancer," he said. "Leukemia."

She felt nausea and pain. Pain everywhere. Needles in her arms and tubes going to all kinds of bags of fluid. Machines beeping all around. The hair on her head had long disappeared, as had her eyebrows and eyelashes. She was dying.

Then she saw Gideon's face, handsome and smiling. He saved her. She remembered that now—when he found her and protected her and taught her. She looked down at her arms and saw the tattoos scrawled along her limbs and torso. Beautiful, curving, black marks, just like Jason's. They had been hers first, and she felt the power that coursed within those tattoos, filling her body with energy and life. The feel of the sword in her fingers warmed her hand, as though she had been born to wield it. A breath of exhilaration escaped her lips as she lifted the sword, fire wrapping from the hilt and around her wrist.

Everything changed, and she felt her hand pull a demon—a drone—from the chest of a woman. The beast fought at her, screaming and spitting, but she decapitated it without hesitation. She was the seraph, the destroyer of demons.

Then she saw Jason, his face different than it looked now, and she remembered why. He had been possessed by the demon Abaddon, who had tricked her. Those red eyes, burning with fire, looked at her. And then she saw those eyes in Gideon's face.

Gideon was Pazuzu, the high general and Lucifer's right hand. She felt a pain in her chest as she struggled to breathe. How could she have forgotten his true nature? Her knees wobbled underneath her, and she dropped to the ground. Gideon was a demon; he had been all along, and he had tried to hide this from her when they first arrived in Garnet Falls. That was the thing she sensed in him the other night in the church when she kissed him and her mark burned.

And Jason knew that Gideon was a demon too.

All the memories came flooding back at her in torrents, all the hate she had for Abaddon, her love for Jason and the mourning she had spent for

Gideon when he had fallen into the Hell portal. Tears flowed down her cheeks, and she cringed at the sobbing she heard in that light, knowing that the sounds came from her own throat.

But she loved Jason. She had no doubt about that now. She remembered his arms around her, his kiss and their first night together.

And then Gideon returned, but everything was wrong. Something had changed.

The truth of it all came to her so suddenly that she felt ringing in her ears as her head swam in a whorl of dizziness. She found herself back in the dark of a room, alone with Gideon, as he forced himself on her. She remembered all that they had tried to hide from her.

It all became clear at that moment when she felt him hold her down, the memory of it painful as she felt the cries from her own throat. She was a seraph, he was a demon, and Jason was human, the future chosen seraph. This child was the product of one of them, either demon or seraph.

The words of the beast in the darkness came to her: "I will have my progeny."

Her fingers clutched at her abdomen, feeling the baby move again as the memories assaulted her senses. The smell of blood overwhelmed her, and she found herself bound in the dark room, nearly naked and Gideon cutting the tattoos from her body. One by one, he peeled away her flesh. She was there again, feeling every agonizing moment of it.

The mark on her chest came alive for the first time as Gideon/Pazuzu, tried to brutalize her again. The power took over her body, energized from the depths of her soul, and it exploded into light. It flowed with such intensity that she felt it tear from her spirit, taking a fragment of it from her.

Then, there was nothing but light and warmth, and the pain had disappeared. Something held her close with love and protection. Her body shuddered, and she opened her eyes to see the tile floor just at her feet, her hands pressed to its cool surface. Tears fell from her eyes and splashed on the ceramic flooring. The warm light had vanished, leaving her in the lodge with the angel, shaking.

"The past is always painful," Samael repeated as he looked down at her.

His warm hands touched her face again, and she flinched at first, afraid that his touch would bring more terrible memories. He held back for a moment but then touched her chin and brought her head up to look at him.

"I found you in that light, the cherubim brought you to me," he said. "My creation. My beautiful seraph. I took those memories from you and placed you in a safer environment, where you and your child would be protected."

"You call me your creation," she said, watching the violet light fade from his eyes. "Why?"

"I gave you this mark," he said, his fingers touching her tattoo again. "Your power is derived from my own. I knew you were special the moment I found you. The only woman worthy to carry the power of a seraph. And I have never been wrong. You wielded it unlike any I have ever seen, and that is why I gave you the power of the archangel as well."

She looked down at her tattoo, the identical mark that Samael wore. The implication of what he said now fell on her like a heavy weight. "You mean—"

"Yes," he said. "You are an archangel now."

Chapter Forty

Nikka

Maybe Samael could read Nikka's mind, but he let her wander around outside the house without hovering behind her. He must have trusted her enough to not run, and she wasn't about to leave now. Not with everything he had just told her. He had so many answers, and unlike everyone else in her life, he told her the truth. With him, she recovered her memories, and he told her all that she asked him, as difficult as it was to hear.

Archangel. He had turned her from a seraph into an archangel, but what did that mean?

She bit at her nails until they were sore as she walked along the leafy paths that meandered around the lodge and down to the lake. The scent of wet wood from the dock that stretched from the shore hung over the water that caught the glimmer of sunshine above. She settled down on the edge of a fallen tree at the water's edge and looked out to the wilderness along the opposite edge of the lake, her mind trying to process all the memories that Samael had just introduced.

Maybe it was the baby moving again, but her stomach felt unsettled by all of this. Gideon had changed so much from the last time she had remembered seeing him until the moment he had arrived in Garnet Falls. She would have hoped to sense the demon inside of him if it was still there, but she had never noticed anything other than the guilt that exuded from him. He definitely wasn't Pazuzu anymore, and he had even tried to stay as far away from her as he could.

No wonder Jason hated him so much—stuck with Gideon, the one who had raped her and tried to kill her.

A wave of nausea flooded the back of her throat. How could she face them again, knowing all of this?

"Are you all right?" Samael's voice came from behind her.

Her hands jolted into fists, and she nearly fell from the edge of the tree. Once she caught her breath and felt her heart rate slow down, she turned to face him. "You scared me to death."

"I would certainly think not," he said and stepped around her. In the time she had been outside, he had found himself a T-shirt. He sat on the tree next to her. "You seem to be alive enough."

She laughed a little. It was the kind of thing Gideon used to say to her when they first met. "It's just a saying."

His eyes bored into her again, like he had never seen the world around him. "You must have questions."

"Yeah, I do." She turned toward him. "Why me? Why did this have to happen to me?"

He looked at the sand and gravel at his feet as though he thought what would be the best thing to say for this situation. "Destiny, perhaps."

"You don't sound like you believe that."

He smiled, and she realized that it was the first time she saw him do that. "You would probably be correct. I was a Watcher, and I saw your potential. You could say that all of this is my fault."

She shook her head. "I think I'm starting to see that. What do you mean by Watcher?"

"A Watcher is a guardian of mankind," he said. "We are the angels that bestow the power to a seraph."

"So you were there the night that Gideon found me."

He nodded slowly. "Indeed. And I could feel your power even at that moment. You took the seraph mantle and molded it in a way I had never seen. I knew then that you could be so much more."

"You gave me the ability to extract the higher order demons."

"Call it an experiment, if you will. I wanted to see if you could actually do it. Only an archangel has ever been able to do such a thing."

She remembered the moment she removed Abaddon from Jason's body, the feel of the demon's throat in her hand, the way it peeled free and unlatched itself from Jason's soul.

"Then you showed me the future, didn't you."

"Again, yes."

She furrowed her brow. "But I could never change it. Why show me?"

"I did not know if it was possible to change it, but I needed to try."

"Well, I failed. Big time." She looked down at the ground and dug her toes into the warm sand.

"All things are as they should be," he said and sat straighter, his eyes turned toward the lake.

She shot him a confused glance. What did he mean by that?

Samael stood and held his hand to her. "Are you prepared to return to the house yet?"

This guy had the ability to quickly turn the conversation and almost make her forget that she had more questions, but she wasn't about to let him off that easily.

"No," she said. "I really need to get back. I'm sure Jason is worried—"

"You can't go back there," he said, his voice steady and firm.

"Why not?"

"It is not safe. I have told you this."

"I know what you said." She stood and faced him, leaving his hand hovering between them. "But I need to see him."

"If you go back to him, it will be the first place that Lila and her demons will go to find you."

"All the more reason to go back. They need to be warned."

Samael shook his head. "I cannot allow it."

"Allow it? You said I'm not your prisoner," she said and crossed her arms over her chest.

"This is true," he said and dropped his hand. "But there is an army of demons looking for you now. As long as you are with me, he cannot detect you."

"He?"

Samael squirmed a little and sighed. "Yes. He. I know you felt him. You saw him. Lucifer himself has come to collect you."

Nikka's mouth dried, and she swallowed the lump that had formed in her throat. The dark form that had tried to engulf her when she stood in the windowless room of the power plant, the evil that she felt when she saw it. Somehow, she had known what it was, even if it didn't have a name at the time.

The dizziness started in her head again, and her ears began to ring.

"Are you all right?" he said.

Of course, she wasn't all right. She had seen the Devil in the flesh, so to speak, and she had barely escaped. Now that darkness hunted her.

"No," she said and looked away from him. She ran her hands over her face, trying to make the dizziness go away. "I saw him. He had me right there. How were you able to get me out of there?"

"He has no body. Not right now, anyway. He burns through them so quickly that he cannot keep them for long. He is searching for another body to possess. When he acquires one, he will be most difficult to deal with."

"Why does that make a difference? He's the Devil. Can't he just do whatever he wants?"

"All of us, demons or angels, have very limited power in this realm. We must possess a body, and through that body, we can channel our powers. Lucifer is one of the first angels; his power is so raw that it decimates most bodies. But when he finds the right one, he will be unstoppable."

"You're saying that all of you possess bodies." She glanced over his form again and then met his eyes. "Angels possess people as well?"

"Of course," he said so matter-of-factly. "We cannot walk among you without one. Our powers are too limited outside of the human form."

She took a step away from him as she watched him. "So you took this body. This man. You possessed him against his will, just like Abaddon. Like Pazuzu?"

"No," he said, his brow developing confused furrows and wrinkles forming around his eyes. "A human body does not reject an angel as it does a demon. They welcome us. We do not abuse them or harm them, not like the Devil's children."

"Wait. This man you possess agreed to this?"

He nodded slowly. "Yes. The moment he placed this mark on his body, he welcomed me." Samael glanced down at the tattoo on his chest.

This was such a revelation to her, and yet it still made her uneasy, speaking to a man possessed by an angel. She watched the way he held himself, upright and proud, with a strong gaze that never wavered.

"And you just possess the beautiful people?" she said with a smirk.

The remark wasn't lost on him. His sharp blue eyes gazed down at her, his jaw set. "We angels make everything beautiful. A body becomes its best self when we possess it. Even now, the mark on your body enhances everything that is remarkable about you." Those eyes bored into her as he spoke, leaving her knees weak, and her fingers trembling.

He held his hand out to her again. "Will you come back inside?"

She broke her gaze free of his eyes for a moment, but still felt the tremors of uneasiness in her chest. Her hand reached to his despite the shaking she still felt. "Fine. For now."

They walked back into the lodge, the quiet, empty place that had been forgotten when the electricity died. He helped her back into the comfortable cushions of the sofa and encouraged her to lie back, lifting her feet onto the pillows he collected for her.

"I will provide some food for you. I am sure you are famished," he said and walked around the couch.

Her stomach grumbled, and she realized she hadn't eaten in a long time, well before she had been taken by the demons. She had even lost track of the days since then. Had it been only one day? Maybe two?

She rested her head back and listened as he stepped out the back door, leaving her in the house alone. The baby moved and bounced around inside her abdomen, which set off a cramp in the center of her belly. The motion took her breath away for a minute and then it eased. Those false contractions had come more often now, and nobody else needed to know about them because they weren't the real deal. It didn't make them any less uncomfortable, though. She closed her eyes when the cramp let up and took in a steady breath. The baby moved again in little rhythmic pulses that lulled her brain to relax, allowing the memories to fade into the shadows of her mind.

A tap on her forearm startled her enough to open her eyes. The room had plunged into darkness, and she saw Samael's form above her, his face lit by a single candle somewhere in the room. For a moment she didn't recognize him, but then the events of the last 24 hours came flooding back to her.

She forced her legs down from the stack of pillows and sat up, her heart racing with the effect of waking up so abruptly.

"I am sorry to wake you," he said. "I have prepared you a meal."

Nikka licked her dry lips and wiped her hand over her eyes. Then she smelled the scent of grilled meat and roasted vegetables. He helped her from the couch and walked with her into the kitchen, where he had prepared the table with candles and the meal.

"You did all of this?" she said and looked up at him. The smell of grilled chicken made her mouth water.

He nodded. "I have learned to cook since being in this body. And I have been able to find the things you might need." He pulled the chair for her and helped her closer to the table. "Proper nutrition is vital during the final weeks of pregnancy."

This was far more attention than she usually received. Most of the time, people just stared at her belly and gave her that pitied look that said, "I'm sorry that you have to go through this during the apocalypse."

"Thank you," she said and picked up the silverware that he must have fished out of the drawers of the kitchen. She cut into the meat and tasted it. Perfectly seasoned. Moist. Just like her dad used to grill it. "Wow, Sam. This is awesome."

He looked at her with a little tilt of his head. "Sam?"

"Yeah. Sorry. Is it okay to call you that?" she said, her mouth full.

The candlelight danced in his eyes, which appeared almost silver in the dark like this. "I suppose so. Nobody has ever called me that before."

"All right. It's settled then. Sam." She took a drink of the water, cold and clean. "This is amazing. Where did you find all this?"

"I have my resources. And I can show you a few things tomorrow when there is proper light."

The baby moved when the water hit her stomach, and she shifted, her hand moving to her abdomen. "It must be hungry too."

"The child will be growing rapidly as it nears the end," Sam said and took a bite of the grilled chicken.

She watched him as he chewed, watching the way he held his shoulders with his spine so straight and rigid. This man, an archangel, had so much power, and she could feel that he still held back some information from her. He had revealed so much at this point, she didn't want to stop it from coming, but she had to ask.

"Sam," she said and got his attention. "What do you know about my pregnancy?"

His brow furrowed again. "I know that you are very close to the end."

Nikka placed the fork down on the table and bit her lip. This was delicate, and she needed to approach the subject with caution. "Yes, but do you know other things? Can you tell if it's a boy or a girl?"

He smiled and sat back against his chair. "It is not in my ability to see such things. Nor can I tell what the child is, demon or otherwise."

She averted her gaze from him. He had figured out her intention as soon as she had said it.

"If you wish to ask me something, please just say it. You have no need to worry about my answers. I will tell you anything you desire."

"Okay," she said and leaned her elbows onto the table. "Tell me this. Will my baby survive all of this?"

The smile slipped from his face. "You ask me about the future."

"Yes."

"I cannot say."

"You've shown me the future before," she said. "I know you can."

"In my true form, that is correct. But in this realm, I have no powers to predict the future. I would need to leave this body in order to do so, and that would make you vulnerable. But know this: I will do everything that I can to keep you and the baby alive and safe."

It wasn't the truth that she hoped for, but it would do for now. She continued eating, both of them silent for the remainder of the meal. She would have thought it awkward, but she was sure that Sam had no idea that the silence felt strange.

Chapter Forty-One
Jason

The weight of the rifle against his shoulder became enough of a distraction to keep his thoughts away from worrying about Nikka. He walked around the edge of the perimeter wall with Dave, inspecting every possible weakness until it was too dark to see anything without their flashlights. The activity around town had become frantic since the invasion the previous night, and rightly so. The little town of Garnet Falls had a weakness after all, and a demon horde out there knew it.

Gideon had pulled him away from the power plant, back into the light after he had seen and felt something so awful in there. And that thing had had Nikka trapped in there. Something had taken her out, but to where? Gideon didn't have any more answers than he did. All he could say was that she was probably safe, but that wasn't much of a consolation.

He walked back to the front lobby of the hotel, which had now become a busy center for all the new people they had brought back with them: almost two dozen pregnant women held in that place for heaven knows how long. Lanterns illuminated the lobby and the few stations that somebody had set up to aid the women. Amy saw him enter the room and met him halfway down the hall.

"Anything?" she asked, her hands full of folded blankets.

"Nothing," he said and continued down the hall toward the storage closets where he had stored some of the supplies from his truck. "Gideon and I searched along the west edge of the lake."

"I'm sure she's safe," Amy said and placed a hand on his arm, stopping him. "Gideon said—"

"He wouldn't know," Jason said and looked at the ground.

"Hey, look at me," she said, and he turned his eyes up to her. "You'll find her. You've done it before. You'll do it again."

She had more optimism in her little finger than he had in his entire body, but that wouldn't be enough to help him search. He forced a smile and nodded his head back to the lobby full of women.

"You don't need to worry about me. You've already got your hands full," he said.

"Yeah. If you guys hadn't gotten to them, I can't imagine what would have happened," she said, a ghost of fear glazing over her eyes. "The things they told me—"

"It was the demons we encountered in Carson City," he said.

The color drained from Amy's face. "The ones who took you and Dylan?"

He nodded. "And they'll come back. I need you to stay prepared. If you hear or see anything, you find Gideon or me. And if you can't, just stay hidden. Don't come out for anything. Do you understand?"

"Okay," she said and clutched the blankets closer to her chest.

"You'll be fine. You and that kid have survived a lot, that's why I know you can take care of these girls."

Before he left her side, he squeezed her hand. He continued to the storage closet, feeling her eyes on him the entire time. The rifle rested against his shoulder, but this gave little consolation. If the horde came again tonight, they wouldn't be ready. This town would crumble. The attack that came the other night was only a fraction of the numbers he had seen at the hive. If they gathered more, they could decimate this place in minutes, and everyone would be taken just as easily as they had grabbed Nikka.

He had figured that the only reason the town still stood is that they already had Nikka in their grasp. Wherever she had been taken, the horde probably now searched for her, but it wouldn't be long before they came back here to find her. But that wasn't his concern. There was no way he could save this town on his own. He just needed to find Nikka and get as far away from anyone as possible.

CHAPTER FORTY-TWO
NIKKA

Nikka awoke with the early morning sun pouring through the window of the upper room. Sam slept somewhere else in the house, and she assumed he slept because he used a human body. She knew that Gideon needed sleep at times, so the possessed had to function at the limits of the person they possessed. As soon as she rose, she felt the baby moving about, and this caused more of that cramping in the center of her abdomen. But the contractions eased, and she breathed them out until they had disappeared.

The house felt empty as she descended the stairs, and she didn't see him lying on the floor again like he had been yesterday. She craned her neck to look around the corner and through the other doors downstairs, but she didn't see him anywhere.

"Sam?" she called out to him, but she heard nothing in return.

She peered through the windows of the kitchen and to the empty driveway but saw no sign of him anywhere. The silence in the house began to eat away at her nerves, and she began chewing on her nails until they were sore. What if something had happened to him? After what he had told her about keeping her safe, she now began to wonder how exposed and vulnerable she was all alone in this place. She hadn't seen another person in the short time she had been here, and the house seemed isolated enough that she was probably safe, but for how long?

"I wish to show you something," his voice said from behind her, making her jump. She almost screamed when she heard him, and she clutched her hands to her chest, feeling her racing heart.

"You've got to stop doing that," she said with a sigh, letting the shaking ease from her hands.

"I am truly sorry," he said as he walked around the kitchen table. "I forget that you cannot yet sense my presence."

"No, I can't."

He extended his hand to her. "Please, come with me."

"What's going on?"

"It is time for me to teach you how to use your power," he said, and nodded to his hand again, waiting for her to take it.

He was so hard to read since his face was always expressionless, except for the brief time she had seen him smile. If anybody could help her, though, it would be him. He promised to show her what new powers she possessed, and she believed him. She took his hand, and he led her outside to the driveway. Her pace quickened to keep up with him, and she stumbled down the dirt path behind him, but he continued forward, frantic and almost desperate.

They walked down the driveway and to a vehicle parked at the end. She hadn't seen it there yesterday, which meant that he must have found it since last night and driven it to the lodge. That also meant that it functioned, unlike so many of the cars that littered the roadside since the EMP had destroyed global electrical circuits.

Sam stopped next to the vehicle and turned to face her, the creases between his eyebrows deeper than she had ever seen. "I want to show you what I can, but you will be quite limited due to your current condition." His eyes flashed down to her belly.

"Yeah, well, there's a lot of things limited because of this condition."

"You will not have your full powers yet, not until the child is born. But I can show you a few things."

"Sam, is everything all right?"

"No," he said and stepped close to her, close enough that she smelled the lavender again. "We are running out of time."

"What do you mean? We're on a schedule?"

"There will be some who want to take you from me," he said. She could tell he wanted to touch her, but he held back.

"Yeah, we established that. Lucifer and his army."

"There are others."

"Others?" She didn't like the way he sounded.

"Other angels know about you."

Her eyebrows rose. "And that's a problem?"

Sam averted his gaze and dropped his head. For a moment, she sensed guilt cloud about him. "When I created you, I was not doing so by their standards. They know about you. I fear they may come and take you, especially now that they know about the child."

Even though she stood in the sunlight, she felt her fingers grow cold. "Are you saying that not only Hell wants me, but Heaven too?"

"I should have foreseen this."

"What will they do to me, Sam?" she said. She wanted to scream at him, but she held back as she felt the shaking move up her spine.

His head rose, and his icy blue eyes met hers. "They will take the child."

Tears threatened to flood her vision. Not this time, she chided herself. "What do we do?"

"I teach you to fight them. All of them."

Before she could say anything else, he grabbed her wrist. The swift way he moved surprised her for a moment as he turned her palm up and opened her fingers. His hands felt warm against hers as the floral scent of his skin drifted over her again.

"This may hurt a bit," he said as his index finger moved toward the flesh of her palm. His finger moved, as though he wrote with invisible ink across her skin. Then the burning pierced through her hand like a white-hot brand. She cried out and grasped at his wrist, but he held her tight and continued to trace a symbol as it burned black into her flesh.

"Stop, Sam," she cried and tugged harder at her arm. The angel never flinched but continued until his finger had burned a sigil into her skin.

As soon as he lifted his finger, he released her hand. The force of her tugging against him almost threw her off balance. She steadied herself and clutched her hand to her chest, feeling the sting of tears in her eyes with the slow ebb of pain that began to dwindle. As she watched his steady and unforgiving gaze upon her, memories bubbled to the surface. This was a familiar pain that she had once felt over every inch of her body when she was trapped in the light. The same pain that had created the tattoos of the seraph.

She pulled her hand away from her chest and opened her fingers to reveal the black edges of the mark he had etched into her skin. The edges of it shimmered with the last remnants of white fire. As she examined each curve of the sigil, it began to fade as though it were invisible ink and it's time had run out. Just as the last vestiges of pain in her hand faded with the ink, she sensed a tickle along her forearm. The very mark that he had burned into her skin now took residence permanently in the flesh of her arm. It flashed a bright violet just as it set inside her skin.

"The first mark of the Archangel. It is the power sigil, the Master over Spirit," he said as she gazed down at the new tattoo. "This is where you start."

This was no different than when she had her power as the seraph. She had learned to direct the energy along her tattoos and into her hands. Gideon had taught her enough about the power, but she learned to manipulate it herself. It had responded as soon as she became comfortable with pulling it from her core and manifesting it at her fingertips.

She glanced up to him. "Why don't you have this mark?"

He held out his arms but kept his gaze steady toward her. Without flinching, his fingers clenched into fists, and a series of marks materialized across his flesh, each one shimmering with violet light. The tattoos appeared progressively up his arms and curved until they vanished under the edges of his T-shirt—so many sigils, covering the majority of his flesh and arcing up his neck like black vines.

"In time," he said, drawing her attention away from the remarkable tattoos, "you will learn to make and use these marks." He let his right fist open, the tips of his fingers shuddering until an orb of purple light began to glow at the palm of his hand, expanding and pulsating like a plasma ball of electric charge. "But for now, just follow my lead. You can do just as I am doing."

She pulled her eyes away from the incredible orb and looked down at her own hand. The angle made it look so easy, but she wasn't fooled. Nikka closed her eyes and concentrated on her center, where she remembered her seraph power once resided, just the same way she used to start. But there was nothing to draw from. The tank had been emptied and never refilled. She closed her eyes and searched the dark for the power, hoping to will it into her arms, but nothing responded.

His fingers closed into fists, and her eyes flew open. "You search within, but that is not where you will find it." The light in his hands had vanished at some point after she had closed her eyes. "You are not a seraph. The power surrounds you. It lives in the earth. In the trees. In the people around you. Draw from that and pull it into you."

Channeling her own power had been hard enough when she was a seraph. How was she supposed to pull it in from elsewhere, from a place that she had never experienced? Sam stepped back, opening her hand once again. Her fingers splayed open, her palms upward, and she let out an anxious breath.

"Feel it in your feet," he said. "Draw from God's creations."

She closed her eyes again and concentrated on the grass against her bare feet, the soil under the grass and rock beneath that. Maybe if she could imagine each stratum that comprised the earth, then it would unveil its energy. She bit her lower lip as she concentrated, imagining that these things carried light that worked through the soil and grass and entered the bottoms of her feet.

Then she felt the warmth course into her muscles and tendons, like fingers that massaged her legs as they moved into her body. The sensation buzzed into her vessels, the blood pushing it into every tissue in her body. The tattoos tingled with the feeling that traveled down her arm.

She allowed her eyelids to open just as the warmth moved into her fingers. At first, she saw nothing, but then her fingertips throbbed until they began to glow with the same purple light that Sam had held in his hands. It grew into an orb with branches of electrical bursts surrounding it like an atom. As she watched the light build, she pulled more of the warmth into her feet, and this fed the orb, making it grow until it enveloped her entire hand.

And she didn't need to look down to know that the tattoos sparkled with violet light, casting its glow against her chin and arms.

"Excellent," Sam said. "That is a good start." He touched his hand to hers and wrapped his fingers around her wrist. The purple light reflected against his face as he maneuvered her hand toward the hood of the car. Her fingers touched the cold metal, and he pressed her hand against it, burying the light against the hood.

"Start it," he said.

She gave him a puzzled look.

"Go ahead." He nodded to her and backed away.

How was she supposed to start it? But just as she thought it, she realized what she had in her hand. It wasn't just light, but energy. This whole thing was so metaphysical that it defied logic, but she remembered something that she had once learned in her AP Physics class: energy is not created or destroyed, but just transformed. When she saw the light in her hand, it sizzled and flashed, just like electricity. What if this energy could be converted to raw electricity?

She willed the energy into her feet again, stronger and faster as she imagined it building a charge. Nikka closed her eyes as the force grew upon itself, folding and curling under her hand. She could almost see the circuitry of the car, the electrical panels with snaking wires that had long been fried when the EMP hit. The energy pulsed in her hand, traveling along these circuits like healing waters. Then she pushed the charge into a sudden force.

The starter turned over, and the engine roared to life in a quick burst.

She jumped back from the car as it rumbled under her hand and opened her eyes. The light had disappeared, and she no longer felt the warmth pulling up from the ground. But the car still ran like it had never died, even when she no longer touched it.

"That's amazing," she said and looked at the palm of her hand.

"Wonderful," he said and leaned through the car door, turning off the engine. Their small area in the woods once again fell into silence. "But it is just a parlor trick."

He stepped toward her again and stopped before her. "Do you recall how to remove a demon?"

She continued looking at her hand, feeling the buzz of electricity in her fingers. "Yes."

"You can still do that," he said and grabbed her hand, catching her attention. He pressed her open palm against his chest. "And you can do it to angels as well."

"Are you serious?"

"Of course I am," he said and planted his feet. "But it is different when you are an archangel. Only the blade can kill them, but you can remove them."

"Wait," she said and stepped back, breaking contact from his chest. "The sword can kill an angel too?"

His stern eyes looked at her, the crease between his eyebrows growing deeper. "Nikka, do you remember learning of the war in Heaven?"

"Yes. Satan left Heaven over a big disagreement with God, and some of the angels followed him."

"In a nutshell, yes. But we are all cut from the same cloth. We are all the same, just soldiers on different sides of the trench. That sword belonged to God and it can destroy any of us."

He approached her again and grabbed her hand, placing it against his chest. "When you remove an angel or a demon, you need not pull it out as you did when you were a seraph. You force it out by your own will. Now, remove me from this body."

"No." Horrified, she tried to pull away from him, but he grasped her hand and held it in place.

"You will not harm me, only disable me momentarily. But this will be an advantage for you. If one comes for you, at least you can disable it long enough to escape."

"Don't make me do this," she said. "And won't you be able to do this if they come?"

"You need to know how to do it," he said, the warmth of his hand on hers growing hotter. "I may not be there to help you, and I cannot leave you vulnerable if you have the ability to do it. Besides, you are human, and you will not fatigue as fast as I will."

"Wait," she said and tried to pull away, but he wouldn't let her. "You said I'm an archangel. How can I also be human?"

His fingers wrapped around her hand and he removed it from his chest. This relieved her as he held her hand and his face softened. "You are still human, just as you were when you were the seraph. That is why your kind is chosen to fight against the demons. Angels, demons—we can't use our full power when we possess. But a human is the perfect weapon. A human has travelled between the realms of life and death as it is born into this world. This experience allowed them to carry the burden of the power without the fatigue. We have not been blessed to do so, and we must rely on you to do that for us."

"I remember the demons have a lot more power than you're telling me," she said as thoughts of her battle against Abaddon and the other lieutenants floated in her memory. She recalled every wound that she received in those battles, but she also remembered that her body got plenty fatigued when she used a lot of her power all at once. She had collapsed a few times, especially when she had manipulated herself to be invisible.

"Now believe me that it is only a fraction of its potential," he said, and the thought of it sent a shiver across her shoulders.

"Wait," she said and furrowed her brow. "You guys have power that is more focused when you possess a body. But then it's only a 'fraction of its potential'? I don't understand."

"Only on earth. We are all-consuming power in our own realms, as well as those in-between."

"In-between?"

"The spirit realms. Purgatory, the fringes of the battlefield. In those places, we are all powerful, without the need for human conduits."

He pulled her hand toward his chest again and splayed out her fingers. She felt his pectoral muscle flex under her hand. "Now, remove me from this body."

"Sam, please—"

"Now." His stare had grown cold, and he released her fingers as he stood with his chest pressed against her hand.

She let out a sigh and pressed the tip of her tongue against the roof of her mouth. The energy moved into her feet as she willed it through her flesh. Sam didn't need to tell her that this would require a lot more power than just forcing a car to start. The power she used when she had exorcised demons as a seraph was extreme even back then. She tried to pull the equivalent of that into her feet and up her legs. The power streamed into her arm, building into a light that flickered at her fingertips. The charge collected in her core, just behind the tattoos, until it throbbed and threatened to burst from her chest. As it pulsed and shuddered, she let it loose, streaming down her arm like a water cannon.

The power shot from her hand and struck him directly in the chest. He grunted as the power hit him and sent him falling backwards in a flash of violet light. His body crashed back against the gravel driveway, and Nikka almost fell backwards with the kick until she planted her feet.

She held her breath as she looked at his still form until his eyes opened and he lifted his head.

"Not strong enough," he said and stood, dusting the dirt and leaves off his jeans. He stepped toward her and grabbed her wrist, planting it against his chest. "Again."

How could that not be enough? The collection of the energy almost burned through her ribs. Any stronger and it would make her detonate like a nuclear bomb. But he wouldn't back away, and he stared her down like a predator, which made her want to toss him into the gravel again.

She pulled energy from the earth into her feet, just like she did before. But this time she drew it faster and harder, dipping into the deeper aspects of the earth. She remembered that he told her to pull it from the trees as well, so she imagined the light flowing from every leaf and branch that surrounded her. The ball of power swelled in her chest, and the pressure there made nausea well into her stomach. When she sensed that it would no longer compress and hold its shape, she let it go again, striking him in the chest.

He fell back hard enough to crash into the gravel and slide into the tree line, leaving a gouge of dirt in the ground where he had landed. But he opened his eyes again and came at her, his eyes angry now.

"Again."

He grabbed her wrist hard enough now that it hurt. When he pulled her toward him, she tried to yank her hand free. The fierce blue of his eyes glared at her with a tinge of the violet light that now shimmered in his pupils, just like the demons that had come for her that night in the rest area outside Las Vegas. They had one purpose that night: to bash her head into the mirror until she could no longer stand.

She pulled back from him, forcing the will of the earth, wind, sky and life that circled her. The power flowed deeply into her chest until it formed a leaden core so compressed that it shuddered in her breast. She forced both of her hands before her and let it loose with the force of a tornado directed through her fingers. The power shot into him as he moved at her, hitting him in the chest. This time, he didn't fall like he had been hit by a train. His head whipped back, and his arms spread wide as he cried into the air. The power moved through his body in a gale of violet-white light so bright that she almost closed her eyes.

The energy dissipated as soon as she had released it, and the drain of it pulled on her insides. She collapsed to her knees and watched as he did the same. He fell back into the grass, limp and unconscious. The last aftershocks of the power ebbed along her arms and into her legs like twitches after an electric pulse. She was too afraid to stand in case she would fall again. And Sam didn't move this time.

She crawled toward him, watching his chest rise and fall with shallow but even breaths. Her shaking hands touched his cold cheek.

"Sam," she said and slapped his cheek, but he didn't open his eyes. "Wake up. I did what you told me to do."

But he only laid in the grass, his eyes closed and his mouth slightly agape, the body just an empty shell without the life-giving force of an angel inside it. The lavender scent that usually surrounded him had vanished. She moved around him and kneeled in the grass, pulling his head up to rest on her thighs as she touched his cheek.

After what seemed like an hour, she felt a twitch under her fingers where she touched his face. She looked down at him, and his chest stopped moving. Her hand began to shake, and she moved her fingers to his ribs again.

Oh no, she thought. *I killed him.*

Then his eyes flew open, and he looked up at her. His black pupils focused on her again, and she saw his smile, even though his face looked upside down to her.

"Very good," he said.

"I thought you were dead," she said, still not sure if she truly believed that he now spoke to her.

"Not dead. Just between worlds for a little while."

The smile on his face scratched at the itch that had built inside her over the last hour that she watched him. It was enough to make her want to slap him. She shoved him off her lap and pushed herself to her feet, but the movement only turned into a jarring waddle as she finally stood. She hurried through the grass and back to the door into the house.

"What is wrong?" he called after her.

"I don't want to do this anymore," she said and slammed the back door as he began to say something else.

Every step into the house seemed to bring on another contraction, the last one strong enough that she had to stop and catch her breath as she leaned on the kitchen table. The door opened and shut again behind her as he walked into the kitchen.

"Is everything all right?" he said.

He stood just a short distance from her, but she shifted further away from him. "Just leave me alone."

"I am sorry if it frightened you."

The contraction eased, and she was able to stand straighter. "I thought you were dead."

"I know, and I am sorry." He pulled a chair from the table and placed it beside her. "Please, sit."

"I don't need to sit down."

"Yes, you do. Please."

She finally looked back at him and saw the worry that had settled into the lines around his eyes. Her hand found the back of the chair, and she settled into it.

"It is enough for today," he said and crouched down to look at her. "I am pleased with what you were able to do, and I will not make you do that again."

"Fine," she said, feeling her resolve soften as she watched him. "Now do we have anything for breakfast? Pregnant lady here. I'm starving."

He smiled, making the blue of his eyes seem to change color. "Of course. Where are my manners? Breakfast it is."

Chapter Forty-Three

Nikka

Just as he had promised, Sam never mentioned any more about the power for the rest of the day. And even more than that, he didn't talk about the demons or the war in Heaven. It was almost like he did everything to avoid it. Instead, he wanted to talk about the baby and what her plans were. He asked so many questions about it that she eventually wanted to change the subject. All that talk about a birth began to make her a little nervous as if those increasing contractions weren't bad enough.

With the use of so much power today, Nikka felt the familiar onset of fatigue begin to build in her bones, similar to the drain she used to have when she was the seraph, but it had come much later. Sam allowed her to go to bed earlier than she had last night, but not before walking her to her bedroom, hovering like she could get assaulted by someone on the way upstairs.

"I'll be fine," she said as she stood at the bedroom door.

"Perhaps," he started, his voice becoming hesitant, "as the birth draws closer, I need to remain nearby at night."

"You're not sleeping in here if that's what you're asking," she said.

"It would be wise if I did."

"No, it wouldn't." She pressed her hand against his chest to separate him from the door frame. For a moment, she thought he might not move, but he took a small step back. "I'll be fine until morning."

"Very well," he said and tilted his head again. "I will be just downstairs."

She closed the door and pressed her hand against the wood. Even though he said nothing, she knew he stood right outside the room. Sam had saved her life, and she must owe him something for that. But in the brief time she had spent with him, she began to feel that little niggle of worry that settled into her thoughts. She didn't really know him, but he knew everything about her, calling her his creation. Something about that felt a little creepy, Frankenstein's monster-creepy. But he had taught her so much today, things that she never knew she could do.

Even though he had said it would be dangerous, she still wanted to see Jason, to tell him that things were okay and she was safe. Maybe she could convince Sam tomorrow. And if he still felt it was too dangerous, maybe he could at least get Jason the message.

But in the meantime, she could only trust herself.

Her fingers slid down the door and to the knob, twisting the lock until it clicked into place.

She moved through the dark to the bed and crawled over the covers. The down pillow nestled around her head and she stared out the windows to the moonlight that fell over the lake. She tucked her hand under her head, feeling the baby move again.

If everything had energy, she wondered what kind of power she could draw from the moon. Sam waited outside, maybe still just on the other side of the door, but she could do this silently. She drew her other hand before her and held open her palm. Although she wasn't standing in the grass, feeling the earth, she closed her eyes and just felt the moonlight against her fingers. It was a strange thing, trying to feel the sensation of the moon. At least in the daylight, she could feel the warmth of the sun against her skin. But moonlight was intangible, at least to most people. And yet, she could feel it, like cold silk sheets that brushed at the tips of her fingers. It didn't enter her body like the power of the earth, which felt definite and abrupt. Moonlight flowed like ribbons of cool silver liquid that filled her hands. It was something she could twist and form like clay just under the tattoo, the edges of it pliant and flexible, not the hard lead of the earth.

The light began to shimmer like silver and violet around her palm, tendrils of effervescence floating like seaweed in water around her fingers. This power moved so different, smooth and salient like a dancer or a song. If the energy of the earth could force a spirit from a possessed body, what could this do?

She remembered when she was a seraph when she first could change her appearance, taking on the image of another person. It was something she had just thought of, right on the spot. Sure, it could have been a divine inspiration, but searched for that now. The first thought of what to do with this power that danced at her finger tips.

> *I once had a sweetheart, I loved her right well.*
> *I loved her far better than my tongue can tell . . .*

The song drifted through her mind, just like it had for days before Jason had come back into her life. And then he showed up in Garnet Falls, the last lines of the song torn from a book that he claims he found. This power wasn't new to her, and she had used it long before she knew about it, back when she removed Abaddon from Jason's body. What if she had been using it without knowing it, calling to him as she slept, leaving that song between them?

She closed her eyes, feeling the liquid silver light between her fingers, and she let the song play in her thoughts. Somewhere under that moonlight, Jason waited and worried for her. She tried to imagine the song like the words in a dream. Now that she had her memory back, she remembered where she had first heard it: at an Irish festival that her mother had taken her to as a child. A woman had sung it acapella on the stage that night, and it had stuck with her ever since.

> *Last night she came to me, my dead love, my dear.*
> *She came in so softly her feet made no din.*
> *And she laid her hand on me and this she did say:*
> *"It will not be long love, 'til our wedding day."*

The light in her palm throbbed, moving with cool vibrancy into her fingers and then it dissipated just as she let her body relax with sleep, the last lines of the song drifting through her thoughts.

Chapter Forty-Four

Nikka

Standing outside in the heat of the day made the contractions more frequent, but Nikka wasn't going to tell Sam about it, not while he was so serious about showing her how to use her powers. He continued to ramble on about the importance of learning it all so fast, but she had so far seen nothing to indicate that they had been in imminent danger, except for him just saying it.

Each of these "sessions" was probably going to begin with a painful tattoo being burned into the palm of her hand, too. He gave her a new one today, a sort-of triangle with curved lines and arcing marks through it. And just like yesterday, the mark disappeared and showed up on her other forearm. Now it itched and throbbed as she tried to focus this new energy into doing what he wanted of her.

"Do you understand what I am telling you?" he said, bringing her out of her daze as she looked up at the sun through the trees.

"Yes, I get it," she said, and held her arm up, palm toward him.

"When you do this, you must stand firmly." He moved behind her and used his boot to shove her foot further back, and his hands rested on her hips while he moved her, something that she wasn't sure that she wanted to allow. As long as he didn't touch her for long, she just looked forward and kept her hand up.

"You direct the power where you want it to go and what you want it to do," he said as he walked around her and faced her. "With this mark," he said and touched the new tattoo on her arm, "you should be able to create a temporary shield around you."

She remembered being able to do something like that as a seraph.

"Now try it," he said and stepped close to her. "Shield us both."

Her toes curled in the bottoms of her sandals as she felt the familiar call of energy rise from the ground. They had been doing this for hours now, and it became a little easier each time as she pulled the power into her core. She allowed the energy to build in her gut, as she did each time. It was just easier that way, but she knew she needed to work on building it faster. Defending herself at such a slow rate really wasn't going to work well.

The core began to expand and curl with energy, when she felt another contraction, strong enough to take her breath away and break her concentration. The energy retracted on itself and zipped back down through her feet, dissipating into the ground. She doubled over as the contraction held tight, threatening to make her knees weaken.

"What is it?" he said and hovered near her, his hand on her back.

"It's okay," she said, trying to speak over the pain, but this one made it difficult to even breathe. "Just give it a second."

His hand moved over her back. He probably tried to ease her discomfort, but his touch only irritated the nerves along her spine. She wished he would just back away and leave her alone for just a minute.

"They are growing more frequent," he said.

The tightening eased until she no longer felt the squeeze through her back and she could take in a deeper breath. She inched back to her upright position.

"I'm okay. Just a false contraction."

"We are done for today."

"I can keep going," she said and waved a hand in the air as she moved back into her stance.

"We are done." His voice grew steely and firm, like an adult scolding a child, as he clasped her hand and pulled her toward the house. She would have tugged her hand free but the way his demeanor demanded the end to their session concerned her more. His pace quickened, and she almost tripped after him going up the steps into the door of the house, almost like he had no idea that she couldn't move as well with a large baby in her abdomen.

At first, his strange demeanor and take on the world around them was a little quirky, but she had just added it all up to him being an angel. She understood that only knowing him for a few days wouldn't be enough to really grasp his personality, but even in those few days, he started to make her uncomfortable. If he had been just any other man, she would have suspected that he might be a little of a control freak. And even the image of a man keeping a woman tied up in his basement came to mind when she watched him behave like this; that was funny to her the first day, but by day three it wasn't so amusing anymore.

He pulled her into the house and to the couch, where he arranged the pillows at the edge of the sofa, just like he had the other day.

"You must rest, elevate your feet," he said, pointing to the pillows. "I will get you water. It is important to stay hydrated."

"Okay," she said, the word falling carefully.

He rounded the couch and stalked back to the kitchen before bringing her a bottle of water that he must have collected during the many times he disappeared for hours on end. Before she could take the bottle, he twisted the cap off and handed it to her as he crouched, watching her drink.

After she took a deep drink, she pulled the bottle from her lips and looked away from his trapped gaze. "Everything's fine. It was just a little contraction."

"Not much longer now," he said, and his hand rose to touch her face. His fingers caressed her cheek, something that would be wonderful if he was her lover, but it only sent shivers down her vertebrae. As weird as he had been acting today, she wasn't going to pull away from him and send him into a bad mood.

"All of this use of power," she said, trying to distract herself and Sam, "is it safe for the baby?"

It must have worked because his hand left her face, only to fall on her abdomen. The baby moved and twitched under his touch.

"Absolutely," he said. "Your power is only minimal right now, anyway. But you need to know it to protect yourself in any way you can."

A burning question still remained in her throat, something that she had wanted to ask only to see his response. He appeared to be so concerned about the baby, but what about her? What was his plan in the next few days? Weeks? It had only been three days with him, and she couldn't imagine staying with him for much longer. She needed to get back to Garnet Falls.

"I need to get a message back to Jason," she said, although her voice had grown weak just trying to say it.

His face hardened, and his icy blue eyes only stared at her. "I do not advise it."

"He needs to know I'm okay."

Sam stood and turned away from her, pacing along the edge of the couch, his head hung but his shoulders tense and firm. The room might as well have felt like a deep freezer with the way he walked back and forth in silence.

His quiet pacing made her dizzy, and she felt the nausea build in her gut as she watched him, waiting for him to speak.

"Sam, say something. You're freaking me out."

He stopped, facing away from her, his back and shoulders moving in slow, steady breaths. "No."

"No? Just no?" she said and felt a lump form in her throat. "You said I'm not a prisoner. I need to talk to him and Gideon—"

"No."

"I don't understand," she said and stood, her knees weaker than she expected.

"You will want to leave if you do that," he said, his voice steady and without emotion.

Her brow creased and she tilted her head. "And why can't I?" She wasn't sure that she wanted to know the answer.

"You belong here, where I can protect you and the baby."

"Then come with me," she said.

Sam finally turned and looked at her, his jaw tight. "You must stay here. The baby will be coming soon, and you must be here with me."

The way he spoke gave her chills again, and she knew then that he wouldn't let her go. She really was a prisoner here, even if he didn't admit it. If she wasn't nine months pregnant, she might be able to outrun him, but as an angel, he would just be able to hunt her down and follow her anywhere.

"Why are you doing this?" The words came out in a near-whisper as her throat narrowed. Tears threatened to blur her vision.

"I created you, built you in my image," he said, his lip twitching with anger as he pointed a stiff finger into his sternum. "I have waited for the moment to take you to The Ascension with me, and we are so close. I cannot lose you now, not to that human or the demon with him."

"What are you talking about? What's The Ascension?"

He marched back over to her and grabbed her upper arms, his fingertips digging into her flesh as he forced her down onto the couch again. "I will not talk about this now. You must rest, and we will discuss it after the baby is born."

His fingers loosened, and his hand moved to her abdomen again as though to make sure his investment was still viable. She only watched him, trying not to cringe as he leaned over her, his icy blue eyes watching her like a predator.

"You will be safe here," he said. "Do you understand?"

She nodded right after he said it, afraid that if she delayed, he might lash out at her.

"Say it."

The words froze in her throat, but she forced them out. "I understand."

He picked up the bottle from the edge of the couch again and placed it in her hand. "Good. Now stay hydrated and rest."

Sam stood up and stepped away from the couch, disappearing somewhere in the kitchen while her eyes stared to the far corner of the room. This was her prison, and the guard had just locked the door.

As he had the last few nights, he made dinner, and she sat across the table from him just as she always did. She only looked down and pushed the food around her plate under the light of the candles on the table.

"Are you not hungry?" he said as he watched her. She could feel his eyes on her, but she didn't want to look at him.

"Not really."

"It is important—"

"I know," she interrupted him. "It's important to have proper nutrition for the baby."

He paused, and she heard him chewing, and she knew he still watched her. "If this is about earlier today, I am sorry if I worried you."

"Why would you think that?" she said, laying the sarcasm on thick.

He placed his silverware down on the table and crossed his fingers over his plate. "This is how things will be for now, and I do hope that you will soon come to see reason about it."

She pushed the food around again with her fork when he stood and stepped toward her. Her fingers wrapped around her utensil tighter and her hands went cold. He stopped beside her, touching his fingers to her face and lifting her chin, forcing her to look at him as he stared down at her.

"I know that your human emotions will wreak havoc on your thoughts. After The Ascension, these things will only be trivial. You will understand why I do what I must to keep you safe." His thumb rubbed along her jaw. "Now eat."

As soon as his hand left her skin, the cold stiffened her fingers again. He stalked back to the end of the table, but she could still sense his presence next to her. Despite her shaking hand, she scooped up any vegetables that would stay on the end of her fork and placed it in her mouth. The bland food moved over her tongue, and he stared at her now, watching as she ate each bite. She hardly chewed anything, just letting her dry mouth swallow as she gazed down at her plate.

The food had grown cold by the time she finished her last bite, and everything she had eaten didn't settle well in her stomach. When she placed her fork down, he stood and walked toward her again. The muscles along her spine tightened into a rigid line as he neared her and stood behind her chair. His hands moved to her shoulders, resting heavily there as his fingers extended to her collar bones.

"Very good," he said, his voice calm and smooth. His fingers curled under, the thumbs kneading into the muscles along her neck. "I know it is difficult, but this will be but a short time. Please, try not to fear me. I only want what is best for you."

His fingers massaged along her neck, but she stayed rigid.

"Relax," he said as his fingers stopped kneading. "All this stress is not good for you."

She tried to let her shoulders fall, but she didn't want him touching her anymore or even to be near her. The candlelight flickered, and she focused her eyes on it until she felt the fingers of his right hand move across her collarbone and creep over her skin to the first rib, then the second. Her shoulders tightened again until he stopped along her sternum. He placed his index finger along the edge of her tattoo and the mark illuminated in a cascade of violet sparkles, like a traitor against her will. The mark thrummed and buzzed just under her skin, sending ribbons of energy into her chest.

"See," he said and lifted his hand. "Your spirit knows its kindred. It feels my essence like its own."

The light slowly diminished into tiny dots of light and then extinguished as soon as he broke contact with the mark. He backed away and stepped into the darkness of the main room, out of the kitchen and leaving her staring into the candlelight, shaking.

CHAPTER FORTY-FIVE
NIKKA

She didn't want to come out of her room the next morning, but Sam arrived and shoved it open, breaking the stop as though the lock was meaningless to him.

"You do not have to hide from me," he said when he walked into the room.

Nikka sat at the edge of the bed and watched him enter. The tightness in his shoulders had vanished, and his face looked softer today.

"I don't feel like training today," she said.

He leaned down and grabbed her wrist, pulling her to her feet. "Then we do not have to. But you need to move. You need food and water."

His grip on her wrist loosened as he walked her out of the room. She followed him down the stairs because she had nowhere else to go now.

The morning sun had lit up the skies and poured through the tall windows into the main room, warming the cushions on the couch. She settled on the sofa, in a patch of sunlight that settled on her skin.

"We will need to be leaving soon. It is not good to stay in one place for too long," he said to her from the kitchen.

Leaving this place and traveling somewhere—anywhere—with him made her veins feel like ice. She wanted to say something, to argue with him, but after last night she knew he would just give her some vague reason about it being for her safety. She thought of only one thing.

"What did you have in mind?" she asked, peering back into the kitchen.

"Tomorrow," he said and turned toward her. She quickly ducked her head behind the back of the couch, hoping he hadn't seen her watching him. "I will gather supplies today. We need to find a place suitable to birth your child."

He rounded the edge of the couch and brought a plate of food and another bottle of water to her. She accepted it as he settled down on the chair across the room from her.

"And what's wrong with this place?" Of course, she definitely didn't want to have a baby in a cabin in the woods, especially with him there. As the contractions increased, she started to worry about having this baby at all.

"We have been here too long. Undoubtedly, those hunting us will converge if we remain here."

"So, you're leaving today," she said, trying to keep her voice even. "To get things for our trip."

"Yes, I will not be gone long. You may wish to prepare a few things to take as well."

"Fine," she said and forced a smile.

The remainder of the morning dragged on in silence as she finished her breakfast and he moved about in the kitchen, gathering things in bags.

Then, he slipped out the door. She heard the car engine roar to life, and she leaned over the edge of the couch to hear the vehicle crunch along the gravel road as it pulled away from the house.

Every panicked thought rushed through her mind at once. He had left her alone a few times already, and she never had the need to escape, until now. But where could she go?

The car, the one he just drove away in: it had Oregon plates. So, they were still in Oregon, and the coded numbers on the plate told her they were still in the same county as Garnet Falls. She wasn't too familiar with the area, but that license plate was enough. She stood, catching her balance after a few seconds with her abdomen protruding awkwardly. The driveway now stood silent behind the house. She rushed to the kitchen windows, peering out for any sign of him.

She was alone with an unlocked door, in a cabin deep in the woods by a lake. This was her one chance to do something to free herself. She slipped the sandals on her feet, collected a few bottles of water into one of the packs lying on the kitchen counter and then strapped it on her back. Wherever she was, she might need a few things to get her a little farther down the road, but at least she would be away from this place.

She rushed to the back door and down the driveway, but she stopped and glanced down the road. Nothing but the sounds of birds and the lapping of the lake shore behind the house. She looked down both ways, and each side appeared equally barren and distant. But the car had gone left. Then right it would be. She turned down the right lane and quickened her pace as she moved down the road. It didn't matter how long or hot it was, she just needed to get away. And he was an angel; he might be able to find her. But she had to take the chance.

The only thing she knew about Garnet Falls was that it resided in the hills in central Oregon. At least she wasn't stuck in some cabin in Arkansas or something. This was within walking distance. A long walking distance, but still do-able. The road curved and she followed it until it turned downhill out of the trees.

She stopped at the top of the hill and looked down to the open fields before her. At the other end of the pastures she could see another bank of trees, but as soon as she stepped down that hill, she would be exposed. If he came back now, Sam would definitely see her.

Then she needed to hurry and get to the other bank of trees.

The faster she moved down the hill, the more cramping she felt in her pelvis. The baby moved more now, sensing that she hurried along the road and the adrenaline pumping through her veins. She almost ran, as much as she could, toward the other bank of trees. Sweat dripped from her forehead with the sun that beat down on her skin. At least her hair was short and didn't heat up her neck.

She neared the other bank of trees as the road curved into the woods, heading west. The shade fell over her, and she stopped to rest against a tree along the shoulder of the road. She glanced back at where she had come from, but it remained quiet and desolate. Now she had the woods that provided enough shade and cover that she could slip away from the road and hopefully head in the direction of Garnet Falls.

Stepping into the thick of the trees, she left the road behind and continued through the woods, keeping the sun tracking where she knew that she still walked westward. The heat of the sun eased a little while she walked under the trees, but the sweat continued to drip from her forehead.

With each step, the baby moved and kicked. An hour wandered by and then another. She wasn't sure how many miles that would have been, but her sore feet began to rebel. Despite the ache in her hips and knees, though, she kept going, walking along a man-made trail that meandered through the woods but always keeping the sun at the end of the path.

A contraction began in her back and crept around her abdomen, making her stop in the path and bend over, her hand on her thigh as she breathed with it. This one made her dizzy enough that she stumbled along the path until she found a tree stump that she could rest on. The contraction continued until it reached its nadir and then eased off. She pulled the pack from her shoulders and found one of the water bottles. The water had grown warm in the sun, but it didn't matter. She drank heavily and felt it hit her stomach. Her hand wiped the sweat from her forehead, and she gazed up to the sky. The sun had tracked a long way since the moment she had left the lodge. Half the day had already passed. Sam must have returned by now and found that she had disappeared.

This made her heart race again. It didn't matter how much her feet hurt or the ache in her pelvis. She needed to keep going.

When she stood, she took in a deep breath, but a thought raced through her head. Maybe she could get a little help. Something to help her find home, or something to take away the pain. She glanced down to the ground and held out her hand, her palm facing upward. Just as he had taught her, she pulled the energy from the ground and into her feet. It moved easily through her muscles and bones, rivulets of warmth coursing into her core. Just as she did when she was the seraph, she closed her eyes and focused on what she wanted it to do. It eased into her joints, every tendril of warm energy settling into her hips, knees and feet. The ball of light coalesced in her palm, and she felt the tingling light begin along the mark on her chest. The pain began to disappear, and she took a step forward without discomfort. She smiled and let the light dissipate from her fingers. Her feet were light with each step, as though she didn't have the weight of her abdomen hindering her progress.

It could work. She could make it home.

She opened her eyes and immediately felt her world spin. Sam stood before her down the path, his stare icy and cold. The breath caught in her throat as soon as she saw him, her knees growing weak again and the pain in her feet throbbing to life. He started toward her, a determined and fierce march as he stared at her. She stepped back, knowing that she could never outrun him.

But she could do something.

She planted her feet and held out her hands, palms facing him as she pulled the energy from the earth into her heels. The power surged as she willed it as fast as she could into her core, building it into a ball of vibrating and pulsing energy. He came at her faster now, sprinting toward her. She pulled the power from the trees and the air as it circled around her, drawn in through her fingers. It boiled and collided with such force that she could no longer contain it. The power broke free, rushing down her arms with terrible ferocity, aimed at Sam's chest. This was the strongest burst of energy she had felt yet, and it left her with such force that she nearly lost her balance.

The burst of violet white light rushed toward him, but he never flinched. He threw out is forearm, creating a brief dome of light around himself just as the energy struck, deflecting in all directions until it vanished among the trees. By the time she had seen it strike his shield, she stumbled back and turned, but it was too late.

He was on her, his arms wrapped around her torso, pinning her arms to her side. She kicked at him, knowing it would be useless. He had held her like this before and knew she could never get away. He pulled her into him and pressed his lips to her ear.

"What were you thinking?" he said with a growl. "You were vulnerable out here. Any of them could have found you."

"I don't care," she said through clenched teeth.

"Yes, you do." He squeezed her tighter as she squirmed and kicked. This made it too hard to breathe, and she cried out. "Stop fighting. You will only hurt yourself."

She hated to admit it to herself, but he was right. With his hold still tight around her, she let her arms fall, and she stopped kicking him. He loosened his grip and let her back onto her feet, but her knees would no longer hold her upright. She went to the ground and let her head fall, tears flowing hot down her cheeks.

"You do not have the strength or ability to stop me," he said as he stood over her. "By using your power, I was able to track you. Are you so naïve that you thought you could leave me?"

Yes, that had been the plan, but she didn't need to say it. He already knew.

"I just want to go home," she said, crying into the dirt path.

He crouched down and touched his hand to her back. "With me, you have no need for another home." He wrapped his fingers around her wrist and pulled her up with him, wiping away the tears from her face. "Now we need to go, you are too exposed out here."

With his vice grip on her wrist, he pulled her down through the trees until they finally opened up to the shoulder of the road, where his car waited. He placed her into the passenger seat and drove back to the lodge as she stared out the windshield, feeling her hope left behind on that trail in the woods.

When they returned to the house, Sam went about things as though nothing had happened, but he insisted that she wash the dirt and sweat from her skin in the lake. She stood at the shore after he led her there, his hand once again on her wrist.

"Clean yourself," he said with a nod and let her wrist go, but he still stood there.

She turned toward the water line and stepped toward it, dipping her toes into the cold water.

"No," he said. She turned back to face him as he approached. "You will need clean clothes." His fingers touched along her back and found the edge of her tank top, pulling it up. She grabbed her top and stepped away from him, keeping it tight around her torso.

"Stop," she said and backed away from him. Her hands shook as she looked at him, the stern stare in his eye.

He stepped closer to her, and she backed away until she stood ankle-deep in the water. "You will do as I say." His hand grasped the edge of her tank top again and forced it out of her hands and over her head.

Her hands reflexively moved to cover her exposed breasts, and she felt her cheeks flush.

"There is no need for false modesty, Nikka," he said. "I have seen everything when I made you what you are."

She looked away from him, even though he stood close enough that the water soaked his shoes.

"I will clean your clothes, but I need them all," he said, and she knew that he wanted her to strip completely down, and he wouldn't go away unless she did it. Even though he stood right there, she freed her right arm to loosen the waistband of her pants, and she wriggled out them until she had let them drop into the water at her ankles.

He stooped to gather them into his arms and turned away from her as though he didn't care what she did at that point. He was smart enough to know that she wouldn't likely run away bare naked and pregnant.

"Wash yourself, and then come back inside for dinner. I will have fresh clothes for you then," he said as he walked away.

She stood at the water's edge and watched him disappear back into the house with all of her clothes. The day had been warm, but standing there naked made the goosebumps start along her arms. At least he didn't stand there watching her anymore, but the thought that he had already seen her naked sent more chills down her spine. She turned toward the water, tears stinging her eyes, and stepped into the cold lake.

Chapter Forty-Six

Nikka

After she had stepped from the water, Nikka hurried back into the house, shivering and naked but clean. Not that she wanted to be around him, but she couldn't bear being outside without any clothes. And if she didn't come in soon, he was bound to come out looking for her. She stepped into the back door, dripping water on the stone tiles. And, of course, he stood there waiting for her with a big towel.

She accepted it and wrapped it around her shaking body just as he turned away and finished preparing the table. Her teeth chattered as she tucked the edge of the towel against her skin and stood at the doorway.

"I have laid out some clothes for you upstairs," he said. "Be back quickly before dinner gets too cool."

This surprised her. She was sure he would make her stand there and shiver while he talked about why it was useless to try and leave. She held the towel close around her legs as she moved through the kitchen and hurried up the stairs to her room. He had found a pair of capris and a thin T-shirt for her that she slipped on, hoping he wouldn't come through the door before she could get dressed. As soon as she pulled the T-shirt over her head, she moved to the stairs, feeling the stone of worry settle in her gut again. Another meal with him at that table, especially since she had just tried to leave, promised to be awkward.

They ate in silence, and he said nothing about the events of the afternoon. She knew that if she didn't eat, he would be there at her side again and eventually force her to do it. So, there was no point in fighting it. She finished her dinner and then took her place back in the main room as he put everything away, and then he walked outside, leaving her alone in the cabin as he milled around the car, loading it with everything for their departure tomorrow.

She rested her hands on her abdomen and watched the sun set outside the window. The unknown plan for tomorrow began to creep into her thoughts. At least in the lodge, she knew how relatively far away she was from Garnet Falls. Tomorrow, he planned to take her somewhere else, somewhere further from home, and no matter how far she tried to run he would find her.

He spent the rest of the evening out there, and she padded back up to her room, closing the door behind her. The lock was beyond repair, and it hadn't kept him out before he broke it. But closing it at least separated her from the rest of the house. She sat on the bed and stared out the window, to the moon that rose over the lake, casting a gray-white light on the surface of the water.

The moonlight gathered around her feet and touched the edges of her fingers as she gazed out the window. She wasn't one to just allow things to happen to her, but she was stuck now. There was no other alternative left but to leave with Sam in the morning, but the thought of Jason and Gideon out there made her sick with worry. She opened her hand and let the silver moonlight shine on her palm, the power of it tingling just under her skin. The fingers of her other hand caressed the skin, as though she could sense the remnants of the tattoo that had once been burned there. Maybe if she knew more sigils, she could harness a power to get her out of this mess, but the only one who could teach her was the crazy angel downstairs.

Her index finger touched the flesh of her palm as she thought about the way his fingers had touched her skin. A sudden surge of pain bored into her skin, and she flinched. When she saw the singe mark on her skin, she drew her hand into the light and examined her hand. Just like Sam, she was able to create a mark. Sure, it was only a burn, but that had to account for something.

She flashed a glance back to the door and held her breath, listening to the sounds outside her room. Nothing. No floor boards creaking. No footsteps on the landing or the stairs. Maybe Sam still had no idea what she just did.

But what could she do with it? Nothing. That's what. She had no idea what sigils she could make and what power they held.

Nikka closed her eyes and clenched her fists again, pressing them to her eyelids. Why did this feel so close to freedom, but it still left her dangling without any hope of reaching the edge?

God, help me.

The tears threatened to come again, as they so often did lately. Blame it on the hormones, but she couldn't help it.

All this power, for what? To hope that Sam would teach her the right sigils to use because she had no other way of learning.

No other way? But there was another way. Her eyes flashed open as the memories came back to her. She did know sigils; a lot of them. There were once so many of them all over her body. The memory of waking up in the basement of the hospital and examining her skin for the first time flooded her thoughts. Black, beautiful marks that inched up her arms and legs, curved over her shoulders and neck. Each one held power, and now she learned that each one gave her very specific abilities. But there had been so many of them. How would she even know what to use?

With her eyes closed, she envisioned the marks that once decorated her skin, trying to remember the details of each of them. A single mark that had been burned into her side lit up into a flare of blue light, like a flashing traffic sign. She recalled its exact form.

Was it possible? She opened her eyes and gazed down at her palm in the moonlight again. A violet light had illuminated the room, and she saw the sparkles of her tattoos shimmer in the darkness. She placed her index finger to her palm again and urged her power into etching a mark on her skin, the same mark she had pulled from her memory.

Please hear me, she thought as she felt the burn of the tattoo enter her hand. As soon as her finger lifted from the skin, the mark vanished, and she felt it take its place along her arm with a flash of purple light.

Jason, please hear me.

It was the closest thing to a prayer that she could find right now, and if this mark had the ability to communicate through time and space, then so be it.

She opened her eyes and watched the light dissipate from her tattoos, fading from violet to silver and then gone. The breath that she had held for so long now released in a slow sigh as she gazed out to the silver moon over the lake. That was all she could do for now.

The stairs creaking under footsteps drew her attention to the door, and the familiar clutching in her chest started again. She pulled the blankets back and eased down onto the pillow. Just as she moved her legs onto the bed, the door opened. She gripped at the edge of the blanket as he stood at the threshold, the moonlight falling over him. For a moment he just waited there, looking at her until he stepped across the room and to the other side of the bed. Maybe he sensed what she had just done, and the thought seized at her lungs, making it hard to breathe again. She pulled her arms around her torso, hiding the mark that had newly formed on her skin. His arm leaned across the mattress, making a deep indent in the comforter. The closer he moved to her, the more she wanted to run. The cringe started along her arms, and she couldn't help but slide away from him as soon as he moved onto the bed. Nikka moved to step out of the bed as his other arm grabbed her wrist and pulled her back.

This was the first true surge of panic she had ever had around him. "What are you doing?"

"Do not worry," he said and crawled onto the bed, situating himself on his side and resting his head back against the pillow. "I will do nothing to you, but I will not leave you alone any longer. You have abused my trust."

With his hand still around her wrist, he tugged her down to the mattress. The knot of worry turned in her gut, but she pushed it back as she eased her body down to rest next to him. She turned to her side, facing away from him and looked out the window, but she could still hear him breathing next to her, and the scent of lavender and trees drifted into her senses.

As his breathing grew even and slow, she tucked her hands under her head and watched out the window. With him sleeping right there, she couldn't get comfortable enough to close her eyes. Her feet still throbbed with the blisters that had formed in her attempt to get away. That, plus the little movements in her abdomen, pulled her to the point of tears. There was no way to get away from him, and the thought of giving birth to her baby with him at her side made her sick.

The new mark still tingled against her skin, but other than bearing a fresh tattoo, she had sensed no other power with it. The hope of letting it communicate with Jason diminished as the last sensations within the mark vanished. Her fingers clenched into fists as she realized that even if she could send a message out to Jason, he may not recognize it. But Gideon might.

She had tried not to think about him ever since Samael gave her memories back to her. All that he had done to her made her nauseous, and she just wanted to put it in the past and never really think about him again. But he was also of the demon realm, and he would know a vision when he saw it.

As she listened to Sam's quiet breathing, she knew he slept. Now was the time to try and use the mark she had just created. The energy around her and in the moonlight that fell through the window was enough to pull into her fingertips as she felt the new mark zap to life in her flesh. She closed her eyes, feeling the power flow smoothly into her hands but keeping it steady and low for fear of waking Sam. Images of her present location formed in her brain. The cabin. The long road she had used to attempt an escape. The aluminum numbers nailed to the mail box at the end of the drive. Anything that would show Gideon where she was living.

Come on, Gideon, she thought. *I know you're out there.*

Chapter Forty-Seven

Gideon

A dark gray mist covered the ground and meandered at the base of the aspen trees along the hill. Moonlight fell through the leaves, but the shadows continued to creep along the floor of the forest, drifting down a hill until they spilled out onto an empty road.

When Gideon opened his eyes, he had not seen the road at first. Only the trees and the mist that trickled through the brush. Everything here was cold and dark, like looking at the woods from another world. Like looking at it from Hell.

Beads of sweat formed on his brow, not from heat but from the possibility that he could be lost again, taken from the world and thrust back into that place he had tried so hard to escape. Only, here there was no sound. Just shadows and silver light that fell on everything, leaving it cold and bleak.

He turned and looked down the road that wandered and disappeared into the woods ahead. The way his body moved felt like he was stuck in water and that if he wanted to run he would never be able to get the momentum.

It was a dream.

But in the dreams he had seen since he had obtained the soul Nikka thrust upon him, he had never been able to smell anything. In all this darkness, he could smell the faintest hint of lavender that laced the edge of the mist.

Something else was here with him.

The mist collected at his feet, falling over the surface of the road and obscuring his path. His feet grew cold and numb as the fog thickened and rose up his shins and to his knees. When he tried to move, the fog held him in place like mud.

Can't leave.

He was sure that he had not actually heard anything, but the sound came from his thoughts, only they were not his own.

I'm here.

Then the sound of the forest came to life as a breeze drifted through the trees, rustling the branches in a murmur of whispers. The breeze turned into a wind, pulling at his clothes and making the mist at his feet whirl around his body as though it was ready to pull him under. A flash of light came from the spinning fog like a burst of lightning, but it was a brilliant violet-white that nearly blinded him with each burst.

Such bright purple light mixed with the scent of lavender meant one thing. An archangel.

Help me.

This time he knew he heard a voice, and he recognized it immediately. Nikka.

He was mistaken. This was no dream. She called to him from somewhere out in the woods, and she showed him what he needed to know. A cabin surrounded by trees. A lake in the back. The vision was weak, but she made the message clear enough.

Gideon bolted up from his bed, the last images clearing from his mind. He breathed fast as sweat had formed on his forehead, but he closed his eyes again, memorizing every detail of the vision before it began to fade.

Chapter Forty-Eight

Nikka

When her eyes opened, she wasn't aware that she had fallen asleep at first, but she must have because the moonlight in the window had dimmed, plunging the room into darkness. She lifted her head from the pillow and realized that she could no longer hear Sam breathing behind her. Nikka held her breath and leaned back enough to see that she was the only one in the bed.

She sat up and glanced at the door, where she could see a faint yellow glow shine in the space between the door and the floor. Not that she wasn't grateful to have him out of her room, she felt the twinge of anxiety that began to build in her chest. At this late hour of the night, he had left her alone and was now downstairs. She rose from the bed and clutched the doorknob slowly enough to keep it silent when she pulled the knob. The door opened without a sound and she peered through the space that looked out to the main room.

The room was lit with a faint light, probably a flashlight or lantern that cast dim shadows over the walls and the fireplace. Nikka pressed against the door frame and let the door fall open enough to look out to the empty landing.

That was when she heard Sam speaking. Her heart raced at first, afraid that he had heard her. But then she heard another voice answering him in return. Somebody else was down there. She let the door open a little more and craned her neck out to hear them better.

A man's voice and it sounded familiar.

She stepped out to the landing and looked down over the railing into the main room. The light had come from the kitchen area, and whoever was down there with Sam stood out of her view.

Her fingers tightened around the railing when she felt a chill rise from the lower room. At first, it was subtle, but it grew as it extended to the landing and chilled her bare feet. It was the kind of cold that she would never forget since she had felt it enough times to recognize it. It didn't matter now that Sam was down there or if he could hear her. There was something with him, but he and the man kept talking.

"We are leaving in just a few hours," Sam said.

"It will be happening soon, then," the other man said.

"Twenty-four, maybe forty-eight hours, but yes," Sam said. "Very soon."

"And we still have a deal?"

"Of course. Once I have the baby, we will make the final preparations. And then we wait for Ascension."

"But our deal? I found her, I told you where she was," the man said. "I will have Redemption at your side."

"Yes. Just as I promised."

She moved out to the stairway and felt the shaking begin in her knees. The tattoo on her chest began to glow, faint at first, but it tingled and sparkled against her will as she descended to the main floor. From the base of the stairs, she saw Sam standing in the kitchen, his back to her and there was someone else across from him, out of her line of sight. The cold grew more intense with each step she took toward them.

As she moved around the couch, Sam finally turned when he heard her step into the living room. That was the moment she saw it.

Sam looked at her, his eyes as icy as ever, and she saw his hands ball into fists. There was no hiding it now. Across the kitchen from him, the other man pulled away from the counter where he had casually leaned until he met her gaze. She would recognize him anywhere: his black hair molded into a near-mohawk with streaks of red, the way he left his black shirt unbuttoned like he was a rock god. Belphagor.

The anger boiled in her chest the moment she saw him and the pleased grin that formed on his lips. A flash of ember orange appeared in his eyes.

"You!" she said the moment she saw him. She remembered that smile when he looked down on her just before he had been ready to cut her baby out of her body. It was the same when he tore her shirt away from her chest in the rain to expose her tattoo.

Sam stepped toward her. "Let me explain."

Nikka took a single step back, her hands shaking more out of anger than fear. Then it built on itself without her even trying. The energy flowed through her feet and into her hands with such little effort that at first, she didn't recognize that it was even happening. Her tattoo shined with a bright violet light, and her vision changed, feeling the light coming from her own eyes.

Sam's face contorted and she could sense that he was coming at her now. But it didn't matter. The energy exploded from her hands, and she braced her feet just as it happened. The power rushed toward Belphagor, and he couldn't move fast enough to escape it. It hit him in the chest, and he fell back just as Sam rushed at her. His arms reached for her and had her on the ground before Belphagor's body hit the floor.

The light left her fingers and her tattoo as quickly as it had formed. The aftershocks of it still rippled along her body, leaving her hands numb and shaking. Sam held her down, but he also glanced back, and his grip wasn't nearly as firm or painful as she had expected.

His eyes turned toward her, and for a moment she swore she could see a glimmer of fear.

"What did you do?" he said, his voice even but with a hint of concern.

The walls of the cabin shuddered, and the cold grew more intense. The windows rattled in their frames, and the shelves along the wall in the main room shook until the trinkets on them fell to the ground. Sam glanced around them to the shadows that stretched across the house from the flashlight's single beam on the kitchen table. A sound like a moan moved through those shadows, bouncing around the walls and then retreating back into the corner like a caged beast.

Sam grabbed her arm and pulled her back up, but he didn't release her. Instead, he dragged her through the kitchen and forced her to crouch with him beside the still body that Belphagor had inhabited. Now it was empty, just like the moment when Sam's body had stilled when she forced the angel from it. He pulled her arm forward and pressed the palm of her hand to the man's chest. Under her fingers, she still felt the in and out movement of air. He was still alive, but just barely.

"That was very good," Sam said, his eyes now flashing to her, excited. She tried to pull away from him, but he held her hand pressed to the body. "Now, put him back inside."

"What? No," she said and tried even harder to pull away. She just had forced the demon out of that man, and not just any demon—Belphagor, a lieutenant. The very demon that had stolen her from Garnet Falls, the one who had tried to take her baby.

Sam's eyes narrowed, changed from excited to grim. "Do it now. Or . . ." he said but was interrupted by the disembodied growl that came from the shadows in the room behind them. Nikka glanced back, afraid that she would see a monster creeping up on them from the dark. "Or he will haunt this place until he gets back in there himself."

His nails dug into the skin of her arm as he held her there. She had no idea how to put a demon back into a human body, and she had never wanted to know. This was against everything she had learned since becoming a seraph. She was sure, though, that Sam would never let her go unless she did this.

"I can always make you," he said, his voice eerie and calm. His other hand rose and touched his index finger to the mark on her chest. "I do not wish to force you into anything, but I will if I have to."

Another tug against his hand made his eyes narrow. The burn of his fingertip started against her chest where he touched her, and she struggled even harder to pull away from him. Despite her cries, he continued to etch something into her skin.

The pain of it was far worse than the marks he had been putting into her hands. This tattoo burrowed into her chest, deep inside her ribs as though it seared against the bone and not just her skin. Her eyes watered as she bit her lip against the pain, not wanting him to hear her screams any longer.

As soon as he lifted his hand, the power of the mark settled further into her body. Ringing sounded in her ears, and the rattling in the darkest shadows of the room plunged into a muffled noise. She stopped tugging against his grip. She wanted to pull away from him, but she couldn't do it anymore, as though her limbs wouldn't respond to her own will.

"Nikka," he said. The words echoed in her brain as though he spoke to her through a long tunnel. "Put him back in this body."

She tried to force her arm to pull away again, but her body was no longer her own. "What did you do to me?"

"A binding sigil," he said. "One of my own creation. Now put Belphagor back into this body."

Her mind screamed at her to stop, but her eyes turned down to the man who lay beside her. The fingers stretched out over his chest didn't feel like hers, but she knew they were. The energy tingled in her hands first, building into a collection just under the palm of her hand, hovering in the space where her hand met the body. She no longer had control of the power that pulled through her center. It tingled and zapped at her fingertips as the power searched in the darkened room behind her for an entity that lingered in there. The demon stayed just out of the light, gaping and writhing in the shadows. Its energy was tainted and sticky, like spoiled tar that would never wash clean from her skin. Like a beacon, her power encouraged the demon to course through her body, along the streams of energy that she became so familiar with, but it left its claw marks along the way. The cold entered her limbs, and she cringed as it moved into her hands. The energy forced it harder, like purging it from her body and emptying it into the man on the floor.

His eyes flew wide, and his mouth gaped with a silent scream as he gasped for air. The orange glow returned to his eyes as his back arched painfully. The muscles along his bare chest flexed as he howled with his next breath.

Sam pulled her away as though he sensed what was going to happen. Belphagor growled and leaped to his feet, his orange eyes training in the dark until he found her. She felt her own will return to her limbs as she reacted to his anger. He leaped toward her, his lips twisted in a snarl, but Sam stepped in the way, shoving him back with the strength that only an angel could gather against a demon. Sam's other hand reached back around to hold her protectively close to him, and the pull to remain close to the angel disturbed her. She knew that even if she wanted to get away from him that she would have no will of her own to do it.

Belphagor collected his strength again and moved to leap at her once more.

"Stop," Sam said and held his arm out toward the demon, but this time she could see ribbons of violet light coursing down his arms.

Belphagor halted his progress, but his orange eyes still watched her. His jaw tightened like a hyena ready to devour its prey.

"You will not touch her," Sam said, his voice booming.

"She'll pay for that," the demon hissed, the muscles in his shoulders rippling with anger.

"I can destroy you." Sam still held his other hand around her, firm and protective. "Do not make me regret bringing you into this."

The snarl slipped from Belphagor's face, and his shoulders loosened enough for him to stand upright, but the orange glow remained in his pupils. "Very well. But I will not allow it to happen again."

The violet around Sam faded, plunging them back into the dim light of the flashlight. Sam's guarding hand softened as he turned back toward her, keeping his eyes on Belphagor as he did so. He reached back for her, and she tried to step away from him, but her legs wouldn't move. His fingers curled around her hand and drew it up to his chest. For the last few days, she had grown concerned about his behavior, and there were times when she was afraid. But now she was too angry to fear him anymore. With the magic of the binding sigil and the presence of the demon in the house, she knew that he had lied to her this whole time. He had been working with Belphagor from the beginning, and whatever their plan was, she and her baby were the central core of it.

"How could you do this?" she said. She was still able to hate him even if she couldn't escape him.

Sam looked back at her and reached his hand to the mark on her chest. "Nikka, I never wanted to do this to you." His palm touched the tattoo, making the mark heat against her flesh. A sudden pulse of light from his hand and the heavy pull in her limbs had vanished. He removed his hand, revealing the original mark. The binding sigil was gone.

A quick gasp filled her lungs as soon as she was free of the spell. His hand moved to touch her face, but she slapped his arm away from him. "I hate you."

His eyes turned cold, his head tilting downward as he stared at her. She backed away from him, but he moved toward her. Just as he came within arm's reach, she saw his eyes change. They turned black, just like the demons' did as they revealed themselves, but a bright purple light emanated from the center of the dark oil, the edges rippling with threads of electric light. The last thing she saw was his hand reaching toward her face when a bright violet light blinded her and then plunged her into darkness.

Chapter Forty-Nine

Nikka

A blanket of fog covered everything, thick and choking and heavy with substance. It poured into her lungs like water in the pool where she drowned. But her ribs fought against it, pulling more of it deeper into her chest. Her feet wouldn't move, wouldn't obey anything that she wanted them to do. At first, she thought that Sam had placed another binding sigil on her, but that couldn't explain the fog. This was the moment she knew that she stood within a vision.

And somewhere in that fog, she felt another person there, just beyond her sight. It wasn't Samael. She would have been able to see his purple and black aura through the murk that surrounded her. For these few seconds, she knew that she lived in that in-between place where he wouldn't find her, but somebody else could.

She reached her hand out into the dark. Whoever waited there looked for her too, and maybe she could at least touch him and let him know she was here. Her hand disappeared into the thick fog like searching through a deep puddle of mud, her arm buried up to her shoulder.

Then she made contact with another hand, the warm fingers grasping around her palm. The other hand pulled at her . . ..

Her eyes flew open with the last tug on her hand. Midday light poured down on her from the large panel of windows that looked out onto a bleak and empty town. She leaned up on her elbows from where she lay on a mattress covered in white sheets, but it wasn't just some normal bed. It had side rails and buttons. A hospital bed.

She squinted against the light and turned on her side, where she saw a dark form standing next to the bed. The blurry figure soon came into view, and she reeled back against the railing when she looked into Belphagor's black-rimmed eyes.

A painful grip tightened around her ankle as she jumped back and the clink of a chain echoed throughout the room. She glanced down to see thick links of steel locked around her ankle, probably tethering her to the bed. Her heart raced enough to clear her head, and she sat up, her back pressed against the wall as she finally met Belphagor's gaze again. He paced around the edge of the bed, watching her like a cat as he glided back and forth. The cold fell from his shoulders and arms as he moved, drifting toward her bare feet.

The wall behind him drooped with torn beige wallpaper spotted with circles of brown water stains. Like a patchwork of the former electronic world, silver-rimmed electrical outlets dotted through the wallpaper, some marked for oxygen connections or a suction canister, standard for any routine hospital room. A single door gaped open to a barren hallway. Even though this place had probably not been used in months, it still held onto the clean, antiseptic scent that laced the sheets.

And the one thing that was missing: Samael.

Belphagor stopped his pacing and leaned his head down as he feigned a look of concern. "Are you looking for him? He's not here. Had to leave and collect a few things to get ready for your big arrival." He shot a glance down to her abdomen. "So he left you here under my watch."

Her fingers tightened into fists as he looked down on her with his smug grin. Just as she felt a surge of energy pour into her arms, he moved fast, climbing over the bed and wrapping his cold hand around her throat. His face was only inches from hers, the orange ember glow of his eyes returning and his lips curled into a snarl.

"Don't even think about doing what you did back in the cabin," he growled at her. "Samael may not want me to kill you, but I can mess you up beyond recognition. He never said I couldn't take an eye or your tongue." His other fingers snapped just in front of her face, acting like he could make true on his promise. His hand tightened around her throat, cutting off her air supply. She clutched at his wrist and bucked against his grip. Those orange eyes burned as he gazed at her struggling for a breath.

His face softened as he watched her struggle against him. As her fingers clutched at him, he finally loosened his grip. The air burned into her throat as she gasped for a breath and watched him back away from her.

"You wouldn't get far anyway," he said and nodded his head to the chain locked with a padlock on her ankle. "Samael's idea, not mine. I told him he should have just replaced the binding sigil."

Her throat tightened into a cough until the gag came, but the oxygen reached her brain and stopped the sparkles that had started behind her eyes. When her throat no longer felt raw, she looked up at him as he had begun his pacing again.

"Why are you even here?" she said through a hoarse voice. "What do you care what he thinks?"

He stopped and looked at her with a wide smile, the strands of black and cherry-red hair falling over his left eye. His hand wrapped over the back of a folding chair next to the bed and pulled it toward him. He straddled it backwards as he looked at her, his arms resting over the back of the chair.

"Well, I know that he never told you about me in all this," he said. "Angels are all so high and mighty on themselves, thinking that they are the only ones who have the right to do anything. But he is just as much a pawn in all this as the rest of us."

"You are nothing like him," she said, each word burning as it passed her throat.

He laughed. "You have no idea how alike we actually are. You see, all this," he said, opening his arms wide, "this is just one big chess game. Samael and I are just pawns. But you, you're the King, and that baby is the checkmate."

The smugness about him made her stomach turn, and the way he was so pleased with himself made her want to hit him just for fun, but he was right. The chain held too tight, and unless he unlocked her, she wasn't going anywhere.

"Whoever captures the King and gets the checkmate wins." His voice dropped, and the smile slipped from his face. "I guarantee that Samael never told you about the plans for the baby, did he?"

The only thing that Sam had ever said was that he intended on keeping her and the baby safe. At least she had believed him on that point.

"What plans?" she asked.

"Oh, this is too rich," he said and laughed again, but his smile had slipped away. "There is a revolution going on in Heaven right now, and it's all because of you."

"What are you talking about?" The baby moved, and this triggered a contraction that took her breath away. Her hand shifted to her abdomen until the cramp released.

"He would definitely not want me to tell you this," he said, and then his eyes narrowed. "But I never promised him anything. This thing in Heaven started because he jumped his place. He was a Watcher. All he was supposed to do was take orders and keep his eye on the next seraph. But he went off and did his own thing because he had already planned it."

"Is there a point to all of this?" she said and glared at him.

"Sweetie, you weren't supposed to be the seraph. Your boy Jason was next in line. But then Samael interfered, sent the wrong message and you were picked instead. That left Jason vulnerable, and Abaddon found him; figured he could take him before the archangels realized what had happened."

The mention of the demon's name sent chills into her core.

"You're a liar," she said and turned her eyes away from him.

"I'm the only one who has ever told you the truth."

Her body shuddered, feeling cold both from his words and the chill that came off of him being so close to her. The memories of Jason being possessed made her head spin. "And why should I believe you?"

"Because that's what got you into this mess to begin with. Samael continued to manipulate you, all of us until he got everything into position just the way he planned. All of this—this apocalyptic world you now live in— this is his doing."

She shot forward, not afraid of him sitting there or the chain holding her to the bed. "That's not true. He warned me about it in order for me to stop it."

"And that was the plan," Belphagor said, leaning toward her until she could smell the decay on his breath. "He worked with certain demon factions to get the EMP in play, to get it where it needed to be. He never intended on you stopping it."

"Why would he do that?"

"Because it put you right in the position he needed. He put you and the other seraph together. It was he that gave you the power to free Jason in the first place. No other seraph had removed a general before. He arranged to keep you two together. And then he could have an offspring of two seraphs, the final piece in the game."

Belphagor was a demon, one of the darkest she had ever seen, and his words made her sick. But how would he know all of this if someone hadn't told him all along?

"That can't be true," she whispered, mostly to herself, but the demon tilted his head to the side. "It doesn't make any sense."

"It does when you know that Samael has been staging a revolt since before he made you. He hated the seraph, someone who always had more power than he did in his angelic form. The archangels can fight Lucifer's forces, and at the gates of Heaven, that's why demons like me can never return. But we can live here. Earth is an open battle ground, free for the taking, but the angels have strict orders to stay out. He's tired of being told what to do, so he made you. You're his little Frankenstein monster, and with the child of two seraphs, it's something he can mold to fight for him."

Maybe another contraction pulled at her insides, but her stomach threatened to spasm on her. She sat back on the bed and pressed against the wall. Belphagor didn't have to say it; she knew what came next.

"But there was a problem, wasn't there?" she said, her words coming out in a sigh.

"You got it," he said. "Lucifer got wind of Samael's little act of rebellion. So he moved his own pawn into place."

She closed her eyes and recalled the memory of the night that changed everything. "Gideon."

"Pazuzu." Belphagor corrected her, speaking the name with great reverence. "Lucifer figured he could do the same thing to have an upper hand here on Earth. He sent Pazuzu in with strict orders to ensure that he had his dice in the game."

"Half seraph—"

"Half demon," he finished.

Her hand covered her eyes. She didn't want to cry in front of this demon, but everything he said made so much sense. The trembling started in her arms and affected her fingers.

"So now we wait," he said.

"And what do you get out of all this?"

"Me?" She heard the smile in his voice. "Redemption. I've been the informant for him in exchange for redemption."

"Why would you want to go back to Heaven? They'll destroy you the moment you get there." She opened her eyes and looked at him.

"It's all in the way you play the game. Truthfully, I don't care whichever side wins, just as long as I'm on the winning team. With a key to Heaven, I at least have a choice. And now, I'm on Samael's right hand."

A contraction tightened again, and she winced with the cramping that started in her pelvis. As it began to loosen, she shot him a glance.

"So what happens to me? What if this baby is Gideon's?"

For only a second, the ember glow flashed in his eyes and then vanished, like it was a single moment of absolute enjoyment for him. "Samael will tear it to pieces."

She looked away from him and down to her abdomen.

"And if it is Jason's, he will take it and raise it as his own. And you—he expects you to fight at his side as his companion. He believes you will be his own special weapon, half-human, half-archangel."

"Why are you telling me all this?"

The smile returned again. "Because I will be on the winning side; so I'm leveling out the playing field. I don't want any surprises. I hate you. I hate him. So I don't care what he wants me to do. I will be the one standing at the end after all the chips have fallen, then we'll see."

A flash of light from the hallway drew her attention, and Belphagor became silent, glancing behind him. Then he turned toward her again, his eyes narrowed and sinister.

"He's back," he whispered with a twisted grin. "And you're not gonna like this."

Chapter Fifty

Nikka

Sam stepped into the threshold of the open door. At first, his eyes glanced to Belphagor and then to Nikka, as if he expected to see that the demon had abused her after all. He remained still for a moment, looking over her and to the restraint on her ankle.

Seeing him standing there made her angry. Everything that Belphagor had just told her rummaged in her thoughts as she remembered the events that had brought her this far. Sam's icy, soulless stare looked her over and then he looked at her abdomen. This made her cringe, and she placed her hands over her stomach.

He stepped into the room and around Belphagor. "Is everything all right in here?"

"A-OK, boss," the demon said with a wink toward Nikka. He stood and shoved the chair aside. "She's all yours."

As Belphagor slipped out of the room, she saw him give her one last glance before he disappeared into the hallway and Sam moved to the edge of the bed.

"I am sorry I had to leave you in his care," he said and moved his hand to her abdomen.

The way he touched her now, as though she was his property, made her want to squirm away. But he had no idea what the demon had just revealed to her. If he only knew, he might act out against her.

Another contraction tightened around her belly. They were coming so close together now and not really letting up much since she awoke in this place. As it tightened, she could only think to protect the baby, no matter what, but how could she possibly do that with a demon and an angel watching her every move?

His hand moved to her face, which had now twisted in a pained grimace with the contraction. "I know, my dear. It hurts, but that means the baby is coming soon."

That's what she was afraid of.

"Just breathe through it," he said. "Let it happen."

The contraction loosened, but the strength of it left her eyes watering. As soon as she could speak, she looked up at him.

"I can't have my baby here," she said, her eyes pleading, hoping that he might at least loosen the chain.

"This is the best place available," he said. "A hospital. It has everything we need. I retrieved some fresh water. I have found clean linens for you. This is the most appropriate place we could possibly be."

"I don't want to do this." She felt her body shudder as tears began to flood her eyes. He moved toward her, pulling her into an embrace that felt like stone against his chest. Although he tried to comfort her, she wanted to be as far away from him as possible.

His hand moved to her abdomen again as he pulled away from her. The icy stare locked her into his gaze. "You must be strong, Nikka." The pressure from his hand grew as his touch warmed. She saw the edges of his hand illuminate with violet light, drawing the heat into her core. Another contraction started, this one even stronger than the last. The light around his hand flashed bright for only a second, triggering a sharp increase in the cramping.

"It has begun," he said and released his touch. He stood at the edge of the bed and watched her as she doubled over her abdomen.

The pain held like a vice around her middle, pulling from her back. She cried out with the cramping as it forced the baby further into her pelvis. Then it began to release, letting her catch her breath again.

"What did you do?" she said, gasping for air.

He looked down at her without any hint of emotion in his angelic face. "I started what needed to be done." His fingers reached into the pocket of his jeans and produced a key. He unlocked the chain at her ankle, letting it fall to the ground with a loud clank. Then he held out his hand to her. "Now come. I have reinforcements that I want you to introduce into this world."

There would be no running from him now, not with the contractions building into such strong cramps that nearly brought her to her knees. She took his hand and stood up from the bed, her legs weak from the last contraction. He put a hand around her back and supported her as they walked into the darkened corridor. He led her toward an open, rounded lobby with large windows that overlooked a bare parking lot. Sofas lined the walls, and dusty framed pictures of women holding newborn babies still hung between the windows. All of these things seemed so benign until she saw the person sitting in a single chair in the center of the room. It was a woman, her face covered by a black cloth sack over her head. Her hands were tied behind her back and lashed to the chair. The woman's shoulders shuddered with sobs that were muffled under the mask.

Nikka's footsteps froze, but Sam pushed her forward with him, his fingers clutching at her side and digging into her flesh.

"One last trial," he said and forced her into the lobby with his new captive.

"What is this?" she said, the tremors starting in her hands.

He released her and stepped behind the tied woman, resting his hands on her shoulders. "I want to see if you can do this as well, and I wish for you to do it willingly. Please do not make me bind you again. I have more of my kind ready to re-enter this world. I want you to help me cross them over into this world, and I have brought her as a host."

"Are you saying you want me to help possess her with an angel?" she said.

"Exactly."

A contraction started in her back and almost brought her to her knees. She groaned with the pain that ripped through her pelvis and took her breath away.

Belphagor stepped into the room, his hands in his pockets as he watched her with a grin. She felt him enter, even though she didn't see him at first. The cold that followed in his wake drilled waves of chills into her back despite the heat of the contraction that started to abate.

"You were able to put a demon back into the body," Sam said. "Now I want to see you put an angel into this one."

As soon as the contraction released its grip on her spine, she stood straighter and looked at Sam. His hand moved to the cloth over the woman's face and pulled it free.

Nikka's knees wobbled for a moment as she saw the woman—her familiar red hair and green eyes.

Sam moved back around behind Nikka as she looked at Amy tied to the chair and her mouth gagged. The angel wrapped his arms around Nikka, his hands moving to her forearms and forcing her toward the woman in the chair.

"What did you do?" Nikka muttered as her feet slid forward under Sam's coercion.

"What I must do," he said, his breath warm against her ear. "As the host to one of my kind, she will be protected and loved. She will welcome my friend's embrace. Is that not what you desire for your friends?"

Amy looked at her, her eyes finally adjusting to the light. The veil of recognition fell across her face as she saw Nikka standing before her. She tugged and pulled at the binds against her wrists, but she could barely move in the chair.

Sam grasped Nikka's wrist and pulled her arm outward toward Amy. "Just as you did with the demon, feel the power of the angel that is here with us now, waiting to enter your world."

Nikka tried to free her arm from his grasp, but he held her so tight now, and she feared that he would just burn another sigil into her chest again. "Please don't make me do this."

Amy's eyes were wet and red like she had been crying the entire time she had been in Sam's presence. Nikka could only imagine it was something like the moment he had found her in the power plant, tied down to the gurney and the demons ready to cut the baby from her. So much light and terrifying noise. Sam pushed her forward until her palm had pressed against Amy's chest, her fingers splayed.

Nikka didn't try to withdraw from him anymore. She felt the trembling movements of Amy's body under her hand as Sam loosened his grip and moved away from her. The baby twitched inside her, a little burst of a kick between the contractions that pulled her deeper into the pain. Her hand didn't waver, though.

Sam and Belphagor stood behind her, waiting to see what she could do. In the recesses of the room, she could feel another presence lingering in the sparkling light that filtered through the windows. Unlike a disembodied demon, it stayed away from the shadows. It felt like a summer breeze that dwelled in the shade of a tree. She sensed its movements from window to window, circling them and waiting for her to act.

She held her arm steady, her fingers pressed to Amy's warm flesh. Nikka knew that if she looked into Amy's eyes, that any resolve she might have to do this would melt away, but with the two that watched her from the other side of the room, she had no choice but to pull that energy into her body. Sam would never let Amy go, not unless she did something now.

Nikka took in a steady breath and did what she knew she had to do. Her eyes drifted up to Amy's. The woman continued to cry, her shoulders shaking and the tears soaking the cloth gag wrapped around her jaw. Nikka locked her into her gaze, and soon Amy stilled long enough to see her through the tears. To really see her.

The first trickle of energy came through the floor, but then she pulled it fast from the sunlight that fell into the room. The angel that hovered in the space between worlds had its own energy as well, something powerful and almost too difficult to contain. But she pulled it in also, since it wanted to be channeled so badly. The power rolled and warped on itself, so strong that she had never felt this much power all at once, not even the time she disembodied Belphagor.

It had to be enough.

The moment the power recoiled on itself, the violet light sparked in her eyes and Amy saw it. Her chest stopped moving as she held her breath.

It was time.

Nikka turned and let the energy flow from her body like a tornado of light and power. The windows shattered with the force as it emanated from her arms and struck both the demon and the angel that stood at watch. They had not been prepared for the impact, and they fell back, striking the wall behind them and collapsing to the ground. The angel that she had held inside her had vanished as well, forced back into whatever dimension it had come through. As strong as it was, though, she knew it would eventually be back.

With the falling of the last shards of glass, she turned back to Amy and pulled the gag from her mouth.

"What did you just do?" Amy said with a gasp.

Nikka moved quickly behind her and untied the rope that bound her wrists. "What I had to, but we don't have a lot of time."

As soon as the rope loosened, Amy shook it free and stood up from the chair. Amy turned back to her when a contraction started, taking her breath away. Nikka doubled over, groaning as it squeezed into her pelvis.

"Oh no," Amy said.

Damn straight, oh no. The power of the contraction made her crouch, taking away her breath, as Amy placed a hand on her back.

"You gotta go," Nikka said with a grunt at the peak of the contraction.

"I know, but I'm not leaving you here like this."

The contraction began to ease as Amy rubbed her back. When she could take in a deeper breath, Nikka stood straighter and faced her. "Let's get out of here."

They moved together into the corridor and down a stairwell to the ground floor. Nikka hoped the car was still in the parking lot because she was certain that she didn't have the ability to walk away like she did last time, and that hadn't worked out so well for her anyway. They emerged onto the main lobby floor and stepped out to the barren parking lot, where the sedan waited for them.

"You got the keys?" Amy said as she looked at the car.

"No need," Nikka said and stepped up to the vehicle, placing her hand on the hood just as she had learned from Sam. She forced enough energy into her body to kick the engine to life.

Amy smiled and headed toward the driver's side. "I'm driving. You're in no condition."

Nikka wasn't about to argue. The last contraction still lingered, the pressure in her pelvis never really letting up this time. She slid into the passenger's seat, and Amy drove out of the parking lot with tires squealing. The car swerved out of the lot and onto a street that plunged directly into the heart of a small city.

"Do you know where we are?" Nikka said, feeling another contraction coming on.

"I think so," Amy said, driving between the abandoned cars along the street. "We're about fifty miles or so from Garnet Falls. I recognize the mountain range to the west."

She banked right down another street, and Nikka moaned as she felt the pain intensify.

"They're pretty close now, the contractions," Amy said, shooting her a knowing glance.

Nikka breathed out through pursed lips, her hands on the dashboard trying to keep her body steady as the car moved. "Tell me something I don't know."

"Need me to pull over?"

"No," she said, louder than she had hoped. "Just keep going as fast as you can."

"Okay," Amy said and bit her lip as she stepped on the gas. The engine roared as they raced down the street of the abandoned shopping district. "Who were those guys? What did they want with us?"

The end of the contraction eased up, and Nikka sat back into the seat. "Angel, demon. They want the baby."

The car surged forward harder as Amy pressed further on the gas. "Jason and Gideon have been out there searching for you every day. I know they can't be far."

"Just go," Nikka said, her mouth feeling dry. "Get as far away from these guys as possible."

"But you killed them, right?"

She shook her head. "Just stunned them. They'll be looking for us."

Amy shot her a wide-eyed glance. She maneuvered the vehicle between stalled cars at a dead traffic light and pressed the gas as the road wound to the north of a large empty parking lot surrounding a shopping mall. Leafy trees lined the road on either side, but the grass along the lawns had grown brown and long. The car came around the lot, and just as she turned on the street heading west, the engine sputtered.

"No," Amy said, her eyes flashing down to the gauges. "No, no. Shit," she shouted.

A contraction started again.

"What is it?" Nikka said before the pain had her in its grip.

The car sputtered again, and the engine began to rattle.

"Gas is empty," she said as the car rolled to a stop. Her fists slammed against the steering wheel as she let out another string of swear words that Nikka never would have thought she could say.

But she wanted to say them now herself as she cried with the contraction.

Amy jumped out of the car. Although Nikka tried breathing steadily with this contraction, she glanced at the side mirror and saw that Amy had opened the trunk. Nikka clenched her teeth as the tightening burned across her abdomen. It squeezed like a vice for what seemed like five minutes before it finally began to ease. When she had caught her breath, the sound of Amy's footsteps around the side of the car caught her attention. The passenger door opened and Amy stood there.

She held out her hand to Nikka. "Come on. We've got to get to some cover."

As Nikka pulled herself out of the car, she saw an orange gun in Amy's hand along with a crowbar. Amy moved with her as they hurried across the parking lot and toward the empty mall. After another contraction made her stop in her tracks, Nikka collected her strength again and ran with her to a side entrance to the building.

Releasing Nikka's hand, Amy rushed to a boarded window and pried back the wood, revealing a large, tinted window that looked into a department store. She smashed the glass in, sending showers of tinted splinters across the ground. Bracing over the edge of the windows, she climbed in first and then helped Nikka inside the dark, closed-up building.

They moved through the aisles of fallen clothing racks and shattered display cases. When the EMP hit, places like this had been looted first, and this department store was no exception. Not that any of this stuff would have value in the aftermath, but it had left the place in disarray. They hurried through the store and emerged out into the wide corridor that arched through the center of the building, the walkway to access any store. Skylights in the ceiling provided enough light to the ceramic tiles on the ground, showing them the main floor and a second floor of shops above that.

The pain started in her abdomen again, and she nearly pulled Amy down with her as she collapsed to her knees.

"Nikka," Amy said, her voice trying to stay calm as she placed a hand on her back. "Just breathe with them. Like this." She pursed her lips and breathed in through her nose and out through her mouth. "You've gotta breathe through it each time. It helps with the pain."

She watched her and tried to mimic it, controlling the breath through the peak of the contraction. It didn't make the pain go away, but she felt better control over the tightening of the muscles in her shoulders and her chest. She watched Amy the whole time as she coached her through the contraction, one hand gripped with hers.

"We need to hide," Amy said, her eyes scanning the expanse of the abandoned mall before them.

Nikka rose on her feet again, the muscles in her legs like jelly. She wanted to go with Amy, but she knew it was futile. She could barely move, and Sam would be looking for them in a short while.

"You need to go. Just run and don't turn back," Nikka said.

Amy's eyes narrowed. "I won't leave you. Now come on, I've got a plan."

She gripped Nikka's hand and pulled her down the corridor. They hurried beyond a silent water fountain in the center of the walkway, tiled in white ceramic that had gone green with algae that now sat in the bottom of the festering pool of water. They moved as Amy glanced at the variety of darkened shops, most with the crisscross metal gates dropped down and locked to avoid any looting. Some of the gates had been torn open, though, with items strewn into the hall and the shops trashed. They emerged into the former food court, and Nikka gazed up at the wide skylight that allowed more illumination of their space. From here she saw a wide staircase that wrapped behind an elevator bank opening to the second floor. She followed Amy's gaze up to the next floor and saw the edge of a sporting goods store.

"Let's try it," Amy said and sprinted up the stairs, letting Nikka take the steps at her own pace until she reached the upper level when another contraction started.

The metal gate to the shop had been locked, but Amy pried it open with the crowbar. The gate ratcheted upward with a sound that echoed down the hallway. Then she plunged into the dark of the store while Nikka hunched over, breathing just as Amy had instructed. By the end of the contraction, Amy emerged from the store and found her.

"It's good," she said, and Nikka stood straighter, following her under the partially opened gate and into the store.

The smell of leather and canvas filled her acute senses as they wandered between the rows of hunting gear bordered by bicycling and running equipment. She followed Amy to the back of the store, collecting some items along the way, but Nikka couldn't see what she had through the rush and confusion. They came upon a door in the back, and Amy flicked on a flashlight, something that she must have grabbed on her rush through the store.

It was an office with a broad cushioned sofa and a single desk with a chair.

"This will do for now," Amy said as Nikka entered the room and settled down on the sofa. Amy moved into the room, dropping the things onto the floor that she had collected. Thermal blankets. More flashlights. A gallon of water and a baseball bat.

"Okay," she said, almost out of breath. "Just stay here. I'll be right back."

"Wait," Nikka said, grabbing her wrist before she could go. "What are you going to do?"

Amy raised her other hand and held out the orange gun in her hand, the one she had taken from the back of the car. It looked like a toy with a large barrel. A flare gun.

"I'm gonna call for back up." She smiled and palmed the gun tighter. "Jason and Gideon are out there. They've got a Humvee, and I know they're looking just outside the city. I need to let them know we're here."

It would be risky, but Amy knew that already. It was the only way to get their attention. Hopefully, Sam hadn't been able to reacquire his body yet and he wouldn't see it.

She let go of Amy's hand and watched as she ran from the room to find access to the roof where she could shoot off the flare and signal the others.

Chapter Fifty-One
Gideon

---

eads of sweat dripped from Gideon's brow as he carried the last gas can toward the Humvee. With Jason driving, it was not unusual to run low on gas or completely empty while travelling the back roads. They were only lucky enough today to end up near a farm with plenty of abandoned vehicles where they could siphon the gas tanks. Gideon walked to the Humvee and placed the can on the ground near the rear bumper while Jason emptied the can he held to the tank.

The nagging feeling of something pulling him out into the unprotected wilderness had not left him since he awoke in the middle of the night. Telling Jason about it did not seem to help, either. What he believed was a vision, Jason only summarized it as wishful thinking. But Gideon knew that Nikka still waited for them out there, hoping for help, even if Jason could not sense it.

He turned away from the vehicle, his eyes searching the edge of the trees and the long road that extended far to the east and disappeared as it curved downhill. The memories of his vision still played in his mind, with a road covered in fog and Nikka lost somewhere in that mist. It was a road much like this one that plunged through the tree line. His eyes focused beyond the trees, to the space past the woods. They had not driven that far yet, and as the hours of the afternoon dwindled away, they could not go much farther if they were to return to Garnet Falls by dark. It was too dangerous to be out once the sun set, and with the population of the town having a sudden growth spurt, Amy had her hands full. She needed the help, and Gideon was usually the one to be at her side. She had come to worry every time they left the walls of the town, and he recognized those lines of concern on her face when he walked away, just as they had early this morning. They had been gone for hours now as they neared the end of the day and still had nothing.

He heard the glug of the fuel as it gushed out of the can and into the tank where Jason stood. The sound grew thin like the can had nearly emptied. Almost ready to get back on the road.

Just as he turned, a flash of orange caught his eye. At first, he thought it was a trick of the fading sunlight reflecting on the horizon. Gideon stopped and watched as the flash grew into something real and bright.

"Hey," he called out to Jason as he kept watch on the light that rose into the sky, burning brighter as it ascended.

"What?" Jason said with a hint of exasperation.

"Hey," he said again, his voice stronger and louder than before. Jason turned to him and removed the can from the tank, his eyes squinting in the afternoon sun. Gideon pointed to the skyline. "What is that?"

The lines around Jason's eyes smoothed as his eyes widened. He dropped the can and hurried to Gideon's side as he watched the light on the horizon.

"That's a flare."

Before Gideon could ask anything more, Jason turned back to the Humvee and rushed to the driver's side. Gideon did not wait another second and climbed into the vehicle while Jason started the engine, his eyes watching the flare as it ended its ascent, leaving behind a trail of smoke.

"That is important, correct?" Gideon said, watching the light diminish.

"Damn right it is. Somebody is trying to get attention."

Gideon kept his sight on the flare as the Humvee raced down the road, the trees rushing past them in a meld of green and shade. The road curved down toward the tree, and he lost sight of the horizon, but he no longer needed it. He would remember where the light had originated, and the churning in his stomach told him that it might be Nikka.

The niggle of thoughts shoved into his brain, what if it was somebody else? Maybe Nikka was lost, far across the country, taken by some angel that had swooped in and saved her. Of course, he would be grateful for that singular act, but he needed to know she was okay and with the vision he had last night, he knew that things were not all right. Those thoughts pulled at him, drawing him further down the road and toward the source of the flare.

The road curved up and down over hills that wound through the trees until it finally opened to a valley. In the distance, the road moved into a thin gray line that traced toward a small city, empty windows of the taller buildings reflecting the late day sunlight.

"That has to be where it came from," Jason said as he pressed the gas pedal deeper into the floor and the Humvee roared down the road.

The vehicle slowed as they neared the outskirts of the town—a city big enough that it would be hard to narrow down the origin of the flare. The road opened into a four lane street dotted with abandoned cars and dead traffic lights. They wound through the maze of cars as Gideon leaned through his window, listening for anything in the ghost town that could indicate any other people.

"You hear anything?" Jason said as he watched out the front window.

"Nothing."

This could not be the end, not when he should have been so close. He knew she was somewhere nearby; he could feel it.

Then another flare rose into the sky and jetted upwards just above their heads. The trail of smoke disappeared behind the row of buildings to the east. When Jason saw it, he turned the Humvee down the next street and pushed the vehicle faster despite the maze of cars that had littered the street. The city opened to a wide parking lot, and through the tree-lined streets, he saw a lone building splayed over several acres of land: a shopping mall. The trail of smoke pointed down to the roof, and the flare still blazed overhead.

The vehicle turned into the empty parking lot, and Gideon scanned the wide open space for any sign of human life. Whoever had shot those flares had disappeared by now, but it had to be from here. Gideon opened the door when Jason stopped the vehicle and moved out onto the pavement. Jason killed the engine and stepped out of the Humvee, listening into the stagnant air around them.

The mall had been abandoned months ago, with no sign that anyone had been here in a long time. Weeds had grown in the cracks of the pavement and along the edge of the building. Gideon stepped around the corner, away from the west-facing wall that looked directly at the sun, and with such a bright light on that wall, he knew that the sun crept awfully close to the tree line.

"Hello?" Jason shouted into the air, to anyone that would listen.

The sound made Gideon jump, the shrill nature of it crawling over his skin. He walked around the corner and saw the front entrance to the department store, and the board over the first window had been torn away.

Tinted glass had scattered across the sidewalk from the breach that someone had made into the building.

A sound moved across the parking lot, a noise like the mewling of a cat but faint enough that Gideon almost missed it. He froze and craned his ear toward the opening in the building. It had been so faint and brief that he wondered if it had been an animal, maybe wandering the streets looking for a meal.

But then it happened again. The sound had come from inside the building, and it was not an animal, but a human cry.

"Jason," he called and ripped back the boards until they broke free and he could climb into the hole in the shattered window. Jason rushed in after him, his boots crunching on the broken glass littering the floor.

Gideon never looked back to see if Jason was close. The last echoes of the sound drove him further into the building as he hurried to trace the source of the noise. He emerged into the dimly lit main corridor, opening to a collection of ransacked shops and broken water fountains. The further he moved into the building, the more he could feel her hiding somewhere in the shadows. It was as strong as the day he first found her and knew that she was the one he had been called upon to turn into a seraph. And just like that day, he could feel her spirit pulling him into the depths of the mall.

His feet quickened, carrying him down the corridor, as he listened to every sound within that space. Jason hurried beside him, his breath quick as they ran together, eyes scanning the broken windows and darkened entryways of each store that filled the lower level of the building. Skylights shone down on them, casting pale silver light onto the floor. The lights opened into a larger atrium filled with overturned tables and chairs.

She had been here; he could still smell the trace of lavender that had come from her skin.

"Nikka," he called into the atrium, his voice echoing down the long corridors.

A shuffling sound came from the second floor. His eyes trailed up the stairway until he saw a flash of light through the windows of a store. A figure emerged from the shadows, but it was not the face he had expected.

"I can't believe it," Amy called down to him, her flashlight still in her hand and shining down the stairs to them.

His heart almost fell to the floor, and he could hardly breathe. "Amy? What the hell are you doing here?"

"Get up here, we've got to hurry," she said, her voice rushed and frantic.

The ground at their feet rumbled, pieces of drywall cracking in the ceiling and falling to the ground. The tiled floor split into a deep furrow that unzipped across the width of the building as though an earthquake threatened to tear the place down. Gideon almost lost his footing and fell against a pillar that stretched up to the second floor landing. A flash of violet and white light erupted from the center of the atrium, bringing a terrible roar that screeched down the halls in all directions. The tremors in the earth continued, raining mortar down on their heads.

Jason fell to the ground beside him. Gideon shouted at him to get back, but the sound drowned out his voice. The light was so bright that he pinched his eyes closed as tight as possible and held his hands over his ears.

He had seen this display on many occasions and knew what it meant.

An archangel had just arrived.

Maybe this was the one that had saved Nikka, but he knew that its arrival was no coincidence.

The sound and light suddenly abated, and Gideon's eyes flew open to see the violet ribbons of electricity that coursed out from the pit of darkness that had overtaken the atrium. The angel that walked in that shadow emanated rage, its power reaching across the building, searching for something. Searching for Nikka.

The archangel stepped out of the shadows, the purple light in its dark eyes glancing toward him. In that instant, Gideon knew who had just arrived. The Watcher Samael.

How was this possible?

Gideon rose to his feet, keeping his shoulders wide and his hands clenched into fists as he faced the archangel that stepped toward him. The violet light around it ebbed away until only it remained in fine points within the angel's pupils.

"Samael," Gideon said, his voice strong across the wide corridor.

Jason moved to his feet, standing beside Gideon but keeping his distance. The seraph knew enough to sense that this was not a peaceful creature standing before them. He pulled the blade free from its sheath, the blue fire extending down the length of the sword and his tattoos sparkling to life.

The angel slowed its pace as he came into the light that cast down from the skylight, as though it were a faint beam from Heaven. It fell on his light blonde hair and fair face, making him look like a gentle creature painted in the frescos of the Sistine Chapel.

"Pazuzu," the archangel said, his face stony and formidable.

Gideon clenched his teeth at the sound of the name, something that he never wanted to hear again. The way Samael spoke it made it sound like poison dripping from his lips.

"I am Gideon now, not the creature you cast out of Heaven."

Samael smiled, but his eyes continued to stare with the violet sparkle still hovering in his pupils. "You will always be one who defiled his name when you followed Lucifer."

"Not any more. I have been offered Redemption."

The archangel laughed, the sound peeling against the walls like a toll bell. "And who hasn't nowadays?"

The shadows around the angel shifted, a cold chill spilling over the broken tile floor. A figure stepped from the darkness with eyes glowing as red as coals. It moved into the light that fell down upon Samael, revealing the mane of long black and red hair, dark eyes and lean physique: a demon, the very one that had taken Nikka away from them.

The archangel had never saved her. He had this planned all along. The demon had taken her out of Garnet Falls, just to give her to Samael. The angel did not need to explain himself—Gideon had figured it out the moment he remembered the mark on Nikka's chest. It had been Samael's mark; the angel had planned this from the beginning.

"You cannot have her," Gideon said, but his hand had begun to shake.

"I can," the angel said, his voice dropping. "And I will. I created her."

"You will never have that child."

"I would not be so sure if I were you."

Samael flicked his wrist, and the rumbling in the ground started again, bucking the floor up enough to knock Gideon off his feet. As he stumbled, he saw the demon move fast, in a flash of black and red to the stairs. The rush of cold brushed over his skin just in time for him to scramble to his feet and dash up the stairs after him. The creature moved swiftly, and Gideon knew he chased after a high-ranking demon, something that he would never be able to stop on his own. But he had to try; Nikka was up there, and the creature followed her scent.

In the corner of his eye, he saw Jason's tattoos flash brighter as he gripped his sword and faced the archangel that began to tear apart the building.

Chapter Fifty-Two
Jason

When the demon moved, Jason almost missed it in the blur of shadows that rushed past Gideon. He wanted to chase it, hunt it down and kill it, just as his power pulled him. But then he saw the creature move before him, the one Gideon had called Samael. The creature, shrouded in light and sound, raised his hands and the entire building shook. Violet threads of electric light crept around his legs and moved to his arms. Samael's emotionless face looked at him, the purple light in his eyes deepening as the space around his eyes turned black and sinister.

Jason held the grip of his sword, feeling the power surge into his arms and down the hilt of the weapon. The ground around him heaved again, nearly knocking him to the floor. Samael took a step toward him, his head tilting downward but his black and purple eyes remained trained on him.

"You will never win," Samael said, his voice booming down the corridors.

This creature, whatever it was, had taken Nikka from him. The anger of it pulsed in his arms, strengthening the power in his core.

Samael forced his forearm outward, ribbons of violet light shooting from his fingertips toward Jason who reeled back, his hand holding the sword reflexively curling upward. The creature's power hit him, and the sword blocked it, but he had never felt this kind of energy before. The force of it drove him to the ground and burned into the sword, scorching his fingers where he held the weapon. He gritted his teeth, biting back the pain. The metal heated under his palm until he could no longer stand it. A howl escaped his throat, and he rolled to the side, letting the force of it career away from him and strike into the ground.

The weapon cooled in his hand as soon as he broke contact with the angel's power. He scrambled around a pillar, out of Samael's line of sight. He knew it wasn't hiding, but it would give him a couple of seconds to gather his thoughts and plan his next maneuver.

"You have no power over me," Samael said. The sound of his footfalls over broken tile gave away his position. "I am stronger than you will ever be."

Jason's heart pounded against his ribs with each step he heard from Samael. This was definitely no demon, at least not one that Gideon had ever told him about. There was only one other explanation: it had to be the angel that Gideon had mentioned. He had half-expected it to have big white wings, a halo and flowing robes. This was definitely different than all the paintings he had ever seen of an angel.

And this angel worked with the demon that had attacked the town, the one he had seen in the hive back in Reno. What angel would join forces with a demon?

The angel stepped closer. Jason darted back into the shadows, toward another pillar that supported the upper floor, but the creature saw him. A jolt of light struck the ground just behind his foot as he leaped into the shadows behind the protection of the pillar. Debris rained down from the ceiling as part of its support began to collapse.

The tattoos along his arms glowed brighter, filling his core with power that coursed down the blade. But would it matter against an angel?

Samael moved again, his footstep echoing against the wall. Jason dodged from behind the pillar as another stream of light zipped past his ear. But this time, he turned, his sword light in his hand as he brought it down toward the angel. Samael flinched as he saw the blue fire descending past him. The edge of the blade caught his ear, sending Samael stumbling backward, his hand flying up to the blood that streamed against the side of his head from the slice in his ear

Jason jumped back and held his sword at the ready as he saw the blood trickle between the angel's fingertips.

It can be wounded with the sword, and if it can be wounded, then it can be killed.

The angel's violet eyes flashed toward him, narrowed and angry. Samael moved his open palm toward Jason, sending another volley of light at him. Jason ducked and swung the sword again, but Samael must have expected it. He moved his other hand, his fist swinging low and then up, striking Jason across the jaw. He fell back hard, skidding across the tiles and his ribs fighting to catch the air that had been forced from his lungs with the blow.

Little points of light sparkled beyond his vision as he looked up at the crumbling ceiling from where he lay. The tang of copper filled his mouth, spilling down his lip and over his teeth in a splash of crimson blood. Footsteps marched toward him, each one making the ground tremble. He had to move, had to get up, but as he rolled to the side, every muscle in his body wanted to spasm and ache. He forced himself to his knees and tried to get to his feet when a hand clamped into his hair and yanked his head back.

The angel pulled him back and craned his neck enough to expose his vulnerable throat. Jason tried to twist, to bring the sword back up, but the angel swung his fist and knocked the weapon from his grip. Samael's fist rose over his head, an orb of violet light forming in his hand.

Jason could feel the strength of the angel's power building, pulling every bit of energy from the darkness and even from his own tattoos. The light along the marks began to flicker and dwindle as the energy rose, coursing through the length of the angel's arm and into the orb in his palm.

This creature, a being that poetry and songs had described as something glorious and beautiful, was no better than the demons. The rage and anger inside this angel was far worse than any general he had ever seen, and the angel wanted him dead and out of the way. Samael aimed to destroy him.

Chapter Fifty-Three

Gideon

The creature ran past Gideon so fast he could only see a blur in the shadows that grew around the atrium. The demon moved up the stairs, headed toward the sound that had come from the closed store at the top of the landing. It ran after Nikka.

Gideon had to move, even if the demon could destroy him with one blow. He scrambled to his feet and bounded up the stairs. The creature left behind a trail of cold that Gideon followed up to the landing. It ducked under the metal gate of the store, plunging into the darkness of the vast space beyond the corridor. Gideon rushed in after it, and then he heard the cry again.

He shoved through the dim light from the front windows, dodging down an open aisle between clothing racks. A shadow emerged from the rest of the darkness, growing large and looming over him with orange ember eyes. The thing had bounded into his path so quickly that he never had time to stop. The shadow twisted and morphed from its human form to a large black beast and wound back. Before Gideon could turn, the beast swung its arm and struck him in the face. The pain of it exploded in his cheek, and he flew across the room, crashing into a darkened display case. Shards of glass crunched around him, cutting into his back as he fell across the wood framing of the case and to the floor.

"Gideon," a voice called out after him, and moments later, he felt Amy's hand on his back. She cried, urging him to get up, but his head swam with stars. He heard her voice again and the sound of something else in the background. *Stomp. Stomp.*

He opened his eyes to see the demon bounding toward them. Amy had her back turned, and she would never see it in time. Gideon pushed himself up and reached his hand out to her to shove her away, but it was too late. The demon grasped the back of her neck and tossed her as though she were only a doll. She fell back against the far wall as the demon leaned over him and curled its fingers around his shirt. It lifted him from his feet, the beast's eyes burning orange as it looked at him. A wicked grin twisted over its lips.

"The great Pazuzu," the demon said. "Look at what you've become."

Gideon kicked at him, landing a solid strike to the demon's abdomen, but the beast never flinched. It only laughed and slammed him back down to the ground. The air rushed from his lungs as it held him down. The stars began swirling in his head again. The demon loomed over him, the cold spilling from its breath.

"That soul inside of you has made you weak," the demon said through clenched teeth. "It's made you human. Too easy to kill."

The demon's fingers extended with the sound of creaking bone and stretching tendons. Thick black claws reached from the end of his fingers, and the demon bent its knuckles, the claws pressed against his chest. Each claw pierced into his flesh, digging deeper as they inched further toward his ribs. Gideon cried out in pain as the nails scraped at his bone, ready to crunch through his chest and pierce his heart.

"Belphagor," Nikka's voice called out to him through the dark, a sound that demanded that the beast listen as it reverberated through the darkness.

The demon froze, its claws stopping their penetration into his chest. Gideon's hands clutched the demon's wrist, praying for an end to the stabbing pain. The beast's head ratcheted toward the dark and faced the woman that called its name. Its lips peeled back, and Gideon could see its teeth had morphed into rows of blackened sharp fangs.

"Get away from him," Nikka said from where she stood in the darkness.

The demon forced its hand back, withdrawing every claw that had pierced Gideon's chest. Gideon groaned and clutched at his chest as Belphagor stood and faced her, his black form coalescing back into the tall and lean body he possessed. Gideon turned to his side, his eyes searched the dark through the sparkles that still hovered in his vision. He found her silhouette in the dark, but she leaned against a door frame.

"It doesn't matter what you do to me. Samael is still going to kill your boy downstairs unless you come with him," the demon said, his voice edged with something that growled from deep inside his chest.

The demon took a step toward her, and Nikka stood straighter. "I'm not going anywhere with you."

"We shall see."

Belphagor's form shuddered in the dark, the skin on his arms turning black with slicks of oil that coursed down his veins. The muscles along his back rippled and expanded, lengthening his spine. The demon howled, and his torso doubled over as his jaw grew into a massive hinge, exposing rows of teeth that looked like blackened glass shards. Its foreleg wound back, ready to drive down a death blow toward Gideon's head.

"No," Nikka shouted.

The mark on her chest exploded in a burst of violet light. The pupils of her eyes flashed into shimmering neon purple as her hands rose, sending a shot of powerful light toward the demon. Gideon covered his head as the energy struck Belphagor hard in the chest, forcing him crashing back toward the front entrance. The light that carried the demon burst through the metal gate, sending the demon careening against the upper level railing and back down to the main floor.

Gideon did not move at first, keeping his arms over his head as the last of the metal gate came crashing down around the entrance. The room once again plunged into darkness, and then he heard Nikka gasp and cry out.

He moved to his feet, every muscle and bone in his body aching with each motion. The glass crunched under his boot as he stumbled toward the back of the store where she stood, hunched over with a hand against the wall as she breathed quickly.

"Are you injured?" he whispered and placed a hand against her cheek. He felt the moisture of sweat and tears on her skin.

She let out a pained breath, her hand wrapped around her abdomen. "No, but I'm sure I'm in labor."

His eyes drifted down to her abdomen, and his hand fell from her face. She breathed in and out in fast bursts. Whirls of uneasiness arose in his gut, making his knees wobble under him. In his thousands of years of his existence, he had seen life come and go countless times, so he wondered why this one made him sick to the point of nausea. He stumbled back against the door frame and watched her breathe.

Because this was the only one he loved, this woman who he had hurt beyond measure—he wanted to do anything to fix what he had done to her, but now her body readied to descend into that realm between life and death to bring forth another soul. And this, too, might be yet another sin he had placed upon her.

She finally opened her eyes at the end of the contraction and stood straighter, but the lines around her eyes still held onto the pain.

This was going to happen whether he was ready or not.

CHAPTER FIFTY-FOUR
NIKKA

From the moment that Samael gave her back her memories, Nikka had been nervous about seeing Gideon again. There had been so many mixed emotions in their history together, and she knew she still loved him. But that stayed so deep and buried now, she wasn't sure if she could even find it again.

And then she saw the worry on his face, the way he looked at her now as though she were dying. Maybe he was in shock or catatonic, but he pressed himself back against the door frame and stared past her into the dark, still and frozen.

A moan sounded in the dark and Nikka turned away from him to see Amy trying to sit up against the wall. At least the contraction had eased up enough for her to walk, but she knew it would only be a few minutes before it struck again. She stepped toward Amy and leaned down to see her.

Amy blinked her eyes a few times and Nikka could see a thin trickle of blood at her hairline.

"I'm okay," Amy said, her voice shaky and uneven.

Before she could bend down to help her, another voice boomed throughout the building, rattling against the windows. "Nikka."

Her heart nearly stopped, and she held her breath as Sam's voice reverberated in her bones. The sound of it made her want to cringe. He knew where she hid, and if Gideon was in the building, then Jason had to be here too.

Nikka stood, the heaviness of the baby in her abdomen hung deep in her pelvis. She stepped toward the front of the store, each footfall uneasy and weak with the strain of labor. The angel's voice called out to her again. The fading light from the skylights cast through the shattered windows of the store and fell on her face as she placed a hand against the window frame. She knew what was down there, and she didn't want to look, but the urgency in Sam's voice forced her toward the demolished gate. She steadied herself against the wall until she came to the remains of the gate, which gave her enough of a view of the mall's open atrium.

The archangel stood in the center of rubble from the collapsing building. Ripples of violet energy surrounded him, as did a pool of black inky darkness that stretched out from his body like bat wings. The darkness had invaded his eyes as well, leaving only violet orbs surrounded by shadow. His shirt had burned away with the intensity of the energy, exposing the illuminated tattoo on his chest as well as the other marks on his arms that he usually kept hidden.

His eyes looked toward her, those angry purple lights that shone within his skull. From this distance, she could still feel the power that surrounded him, and it made her own tattoo sizzle and spark to life with dots of light.

In all the shadow and ribbons of light that surrounded him, she followed his arm down to the person he held to the ground. Jason knelt before him, Sam's hand grasping his hair and forcing back his head to expose his neck. The moment she saw the pain in his eyes, she felt the catch in her throat. Although Jason's tattoos had illuminated to a bright light, his sword had fallen away, leaving him defenseless. His chest moved fast as he breathed against the pain. Blood spattered against the left corner of his mouth and bruises had bloomed along his cheek and neck.

Nikka's hand moved to her mouth as she felt the tears begin to blur her vision.

"It does not have to be this way," Sam said again, his eyes locked on her. "You are my companion, and when we reach Ascension, you will understand that this is how it had to be all along."

He pulled back hard on Jason's head, and he grunted through his tight jaw. He tried to be strong and not give into the angel, but Nikka could see the strain in his face.

"Nikka," Gideon's voice came to her as soft as a whisper, but she couldn't turn away from Jason. "If you go down there, Samael will kill him anyway."

The angel's violet eyes bored into her as his arm held fast to Jason's hair.

"You and Amy need to go," Gideon said as his hand touched her shoulder. "Get out of here while you can."

"I can't leave him."

Gideon's hand moved down her arm and grasped around her fingers the same way he used to when they lived in the abandoned monastery. It was warm and firm as he pulled her away from the front of the shop, breaking her eye contact with Sam. She tried to pull away from him, but he forced her around to face him, cradling her face in his hands. He made her look into his eyes as he spoke.

"You need to go," he said, but she could hear the break in his voice.

Gideon had been so many things in thousands of years, but first, he was the protector of the seraph, and that was his protégé down there, just as she had been. His one job was to keep Jason safe, but she could see the truth in his eyes. He could do nothing now. The archangel was going to kill both of them if they tried to stop him.

Her fingers wrapped around his wrists and drew them away from her face as a tear streaked down her cheek. Every memory came to her again, just as it had when Sam allowed her mind to remember. The first time she met him, the way the wrinkles around his eyes grew deeper when he worried. They looked that way now. The furrows between his brows. The sorrow in his hazel eyes. He appeared this same way the day she met him, as he looked down on her death bed. Gideon knew then that she had less than eight hours to live that day. He had been running out of time, just as they were now.

The other memories flooded back to her as well, things that she wished she could forget again. That singular moment when they had kissed in the church, when her mark had burned, and she knew that something had happened to him. But she remembered his ferocity when he had that orange-red glow in his eyes. There had been such violence, such cruelty.

For a moment, she gasped as she thought about it and stepped away from him as he watched her.

The angel's voice echoed through the building. One last warning. She looked back to the fading light of the atrium.

Before she knew anything about her new power, she had almost done it, but could she do it again?

Her eyes flashed back toward Gideon as the dreaded thought came to her, scratching and clawing at her willpower. It was a dangerous proposition, after what had happened only seven months ago.

But the archangel was too powerful for her or Jason.

She needed to match that power.

Gideon's brow furrowed as he saw the change in her countenance. "What are you thinking?"

The guilt of what she needed to do boiled inside of her. In all the time she had known Gideon, she watched him struggle to fight his true self. But she had no choice.

"I'm sorry," she said and tilted her head.

"About what?"

"About what I'm going to do to you," she said. "But we need a touch of evil."

She moved toward him, her hands grasping behind his neck as she pulled him closer to her. Her lips touched his, kissing him deep enough that she felt his gasp, the same kiss she had felt the night they were together in the church before the demons had taken her from Garnet Falls. The same night her tattoo had come to life for the first time.

The power of their kiss stirred the energy just behind the tattoo, pulling in the life force of anything around them. Sunlight. Air. Earth. It flowed between them, and Gideon wrapped his fingers around the back of her head, pulling her closer to him. The energy moved fast, taking his body and searching deep behind his soul for that hidden door, the one place that nobody was allowed to see. For that moment, time stood still, and nothing else existed outside of their embrace.

The energy ripped open the hidden space inside Gideon that he had kept locked for so long. He suddenly pulled away from her, breaking the flow of her power, but it was already done.

"What did you do?" he said with a gasp, an ember glow starting in his eyes. He fell to his knees and cried out as his back arched in pain.

Nikka stepped back from where he writhed, his arms shaking and the muscles rippling with flashes of red light that pulsed in his veins. The ground below her feet quaked, sending a shower of debris onto them. Gideon cried out, but his cries were laced with a deep and guttural growl that rose from his chest.

Amy stood as she watched it all unfold, and the ground quaked again. She tried to rush toward Nikka, but she held out her hand to stop her. Nikka couldn't afford to have Amy in the way if everything fell apart now.

"Nikka," Sam's voice shouted toward her. The sound had changed, becoming dread instead of fury. "What have you done?"

She knew the archangel had felt the change in the air as Gideon howled in pain and anger where he crouched on the ground. The skylights began to dim with the coming black storm clouds that gathered outside, the earth growing restless with the unleashing of such a powerful and evil force. The ground rumbled and heaved, nearly knocking her off her feet.

Then everything grew still and quiet, the dim lights growing darker. The temperature in the room plummeted enough for her to see her breath as her heart raced. She could feel the spark of terror that had filled the store, like the aftermath of a lightning storm. Gideon's back no longer arched and writhed with pain. He remained motionless where he crouched on the ground.

The chill bit at her lips and ached in her throat with every breath like deep winter as she watched him. The shadows in the room deepened, stretching closer around Gideon's still body. The hair on her neck began to rise.

Gideon twitched, making her jump back. Then his back curled forward, and he stood, each vertebrae clicking into place until his hung head lifted with the grace of a cat. His mouth opened with a deep gasp as his eyes turned toward the crumbling ceiling. His shoulders locked, broad and powerful when his head turned down, and his eyes opened to look at her. Bright red light filled his pupils. The wrinkles of concern that had settled around his eyes had vanished, leaving only the harsh and smooth look of danger. A viper ready to strike.

She remembered that look all too well.

A crooked grin spread over his lips as he stretched his neck like he had been cooped up for far too long. "You brought me back."

Quick puffs of air moved past her lips as she watched him.

He stepped toward her, those embers trained on her now. "Couldn't get enough the first time?"

She moved back as he neared her, but then he rushed through the darkness, and she felt his cold hand around her throat as he pressed her back against the wall. His face neared hers, his fingers like ice against her skin.

"You locked me in there? Why would you bring me back?" he growled.

Nikka shuddered under his grasp, the memories of their last meeting still too fresh. She tried not to close her eyes because she had to keep his focus on her. This wasn't just the demon, high general and right hand to Lucifer. He had the ability to be so much more.

"Because I trust you, Gideon," she said, her trembling fingers reaching up to touch his face.

His eye twitched for a moment as she touched him and he stood still, his hand tight around her throat. The smile almost slipped from his mouth.

The embers burned brighter in his eyes. "My name is not Gideon."

And she realized that she couldn't smell the rancid odor of decay that accompanied the other demons.

His grip on her throat slipped just a little, and then he moved in swiftly toward her. His lips touched hers, kissing her hard and fierce. There was nothing gentle about it, and it took her breath away until he pulled back, the light still in his eyes.

"I hope you are right, for your sake," he said.

Then he rushed into the darkness and out the front of the store, leaving her cold and trembling just as another contraction began to tighten around her belly.

Chapter Fifty-Five

Jason

Samael pulled his head back further when the first rumbles shuddered beneath them. Dark clouds gathered overhead, darkening the light that had shone down from the skylights. He tried to glance back up at the entrance of the store upstairs, but he could barely see the landing. Something had crashed through the gate and collided with a fountain down below, but he couldn't see that either.

Then he felt the chill in the air, the kind of cold that only accompanied the highest level demons. It frosted everything around them, coating the surfaces with a sheen of sparkling white. The shadows deepened as he felt the angel shift behind him, his hand tightening in his hair. Samael had called out to Nikka, and now he waited for something that dwelled in the space above them.

A blur of light and dark moved from the broken gate above, and then Jason saw Gideon's form leap over the railing and land on the ground before them in a crouch. The air chilled further as Gideon lifted his head, but his eyes now glowed an orange-red. Gideon no longer had the look of a fallen and guilty man. He stood tall and powerful, like a battle-hardened soldier. He stood as a strong and full demon, just as Jason had seen him seven months ago when he had tried to kill Nikka.

Gideon rose to stand, his shoulders wide and his arms strong. He held his palms up and forced a crimson energy down his arms and into his palms, the same way the archangel had drawn on his power.

"Pazuzu," Samael said with a hiss.

"None other," Gideon said, and a wicked smile formed across his face.

The archangel twitched again, and Jason's head pulled back further. A gathering violet light rushed into Samael's hand, ready to come down on his throat when a harsh red force hit the angel in the chest. His hand loosened from Jason's hair enough that he pulled free. He sprang forward and clambered toward the sword. His fingers found the hilt, and the blade erupted into blue flames. The beat of his heart pounded behind his sternum. A terrible crash sounded behind him as he turned on his hip and pointed the sword back toward the angel.

But he saw Gideon, who glanced back at him from where he stood, his eyes still aglow. "Get them out of here."

The red light still flowed down Gideon's arms and into his hands like a gun that smoked after it had fired. The angel stood from a fresh pile of rubble, the dust settling around him as he faced the demon.

"What about you?" Jason said, the sword shaking in his hand.

"I will catch up," Gideon said with a smile and turned back toward the angel.

He wasn't going to ask any questions—like how in the world did the demon infect Gideon again? Jason hurried to his feet and bounded up the stairs as the sound of crumbling walls echoed down the halls. Violet and red light flashed up from the atrium as he ran across the landing and rushed through the collapsed gate of the dark store. He didn't let his eyes adjust to the darkness before he sprinted down the aisles, toward the silhouette of Nikka and Amy at the back of the large room.

Nikka stood against the wall, her hand around her abdomen and breathing fast. The way Amy's wide eyes watched him as she held Nikka upright told him enough. Things had changed in the week or so that she had been away, and this looked serious.

"We need to get out of here," he said.

Amy nodded. "There's a stairwell in the back, goes down to the loading bays."

Jason stepped up to Nikka and pulled her arm around his shoulders as she breathed, her face pinched in pain. But she planted her feet and tried to pull away from him. "What about Gideon?"

"Don't worry about him," Jason said and forced her arm around his shoulder again. "He's got this."

He could tell she didn't have the energy to argue with him. As he tugged her toward him, she began to walk faster when the contraction eased. Amy led them to the back of the store and through a dark stairwell. She turned on the flashlight, but the weak light barely shone enough to light the step before her. They emerged onto another floor that opened to a corridor that appeared to run the length of the building. Rims of light surrounded each locked corrugated metal door lining the walls. Amy tried each one as they ran, the echoes of the battle in the center of the mall rattling against the hinges of the doors.

Nikka held close to Jason as he supported her, her fingers wrapping around the back of his neck.

Amy shouted far ahead of them as she opened a door, but Nikka's footing slowed, a groan coming from her throat. He stopped as she doubled over her abdomen, her breathing fast. Her fingers moved away from his neck as she found his hand and squeezed.

The pain that moved through her made his hands shake. "What do I do?" he said to her as he kneeled before her, holding her hand.

"Just . . ." she said, but she couldn't finish as she held her breath at the peak of the contraction.

"I don't know what to do," he said.

He couldn't take away her pain, even though he would do it in a second if he could. The only time he had felt so helpless was the night she had been taken away from him when Pazuzu had nearly killed her. Now, she was here with him, and he could do nothing to help her.

Her eyes turned up toward him, and her breathing slowed. The pain lingered around her eyes, but she forced a smile. "Just stay with me."

As she stood taller, the pain easing in her abdomen, he pulled her close and kissed her. When he pulled away enough to look at her, he spoke. "I'm not going anywhere."

The ground quaked again with the sound of terrible destruction behind them, as though the entire building was ready to collapse on them at any second. Jason took Nikka's hand, and they moved together down the corridor toward Amy's opened door.

They emerged at the rear parking lot in a gust of wind that had picked up with a coming storm. The Humvee wasn't far, but they still had to run down the length of the mall and around the west side of the building. As they rounded the corner, the sounds of metal on metal screeched from behind them. The ground heaved again, making Jason almost trip on the buckling pavement before him. The metal screeching grew until the building began to fall, a cloud of dust and debris erupting from the base of the mall and mushrooming out onto the parking lot.

The cloud rushed toward them as they approached the vehicle. Amy and Nikka climbed into the back seat as Jason jumped into the driver's seat. He turned the key, praying that the engine would start on the first try. The engine roared to life as the cloud passed over the Humvee, enveloping it in a fog of brown and gray debris. The passenger window was still rolled down, and the fog spilled into the car as Jason put it into gear and stepped on the gas.

The tires spun as the Humvee rushed across the parking lot toward the edge of the choking cloud. The ground buckled again, catching the tires of the vehicle and tossing it up. The Humvee caught the pavement again and rushed over the uneven terrain as it bucked.

Something crashed down on the hood of the vehicle and Jason slammed on the brakes. The wind brushed enough of the cloud away for him to see Gideon's form, rising from a crouch, his burning eyes turned up and gazing at him through the windshield. Gideon glided over the hood and to the running board along the passenger edge of the Humvee.

"Go," he shouted over the roaring of the engine and the crashing of the building behind them.

Jason didn't wait for anything after that. He slammed on the gas pedal and the vehicle shot forward as Gideon clung to the side of the vehicle. The car raced through the parking lot and beyond the cloud that had stretched out from the fallen building.

He kept the Humvee on the road, swerving through the maze of abandoned cars until the road opened up down the center of town. The wind that blew in from the coming storm knocked at the side of the car. Gideon had climbed into the passenger seat, and his presence only made the interior of the Humvee feel like a deep freezer.

While Jason drove, he glanced into the rear view mirror and saw only the skyline of the empty city and the dark, black clouds that had formed in the sky. No angel following them. The other demon that had been there had run away, leaving them with the demon he knew: Pazuzu. He shot a careful glance at Gideon, who had turned and watched Amy and Nikka in the back seat. The demon had gotten them out of that tight spot, but what was Jason to do about him now? Having him that close in the car made his tattoos burn and itch like crazy and this space was a little too confined if he needed to use his sword.

Nikka cried out again, and he could see her face twisted in a grimace through the rear view mirror as he drove.

"We've got to find somewhere to stop," Amy said.

Wind battered the door and rain began to pelt the windshield. The clouds had taken over the last of the light from the setting sun, leaving the landscape in a blue haze of twilight. He had only ever seen one tornado in his life, and he remembered the sky collecting the black and blue clouds just like this. That, combined with the fact that an angry angel now chased them, made it a little difficult to listen to Amy.

"Where do you propose we stop?" Jason said, his voice rushed.

"I don't know," she said, her voice raising to a shout. "But this baby is coming."

Nikka cried out again, and it halted in her throat for a moment. She glanced down at her abdomen, and everything fell silent in the back seat.

"What was that?" Nikka said. The shaking in her voice worried him.

Amy sighed, a quick sound that made the hair on Jason's arms stand up. "Your water just broke."

The rain pounded on the vehicle, leaving the road dark and difficult to see even with the headlights.

Gideon turned back to look at him, his face emotionless and his eyes burning red. "She is correct. Out here, we are too vulnerable, and there are more coming." His voice had dropped enough that Jason knew he spoke so the women couldn't hear him.

"More? What do you mean more?" Jason said and flashed him a glance.

"This storm," he said as he glanced up to the sky through the windshield. "This is not my doing. A horde is coming our way. They know what is about to happen."

The rain poured over the car, and the wind battered the side again. Nikka cried with the onset of another contraction. An archangel would soon rise from the rubble of the fallen building, and a demon army came with the storm. How could he possibly protect Nikka with all of this against him? Even with Pazuzu at his side, the odds were too great, and he couldn't exactly trust the demon, either.

His fingers curled around the steering wheel as he felt the well of anxiety build in his chest. He needed a miracle.

CHAPTER FIFTY-SIX

NIKKA

Even though Gideon tried to speak below the sound of the rainfall and the engine, Nikka heard every word Jason said. Since the contractions had started, every sense in her body had grown stronger, including her hearing. And she had felt everything change as soon as her water broke. It heralded that this baby was close to coming. The contractions grew stronger now, something that she had thought impossible after she had suffered through enough of them already.

Jason still gunned the engine, and every bump in the road took her breath away as it beat against the weight in her pelvis.

The coming storm brought a demon horde on the horizon. She didn't need to see them to feel it getting closer. Sam would find them; he always would. All of them would battle to take her baby, and her friends would die in the crossfire unless they could find a way to protect themselves.

"Wait," Gideon said. He craned his neck to look through his window. "Turn here. Now."

Jason didn't hesitate and turned the Humvee to the right. The vehicle banked hard at that speed, but he pressed the engine harder. Road signs zoomed by, but the rain-streaked windows made it too difficult to see where Gideon had led them.

She felt the car slow, the headlights landing on a tall iron fence that stretched into the darkness.

"This may work," Gideon said and stepped from the car.

Jason came around to the side of the vehicle and helped Nikka to her feet. She stepped out into the twilight and rain that had covered the landscape and gazed onto the iron gates that closed the entrance to a vast cemetery. Large trees dotted the field of tombstones that disappeared into the darkness beyond the fence. Deep into the heart of the place, though, she saw a building, white walls and stained glass windows standing silent in the rain.

"It's a cemetery," Amy said, exasperated. "How is this going to help?"

Gideon turned his burning eyes toward her. "Because this is a blessed place. Hallowed ground. Unless the threshold is broken, no unclean spirit can enter." He raised his hand and pointed toward the quiet building. "And the mausoleum is protected. You can take Nikka in there."

Jason looked out over the place, his face wet with rain. "Hey, it's the best plan we've got." He moved to Nikka's side and put her arm around his shoulders again.

They started toward the gate, her arm around Jason and Amy ahead of them, but Gideon stood by the car. Nikka stopped and turned toward him.

Jason glanced back with her. "Are you coming?"

"He can't," Nikka said, the realization of it hitting her. She pulled away from Jason and faced Gideon as his red eyes watched her in the fading light. "He's an unclean spirit. He's never been given Redemption."

His eyes never wavered from her as she stepped toward him.

"You must go," he said as he watched her approach.

The thought of leaving him here, alone in the rain to face the army himself, made her heart ache. She had forced this upon him and whatever happened to him now was her fault. Gideon had had the demon under control and locked away, but she allowed it to escape and taint the soul she had given him.

"Not without you," she said. She reached to touch his face, but he grasped her wrist, the force of it painful.

"Go."

Jason stepped up to her and grasped her arm, trying to encourage her to come with him.

She yanked her hand away from Gideon's grasp as she looked at him, his red demon eyes watching her. This was not the Pazuzu that had hurt her so many months ago. Gideon still hid there, holding onto his soul with bleeding hands. If he stayed out here, he would die. But he couldn't cross the threshold that had been blessed.

Blessed to be protected by angels.

And angels had the power to let in the ones that deserved to enter. They had the power to give a seraph the abilities that he had. And Samael had been able to alter any of that at his own will.

And she had Samael's power too.

Her eyes grew wide as she pulled the energy into her feet. The power had a strange feel in her body as it drew in from the storm and the wind. But it wasn't that. This was more primal, like something that had once created the earth. Sam had told her to pull it from all the life around her, but there was power in death as well. The energy flowed from the cemetery, from those that watched just beyond this veil of life. It was the strangest thing she had ever felt as it flowed into her core and tingled along the edges of her tattoo. Master over Spirits. That's what Sam had called the mark.

The power coursed into her arm and she raised her hands, her fingers splayed out and touching both Jason's and Gideon's chests, locking them in place. Just like her seraph power, she told it what she wanted it to do, and hoped that it worked. The energy flowed from the thousands of the dead that lay in the rain-soaked ground, waiting for their chance at life again.

Jason grabbed her wrist as the energy rushed into his body, his eyes closing and his face twisting in a grimace. The light along his tattoos sprang to life in a shimmer of blue.

Gideon's red eyes just watched her as her power poured into him, the violet light from her fingertips blending with the crimson glow that throbbed in his arms now. The power glimmered as a purple light in her eyes, mingling with both a demon to her right and a seraph to her left, like a super-charged battery that increased its voltage. The blue light of Jason's tattoos began to shimmer and spark with violet energy as she continued to pour more of her power into the both of them.

Then a contraction started again, and the force of it broke her concentration. The light blinked out, extinguished as she doubled over in pain. Jason stumbled away from her, gripping his chest with the agony of the touch she had just given him, but he caught his breath and looked up at her through the rain. Gideon stood beside her and gazed down at his chest, at the place where her hand had just touched him.

He pulled down the neck of his T-shirt, exposing a new tattoo that had been singed into his skin.

Jason watched him do this and glanced down at his own chest as well, the same mark branded into his flesh.

They both matched the only mark that Nikka bore on her chest.

Jason stepped back as he looked up at her, reaching back and finding the sword. His eyes were wide with amazement as the blue flames erupted down the length of the blade, now intermingled with ribbons of electric violet light. His tattoos glowed blue with a hint of purple light.

As Nikka stood straighter from the contraction, she felt her knees get weak. Amy stepped to her side, supporting her as they both looked at Gideon and Jason.

"What did you do?" Jason said, the violet blue light of the sword illuminating their space outside the cemetery.

"Redemption," Gideon said as he looked at Nikka, the crimson glow of his eyes hallowed by a ring of violet. "She gave us the power of angels."

CHAPTER FIFTY-SEVEN
NIKKA

They moved into the cemetery as the rain poured down, leaving puddles across the grass and tombstones. Jason kicked in the door of the mausoleum, which breathed out a gust of stale air. Lightning danced across the sky, casting stark shadows through the door and into the long room lined with cemented caskets. He supported her as they moved into the space and settled her to the floor in the center of the large room. Her knees didn't want to keep her upright any longer.

Thunder rattled the windows as Amy knelt down beside her. The pain in her pelvis began to burn, a pressure that wouldn't let up.

Beyond the cramping in her abdomen, the crack of thunder that spread over the valley, and the rain pattering at the windows, she could feel something else in the darkness around them. The storm settled over the valley and beat down on them, but a darker force loomed just at the edge of the trees, even if she could no longer see them. The army had approached, and she felt Belphagor's presence just outside the iron fence of the cemetery.

He had planned to be on the winning side, and when she had introduced Pazuzu into play, he had run and tried to even the playing field yet again.

Gideon stepped to the open door of the mausoleum, the wind blowing past his shirt and sending it in wet waves over his muscled back.

"It is time," he said over the sound of the wind.

Jason looked back at him, his sword still in hand. He then glanced back at her. Water dripped from his wet hair and across his goatee. His hand touched her face. "I have to go now."

"I know," she said, trying to hold back the ripple of pain that began in her lower back.

He leaned down to kiss her, and she reached behind his neck to hold him. The hand against her cheek felt hot as he tried to hold her as long as he could.

The pain grew, and she pulled back. "I love you."

"Back at ya," he said with a forced smile and stood, the sword lighting up the room. He backed away from her before he finally turned and walked out of the mausoleum with Gideon at his side. The doors latched closed, leaving Amy and her alone with the windows rattling and the pain growing in her abdomen.

The contraction tightened and forced the pressure like never before into her pelvis. She cried heavy tears this time, unable to breathe through it anymore. Her spine locked into a curve around her belly, her arms shaking as her hands tried to support her against the floor. So much pressure. She held her breath as her abdominal muscles tightened into a spasm.

"You've got to breathe," Amy said as she touched her back.

"I can't," she cried and hung her head as the pressure built on itself.

The cramp in her abdomen let up, but the pressure down low would not ease. Nikka cried, her head between her shaking arms, as Amy's hands worked at her waistband. In any other situation, this would be weird, but she didn't care anymore as Amy worked her capris down her legs and then tossed them aside. Her bare skin shivered in the cold of the mausoleum, feeling the chill descend upon the cemetery as a demon army collected just outside the fence.

Amy moved around her and forced her head up to look into her eyes. "You're so close now, I can see the top of the head."

Not like this. Not like this, she wanted to cry. This was the last place she would have ever thought she would bring the baby into this world. Surrounded by death and destruction.

Amy's cold hands touched her arms and pulled Nikka upright into a squat, with her long wet shirt falling down over her hips and thighs.

"Okay," Amy said, almost out of breath. Her eyes were wide now, and she could feel the tremble in Amy's hands. "Just look at me. You've got to push with the next one."

Nikka tried to catch her breath, but the pain down low was constant and burning.

"I can't do this."

"Yes, you can."

Her head slipped down again, but Amy brought her chin up and forced her to look into her eyes.

"I don't want to."

"I know," Amy said, the lightning flashing in her green eyes. "But you've got no choice. It's going to happen no matter what. You just need to be fierce, okay?"

Nikka nodded her head, hoping that she could find the ferocity that Amy believed she had. The contraction started in her back again, pressing the thing down that burned below her pelvis even deeper.

The burning erupted, and she cried out as she felt the strain in her abdominal muscles. They were pushing against her will now, forcing that thing further down. Her fingers dug into Amy's arm, and she closed her throat as she pushed with all the power she could gather.

Chapter Fifty-Eight

Jason

Shadows moved in the dark, thickening beyond the light of Jason's sword. The rain had diminished as the horde moved closer, red eyes shifting in and out of the dark, as they moved toward the cemetery, drawn to it like predators. His heart raced, and his fingers twitched around the hilt of the sword. Bodies approached the iron fence, the legion deepening with every second that passed.

He glanced back over his shoulder and saw Gideon standing on the other side of the cemetery, facing east where a white and violet light grew from the darkness. He had expected Samael to show up, but more than just a single angel approached the cemetery now. Other creatures stepped among the purple light that illuminated just beyond the fence, things that he had seen before. They were large beasts with thick shoulders and arms that extended into claws. Their white manes drifted in the wind, playing along their heavy jaws and feline eyes. Gideon had once called them the cherubim. Samael had brought reinforcements.

And Gideon stood to face them, threads of violet and crimson light spilling down his arms as he readied for the onslaught.

A cold breeze danced across the tombstones and caught his attention. He turned back to the demon horde that grew along the fence line. The sun had already set, and with the storm clouds overhead, everything fell into a premature darkness, but the shadows in the center of the horde grew deeper as if it drew in any available light in the cemetery.

He had seen it happen once before, back in the depths of the power plant. There had been a shadow there that followed them, something that even

Gideon feared to face. Now it had come for him, and he remembered that Gideon had called it the First Evil.

This was Lucifer, come to sit ringside for the big event.

The shadow extended over the cemetery and threaded its dark arms toward the light of his sword. The cold that came off it hurt his joints, and he backed away, but the thing still shivered around the sword, inspecting this new creation of blue and violet.

The Devil couldn't breach the fence, but his influence definitely moved beyond the tombstones, stretching his will around him.

The horde moved like a single organism, pressing against the fence and waiting for a breach that would allow them in. Each of them tasted the air, feeling for the scent of a child about to be born. A thousand faces watched him in anticipation with black and red eyes that searched the walls of the mausoleum. Nikka's cries called out to them like a dinner bell.

Jason gripped the sword tighter and straightened his spine. This was not the time for fear, despite the army that grew in numbers all around the perimeter. Each sound he heard coming from the mausoleum steeled his muscles, forcing his anxiety to the back of his mind. The weapon felt hot in his hand, ready to strike and taste demon blood.

Chapter Fifty-Nine

Nikka

The pressure pierced into her pelvis, and Nikka screamed as her abdominal muscles tightened. A burn like fire filled her pelvis, and Amy's eyes turned downward. She let go of Nikka's hand and reached between her legs. Tears flowed down her cheeks.

"One more time," Amy said.

She held her breath and pushed into the burning. Warm liquid gushed around her legs and then she felt a release from the pain. She gasped when she felt the loss of the pressure, but her legs wouldn't hold her upright any longer. She eased herself to the ground and looked down toward Amy's hand.

Then she heard the peal of a cry echo into the large room of the mausoleum.

Amy held the baby, its skin covered with streaks of blood. Lightening flashed against its wet skin, glistening with amniotic fluid. The sound from the child's mouth came out in shuddering cries. Amy wrapped the baby in her jacket as Nikka sat back.

Her head began to swim, and her ears rang while Amy worked to get the baby protected, and then whatever else she was doing down there. Nikka lay back against the cold stone floor, the weakness beginning in her arms and then working into her core. The pain had vanished, replaced now by an overwhelming need to close her eyes. The sound in her ears rushed as she felt warm liquid pool around her back.

"Nikka," Amy called her name, but it sounded so hollow and distant, too far away for her to care anymore.

She forced her eyes open and looked at Amy, but her face had grown pale, and she shouted, but Nikka couldn't hear anything. Bright red blood covered Amy's hands. Nikka searched beyond her, along the ground to where the baby lay, wrapped in the dark green jacket that Amy had once worn. Between her and the soul that cried on the floor, she saw an ever-expanding pool of blood. She knew it belonged to her; she felt it flowing out of her like a faucet of water.

The baby continued to cry, but she could no longer hear it beyond the rushing sound in her ears. Her heart beat raced faster than anything she had ever felt.

She just needed to close her eyes. Too tired.

Then everything went black.

Chapter Sixty

Amy

The baby had cried quickly, and from her own experience in the delivery room with Dylan, that was a good thing. But it needed to be warm. Not it. He. A boy.

She pulled her jacket from her shoulders and wrapped the child in it, pulling one of the hood ties free and tying off the umbilical cord. Nikka collapsed back against the cement ground while she worked to cut the cord. As she turned back to her, though, she saw the blood pooling between her legs, flowing fast. She had never seen so much blood, not even when she delivered Dylan.

It just poured with the sound of running water.

Nikka fell back, her skin paling by the second.

This can't be happening. She felt her heart racing in her chest as she freed the placenta, but the blood coated her hands, pooling around them. It just wouldn't stop. The baby's cry ascended into the room, and Nikka closed her eyes.

"No, no," she shouted to Nikka. Her hands shook so badly now that she couldn't feel anything in her fingertips.

"Please, don't do this," she cried and pressed on Nikka's abdomen. She remembered the nurses doing this for her after she delivered her own baby. There was supposed to be a hard knot there just under her belly button, but everything was soft and still. "Nikka, please."

She had lost enough people in her life, but she had never seen anyone actually die before. There one minute, and then gone the next. As she screamed at Nikka, she heard the gushing of the blood begin to slow, and her skin grow colder under her touch, all while the piercing cry of the baby rose into the mausoleum.

Her fingers clenched into fists, and she pressed harder on Nikka's abdomen, but there was nothing else to do. Tears streamed down her face when she finally sat back on her heels, her hands coated in blood. The cold in the room stabbed to her bones.

The sound of the baby drew her attention away to the body just a few feet from her, the one lying in a pool of her own blood. Amy picked up the screaming child and held it close to her chest as she rocked it, hoping her own body heat would keep the baby warm enough. Her eyes fell on Nikka's body again as she cried.

A peal of thunder tore through the valley again, rattling the windows. A gust of wind beat against the building, whistling along the rafters. Amy felt every jarring sound in her core, tearing at her as she watched for any movement of Nikka's chest, but she had gone still.

The baby's crying eased as she rocked it.

The chill receded from the room despite the wind that rocked the foundation. She no longer felt the piercing cold in her fingertips or the puff of white at her lips with every breath. The sound of the rattling windows vanished, and everything became deathly still in that small space. Amy was sure that the sound of her heart beating would break the quiet that had fallen on them.

A faint violet glow glistened along the windows and Amy realized that it came from the tattoo on Nikka's chest. At first, it was faint, but it now shimmered and filled the room with such brilliant light that she squinted against it and covered the baby's eyes. The light intensified, and she scooted away from the body, fixing herself in the corner as she held the baby away from the light.

The body elevated from the cold floor like it was pulled on a string from the center of Nikka's torso. Her limp arms and legs, splashed with smatterings of blood, hung down until they no longer touched the ground. The light burst with such intensity that it enveloped the body. Amy closed her eyes against the brightness of it and tucked the baby's head into the crook of her neck.

A roaring sound filled the mausoleum and Amy screamed against it, but she could no longer hear her own voice.

Then the light and sound disappeared as fast as it had started.

When Amy opened her eyes, she saw only shimmering light in the center of the room, hues of white and blue and purple that coalesced into a solid being. She held her hand up to the light to shield her eyes when she saw the being step toward her. The light dissipated and she saw the edge of the person that stood there as she let her hand fall.

It was Nikka's eyes and her face, but she had hair that cascaded down along her back in waves of light blonde. Any blemish that she once carried had now vanished, leaving her eyes bright and blue and her skin perfect. Nikka's flesh seemed to glow almost white. Beautiful. Like an angel. The mark on her chest glowed with bright electric light as she reached her hand out for Amy to take. That was the moment Amy saw the rows of new tattoos marked along Nikka's arms, ascending up and beyond the sleeves of the T-shirt.

The long, white shirt still clung to her slender frame, no longer stained in blood.

Amy took her hand and stood on wobbling knees. Nikka looked at her and Amy could see her irises were no longer blue, but a brilliant shade of purple.

"I thought you had died," Amy said, ready to faint at any moment.

The baby made a keening sound, and Nikka glanced to the child, placing a hand on his smooth head.

"I think I did," she said. She no longer carried the look of fear that Amy had always seen from the moment she met her.

"What are you?"

Nikka turned her eyes up to her. "I don't know, but I think I might have seen Heaven. Just for a moment."

The ground quaked and the center of the floor split, sending a deep furrow down the length of the mausoleum. A great roar sounded from beyond the walls. Amy clutched the baby tighter as bits of cement rained down from the ceiling.

Nikka looked up to the rafters. "It's time to end this."

Chapter Sixty-One

Jason

The sound of the baby crying made Jason turn his head back to the mausoleum, and he saw that Gideon had done the same. He could hear it beyond the wind and the noise outside the gate. Then a bright flash erupted from inside the mausoleum, spilling light through the stained glass windows. He felt a stone settle in his stomach. Something wasn't right.

The fence that lined the perimeter of the cemetery shook, and the sound of tearing metal echoed through the valley. He turned back to see the horde rushing through the fence as though the threshold had vanished. The army tore the fence down, and a legion of a thousand red and black eyes raced toward him. He gripped his sword tightly and felt a surge of power in his core, something that had moved so quickly and responded to his guidance. It coursed down his arms, and he collected it in his hand. The orb of blue light grew until he could no longer contain it and then threw it like a hand grenade toward the mob that infiltrated the cemetery.

The orb exploded in a flash of light, disintegrating a hundred demons that rushed his way. But the army dodged the light, and the ranks closed around the gap in the fence. The first front came toward him, and he collected another round of energy as the fastest demons neared him. He threw the orb back into the crowd and swung his sword as the first demon leaped into the air at him. The blade sliced cleanly, disintegrating the creature into ashes.

He turned and ran back toward the mausoleum as the ground shuddered, heaving upward enough to drop him to the ground. The sword slipped from his grasp. The sound of the coming army spurred him forward, and he scrambled to his feet and grabbed his weapon as he glanced up and, catching sight of Gideon. A dozen figures shrouded in black and purple light raced toward him, and the demon had extended his power into his arms, ready to fight.

The horde closed in tighter as Jason backed toward the mausoleum. The darkest shadow in the center of the army moved with singular purpose toward him, his blackened tentacles moved like smoke through the tombstones. The front crushed inward, and he turned with the sword in hand, cutting through the bodies that rained down on him. Blood like oil splashed down the length of his weapon. His power rose inside his core again as he sliced through another wave of bodies. He slammed his hand to the earth, sending a shockwave of energy across the cemetery. The first front of demons fell to the ground as the wave of light passed through them, carrying the demons from their hosts.

He rushed forward through the front of fallen bodies. He wasn't going to get pinned against the mausoleum walls, unable to fight the coming waves. A new onslaught came at him, and he turned, the sword spinning through the dark in a swirl of light. He crouched down as the next head rolled off the end of the blade. The energy flowed into his center again, and he formed it into an orb that collected in the palm of his hand. Another wave of demons came at him, drones with their faces twisted just under the mask of their hosts. He let the orb go, and it exploded with enough energy to take down another hundred bodies.

A foray of demons came at him from the left flank, bearing down through the shadows under the trees. His blade swung, catching them, just as he saw a flash of red light.

Something struck him from behind, and he collapsed to the wet grass, but his fingers tightened around the blade. He turned on his back, bringing the sword around with him and slicing it through the air. The demon that struck him jumped back just as the tip of the sword caught the edge of his black jacket.

The orange-red glow in his eyes moved like two dots in synchrony in the dark, but Jason could see the demon's face and his long black locks that fell over his eyes.

Belphagor.

The demon smiled as he stepped back and watched Jason rise to his feet. He twirled a rod of iron from the fence in his hand as though it were a bow staff, the same thing he used to strike Jason. The demon moved in the shadows around him, the edge of the iron catching the light from his sword.

Jason stepped to the side, and Belphagor lunged at him. He swung the sword, but the demon blocked it, the strike ending in a shower of sparks. The demon forced the rod to the side, pushing the sword away from his body. Jason almost lost his footing, but stepped back and came at him again.

Belphagor dodged the strike, sliding to the side like a spirit in the shadows. Jason wound his arm back, building another orb in his hand that he let loose as soon as the demon righted itself. The orb rushed at him, but Belphagor leaned to the side as it zinged beyond his touch.

The demon faced him and planted the staff in the ground as he straightened his stance. "You can't win this."

"Yes, we will." Jason reeled back again, the power in his core now bleeding through his tattoos in bright light. He swung his arm out, ready to release it at Belphagor.

Then something landed against his back, knocking him to the ground. The sword slipped from his hand and the energy that had built inside of him dissipated into the grass. The pain of the strike throbbed in between his shoulders.

A clawed hand pulled him back, lifting him to his knees as Belphagor stepped closer to him, the orange eyes shining in the dark.

Chapter Sixty-Two
Gideon

The fence collapsed all around Gideon, and the creatures that came at him melded into swirls of black and violet light. They were all beings he had not seen in millennia—angels and cherubim that had watched his fall from grace. They moved toward him with singular purpose: to destroy him and get at the child they heard crying in the mausoleum.

He called forth the power in his body, the force of the demon and the new power that Nikka had given to him, and it rushed into his arms. He watched the army of archangels that came toward him, and Samael stood in the center, his dark eyes turned toward him with such malice.

Gideon pushed the power into his fingertips, extending it well along his body in the form of two whips that surged with licks of red fire. They came alive at his bidding, curling and gliding at his side like two cobras. He had once carried these weapons during the Great War in Heaven when so many of his brethren had fallen, and these whips had taken enough of his enemies down to know that he had trusted them.

"There is no place for you here, Pazuzu," Samael said as he crossed over the fallen fence. The angel's pace quickened as he rushed at him.

Gideon planted his feet and faced the group that now came at him, the cherubim roaring with their enormous teeth. He flicked the whips in his hand as they sprang to life in threads of fire. The first cherub closed in on him, and he jerked his hand, lashing the whip through the darkness. The end of it cracked against the creature's body, creating a flash of red light. The creature howled and tumbled against a row of headstones. It righted itself on its four feet and roared into the coming night.

Samael raised his forearms and forced his thread of energy toward him in a flash of violet light. Gideon dodged the light and cracked the whip in his left hand toward the angel. The tip grazed his cheek, leaving a jagged gash in his pale flesh. The others came toward him, flanking him on both sides. The whips lashed through the air and crashed into the bodies of the initial front.

The power in his weapons diminished as more angels descended upon him. He pulled his power from his core again, feeling the mark on his chest glow with the effort. The black tattoo turned red, filling his limbs with energy that coursed into his muscles. The whips suddenly vanished into puffs of smoke. He crossed his forearms before him, amplifying the power that surged from his arms. The force of it shot toward the first wave of angels that rushed at him, striking them down in a semi-circle of bodies that turned to ash.

Samael turned his head down as he watched his soldiers fall with Gideon's power. The violet eyes trained toward him, and he stepped over the piles of ash as he sprinted toward Gideon. His hands extended, his fingers splayed, until a light erupted from his fingertips into two long swords that rippled with violet fire, just like the seraph's weapons.

Gideon leapt back as the archangel came at him. The swords swung through the air in parallel, striking down as Gideon dodged out of the way. He felt the whip form in his left hand in a zing of fire from his palm. The whip curved into the dark and cracked against the angel's back. Samael arched and howled in pain as the fire sizzled against his skin. His hand moved, slicing the sword back toward Gideon.

The blade whistled past Gideon's ear as he pressed himself back to the ground, but he scrambled to his side in time to get the whip back into the air. The angel righted himself in time to find Gideon in the dark again. He swung the blade back at him, and Gideon flicked his wrist. The whip curled into the dark, lashing about Samael's wrist. The archangel cried out in pain, but he remained focused enough to swing his other arm around, the sword catching Gideon's side.

Gideon grimaced, his teeth clenched as he felt the sword slice along his flank. His eyes burned brighter as he watched the angel reel back again for another strike. He pulled the whip back, and it carried Samael forward into a lurch. Gideon planted his feet and howled as he plunged his fist forward with all the power that the tattoo energized for him. It struck the angel in the chest like a barreling freight train. The ground quaked with the impact of the unearthly force that sent the archangel back into the front line of his kind.

The impact knocked Gideon backward as well, sending him careening into a thick granite tombstone that shattered underneath him. The shards of the stone rained down on him as he took in a breath and rolled over, where he felt the pain of the wound in his side. He moved to his knees, one hand on the cut. Blood flowed over his fingers, pulsing with each beat of his heart.

In his peripheral vision, he saw the onslaught of angels and cherubim bearing down on him, and there was nothing he could do as his energy slipped away with the flow of his blood.

Chapter Sixty-Three

Nikka

The power that flowed through Nikka's veins moved cleanly and responded to her every command, easy and smooth as though it were as natural as breathing. She no longer needed to pull it from the earth because it came from within her. She raised her head and looked away from the baby she touched. The sounds of the battle surrounded the mausoleum, and she could feel the power on both sides. The force of angels that had come to take her and her baby away bore down upon them. And the legion of demons rushed at them from the other side, ready to collide in a struggle as powerful as the day they clashed in Heaven.

She grasped Amy's arm and looked toward the closed door. The walls of the mausoleum buckled and cracked just as she moved with her. She raised her hand, and the door flew open as they stepped out of the crumbling structure. Amy clutched the baby closer as Nikka forced her to the ground when they emerged in the center of the fierce battle that surrounded the entirety of the cemetery.

A horde of demons rushed her way, and she looked through the darkness toward them. She raised her hand, her fingers open as the power flashed around her and Amy in a protective shield. Another battle cry came from the opposite end, and she watched Gideon staggering to his feet, his hand clutching his side as the full force of the angels came down toward him. Nikka raised her other hand, and the violet light rushed to protect him, enveloping them in her small sphere of defense as Gideon crawled to her side.

She held the power steady, no longer feeling the strain that something like this would have taken on her as the seraph. But it could only keep out the hordes. It did nothing to stop them, and she couldn't keep this protection in place forever.

The onslaught of demons slowed and surrounded them until the angels approached on the opposite flank. Each army stopped their advances when they knew that all their efforts would collide in one grand destruction.

An archangel stepped forward, someone she had never seen, but she recognized the power that had come off his body. He must have been the one that waited in the light for Samael to bring him into a body, and it appears that he had found one after all: a man with short brown hair, broad shoulders and a muscular physique. His violet eyes watched her through the shield, although he kept his distance.

"Come with us," he said to her, the light pulsating around his body. "You and your child will be protected."

The demons, drones and generals and lieutenants that gathered on the other side of the cemetery hissed and slithered around in the dark, red eyes glowing, flashing between her and the angels across the way.

With all their light and power, she wanted to believe the archangel that stood on the other side of her shield. Samael had been one of them, and they all fought for the same purpose though. They had all played a part in the events that unfolded and led to this very moment.

Movement within the demon ranks caught her eye, and she watched as the shadows grew deeper. It was far too familiar, this thing with arms of darkness that reached toward her, testing the boundaries of her shield. Even through her own power, she felt the cold trickling from its form and descending like frost against her skin.

Lucifer himself had come to witness this.

The shadow folded in on itself, the wisps of smoke tendrils pulling inward until she saw a form emerge from the shadows. The dark spilled into the eyes, ears and mouth of a man that walked toward her. He carried the spirit of the Devil in his eyes as he emerged, his muscled form strong with long black hair that fell down his back. His skin was tanned darker like the man had been living among the warm and sunny beaches when the Devil had taken his soul.

This meant that Lucifer had finally found a vessel that could channel his power.

"I have a better offer," he said, his voice smooth and confident, as he smiled under a black goatee.

From the corner of her eye, she saw the front line of angels back away as the Devil emerged.

Lucifer snapped his fingers, and the demons around him stepped back to let someone through. At first, she saw the one creature emerge that she knew would have a hand in this entire thing. Belphagor stepped forward, the same smirk on his face he always seemed to have and his rock star swagger as he moved toward her. But this time he had someone behind him. The demon turned when he stepped beside Lucifer and reached back to bring that other individual forward.

She felt her breath catch in her throat when she saw Jason, his face bruised and bloodied. The demon pushed him forward and threw him to the ground. The sword wasn't in his hand, which meant it must have been taken from him in the battle. Jason fell to the ground but caught himself with his hand. Belphagor stepped around him as Lucifer watched all of this with a wide grin on his handsome face. The demon reached down, wrapped a hand around his throat and lifted him up to his knees. He held the grip as Lucifer stepped closer.

"Checkmate," Belphagor said as his glowing red eyes turned to her.

Nikka met Jason's eyes as he watched her from the demon's grip. For the first time since she awoke with this power, she felt it waver, and her arms shook with the strain of it in her body. The baby began to cry, and Jason's eyes flashed toward the child, seeing him for the first time.

At her side, Gideon crawled to her and lifted his head, his eyes looking toward Jason.

So many lives now depended on her to do the right thing.

Jason's eyes moved to her again, but he couldn't turn his head. He could only watch her as the demon held him fast and Lucifer came to stand beside Belphagor. His eyes glistened at the sound of the baby's cry.

"You can leave," he called out to her. "Go now."

Gideon pulled himself up to kneel at her side and watch him. "It is true. You can get free of this, right now."

As he said it, she knew it to be true. She had seen Sam do it, move himself so fast from one location to another. A transport through time and space. The bodies that were the closest to her could come with her, those within her sphere of protection.

But she couldn't get to Jason.

"I can't leave you," she said, feeling the hot tears build in her eyes.

"Go, before it's too late," he said.

Belphagor laughed and squeezed tighter around Jason's neck.

"Come with us," Lucifer said, his eyebrow raised in a sharp curve. "He doesn't have to die. You could be together forever."

Her eyes watched Jason in Belphagor's grasp, but she knew the truth as she heard the baby cry. She forced her arms to stay straight and concentrated on letting the shaking ease out of her body. A tear fell down her cheek as her eyes narrowed, and Jason nodded when he saw the resolution pass over her face.

"It's okay," he said. "You'll be okay."

"I love you." She opened her fingers wider, the shield growing brighter around them.

The moment Belphagor realized what she was doing, his eyes widened, and he threw Jason to the ground as he bounded over him and rushed toward her. The demons around him responded to his swift action and leapt at her as well.

She closed her eyes, feeling the power that filled her body and surrounded them, powered by the tattoos along her arms and the mark on her chest. She concentrated on the three other souls that she held under her shield.

"Anywhere but here. Anywhere but here," she muttered under her breath.

The light around them flashed, burning brighter than the sun in the dark cemetery. It strobed once, filling her body with a rush of light that powered her will. Their space in the shield burned hot and then flashed out, lifting them away with a rush of wind and light, leaving that small area in the damp grass empty.

Chapter Sixty-Four

Nikka

It was already three months since Nikka left the cemetery behind, but every day had proven to be harder than the last.

Here, along the Caribbean coast, they rarely came across another soul these days. The effects of the EMP had even reached Central America. When they had first arrived, the disorientation of it soon faded to grim acceptance that they had landed in the quiet and desolate jungles of Belize.

Nikka looked out over the darkening waters of the sea, fading into deep blue with the coming night. Water lapped along the stretch of sand, leaving threads of glowing blue and green sparkles in the sand, bioluminescent algae that stretched along the length of the beach.

The baby grunted and smacked his lips in his sleep as she held him, his small head resting against her collar bone. The warm, humid nights didn't give them much release from the heat of the day, and although Nikka welcomed the drop of the sun, she needed to get back to the house, an empty shell of the former world in this Caribbean paradise. She stood, trying her best not to wake the baby, and she wrapped the long shawl around her body to envelop the child and leave her hands free.

She moved back across the sand, her bare feet sinking into the beach with each step. The sound of the water had become a welcome solace, calming since the chaos of that night in the cemetery. Gideon didn't like it when she took these walks to the beach by herself. But she had to get away sometimes.

Away from Amy, whose depression had pulled her into a disturbing quiet that neither Gideon nor Nikka could break. In their escape to the far ends of the world, Amy had left her child behind, and she couldn't just run back there.

The world had become a much more dangerous place. Garnet Falls would be the first place the forces of Heaven and Hell would look for them. They all had to hope that the town was still safe.

But Nikka had promised her that she would find a way to get Amy back home. She wasn't sure how to keep that promise. Any more use of her angelic power would be like a homing beacon to any angel or demon out there searching for them. If they were going to ever go back, it would have to be under their own human intuition and know-how.

They each had left something behind that night.

When she thought of Jason, beaten and bloodied and on his knees at the edge of the demon army, it would often shake her resolve to keep her powers hidden. Maybe he was still alive out there. Maybe not.

The baby shifted in the wrap, and her hand instinctively touched his back. He would be hungry again soon, and she wanted to get back to the camp before she fed him, especially when Gideon would be anxious to have her back in the protection of the house. He worried too much now when she was out of his sight, but he had never reverted back to the quiet and passive creature she had known in the monastery. Pazuzu still lingered there, savage and intense but protective of her and his redeemed soul.

The baby lifted his head as she heard him vocalize again. Her fingers slipped around the back of his head, and she glanced down to him, his eyes looking back up at her with the same wonder he always had when he watched her.

She smiled at him, and he studied her face, a faint grin playing at the edge of his perfect little lips. The baby gurgled and kicked inside of the wraps. His eyes watched her, and for a moment, she saw the flicker of orange-red demon light in his pupils as it often did when he got excited or angry. And every time it happened, the ground seemed to quake just a little under her feet.

About the Author

When she isn't delivering babies, **Carrie Merrill** is a prolific writer who has been putting pen to paper since the age of 8, when she wrote her first story about a dragon that lived in a cave across the river from her house in Idaho. A day has not gone by since that time when she didn't have a story floating around in her head. She is currently a full-time OB/GYN in the Rocky Mountains with her six rescue cats when she isn't writing about the things that lurk in the dark. *Archangel* is the third volume in her *Angel Blade Series*.

The Angel Blade Series

Book 1: *Angel Blade* is a new adult paranormal novel that involves a strong female protagonist in a supernatural setting, but dealing with issues such as loss of home and family, the burden of being female in a male-dominated realm, and romantic entanglements that can jeopardize her future.

Nikka is dying of cancer until a stranger provides her with a cure, but it comes at a steep cost: she must become a Seraph, an angelic being with the power to exorcise and destroy demons. With Gideon, the stranger who introduced her to this life, she learns of the battle between Heaven and Hell and about the part she must play to fight the demon horde and destroy Abaddon, the Prince of Demons.

Then she meets Jason, a man with a troubled past who also brings the promise of a normal life, and his offer may be too good to let go.

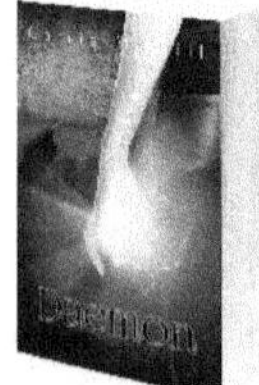

Book 2: *Daemon* In this sequel to *Angel Blade*, Abaddon has fallen, and Nikka, the seraph, and Jason go into hiding as the rest of the world makes sense of the chaos that had occurred in the battle. But as Nikka struggles to face the impact of the events that took Gideon from her, she receives a disturbing vision about the end of the world.

Now, with Jason at her side, she must find another ally foretold in her vision and fight to stop the demon horde from bringing about the final Apocalypse.

Book 3: *Archangel* Demon hordes now rule a post-apocalyptic world. As the new seraph, Jason is bound to Gideon, even though Jason blames him for Nikka's disappearance and the loss of her unborn child. Someday, he will kill Gideon or die trying. Until then, he must wait and learn all he can about being a seraph.

When he sees a vision of Nikka, alive and well, Jason is determined to find her despite the demons hunting them. And with the help of a woman they meet along the way, they may be able to answer the question of Nikka's vanishing.

Copies available from local bookstores, online or from
www.christophermatthewspub.com